The
COMING
STORM

——— HEIRS OF MONTANA ———

The
COMING
STORM

TRACIE PETERSON

BETHANY HOUSE PUBLISHERS
Minneapolis, Minnesota

Cover design by Jennifer Parker & Ann Gjeldum/Cadmium Design

Published by Bethany House Publishers
11400 Hampshire Avenue South
Bloomington, Minnesota 55438
www.bethanyhouse.com

Bethany House Publishers is a Division of
Baker Book House Company, Grand Rapids, Michigan.

Printed in the United States of America

ISBN 0-7642-2770-X (Trade Paper)
ISBN 0-7642-2907-9 (Large Print)

Library of Congress Cataloging-in-Publication Data

Peterson, Tracie.
    The coming storm / by Tracie Peterson.
      p.   cm. — (Heirs of Montana ; 2)
    ISBN 0-7642-2770-X (pbk.) —ISBN 0-7642-2907-9 (large-print pbk.)
    1. Women ranchers—Fiction. 2. Triangles (Interpersonal relations)—Fiction.
3. Indians of North America—Fiction. 4. Indian captivities—Fiction. 5. Bear
attacks—Fiction. 6. Ranch life—Fiction. 7. Montana—Fiction. I. Title II. Series:
Peterson, Tracie. Heirs of Montana ; 2.
    PS3566.E7717C658   2004
    813'.54—dc22   2004002026

To Tom and Dexter,
with thanks for your friendship and
the wonderful house you have built us.
I pray God will richly
bless you both.

Books by Tracie Peterson

www.traciepeterson.com

The Long-Awaited Child • Silent Star
A Slender Thread • Tidings of Peace

BELLS OF LOWELL*
Daughter of the Loom • A Fragile Design
These Tangled Threads

LIGHTS OF LOWELL*
A Tapestry of Hope

DESERT ROSES
Shadows of the Canyon • Across the Years
Beneath a Harvest Sky

HEIRS OF MONTANA
Land of My Heart • The Coming Storm

WESTWARD CHRONICLES
A Shelter of Hope • Hidden in a Whisper
A Veiled Reflection

RIBBONS OF STEEL†
Distant Dreams • A Hope Beyond
A Promise for Tomorrow

RIBBONS WEST†
Westward the Dream • Separate Roads
Ties That Bind

SHANNON SAGA‡
City of Angels • Angels Flight
Angel of Mercy

YUKON QUEST
Treasures of the North • Ashes and Ice
Rivers of Gold

NONFICTION
The Eyes of the Heart

*with Judith Miller †with Judith Pella ‡with James Scott Bell

TRACIE PETERSON is a popular speaker and bestselling author who has written over sixty books, both historical and contemporary fiction. Tracie and her family make their home in Montana.

CHAPTER 1

Montana Territory
January 1870

DIANNE CHADWICK GAZED OUT ACROSS THE VALLEY FROM her favorite perch atop a hill on the Diamond V ranch. Gray clouds stretched across the skies from south to west, and biting cold winds whisked down from the mountains, announcing the coming storm. Uncle Bram promised it wouldn't be all that bad; how he knew, Dianne could never tell, but he seemed right more times than not. Perhaps it was the fact that Bram Vandyke had spent over twenty years in the wilds of this rugged, sometimes hostile, land. Perhaps it was because he listened to the intuitive nature of his wife, Koko, who happened to be half Blackfoot Indian.

No matter the reasoning, Dianne knew both Bram and Koko possessed a strong understanding of the land and the elements in Montana Territory. Dianne wished she could claim the same intimacy with the land, but like a suitor toying with her affections, Montana remained a mystery to Dianne in many ways.

The horse beneath her snorted and gave a toss of his head. He was a young stallion, one Dianne had been working with for the past few weeks. Fiercely independent and stubborn, the young horse had given her nothing but trouble. Still Dianne persevered. She saw something in this horse—signs of strength and quality—that encouraged her hard work. But beyond that, Dianne felt the animal would one day be a good friend. She couldn't explain her thoughts, but ever since coming west on the Oregon Trail, Dianne had come to discover an affinity she had with animals, particularly horses.

When she looked at this black—really looked at him—she saw a long-term companion. Her uncle laughed at this idea. A stallion was much too temperamental for a woman, he'd say. Dianne would only smile at this.

"I'm much too temperamental as well," she murmured. "Aren't I, Jack?"

The black seemed to understand the question and pawed the dirt in a little dance of affirmation. Dianne laughed. She'd named him Jack after her mother's favorite Southern general, Stonewall Jackson. The name seemed appropriate for the horse. He emitted not only a powerful, striking nature, but a fearlessness that impressed most everyone who'd dealt with him.

He reminded Dianne of Cole Selby, the man she loved. The man from whom she'd been separated now for much too long. Cole had decided, after much prayer, to remain in Topeka for at least a year. He'd gone to Kansas to see his parents and to try to straighten out their difficult past. Dianne had encouraged him and understood the need for him to make the trip; however, Cole's decision to stay on and help his father establish a farm had been difficult for Dianne to endure. Part of her was fiercely proud of her husband-to-be. She knew his actions revealed his faith that God could heal the bitterness of the past. Yet she longed for his presence.

"He'll be home this summer," she told herself.

Just across the valley the heavy slate gray clouds pressed in.

"Come on, Jack. We'd best head back. That snow will be here before we know it."

Dianne maneuvered Jack back to the trail and sighed. It was only January, and it would be at least June before she saw Cole again. Determined to push aside her loneliness, Dianne tried to focus on the many blessings she had at hand.

Koko, who'd become such a dear friend, was expecting her second child, though the pregnancy had not gone as well as it had when she'd carried little James. The boy, now a rambunctious two-year-old, held a very special place in Dianne's heart. She fulfilled her longing to be a mother by giving her love to Jamie.

"My day will come," she reminded herself aloud. "It's all about God's timing."

But God's timing was sometimes so hard to wait for. At twenty-two, Dianne found her patience weakened by letters from friends back in Missouri. Her girlfriends were married and happily settled in homes of their own. They wrote about the blessings of their new lives—of plans for large families. It cut Dianne deeply, while at the same time she rejoiced for them.

"I just need to keep myself busy," Dianne murmured. "That's the secret to enduring loneliness."

As she neared their cabin, Dianne was surprised to find Uncle Bram rushing out to greet her. "It's Koko. She's having the baby."

"But it's too early," Dianne said, kicking her boots out of the stirrups. She slid down Jack's muscular side as Bram took hold of his reins.

"I know. I think something's wrong," he said, the worry contorting his expression.

"Will you see to Jack?" This bear of a man, who would think nothing of staring down a cantankerous bull or dealing with a rattlesnake, appeared terrified by the prospect of what might come.

"Of course. Just help her," he said. "I can't lose her."

Dianne knew Bram had been very concerned ever since Koko had taken sick with a cold just after the new year began. The cold had gradually worsened, and Dianne herself was worried that perhaps Koko's sickness had developed into pneumonia. The last few days the poor woman had struggled with a deep, painful cough and a tightness in her chest that left her breathless.

"Maybe the coughing has brought things on," Dianne suggested.

Bram's brow wrinkled. "She's just so weak. I hate to see her like this."

Dianne squeezed his arm. "It's not the best thing for the baby to come early, but these things can't always be helped." By Koko's calculations, the baby wasn't due for another four or five weeks. Dianne could only pray the baby would settle down and wait out the time. The frontier was hard enough on children. "I'll see what I can do for her."

Dianne couldn't help but remember the little sisters she'd lost on the wagon trail coming west. Ardith was only ten when she was swept away in a flood-swollen river. Betsy was six when a mule kicked her in the head, killing her instantly. The losses were hard for Dianne to bear. Hard, too, for their pregnant mother, who died later that same year, taking the unborn Chadwick sibling with her. That left Dianne only her older brothers: Trenton, whom she hadn't heard from in years, and the twins, Morgan and Zane. Zane was nearby, living the life of a frontier army soldier, while Morgan remained at the ranch.

Dianne made her way to the house, lost in thought. Morgan wouldn't stay on for long. Over the last few months he'd taken to going off for days, sometimes weeks, by himself. He'd heard about some caves to the northwest and had gone to explore

them. Before that, he'd traveled to the Yellowstone River country, anxious to see some of the wonders he'd heard about. He'd
been turned back by hostile Indians, barely escaping death at one
point. No, it wouldn't be long before Morgan left for good.

The cabin was deathly quiet. Dianne threw off her coat and
gloves and made her way quickly to her aunt and uncle's room.

"Koko?"

Dimly lit by a single lamp, the room portrayed ominous
shadows as Dianne moved to Koko's bedside.

"The baby's coming . . . early," Koko said, her upper lip
beaded with sweat in spite of the chill in the house. She said no
more, as a wracking cough overtook her. Dianne went to her
and helped Koko sit up until the cough subsided. Pain marred
the pretty woman's features, but Dianne wasn't sure if it was from
the contractions or the pneumonia.

Regaining her ability to speak, Koko leaned back wearily. "It
started a couple hours ago, but I thought it would pass. Now I
know it's too late. I can feel the baby coming."

"I'll get the fire going." Dianne looked around the room.
"Where's Jamie?"

"Morgan took him to help get the milk cows into the barn."

"Good. That will keep him occupied for at least a short
time," Dianne said as she went about the room gathering some
of the things they'd need for the delivery. "You just rest as well
as you can. I'll be back in a few minutes."

Dianne remembered from when Jamie had come into the
world that birthing generally took hours. She calmed her hurried
steps, reminding herself that her anxiety would do nothing to
help Koko.

"How is she?" Bram asked as he burst into the house.

"She's feverish and seems very weak," Dianne admitted.

"She hasn't slept well in days. The sickness, you know."

"I know. She was telling me that just yesterday." Dianne held back from saying anything more. She didn't want to unduly worry her uncle. Koko's failure to improve had concerned Dianne so much she'd thought of riding to Virginia City or Ennis for a doctor—but she wasn't sure anyone would make the trip for a woman who was part Indian.

Koko gave an uncharacteristic scream, sending both Dianne and Bram rushing to the bedroom.

"It's the baby—now!" Koko cried. Coughing again overwhelmed her. She doubled up on her side and made a gasping, wheezing sound as she tried to clear her lungs.

Dianne turned to Bram. "This is much quicker than expected. Bring me some of the heated water from the stove." She then turned to Koko. "Don't worry. Everything will be all right."

Dianne rolled up her sleeves and checked on the baby's progress. Sure enough, the head was already crowning. A few pushes and this baby would be born.

There was no time for panic or worry. Dianne gently guided the infant's small head as Koko bore down to push the baby from her body. A tiny, squalling girl emerged. Dianne thought the baby seemed quite mad about the interruption to her warm, quiet existence.

Laughing, Dianne cut the cord just as Bram returned with the water. "Congratulations, Papa. It's a girl."

"Sounds like a girl," Bram teased. "She's already caterwauling about something."

Dianne laughed and worked quickly to clean the baby and get her wrapped warmly. The little girl was half the size Jamie had been at birth. She probably weighed no more than three or four pounds.

Bram remained at his wife's side. "You did a fine job, Koko. I'm so very proud."

Dianne glanced up to see Koko offer a hint of a smile. "She's our little Susannah," Koko replied.

Dianne started at this. "You're naming her after Mother?"

Bram nodded. "We decided if it was a girl, we'd name her after my sister and Koko's mother. The baby will be called Susannah Sinopa."

Dianne brought the baby to her mother. "What a pretty name. Sinopa means *fox,* right? Perhaps she'll be wily and graceful like a fox." She placed the infant in Koko's arms and pushed back a strand of hair that had come undone from Koko's braid.

"Susannah seems much too long for such a little one." She gently touched her finger to the baby's cheek.

"I'm bettin' she'll grow into it," Bram said, smiling.

"You could always call her Suzy," Dianne suggested. "At least while she's little. Jamie and Suzy sound good together." She smiled in admiration for the little family.

After tending to Koko, Dianne built a fire in the bedroom fireplace. The baby seemed unable to maintain her body temperature, so Bram suggested they heat the room well and move the bed closer to the fire. Morgan arrived to help with the move, and Jamie got his first view of his new baby sister.

"She's too little," he said firmly. "I want a bigger one." Jamie, who'd spoken with a great vocabulary since his first words, was not shy about sharing his opinion. Nearing three years of age, he appeared to be quite the authority on such matters.

They all laughed as Bram scooped up his son. "She's just the right size. If she were bigger, you wouldn't be able to look out for her as well. We're going to need you to help us keep little Susannah safe from harm. You'll help, won't you, son?"

Jamie nodded solemnly. "I help."

"Good boy. I knew we could count on you."

"If she . . . if she . . . gets bigger," Jamie chanted, "we can play."

"That's true," his father agreed. "But this is how God sent

her to us, and God always knows best, right?"

Jamie looked at his sister and then at his father. "I talk . . . I talk to God. He can . . . make her bigger."

They all laughed at this. Dianne moved across the room to ruffle her nephew's hair. "I think it would be just fine to pray that, Jamie. We want Susannah to grow bigger and stronger every day. I think it would be perfect if you would pray for your sister and ask God to make her bigger."

Jamie seemed delighted by this news and despite Koko's illness and the early delivery, the household in general was joyous in the celebration of this new life.

As evening came on, however, the wind picked up with a ferocity that surprised everyone. The howling sound was enough to put everyone's nerves on edge, but as the temperature continued to drop, Dianne worried about the baby's ability to stay warm.

She worried, too, about Koko, who showed no signs of recovery. Every time Koko tried to put Susannah to her breast, the poor baby was interrupted by the coughing. She'd had far too little nourishment today. If she wasn't able to adequately feed the baby soon, Dianne feared the child wouldn't thrive.

Dianne glanced out the kitchen window, praying it wouldn't snow. There was just so much to worry about all at once. Uncle Bram had been confident the storm wouldn't be that bad. Still, Dianne knew he worried about his stock. Would they be all right? Would a sudden blizzard come up and threaten them all?

Bram had already arranged for some of the hands to bring in extra firewood. Dianne knew they'd have to conserve fuel in case things remained unusually harsh. She had the fire in Koko's bedroom stoked but otherwise had limited the rest of the house. She had a nice blaze going in the kitchen stove, which was why she hadn't yet retired to her own bedroom. No doubt it would be very cold in that part of the house, but Koko had made her a fine buffalo cover. Dianne knew once she was buried under its warmth she'd sleep quite comfortably no matter how low the temperature dropped.

She yawned and pulled away from the window. It was times like these when she really missed Cole. She worried because she couldn't remember the sound of his voice. Did that mean she didn't love him as deeply as she believed? Wouldn't true love always remember the tiniest of details?

She could still see his face—every line and feature. She imagined his windblown hair and his lopsided grin.

Dianne felt despair wash over her. "So why can't I remember his voice?"

Just then Bram came in from checking on the livestock. "Everything out there seems to be just fine. How about in here?" he asked, stuffing his gloves into his coat pockets.

"They're both sleeping. I gave Koko some tea mixed with the herbs she suggested. It eased her cough and allowed her to nurse Susannah just a bit." She hesitated but knew she couldn't lie to her uncle. "I'm worried about them both. Susannah won't thrive if Koko can't nurse her. And Koko's sickness continues to weaken her."

Bram nodded solemnly. "I know."

Dianne saw the worry in his expression. "I'm doing all I can, but I wish we had a doctor."

"It's not likely one would come in the dead of winter—much less for a woman who's half Blackfoot."

"Yes, I already figured that. Maybe if the weather gets better, you could . . . well, this may sound crazy, but what about trying to locate her mother's people? Perhaps a tribal doctor could help."

Bram shook his head. "No, they're too far away. Hundreds of miles. No, what we need is a miracle. An honest-to-goodness miracle."

Dianne knew the truth of it. "Then that's what we'll pray for."

———————

The next day the winds died down and the skies were a clear icy blue. They had received only a dusting of snow, much to everyone's relief. Koko seemed no better, however. Her fever refused to abate, and the cough was still relentless. Susannah seemed weak, and although Dianne tried to spoon fresh milk into her mouth a few drops at a time, it just wasn't enough. Feelings of helplessness overwhelmed Dianne at times.

"I brought you two pails of milk," Morgan announced, coming in from the back porch. "Oh, and we spotted a couple folks walking this way—maybe a mile or more off. I can't imagine what would bring anyone out in this cold, but there they were. Uncle Bram spotted them first."

Dianne checked the coffee pot. "There's plenty of hot coffee to thaw them out. Who do you suppose it is?" She went to the woodbox, realizing she'd better get the morning meal cooking if they were to have guests.

"I couldn't say. They were still a ways off. Uncle Bram decided to drive out and fetch them back."

Dianne nodded. "They must be very cold." She threw extra wood in the stove. "Hungry, too, I'd imagine. I'll get breakfast on and make enough for them as well."

She hurried to cut thick slabs of ham. The meat had hung on the back porch all night and was frozen clear through. Nevertheless, Morgan had given all of her knives a fine edge, and the one she used sliced the meat as though it were nothing more difficult than bread. With the meat cut, Dianne pulled two cast-iron skillets from the wall and began heating them atop the stove. She tossed the ham in to begin cooking, then directed her attention to the rest of their meal.

The biscuits were already prepared and sat in a covered basket on the table. Dianne hadn't planned on making gravy but decided with visitors coming she'd whip some together as well.

"Would you take this pitcher and bring me back some milk?" she asked Morgan.

"It hasn't been separated yet."

"That's all right," Dianne replied, turning the ham so it wouldn't burn. "We've got plenty of butter, and a rich gravy will stick to the bones. Just bring me the milk as is."

Morgan did as she asked, and soon Dianne had the ham steaks stacked on the platter and the gravy bubbling in the skillet. She'd no sooner added salt and pepper than the back door opened to reveal Uncle Bram.

"Ummm, smells mighty good in here." He pushed the door back and stepped aside. "I've brought you a surprise, Dianne."

"Me?" she asked, turning to see what he could possibly mean.

As the two frozen figures unwrapped their faces and pulled away thick knitted scarves, Dianne could see exactly what her uncle was talking about.

"Faith! Malachi!" It was the two former slaves she'd met on the wagon train. Going to her dear friend Faith, Dianne embraced her. "I can't believe you're here."

"I can't either. We prayed we'd find you," Faith said between chattering teeth. "Been asking all over the valley." Her skin, generally a beautiful coffee color, had grown pale, almost ashen.

"Come warm up by the stove. We haven't had our breakfast yet, so I made extra when I heard we had company coming." Dianne stood back as Malachi joined his wife. "I'm so happy to see you both."

Malachi nodded. "Thank ya kindly, Miz Dianne."

Dianne waited until they'd had a few moments to warm by the fire before making introductions and taking their coats. Faith and Malachi remembered Morgan from the wagon train, and they squatted down to greet Jamie.

"We'll get some hot food and coffee into you, and that will warm you up to be sure," Dianne said as she hurried to hang up their things on the pegs by the back porch door. "Everyone sit down, and I'll bring the food."

Malachi and Faith were too exhausted to argue. Dianne smiled at her uncle. "I think we just might have our miracle. Faith knows a great deal about sickness and such."

Bram's face brightened. "Truly?"

Dianne's smile broadened. "Truly."

She served the breakfast quickly and waited impatiently as Uncle Bram blessed the food and prayed for the well-being of his family. Dianne had a million questions to ask Faith, and it was so hard to be patient. She wondered where Faith and Malachi had come from, how they'd managed in the gold fields, and what had happened to the baby they'd been expecting when they'd parted company some five years ago. Knowing, however, that they were probably half starved, Dianne held her tongue.

They ate in silence for several minutes, with only an occasional comment about the delicious food being added to break the stillness of the meal. Finally Dianne could wait no more.

"Where did you walk in from?" she asked.

"Can't really say," Faith replied. "We were up north for a spell. Then west. We've been so many places, I can't even remember their names."

"You were going for gold," Morgan stated. "How did that work out?"

"Oh, we found da gold," Malachi assured. "Not much. Jes' enough for us. But we no sooner had it den somebody would come to take it away. We was robbed mo' than five times."

"Oh no!" Dianne gushed with great sympathy. "How awful."

"There were worse things," Faith said softly.

Dianne met her pained expression and instinctively understood. "The baby?"

"Three babies," she admitted. "I miscarried two, and one was born stillborn last week."

"Last week! Oh, Faith. You should be in bed." Dianne looked to her uncle. "They can stay in my room, can't they?"

He nodded. "Of course."

"We gotta earn our keep," Malachi said, pushing back his plate. "I come lookin' fer a job. I'm a hard worker."

Dianne nodded. "And not only that, Uncle Bram, but he's a smithy."

Morgan smiled. "And a right good smithy. I saw him mend many a wagon wheel on the trail west—not to mention shoe horses and oxen. He knows what he's doing, that's for sure."

"We could use a good smithy," Bram replied. "I've long wanted to set up my own blacksmith shop here on the ranch. I'd be happy to give you a try."

And before Dianne knew it, the entire matter was settled. But when Dianne turned to smile at Faith, she recognized her friend showed signs of exhaustion. "I'm going to put Faith to bed," Dianne said as she helped her stand. "You go on and finish your breakfast."

No one argued, especially not Faith. She allowed Dianne to pull her along until they reached Dianne's bedroom. As Dianne helped her into a warm flannel gown, Faith offered her thanks.

"I thought we'd die before we found you. I prayed for a miracle."

Dianne laughed and tucked Faith into bed. "We were praying for a miracle too. You see, my aunt Koko had a baby girl yesterday, several weeks early. I fear my aunt may have pneumonia, and the baby isn't doing very well either. I don't have enough understanding of such things to really know what to do."

"Can she feed the baby?" Faith asked, her voice breaking with emotion.

"No, not really. And the baby isn't thriving." Dianne saw tears come to Faith's eyes. "I'm sorry. I shouldn't talk about it, what with you having just lost a little one. I'm so sorry."

Faith shook her head. "No. God has a purpose, even in this. Don't you be sad—I'm sad enough for us both." She paused and wiped the tears from her eyes. "Bring me the baby."

"What?" Dianne shook her head. "You need your rest."

"Bring her to me. I can wet-nurse her. I have plenty of milk. Plenty so as it hurts to bear." She looked away from Dianne, tears streaming down her brown cheeks. "My heart knows my baby boy is gone, but not my body. Bring her to me."

Dianne reached out to squeeze Faith's hand. "You truly are my miracle. You can't possibly know how hard I prayed for help."

Faith turned her face upward and met Dianne's gaze. "I know," she said sadly. "I know."

CHAPTER 2

ZANE CHADWICK HUNKERED DOWN IN HIS COAT AS HE awaited orders to attack the silent Indian village below. Dismounted and positioned on the snowy bluffs overlooking the Marias River, the cavalry under Major Eugene Baker had their orders to annihilate the camp of Mountain Chief.

Zane thought of his uncle Bram's wife, Koko. She was Pikuni Blackfoot, just like the Indians they were about to slaughter. Her brother, Takes Many Horses, might even be among them. Somehow, when his duties had consisted of killing hostile Sioux and Cheyenne, Zane had been able to justify the situation. Those groups were warring against the wagon trains and refusing to follow government instructions. Many tribes saw the whites as an impossible threat, refusing to even try to get along. But the Blackfoot had been friendly. For the most part.

Mountain Chief needed to be dealt with, to be sure. He and some of his men were guilty of killing a white fur trapper turned rancher named Malcolm Clarke. Zane had no problem in taking the hostiles captive and returning them to Fort Ellis, but to attack the entire village was rather like killing everyone in Virginia City for the sins of one or two highwaymen. But reason wasn't a part of this war. Baker had his orders to "strike them hard," which every soldier knew meant leave no one alive, if necessary.

"If they resist at all," Baker had explained only moments before, "shoot them."

Zane pulled his Springfield rifle close and tried not to think about the half-inch-thick bullets that would rip through the flesh of living, breathing human beings. Of course, he was probably one of only half a dozen present who thought of the Indians, any Indians, as human. Time after time he'd listened to his men and his commanders. The Indians were subhuman, to the thinking of most. They were a nuisance to be rid of.

"Sir, if our reports are correct, most of the warriors are away hunting," army scout Joe Kipp announced to F Company commander Lieutenant Gus Doane.

Zane looked up from where he'd taken position with the others in nearly two feet of snow. January would finally be over in another week. He'd never been colder in his life, but at least the snow afforded a bit of protection from the wind. Someone had mentioned it was nearly forty below zero, and from the numbness in his face, hands, and feet, Zane could well believe it.

"Maybe we won't need to go in guns blazing," the lieutenant replied.

Zane hoped that might be the case as well.

"There's more than that, sir," Kipp continued. "This isn't Mountain Chief's camp. Best as I can tell, this is the camp of Heavy Runner."

"But he's a friendly," Doane said, looking thoughtfully across the valley below. He lifted his field glasses to assess the situation for himself, although it was surely hard to make out much detail in the early-morning dawn. "Does the major know?"

"Yes, sir. He said I was most likely mistaken, but that on any account we were going to attack."

"Attack? Even though we have the wrong Indians?"

Kipp shook his head. "You know the major. There's no wrong Indian when it comes to killing them."

Zane felt sick to his stomach. Kipp spoke the truth. Both men looked to Doane as if expecting him to suddenly make everything right.

"I'll go speak with him," the lieutenant offered. "Joe, you come with me. Sergeant Chadwick, you keep watch. If anyone stirs, send word to me right away." He tossed the field glasses to Zane.

"Yes, sir!" Zane said, catching the binoculars with one hand while maintaining his grip on the rifle. The impact of the glasses stung his icy fingers.

Zane rolled back over to give his full attention to the still silent village. Hopefully Doane would talk sense into Baker. But deep inside, Zane wasn't counting on that. When it came to the Indians, Baker lumped them all together, never considering tribes or individuals. They were heathens—undeserving of any consideration or understanding. Zane had once seen Baker push a Crow child aside as if she were nothing more than a stray dog. His surprise had come in the fact that Baker hadn't kicked the child on the way by. The man's attitude definitely left Zane rethinking his plans for making the army a career.

It wasn't long until the lieutenant returned. He was clearly perturbed and ill at ease with his orders. Joining his men, he motioned to Zane for the return of the binoculars. Zane handed them over, eyeing the man with a raised brow—the unspoken question quite evident.

"He said it's immaterial. We'll get Mountain Chief after we take care of Heavy Runner."

"Begging the lieutenant's pardon," Zane began in a low voice, "but Joe said there were mostly just women and children in that village. Surely we aren't going to unleash war on women and children."

Doane met his gaze. The pained look in his expression was almost more than Zane wanted to see, because in it was the harsh reality.

"Nits make lice," Doane whispered, offering no other comment.

Zane cringed. He'd heard Baker use that phrase over and over since his first encounters with the man. It was his way of saying, "Kill the children—they'll only grow up to be adults we'll have to fight."

Zane struggled to keep down the contents of his stomach. He knew he didn't have it in him to kill a child. Perhaps joining the army had been a mistake. He'd seen it as a brave and noble thing to do. He'd thought of himself as a peacemaker . . . but now that was clearly about to change. He gripped the Springfield even tighter in his frozen hands and prayed for God to somehow intervene. *We're supposed to be the civilized ones,* he thought. *Surely we can't go through with this.*

As the sun rose, word came that the attack was on. In the eerie silence of the frigid morning, F Company and the others moved with great stealth down the slippery slopes. Zane could hear the blood rushing through his ears, could feel his heart pounding harder and harder. Somewhere, a baby cried and then was silent. No doubt its mother had been close by to tend its needs. But in a short time, many babies would be silent, cut down by the white seizers who had come to raid this village of innocents.

"Nits make lice." The words rang in Zane's ears. He thought of his little cousin Jamie, Bram and Koko's son. With only a quarter Blackfoot blood running through his veins, Jamie was still considered an Indian by white man's standards. No doubt Major Baker would be more than willing to kill Jamie, just as he was

willing to take the lives of the children in Heavy Runner's camp.

Zane slowed his steps and gave serious thought to walking away. To simply turning around and marching back up the ravine. Past his men—past Doane—past Baker. *I can't kill women and children. I can't slaughter innocent lives.*

But the moment passed. The charge sounded and the soldiers moved en masse down the snowy bluffs. What happened after that seemed to occur in slow motion for Zane.

To his left, an old man came running from his tepee. Zane knew the man to be Chief Heavy Runner. He'd encountered the man on more than one occasion in the past. The old man was notably alarmed but smiled as he held up his arms. He announced in Blackfoot that he and his people were friends to the whites. Then he repeated the declaration in English.

"Friend," he called while waving a paper in his hand.

Zane wasn't about to shoot the man. He reached out to take the paper, but before he could do even that much, one of the soldiers fired his gun into the old man, killing him instantly.

After that, the war came to life. Screams filled the air, along with gunfire. Pikuni came pouring from their lodges, desperate to escape certain death. Women ran with their children for the cutbanks of the Marias, while old men and young boys attempted to fight back.

Zane fired into the air as his comrades fired into old men and women. The stunned brown faces were permanently etched in his mind as the battle continued. He felt numb, but not from the cold. His mind refused to accept the horrific sights before him or to listen to the question his heart kept asking: *How can I be a part of this?*

The firing seemed endless as the shells ripped through innocent people. Some of the soldiers collapsed the tepees and set them ablaze. Zane was standing in front of the opening of one lodge when a young woman, babe in her arms, emerged. She looked directly into Zane's face, crying out in her native tongue.

"Please don't kill my daughter." She held the infant up for Zane, as though offering the baby to him.

He shook his head and fired his rifle into the air as he said, "Get out of here. Go to the river."

She looked confused for a moment, so he repeated the order in Blackfoot. She nodded and pulled the infant close before running for her life. Zane tried to comfort himself with the knowledge that he'd saved one woman and her child, but it did little to ease the misery of participating in the worst massacre he'd ever known.

Zane moved out, stepping over the dead as he went, trying his best to direct women and children toward the river. Baker might well believe they should all be killed, but Zane would rather face a court-martial than commit murder.

The fighting stopped almost as quickly as it began. With a few of the lodges burning in a bright blaze as evidence of Baker's hatred, Zane could feel the heat begin to thaw his frozen face. The painful prickling on his cheeks made him only too aware that this was no heinous nightmare. This was real.

"Round up the strays," Baker called, as if they were on a cattle drive.

Zane moved toward the river, knowing that other men might not be as compassionate. Women and children, some looking quite ill, were pressed together in the sheltering banks of the river. Zane approached one group and began conversing with them in Blackfoot. The women seemed surprised but almost grateful.

"We're sick," one woman told him. "The white man gave us sick blankets." She pulled back her blanket to reveal a pox-covered child. The girl couldn't have been more than two or three years of age.

Zane swallowed hard and searched the area until he spotted

his commander. "Lieutenant Doane!"

The man came to Zane, the expression on his face appearing to match the same confusion in Zane's mind. "What is it, Sergeant?"

"They've got smallpox." Zane motioned to the woman, who once again revealed her child. Several other Pikuni opened their blankets to reveal they, too, bore the disease.

Doane swore softly. "Round them up anyway. I'll go to the major and explain."

Zane motioned the women to bring their children and move back to the village. He hated that they were forced to march back past the bodies of their dead loved ones. He hated that they were sick and probably hungry as well. He hated that the obliteration of this people seemed the only sacrifice acceptable to appease the leaders of the army.

As dozens of survivors gathered at the edge of the camp, soldiers set fire to the tepees that were still standing. Zane noted the body of the old man who'd come out to them shouting the word *friend* and waving his piece of paper. Stooping down, Zane closed the old man's eyes and breathed a prayer. Blood from the chief's wounds stained Zane's palm and the cuff of his uniform.

"What's he got in his hands?"

Zane looked up to find Major Baker and Lieutenant Doane standing only a foot away. Taking the paper from the old man's stiff fingers, Zane glanced at it quickly, then stood. He had no interest in the formalities of greeting his superiors in proper order. Instead he shoved the paper at them.

"It says he and his people are not to be considered hostile," Zane relayed evenly. "They are a friend to the whites and are to be treated as such. It's from our government."

Zane didn't wait for either one to comment. Instead, he stalked away, rage threatening to overcome him and cause him to do something he'd regret.

There were over two hundred dead. Two hundred innocent souls whose only crime was the fact they were Blackfoot. The sight of all those dead and dying was difficult to comprehend. Zane tried to put it into perspective, but he couldn't. How could there possibly be a perspective that could offer reason and justification for this massacre?

Zane looked around the camp, wondering if he'd find Koko's brother. He knew the man sometimes lived among Heavy Runner's people, but there was no sign of Takes Many Horses. Something akin to relief washed over him. At least he wouldn't have to tell Aunt Koko that he'd been party to the killing of her brother.

Of course, Zane was the only one who knew the truth of the matter when it came to the killing that day—at least concerning his own involvement. He'd not killed anyone. He'd refused to, but it was small comfort. He'd still managed to be a part of it. He still had blood on his hands.

Two hours later Major Baker led all but Company F downstream to where scouts assured him they would find the hostile village of Mountain Chief. He wanted nothing to do with the remaining people and their sickness. Lieutenant Doane and his men were left to finish destroying the village, burning to the ground anything that might prove useful to the remaining Pikuni.

They burned the bodies of the dead as well, something that didn't settle well with the living tribal members. They wanted to prepare their own dead—to hold their ceremonies, even in this bitter cold. The women howled and cried out in their misery, while the few old men who remained stared at soldiers with looks that still registered disbelief.

Many of the soldiers began looting, stripping the dead of anything valuable. Zane ordered his men to cease and desist, and while some did, he caught others continuing.

"Sergeant, take your men and go round up the Indian ponies," Doane said as he caught up with Zane.

"Yes, sir." His lack of enthusiasm was well noted.

"Sergeant, wait." Doane pulled Zane aside. "I'm no happier than you are about this. It wasn't my desire that these Indians be butchered. This is by far and away the greatest slaughter of Indians ever made by U.S. troops, but it's over now."

"Is it?"

The man eyed Zane momentarily, then dropped his hold. "Round up those ponies."

For a moment Zane had actually thought Doane might break away from his role as commander and bare his soul. But instead, the man quickly recovered from his moment of weakness and moved away, shouting commands to some of the others.

"It isn't over," Zane murmured, glancing from the huddled, crying survivors to the funeral fires of the dead. "It's just begun."

————

That night, after trying without luck to fall asleep, Zane wrestled with his choices. He could stay and try against the odds to make a difference, or he could leave. Desertion seemed far more honorable than continuing with a man like Major Baker. After all, Baker had turned the remaining Pikuni people loose without food or proper clothing. Certainly, without shelter in forty-below temperatures, they would all be dead by morning. The man's cruelty was more than Zane could comprehend, and it didn't matter that some suggested Baker's thinking had been clouded by liquor. If anything, that only made it worse. If Baker had to drink to forget who he was and what he'd done, then maybe he should reevaluate his choices.

And that's exactly what Zane was doing for himself. Reevaluating. He could still smell death everywhere, and it made him half crazy to leave. Pulling on his boots, Zane ignored the reality of the moment. Yes, he would probably be caught and court-martialed for what he was about to do, but it didn't matter.

"Something wrong?" one of the men in the tent muttered, rising up on his elbow.

Zane felt his heart skip a beat. He steadied his voice and tried to sound authoritative. "Go to sleep, Carson. It's at least two hours until first call."

"That's a relief," the man said, then yawned and fell back against his makeshift bed. "Night, Sarg."

Zane waited a couple of minutes before gathering his things. It wouldn't be easy under any circumstances to slip past the guards nor to get to his horse without detection. If Private Mueller was on guard duty, Zane knew he could be bribed to look the other way. There seemed to be nothing sacred to that man. But if one of the by-the-book soldiers were on the line, then Zane knew he very well might have to hurt someone before it was all said and done. Either way, he was leaving this valley of the shadow of death and going home.

CHAPTER 3

As the end of February drew near, Dianne and the rest of the household fell into a routine that seemed to serve everyone quite well. Koko was on the mend, although she was still very weak. She coughed less frequently but still required a great deal of bed rest. Susannah thrived under Faith's tender love, and in turn Faith seemed blessed by the child's need of her care.

Koko had alternated with Faith in nursing Susannah so that her milk wouldn't completely dry up, and now that the feedings were more routine and her milk more established, Koko was able to take over the task altogether. Dianne saw Faith withdraw and grow silent as the baby's care returned to her mother. It was hard for Dianne to see Faith this way; the woman had been so encouraging and vibrant on the wagon train west, and Dianne knew in her heart she might never have survived the journey had it not been for Faith.

As Dianne stood outside the open door to the bedroom she'd given over to Faith and Malachi, she prayed for the wisdom to deal with Faith's sadness. *Lord, I don't know what it is to lose my own child, but I know what it is to suffer loss. Maybe I even endured*

*those ordeals for such a time as this—a time when I can minister hope
to my friend.*

Knocking lightly on the door, Dianne entered. "I'm not
going to let you hide away and be sad," she announced. "I know
you're hurting, but you can't shut out the world and hope that
the pain will ease. It doesn't work that way."

Faith looked up from where she sat rocking silently. Her
complexion had still not regained its rich coffee-and-cream
color.

"I know."

Her face lacked the sparkle Dianne had seen on the trail.
Back then, Faith had been enthusiastic and alive with a passion
born of new freedom from slavery. She and Malachi were just
starting their life together, and nothing was too big or too frightening to stare in the face and deal with head on.

Dianne sat on the edge of the bed and leaned against the foot
post. "It's really hard on you, isn't it?"

"What?"

"Giving Susannah back to Koko."

Faith bowed her head and gripped her hands together.
"Hurts almost like losing my babies. I don't know why. I know
that Susannah belongs to Koko. I'm rejoicing, truly I am, that
Koko is recovering. I wanted nothing more." She paused.
"Well . . . maybe there were other things I wanted more."

Dianne wanted so much to say the right words of comfort,
but instead she said, "Tell me about the babies, Faith. Tell me
everything."

"Not all that much to tell. Life up here is just hard, plain and
simple. I lost my first baby shortly after we left Virginia City. Just
came on me one day. I hurt something fierce and next thing I
knew I'd lost my child." Tears streamed down her cheeks, but
she refused to look Dianne in the eye.

"That must have been terrifying," Dianne whispered. "I'm

so sorry I wasn't there to help you through it. You were so good to help me when my sisters died . . . and my mother. Your words to me were the main reason I was able to have an understanding of who God is and why my ways were wrong. I don't think I would have come to that knowledge quite so soon had you not offered me such wise counsel."

"Words are easy," Faith said, finally looking up. Her eyes spoke of pain so deep and raw that Dianne actually winced.

"What happened after you lost the baby?"

Faith shrugged. "We went about our business like nothing had happened. I knew Malachi grieved, but it was impossible to offer him comfort when I had none for myself. A year later I was expecting again. I thought this time nothing would go wrong. We were settled up near Fort Benton. Malachi was working fairly steady doing odd jobs for one of the liveries.

"I was sure everything would be different, but it wasn't. One night I woke up and knew it was happening all over again. I lost the baby by morning. Shortly after that we moved on. Malachi heard about another gold strike, and the fever was upon him again. I didn't want to move, but I figured it might help us both to get to new scenery, so we left."

Faith went silent and began rocking. She stared past Dianne to the window on the opposite side of the room. "When I found out I was expecting again, I just wanted to die. I was terrified that it would all just be the same. I prayed and prayed and watched every step I took. I didn't raise my hands above my head or carry anything at all. I didn't walk any faster than a funeral procession would go—no matter how much of a hurry I was in.

"When I passed the time where I'd lost the other babies and this one kept on growing strong, I figured the worst was behind me." She looked again to Dianne and shook her head. "But I was wrong. The baby was due the middle part of January. I felt strong and healthy as an ox. I just knew everything would be good."

"What happened, Faith? Why did the baby die?" Dianne felt close to tears but held them back. She didn't want to add to Faith's burden.

"The cord was wrapped around his neck just as tight as it could be. He came too fast to get it cut or taken off before it strangled him. I just stared at the midwife and screamed. I couldn't understand why she'd let this happen—why she'd let my baby die. I said horrible things—things I had to repent of." Faith closed her eyes and leaned back to rest her head. "I was so angry."

"You were lost in your sorrow," Dianne said softly. "Just as you are now."

"I can't take any more pain," Faith said matter-of-factly. "I can't go on hurting like this. It's killing me. I don't even want to be with Malachi."

Dianne shook her head and reached out to touch Faith's knee. This caused the woman to stop rocking, but she didn't open her eyes.

"I can't be a wife to him—not again. I can't risk going through all this again. I can't, Dianne."

"Faith, you have to give yourself time. You have to let God heal your hurts." She fell silent, unsure of what to say next. She imagined a tiny boy who looked like Faith, and the pain was acute. How—or even more, why—did God let this happen? He could have stopped it. He knew how much Faith would love this child.

"What did you name him?"

Faith looked at Dianne and offered just a hint of a sad smile. "John. John Michael Montgomery. Malachi made him a little wooden headpiece. There just wasn't money for anything else."

"If you'd like, we could order a stone. I'd be happy to pay for one."

Faith shook her head. "No. It'd just be a waste. Malachi said we had to leave it behind . . . forget. I know he means well, but he doesn't understand my grief."

Dianne moved to where Faith sat in the rocker and got to her knees. "Faith, no one but God knows how much you hurt. As much as I care about you, and even though I've suffered the loss of my mama and sisters, I can't know what it is to bury a child. I pray I'll never know." She drew a deep breath and continued. "But even so, you can't push God away. He'll just keep coming back. Remember, you're the one who first showed me verses in the Bible about His faithfulness."

Faith sniffed and nodded. "Lamentations."

Dianne patted her hand. "Yes. Lamentations chapter three. 'It is of the Lord's mercies that we are not consumed, because his compassions fail not. They are new every morning: great is thy faithfulness. The Lord is my portion, saith my soul; therefore will I hope in him.'"

Faith continued the quote, picking up where Dianne stopped. "'The Lord is good unto them that wait for him, to the soul that seeketh him. It is good that a man should both hope and quietly wait for the salvation of the Lord.'" Her voice was soft, but her tone suggested her convictions were just as strong as they had been when she'd first shared those verses with Dianne.

"Yes," Dianne whispered. "We have to wait for the Lord and hope in Him. He won't leave you, Faith. He's never asked you to bear this on your own."

"I wish He'd never asked me to bear it at all."

"I wish He hadn't either."

"I just don't understand," Faith said, shaking her head. "I would have loved that baby good. I would have given him a loving home. Malachi would have been a good father. I just don't understand."

Dianne smiled. "You sound just like me most days. I don't understand why God allows half the things He does. Why did

Ardith fall in the river? Why didn't someone save her? Why did Betsy have to get kicked in the head by a mule? Wasn't God able to still the animals—keep that mule from kicking? Surely that wasn't too big a job for Him. Then my mother died, just days before she was to give birth, taking my baby brother or sister with her. I don't understand a good portion of what God allows."

Faith nodded and for the first time since Dianne had entered the room, her expression seemed one of compassion and tenderness rather than sadness. "It's hard to trust when bad times come. It's hard to have hope when hope keeps getting killed along the trail." She gripped Dianne's hands. "I'm glad God brought us to you. Glad we found you when we did. We might have frozen to death out there, but beyond that, I know my heart would have froze shut. You and little Suzy have kept that from happening."

"It's hard to hurt this much," Dianne said, meeting her friend's dark eyes. "But the alternative is to feel nothing at all, and that's hardly the answer. I guess in spite of everything, I'd rather go through life feeling everything in all its intensity than feeling nothing whatsoever."

Faith nodded. "I suppose I feel the same way. It's just so . . . so hard."

"But you have people here who love you—people who will help you through this. And there's always work." She grinned. "There's always plenty of work around this place."

Faith smiled back. "There's always work."

Dianne sobered. "Faith, you are a dear sister to me. I hope you know that I love you as such. You will always have a home with me for as long as you desire."

"I know you care, and I cherish you too. I never would have imagined being friends with any white woman—it didn't seem likely that a white woman would want to be friends with a slave, even an educated one. But when we met up on the trail, I liked you from the start. You weren't like other white girls. You didn't seem to care about any of the things that others worried over. I remember talking to the Lord and telling Him that if there were more people like you, we'd have never had to fight the War Between the States."

"I don't deserve such praise," Dianne said. "I didn't even care about the war except to hope that my brothers would stay out of it. I never gave slavery much of a thought at all, though I grieve that now. No man should be slave to another. No man has the right to own another man, yet I turned a blind eye like so many folks. It didn't concern me—at least I didn't think it did—so I ignored it. We had such a good life in Missouri; my father had his own business and the people of the town were good neighbors. Then the war came and all of that changed. We all changed."

"But you changed for the better."

"Maybe I just grew up—opened my eyes to the realities of the world."

"It's a hard world to wake up to, that's for sure," Faith said. "Not everyone had a change of heart. Malachi and I still face people's hatred."

"Well, you won't here. Life here will be different. Malachi can earn his keep and do the job he loves. Folks here won't care what color your skin is—Uncle Bram's made sure of that. Because of Koko."

"And you don't mind that your aunt is half Indian?"

Dianne shook her head. "No. I don't mind at all. Koko is the dearest and sweetest woman. Her love for people runs deep, no matter the color of their skin. I know she loves having you here as well. Uncle Bram has been planning to build a big house. Seems like he's been planning it forever. But in truth, he wants it to be perfect. He wants it to honor Koko."

"Making provision for your family is important. That was

why Malachi wanted to leave Virginia City all those years ago when I was expecting our first child. He didn't want his baby born in a shack no better than what he'd lived in on the plantation." Faith sighed. "Now he doesn't have to worry about that."

They were back to the sorrow of Faith's lost children, and Dianne had no idea what to say. She knew she couldn't just snap her fingers and eliminate the woman's grief, but for a moment she'd been confident that Faith's sadness had lifted just a bit. Now they were steeped in it again.

Dianne got to her feet, struggling for the right thing to say. "Faith, I know it's hard right now, but God will ease your pain. You have to fight against it, though. You can't just give in to it. Koko still needs help. We need you to help with the baby and with Jamie. I even need your help with the house so I can be freed up to help more with the livestock. We don't have a full crew right now—winter is always the time when Uncle Bram lets men go. And some of the men are up north with the cattle." She felt almost cruel for suggesting Faith stop grieving enough to be useful, but the words just poured out of Dianne's mouth.

"I need you, Faith. I can't do this alone. Koko did the work of ten women, and with her sick, everything has suffered."

Faith drew a deep breath and stood. "You don't have to do this alone," she whispered.

Dianne looked deep into the woman's eyes and smiled. "Neither do you. Not so long as I'm around. Not so long as you remember that God will never leave you."

CHAPTER 4

MARCH BURST ON THE SCENE WITH BLUSTERY COLD DAYS that reminded Dianne of January. After a week or so, however, the weather tempered and the air warmed with the promise of spring. By the last week of the month the snow melted and there were hints of green in the grass. Dianne generally refused to let herself get too excited about these early thaws. Back in Missouri the farmers were already planting and enjoying spring flowers and greening trees, but here in Montana, especially in the mountains, the weather was completely unpredictable. Dianne had even seen it snow in July. Of course it didn't last, but it snowed nevertheless.

March also meant that Cole would soon be home. Dianne hadn't allowed herself to dwell too often on how much she missed him. Faith's arrival and the new baby helped to keep Dianne's thoughts occupied, but on days like this she couldn't help but think of a lovely summer wedding and Cole by her side for the rest of their lives.

Taking Pepper, the gray-and-white she'd worked with since he was a colt, to the top of the ridge, Dianne felt the exhilaration of a land about to be reborn. She shared the sentiment. Winters were hard and long, but there came a frantic release with each new spring. As if all creation in the Madison River valley recognized its potential all at once and knew it must act fast or lose its chance.

Shifting in the saddle, Dianne imagined the ranch as it would be in another month. By then it would be nearly May. Cole had written her to say that he should be back to the ranch by July. Her heart quickened at the thought, and Dianne allowed her mind to wander for a time. She wondered what he would look like—how he'd changed. She knew she had changed—hopefully for the better. She'd lost most of her youthful chubbiness, and at twenty-two, she bore the mark of hard work in a slimmer, more muscled figure. Faith had told her she'd grown into a handsome woman, but Dianne only cared that Cole might think so.

"I miss him so much, Lord. Some days are much harder than others," she said, looking up. "When I think of all the time that has passed, I worry that he won't feel the same. That he'll change his mind and remain in Kansas." She smiled and added, "Then I worry that he'll come back a different man, that he won't have resolved his differences and that he will have given up on you, Lord. That makes me worried that I'll change my mind."

Shaking her head, she urged Pepper back down the path toward home. "I'm a silly woman, Father. I don't mean to fuss and fret. I think that's why I've tried not to even give it consideration. But it's so hard."

Dianne took her time making her way home. She had plenty to think about, not the least of which was her longing for materials to make a wedding dress. Faith had brought up the idea of making plans for the big event just the other day, and up until then, Dianne had tried not to even think about the wedding for fear it might not come true.

She didn't know when she'd become so cynical about daydreaming, but she'd been afraid of putting much store in her wedding. In the frontier it was difficult to plan. You never knew what problem or complication might arise. Dianne had been disappointed so many times when she'd plotted and planned for a specific event, only to have it fall apart on her because of the weather, sick animals, warring Indians, or some other interference. Uncle Bram said that in this land it was better to take one day at a time. It was okay to make your plans, but you couldn't allow yourself to get caught up in them. Now Dianne carried that same mindset into preparations for her wedding. Several times Faith had asked her about the arrangements, and Dianne had to admit she'd made no plans.

Truth be told, it was Faith who set Dianne's mind to thinking about a wedding dress. Dianne imagined something simple yet lovely. She didn't want to be married in her old everyday clothes. Koko and Faith had both promised to help her design and make a gown as soon as Dianne felt the time was right.

"Well, maybe this is the day," she mused, imagining yards and yards of soft material flowing gracefully from her slender frame. "Maybe working on the gown will keep my mind busy for a time—at least a couple of months. And after that, maybe he'll be home. Maybe Cole will finally be here and my waiting will come to an end."

———

"Koko, I believe this baby is going to take after you," Dianne declared, lifting Susannah. The baby yawned and looked up at Dianne as if to consider her words.

"I think so too," Faith agreed. "She sure has grown."

Koko smiled at the two women and went back to her leatherwork. "She'd never have made it without the two of you. I've never really had a chance to thank you properly."

"No need," Dianne said, putting Susannah back down beside

her mother. "That's what family is for."

"And friends," Faith threw in.

"Faith is right. It's the way Jesus tells us to be. To love our neighbor as ourselves. Living all cramped up here," Dianne said with a smile, "it doesn't get much more neighborly."

Koko laughed and so did Faith. "Bram says he'll start the cabin for Faith and Malachi as soon as he can get the cattle back and settled. It won't take long," Koko declared. A new two-room cabin was Bram's gift to the Montgomery family for all they'd done. Half of the structure was to provide housing, while the remaining half would be the new blacksmith shop.

Dianne finished tidying the kitchen area. "I know. He told me about a shipment of housing materials coming up from Virginia City. He plans to start the new house this summer as well. He told me that if everything goes well, he'll have the main structure built by fall. He even plans to have some of the rooms ready so we can move in before the first snows. Isn't that exciting?"

"I wish he wouldn't worry about such things. He wants a nice big house for all of us, and I completely agree with that. But he wants so many nice things that we just don't need. Lots of windows and special lamps built into the wall. I told him he didn't need to fuss about such things, but he won't listen."

Dianne smiled at her aunt. "He wants you happy. That's all."

"But he knows me well enough to know that I am happy. This is all I could have wanted from life. I don't need lamps built into the wall."

Dianne laughed. "I'm sure one day we'll all come to appreciate Uncle Bram's efforts and wonder how we could ever do without him."

Koko put down her needle, and her expression became quite serious. "I couldn't do without him."

Dianne recognized the look of panic on Koko's face. "You

aren't going to do without him, Koko. I didn't mean to upset you . . . it was just a figure of speech."

"You don't understand," Koko said softly. "I've had this dream. It's always the same. It's always dark and frightening and Bram is wounded." She shuddered.

Dianne gently squeezed Koko's shoulder. "It was just a bad dream. I sometimes have them about Cole, but I refuse to give them any credence. Both men are in God's hands and we mustn't fret."

Koko started to reply, but the sound of a horse approaching silenced all three women. Dianne went to the door and peered out. To her surprise, the rider was none other than her brother Zane.

"What's Zane doing here?" she questioned. "I thought the army was off on some big campaign to the east. Didn't Morgan say something about that?"

"He did," Faith replied, "but maybe they returned early."

Dianne stepped out onto the porch as her brother dismounted. Koko went to tend to Susannah, who had just started crying.

"You're a sight, to be sure," Dianne greeted. "Looks like you've been on the trail for a month of Sundays."

Zane met her expression and frowned. "Afternoon, Dianne. I've come to talk to Uncle Bram. Is he around?"

Dianne's enthusiasm faded. Zane's tone suggested something was very wrong. "Are you all right?"

"I just need to talk to Bram."

"He's in the horse barn. Why don't you go ahead and visit with him and I'll prepare you a plate of food. You're hungry, aren't you?"

Zane seemed hesitant, then nodded. "I'm starved."

Dianne smiled. "Then go have your talk and afterward wash up and come eat." She wanted to say something more, but Zane made it clear he wasn't interested in talking. As he led the horse away and headed to the barn, Dianne could only contemplate what might be wrong. Maybe the Indians were attacking nearby. Maybe some hideous disaster had struck the town of Bozeman.

Dianne remained outside, watching her brother. There was something odd going on. He was disheveled and not up to the standards of a soldier. And while she'd never been very close to the twins or understood their way of thinking, it was clear that Zane was troubled. Perhaps life in the army was more difficult than he'd anticipated, or maybe he'd had some sort of ruckus with his commanding officer.

"He's not wearing his uniform!" Dianne exclaimed as the realization struck her. Had he resigned from the army? Something had happened, and she intended to know what it was.

Following after Zane, Dianne eased in through the open side door of the barn.

"I didn't think we'd be seeing you anytime soon," Bram declared in greeting.

Dianne eased alongside the corner stall and listened for a moment. She didn't think it proper to eavesdrop, but something told her to hold back—to wait.

"I've deserted," Zane said without further explanation.

Dianne put her hand to her mouth to keep from gasping aloud. Deserted? Why in the world would he do that? Weren't men shot for such things? Zane was such a man of honor, and since coming west, he'd wanted nothing but to join the army. Why would he desert?

"Why don't you tell me what happened," Bram said softly.

"It's so awful—the worst thing I've ever seen or been a part of," Zane began. "We were up on the Marias going after a group of Blackfoot who had murdered some whites nearby. Our major was adamant that we catch and kill these men. He cared nothing about bringing them back for a trial or hearing their side of it.

That bothered me enough, but when we came upon the wrong group of Pikuni and Major Baker insisted we attack anyway . . . well . . ." His words trailed off.

Dianne felt a deep sorrow for her brother. He sounded absolutely heartbroken. She knew he would never tolerate innocent lives being slain. No wonder he'd deserted.

"It was Heavy Runner's village," Zane began again. "I feared maybe Takes Many Horses would be there, but most of the warriors were gone on the hunt."

"They came to visit us just before the baby was born in January," Bram told him. "They were heading south, as the buffalo were scarce in these parts."

"Most of Heavy Runner's band were old people, women, and children. Not only that, but they had smallpox. Baker still didn't care. He turned the troops loose to kill and plunder. He wasn't content just slaughtering innocent lives. He destroyed everything they had, then left more than a hundred people out in the snow in forty-below temperatures. Some weren't even properly dressed—hardly any had buffalo robes to keep them warm."

"I'm sorry, Zane. I know that must have been hard."

"It wasn't just that."

Dianne could hear the exasperation in her brother's voice. She longed to go to him, to offer him comfort, but she remained frozen in place, desperate to hear every detail.

The sound of something slamming against the wall caused Dianne to jump.

"I'm sorry," Zane apologized, "it's just that even remembering it makes me so angry."

"It's all right, son. You're among family and friends here. You can take your time and just tell me what you need to."

"What I need, I can't find. I need absolution for what I did— and for what I didn't do."

"And what's that?"

"I didn't try to stop them," Zane said, his voice breaking. "I knew it was wrong. I even refused to shoot anyone. I headed women and children to the river for safety, but I didn't try to stop the attack."

"What could you have done? You weren't in charge."

"Maybe not, but I could have protested the attack. I could have confronted the major."

"And would he have listened?" Bram asked.

"No . . . probably not. The man was mostly likely well into his cups. Several men said he was drinking before the attack."

"A drunkard is not easily reasoned with. Especially one who has no standard of justice."

"I don't know what to do, Uncle Bram. I've been gone since that night. That was over two months ago. My conscience is eating me up. I feel like I should go back to the fort and face my punishment for desertion, but at the same time, I don't wanna go."

"Have you prayed about this?"

"Yes, sir. That's why I'm compelled to go back. I gave my word to the army, and I know it's only right that I turn myself in."

Dianne bit her lip as tears came to her eyes. Her brother sounded like such a broken man. She was thankful he'd come to their uncle for counsel.

"I just keep seeing their faces," Zane said, picking up the memory again. "I see the women shielding their children and the bullets ripping through their flesh as though they were made of nothing more substantial than cobwebs. I can hear the children crying and the women screaming. It's driving me mad." He began to sob.

Dianne wanted to run away. Her brother's cries pierced her

heart. How could anyone be so cruel as to wage war on children—defenseless children?

"Son, things like this have been a part of human life since the beginning of time. Man is sinful and selfish. His motives are not always pure. Still, you couldn't have stopped this from happening. You did the best you could."

"I don't feel like I did my best. I know God must be disappointed in me. Can He forgive me, Uncle Bram? Can God forgive me for being part of such a hideous thing and then running away?"

"Of course He can, but that doesn't mean the memories will go away. It was no accident that you were present in that situation. I don't believe things happen by chance. You were a witness to this atrocity for a reason. I'm not sure what that reason could be, but it's important that you learn from this."

Dianne heard Zane sniffing and decided to slip away while the two men figured out what was to be done. She prayed all the way back to the house that God might ease Zane's grief and give him peace.

Faith didn't question her when she came into the kitchen. For this, Dianne was grateful. She went to work immediately, putting away the canning jars she'd been tending to earlier in the day. When Zane and Bram came in nearly half an hour later, neither one seemed upset or out of sorts. Bram, in fact, was chuckling about some antic of Jamie's, telling Zane how his son would make a first-rate horseman someday.

Dianne helped Faith serve Zane his meal, then sat down to join her brother. "What have you . . . uh . . . been . . . I mean where have you . . . been? It's been quite a while since we . . . saw you," she began tentatively.

"I know. Looks like the ranch has changed quite a bit. How are you?" Zane asked, then focused his attention on the food.

"I've been good. And you?" Dianne asked nonchalantly.

Zane shrugged. "Guess I could be better."

"What causes you to say that?" she asked, hoping he'd confide his ordeal to her.

He shook his head. "It's not important. Guess you must be just about busting a button waiting for Cole to get back. Uncle Bram told me he's due before long."

Dianne knew her opportunity to hear the truth from him had passed. "I am anxious for Cole's return. Should be soon—about three months, I figure."

"Will you two marry right away?"

"That's the plan," she replied.

"If they'll wait until fall, we might even have the new house built," Bram declared as he brought a cup of coffee to the table and joined the conversation. "I figure we'll have a big enough front room that you could have the wedding there if you wanted."

"I'd hate to wait that long," Dianne said. "It's already been long enough."

"It was honorable of him to stay and help his pa," Bram said after a long sip of coffee. "You've got a good man there, Dianne. No need to rush it. He'll keep his word and do what he's got to do, and in turn that will make him a better person."

Dianne looked up and nodded, but when she met her uncle's gaze, she froze. He held her eyes, speaking to her in the silence of the moment. He knew. He knew she'd overheard the conversation in the barn. Dianne wasn't sure how he knew, but he did. There was something in his look that made it clear she should say nothing, however.

She nodded just slightly—just enough to let him know she understood.

Bram smiled. "Well, maybe Zane will be able to get leave in the fall to come celebrate the festivities. Summer's not the best time for getting away from the army, you know."

Dianne nodded. "Maybe we will wait until fall. If it helps you, Zane."

He shrugged again. "Not sure what will help me."

Koko emerged from the bedroom with Susannah all bound up in a cradleboard. The baby seemed to love being wrapped up securely. "Welcome back, Zane. It's so good to see you," Koko said as she approached Zane. "You haven't met your new cousin. This is Susannah. We named her after your mother."

He looked up to Koko and paled. It didn't immediately register in Dianne's mind what was wrong, but when she took a good look at her aunt, it became clear. The woman was dressed in native fashion, wearing a long deerskin dress, her hair bound in two braids. Added to that, baby Susannah definitely looked the part of a Pikuni infant in her bindings. Dianne cringed.

Zane swallowed hard and looked away. "She's pretty," he said, seeming to gasp for air. He looked to Bram and got to his feet. "I need to be on my way." He glanced back at Dianne, who by now had stood as well.

"Zane, are you all right?"

He met Dianne's gaze and nodded. "I'm fine. I have to get back to the fort."

———

Dianne stood at the corral fence later that evening. The sun had set and the last hints of light were fading in the west. Concern for Zane plagued her thoughts.

"I thought I might find you out here," Bram said as he came up from behind her.

Dianne turned at the sound of his voice. She didn't even bother to try to hide what she knew. She desperately needed to talk to someone. "Why, Uncle Bram? Why did that attack have to take place? Why did Zane have to be a part of that?"

Bram put his arm around her shoulder and hugged her close.

"It's always the *why*s that give us fits. I don't have answers for you, darlin'. Men are men, and they will make their war. Sometimes the war seems just and honorable, but more times than not it's simply a matter of one side wanting something the other side has. In the case of the Indian wars . . . well, the whites want the land. Settlers are restless to move west. I've heard talk of wagon trains that stretch out for miles on end—you've said before that your own wagon train was hundreds of wagons long."

"Yes, it was. And when you watched it move across the open plains, it was a sight to behold," Dianne remembered.

"Imagine being the Sioux or the Blackfoot and seeing that. Seeing their way of life suddenly intruded upon. I'm guilty of doing just that myself. Like most, I saw what I wanted and took it—no matter the cost to others." He grew thoughtful. "Times are changing and bad times are coming. Probably more wars, more death. The tribes won't just give up their land, and I can't blame them. Look around you—it's beautiful, vital, and full of everything a person needs to live. Why would you give that up without a fight?"

"I guess I wouldn't," Dianne said, realizing how very much she loved this land. "Will Zane be all right?"

"He's seen bad things, Dianne. It won't be easy, and I won't lie to you or him and say that it will. But we all have to live with bad things—ugly things. Life isn't always the beauty you see here . . . as well you know."

"I wanted to help him."

Bram shook his head. "You can't. He has to make these decisions for himself. He's made a good choice. He's going back to face his superiors. Whatever happens, his conscience will be clear."

"Do you think he'll quit the army?"

They began walking back to the house. "I can't say. I kind of doubt it. Zane knows that as bad as things were, the army needs good men to balance those who lead such massacres. Someday, Zane may well be the one upon whose shoulders it falls to lead such an attack. Maybe he'll make a stand and maybe another destructive act will be avoided. Who knows? Maybe he'll get involved in the politics of the country and get laws changed so that Koko and the children won't have to live in fear of being rounded up and put on reservations."

"I hope he'll be all right. I hope he knows how much we love him."

Bram squeezed her close. "He knows. That's why he came here."

CHAPTER 5

COLE SELBY GAZED UP TO THE NOON SUN AND WIPED HIS brow. This was his last day in Topeka. Tomorrow he'd rejoin Daniel Keefer and head home to Montana. It seemed like it'd been forever since he'd been under the big sky of that territory. He relished the feel of the dry mountain air and the heady scent of pine. He also longed to be in the arms of Dianne Chadwick.

He thought of Dianne a great deal. Especially on days when he was out in the fields, like now. Working the land gave Cole plenty of time to contemplate his life and the memories of the woman he loved. It was because of her love that he was here. Here in Kansas, on his parents' farm.

Dianne's love and faithfulness had helped Cole to set his heart right. He'd made his peace with God, and over the last year he'd grown in his understanding of God's love and direction.

Cole looked out across the newly planted field, back toward the small farmhouse his folks now called home. They were only a few miles outside of Topeka, where Cole's two sisters lived with their husbands and families. Everyone was happily settled. Everyone but Cole.

It'll come soon enough, he told himself. But until he was back in Montana—back on the Vandyke ranch—with Dianne, Cole knew he wouldn't be completely at peace.

"Your ma's got lunch almost ready!" Cole's father called as he made his way across the black river-bottom dirt.

"Field is finished. You ought to have a good crop of corn if the storms aren't bad this year."

"And if the rains come and if the sun doesn't get too hot and if the pests stay away," Hallam said with a chuckle. "Lots of *if*s in farming."

"Yep," Cole agreed, "but you've done a good job with it. You've made a stand against nature, and I think you're winning the battle." He wiped his forehead again, then tucked his handkerchief back in his pocket.

The two men walked toward the house in silence, but in Cole's heart he knew he needed to speak. With his departure so close, Cole wanted to assure himself, and his father, that all was well and forgiven. He knew his father understood his coming—knew that by staying on and helping his father establish the farm that Cole was showing his approval and love. But Cole also knew that words needed to be shared.

"Before we go in," he began as they reached the water pump, "I'd like to say something."

Hallam stopped and nodded. "I figured you might."

Cole pumped cold water from the well and washed up as he contemplated his words. It wasn't the first time he'd considered what he might say. Many a night he'd lain in bed practicing a sort of speech he planned to give his father.

Turning to his father, Cole drew a deep breath. "I came here to make my peace with you—you know that."

"Yes," Hallam admitted. "You said as much when you came here. I've never wanted to push for more."

"Maybe you should have," Cole said with a hint of smile.

"We Selby men seem to be poor in communicating our problems."

"To be sure," his father agreed.

"Well, so much has happened to me . . . to change me. You know, too, that God managed to get ahold of me. That made a big difference. I was really angry with God for a long time. I felt like He must have hated me—otherwise why would He give me so much grief? I didn't want to be close to a God who would allow innocent people to pay the price that rightfully belonged to the guilty."

Cole walked away from the pump and sat down on a small bench not far away. Hallam followed his son and leaned against an oak that shaded them both from the heat of the day.

Pain-filled memories began to flood Cole's mind. "When we went with the vigilantes that day so long ago, I had no desire to be a part of taking the law into my own hands. I agreed those robbers and murderers had to be stopped, but I felt like there had to be a better way. . . . Still, I went because I knew you expected it of me—that you would be shamed if I didn't go."

"I should never have joined them," Hallam admitted, "but I wanted very much to see justice done. A lot of folks were suffering at their hands." He paused and kicked at the dirt. "I also wanted the respect of the townsfolk. Figured if I joined in ridding the land of such a plague as those highwaymen, then I'd finally be a man folks could look up to—that your ma could look up to."

Cole had always felt this was the reason for his father's actions. Scorned by most, Hallam Selby had never fit in, no matter where they moved. He had a variety of skills but wasn't really good at any one thing. He'd tried ranching and storekeeping, law enforcement and grave digging, but nothing truly suited the man. Then they went to Montana to look for gold, but even that proved to be a bust.

"When we went out to deal with Carrie's father," Cole said, allowing himself to speak the name of the woman he'd once loved, "I knew there'd be trouble. I arranged for Carrie to receive a note from one of her friends in Virginia City. I calculated that if she went into town to see her friend, she'd be gone while we dealt with her pa. I wanted to keep her safe—I loved her and didn't want anything to hurt her."

"It was going to hurt no matter what," Hallam said thoughtfully. "We intended to hang her pa, and that's what we did. We didn't intend for her to die, but she'd always bear the scars of that moment."

Cole nodded. "But I figured I could make it better by marrying her and taking her away from the sorrow."

"I'm sorry, son. I'm sorry it was my bullet that killed her."

Cole remembered the scene as if it'd been yesterday. His beautiful Carrie had come back too soon and, desperate to save her father, had thrown herself into the midst of the vigilantes, only to be shot. Cole knew his father had not intentionally murdered Carrie, but it didn't matter. It had still devastated him. Even now, he could remember holding her in his arms and feeling the life go out of her.

"I know you'd take it back if you could," Cole said softly. "It's taken me a long time to get to the place where I can say that. Over six years, in fact." He looked to his father and shook his head. "I'm sorry, Pa. I was just so angry and nothing made sense."

"I know that, boy. I knew it then. There hasn't been a day gone by that I haven't had to live with the memory of what happened. I'd give my life to undo what's done."

Cole nodded. "I know you would. Dianne helped me see that. I guess I would never have known her had things not happened as they did. I never thought I'd love again, but Dianne is a very special woman."

"She sounds like a good woman too."

"She is. The very best. I've never met a woman with more determination."

"Unless it was your mother."

Cole smiled. "Yes, I suppose Dianne's determination does remind me of Ma. She never seems to be defeated for long. It's amazing to me. I'd like to have half her strength."

"You're stronger than you give yourself credit for."

A silence fell between them as the two men eyed each other. Cole got to his feet and stood directly in front of his father. "I'm sorry for everything. I hope you'll forgive me."

"Son, I did that long ago when you asked for it the first time. I pray you've forgiven me as well."

Cole nodded. "Before I ever came here. I'm sorry it's taken me so long to speak it all out."

The men embraced and Cole felt that finally everything had been set right. "I'm glad," Cole said, pulling away, "that we've had this year together. It's been hard to be away from Montana, but I know it was the right thing to do."

"So now you'll head out with the wagon train tomorrow?"

"Yes. Daniel Keefer, the wagon master I worked for before, is leading a group out of Independence. I'm joining up with him just north of here. It's a good way to earn some money and make my way back. Safety in numbers, you know, and now with the Indians warring almost constantly, these wagon trains are the only way to get across the country alive."

"I wish there were a better way for you. Maybe you could take the train," his father suggested.

"Too expensive. I wouldn't begin to have the means."

His father reached inside his shirt and pulled out an envelope. "I was planning to give you this at lunch, but now's just as good a time." He handed it over to Cole and smiled. "It's to help you get started in your new married life, but you could sure use it to buy a train ticket home."

Cole looked in the envelope and then raised his gaze back to his father. "There's a good deal of money in here."

"A year's wages," his father replied. "I didn't want you working for nothing, and since last year's crop paid out so well, I just tucked this aside for you."

"I can't take it, Pa. I didn't help you so you'd feel obligated to pay me."

"I don't feel obligated to pay you. It's a gift. Just like this last year was for me—and for your ma."

Cole looked back at the cash and shook his head. "It doesn't seem right."

"Well, obeying your pa is right," Hallam said with a grin, "and I'm telling you to take it. Do with it as you will. If you wanna take the train home and get back to that little gal of yours all that much faster, then so be it. As I understand it, you can take the train to just around Salt Lake City. Then go north on the same trail that took us into Virginia City."

"I can't let Daniel down, or I would do just that," Cole said, regretting that his choice was already made. "But thank you, Pa. Thank you for this and everything else."

A peace settled over both men, evidenced by their smiles. "Let's go eat," Hallam said, pulling Cole alongside. "Your ma's spent all morning putting together a great meal for your going away. Tonight a few folks from the church will come by to say their farewells, but for lunch you belong just to us."

Cole smiled. It felt good to belong.

————

The next morning, Cole loaded his saddlebags and readied his horse for the trip home. He was surprised when his mother came out to the barn to say good-bye in private.

"I made these for you," she said, holding up a flour sack. "Oatmeal cookies. There's enough here to last you quite a while."

Cole took the bag, noting the gray in his mother's hair and the wrinkles around her eyes. She'd had a hard life, but now at least she seemed content. "Thanks, Ma. I doubt they'll last that long if they're as good as usual."

She smiled and looked down at her empty hands. "I'm glad for the time we've had. It couldn't make up for the lost years, but I feel like I've finally been able to know you . . . to . . . well, to love you." She looked up and met his gaze. There were tears in her eyes.

"I know, Ma. I feel the same way. I can't tell you what it's meant to me, being here with you and Pa. I've missed Dianne," he said with a grin, "and I've missed Montana, but I wouldn't trade being here for all the gold in the territory."

"Will you marry right away?"

"I hope so," Cole said, securing the cookies with a string and tying them around the horn of his saddle. "I hope she hasn't changed her mind, what with me taking all this extra time."

"If she's the woman you say she is, she'll be watching and waiting."

Cole reached out and touched his mother's shoulder. They'd never been much for physical contact, but she seemed to relish the moment. "I'll miss you, Ma. I hope you and Pa will come to visit us. You'll always be welcome."

"Well, farms don't run themselves, so I doubt it'll be anytime soon," she replied, a tinge of regret in her voice. "But you'll be in our prayers, and I'll write."

Cole nodded just as the rooster began crowing. "Looks like I'd best be on my way. I've got a good piece to ride before I catch up to Mr. Keefer."

Mary Selby uncharacteristically grabbed hold of her son and

embraced him long and hard. Cole couldn't help but sense desperation in her action. "Please be careful. Let me know as soon as you can that you've arrived safely."

"I promise," Cole said. His mother's uneasiness momentarily unnerved him. He shook it off and tried not to overreact. "I'll probably be there about the time the corn gets as tall as you. So just think on that and start looking for a letter a few weeks later."

She nodded and let him go. Cole mounted his horse and looked around for his father. "Where's Pa?"

"Waiting by the gate. I told him I needed a moment with you. He said he'd meet you there."

"Thanks. Thanks for everything. I hope we see each other again . . . soon."

"I pray that as well."

Cole hated that his mother sounded so worried, but he urged Buddy, his faithful sorrel, out of the barn and down the path toward the front gate. There were really no words of comfort he could offer her, so instead he prayed that God might ease her worry.

Spotting his father, Cole dismounted and walked the remaining few yards. "Guess it's time for me to get going," he said. The morning dawn was lighting up the day and soon it would be warm, maybe even hot. In Kansas, his father liked to say, a fellow never knew whether to wear a heavy coat or a straw hat.

"Your ma found you, then?"

"Yeah. She seems really worried. I hope you'll be able to put her mind at ease."

"She heard tell of wagon trains being attacked by Indians. Someone from the church mentioned it last night. It's all she's been able to think about ever since."

"Well, that explains it," Cole said, trying hard to sound light-hearted. "Silly gossips. Don't they know the Bible teaches against that kind of thing?"

His father met his gaze and nodded. "Be careful."

"I will be, Pa. You should have word back from me no later than September. I'll even try to drop you a few lines along the way."

"All right, then. Be off and give that little lady of yours our best." He extended his hand, but Cole pulled his father into an embrace instead.

"I will. Give Ma my love and know that you have it too."

He quickly released his father and remounted the horse. If he didn't leave now, he'd get all weepy—something he was definitely not used to.

Cole moved out the open gate and headed to Topeka. There was still something he had to do. The telegram Daniel had sent confirmed that the wagon train had left Independence on the twentieth of April. But it also asked Cole to pick up additional ammunition and maybe an extra rifle or two.

Apparently the Indians were on the warpath.

CHAPTER 6

"ARTICLE FIFTY-TWO OF THE ARTICLES OF WAR DECLARES, 'Any officer or soldier who shall misbehave himself before the enemy, run away, or shamefully abandon any fort, post, or guard which he or they may be commanded to defend, or speak words inducing others to do the like, or shall cast away his arms and ammunition, or who shall quit his post or colors to plunder and pillage, every such offender, being duly convicted thereof, shall suffer death, or such other punishment as shall be ordered by the sentence of a general court-martial.'"

Zane listened to the words of his superior as the proceeding against him concluded. He'd prayed about doing the right thing and knew that being here—admitting to desertion—was the right thing. But knowing that didn't make it any easier.

"Sergeant Chadwick, do you have anything to say in your own defense?"

Zane cleared his throat. "Yes, sir." He eyed the thirteen uniformed men who would ultimately determine his fate.

"Proceed, then."

Zane paused for a moment and threw a glance toward Major

Baker. Rumor had it the man had faced his own displeased superiors but nothing had come of it. Yes, he had waged war on an innocent band of friendly Indians, but that's where any concern ended. After all, they were only Indians.

"I know what I did was wrong," Zane began, "but I also know what we did that day to Heavy Runner's village was wrong." He squared his shoulders and drew a deep breath.

"I joined the army because I wanted to defend the nation and keep the peace. I wanted very much to be a good soldier, and in my time here, I believe I accomplished that. However, when I joined this army, I swore an oath." He pulled a piece of paper from his pocket.

"'I, Zane Chadwick, do solemnly swear that I will bear true allegiance to the United States of America, and that I will serve them honestly and faithfully against all their enemies or opposers whatsoever, and observe and obey the orders of the President of the United States, and the order of the officers appointed over me according to the rules and articles for the government of the armies of the United States.'"

He put the paper down and looked back into the faces of his accusers. "I've kept that oath to the best of my ability. However, on that January day on the Marias, I was not fighting enemies of the United States. I was asked not to defend against an opposer but rather to murder a band of Indians considered by our own government to be friends.

"Major Baker went into that battle knowing full well he had the wrong group of Indians. It wasn't a case of mistaken identity. He knew well ahead of time, and instead of murdering innocent people, most of which were women and children despite the report sitting on your desk, he could have simply moved on to capture or kill the true culprit he sought."

Zane knew this would be his only chance to speak and decided to make it worth his while. "I don't care why Major

Baker made the choice he did. It doesn't matter to me if he was drunk or misguided or simply afraid. What matters to me is the choice I make. I don't have to answer for Major Baker's choices, but I do have to answer for my own. My faith tells me to obey my authority, but it also tells me to obey God first. I didn't kill anyone that day, because I chose to obey God first. I left the army rather than continue in pursuit of other Indians who might also have been innocent and friendly. My judgment was perhaps in error, but my motives were not born of cowardice." He fell silent, keeping his gaze even upon the men before him.

"We will recess for dinner and reconvene at thirteen hundred hours. The prisoner will be confined to general quarters until such time that we reconvene. Dismissed."

Zane and his escorts headed back to his room. He knew he could face death for what he'd done, but for the first time in a long, long while, he was at peace with the entire matter. Come what may, his fate was in God's hands. No matter the decision of the court-martial, Zane could rest in that knowledge.

"Sergeant Chadwick?"

Zane looked to the corporal who was escorting him back to his quarters. "Yes?"

"For what it's worth, there's a bunch of us who agree with what you did. It wasn't right to take innocent lives. Major Baker should never have ordered that attack."

Zane stopped and looked at the man. "What I did was wrong. I should have gone through the proper channels and dealt with it in a more honorable manner. I tried to take an easy way out. Don't agree with that."

The corporal suddenly looked embarrassed. He lowered his gaze and shook his head. "No, sir."

Zane touched the man's shoulder. "I appreciate the support. What we did up there was wrong—there's no doubt about that."

The corporal seemed renewed. He looked up and met Zane's

gaze with great enthusiasm. "Maybe justice will be done because of what you did."

Zane sighed. "Justice won't bring the dead back to life."

————————

"Just look at all those tulips," Faith declared as she and Dianne walked toward the house. "Aren't they lovely? I've never seen so many colors."

Dianne smiled and enjoyed the warmth of the day. "Uncle Bram has a second cousin who sends them from Amsterdam. Ever since she found out he'd settled down and married, she's been mailing them over."

"Well, they're the prettiest things," Faith said, bending down to touch one of the velvety petals.

"I wish they'd bloom longer. One bloom each year. That's all we get. You have to really cherish it when it comes."

"Lilacs are that way too. You get a few weeks of lovely blossoms, then a nice green bush until winter strips it bare. But the fragrance is marvelous."

Dianne recalled the lilacs in Missouri. "Oh yes! I remember them. Lilacs were always one of my favorites."

"You need to plant roses," Faith said, straightening. "Roses will bloom all summer."

"I think I'd like that. Maybe I can order some. Lilacs too. I'll check with Uncle Bram. He'll know what we can get shipped out here. If there were more time, I'd just write to Cole and ask him to bring some plants along." Dianne glanced up the road to the ridge where she'd first gazed down upon the ranch. Someday she'd look up there and see Cole riding home. Someday.

Faith reached out and touched Dianne's hand. "I know you miss him a great deal, but he'll be home soon."

"I know. I keep telling myself that. The spring roundup is done, the cattle are back to summer pasture, and the men are already working to put your cabin up. It won't be long now." She smiled at Faith. "At least that's what I keep telling myself. But honestly, each day is like a month. It drags by so slowly."

"But we've needed the time. Your wedding dress is coming along nicely."

"Thanks to you and Koko. I'm so nervous, I can hardly put in a straight stitch."

Faith laughed and it did Dianne's heart good to hear. Dianne knew Faith was healing little by little. By helping keep house at the ranch and assisting Koko with the children, Faith had put aside her own tragedy. Dianne wasn't sure if things were better between Faith and Malachi, but the man seemed happier. Of course, it could be Uncle Bram's promise of blacksmithing equipment.

Dianne decided to press for information. "Why don't we sit a minute on the porch."

Faith shrugged. "I guess since the clothes are drying on the line and the kids are down for their naps, it wouldn't hurt to take a minute or two."

Dianne patted the seat of the bench Uncle Bram had made for just such occasions. "I want to know how you're doing. You seem happier."

Faith nodded. "I'm better. Something about this place just seems to bring healing. Probably the good company."

"I'm glad, Faith. I was so worried about you."

"Some days are better than others. Still, I've been spending a good deal of time in prayer, and at night I've been teaching Malachi to read. We're using the Bible, of course, and God always seems to have a way of getting my attention. Just yesterday I came across Hebrews chapter eleven. I remember hearing a preacher talk on this once before, but for some reason, reading it last night seemed like the first time."

Dianne wasn't familiar with the chapter, so she pressed Faith to continue. "What did you learn?"

"The whole chapter is about faith—the faith of our fore-fathers. It tells how each one showed faith through his or her deeds, including the harlot Rahab. I suppose it caught my attention because of my own name being Faith. Anyway, I memorized some of verses. It says, 'Now faith is the substance of things hoped for, the evidence of things not seen.'"

"I like that," Dianne said, mulling the words over. She could only have faith that Cole would return—it was the substance of her hope—the evidence of what she couldn't see. Her faith in God was often like that. She could see His handiwork, but she couldn't see Him face to face. That was where faith came in. She had faith that God existed—that He cared and listened.

"Me too. I thought about my babies and about how much I want to have children. I thought about our years in captivity and how we used to hope for the day to come when we'd be free. That chapter also talks about how some of those folks—Abraham and Sarah, for example—died in faith, not even having received the promises. But they'd seen them down the road and were confident of them—confident of God's ability to make them come to pass." She paused for a moment, then spoke more softly.

"I didn't realize some of the sin I'd harbored in my heart."

Dianne looked at her in confusion. "You? I've never seen you be anything but loving and giving—always pointing others toward the Lord."

Faith shook her head. "But in my heart, I held bitterness. It was hard for me to take help from white folks. I figured I'd lived at the mercy of white folks all my life. I know Malachi felt the same way. You have no idea how hard it was for him to come here—to ask for help. But if we hadn't, we would have died . . . and all for the sake of pride."

"I had no idea you felt that way."

Faith met her gaze, and the pain in her heart was evident in her expression. "You don't know what it's like, so I can't blame you. We used to dream of the day we could walk about free. We whispered about it at night, like white folks whisper about presents on Christmas morning. We prayed for freedom—for the chains of oppression to be broken. We prayed for prosperity and a chance to prove ourselves worthy of freedom."

Dianne held back from saying anything. Faith was absolutely right. She didn't know what it was like.

"When freedom came, no one wanted to be obligated to another white man or woman. We wanted to pick up and leave and be gone. Malachi and I decided to just hightail it out of the war and all that was around us. But we were the lucky ones. Most other black folk had no choice but to stay on where they were. Where would they go? How would they pay their way? Besides, many masters didn't care about what Mr. Lincoln had to say. They didn't figure to set anyone free.

"We were lucky—blessed because the Union needed Malachi's skills for shoeing and mending their wagons. They even tried to talk him into joining up for the war, but Malachi would have no part of that, and I was mighty glad. My master had given me a bit of money, so when we had enough, we were able to join up on the wagon train. But we were different than most." She looked away again and this time her voice sounded sad.

"We came to the promised land—or so we thought. But the promise was for everybody else. The gold was there for those who wanted to put in the back-breaking hours of labor, but then there were folks who stood by happy to steal it away from you once you had it. And of course, there were still the same old attitudes and prejudices. No one trusts a black man to be telling the truth about the gold he's been robbed of. No one believes a black woman is capable of running a store counter. We sure can't be hired to teach school, no matter how good we are at reading and writing."

"I'm truly sorry, Faith. I had no idea—just like you said," Dianne felt deeply apologetic. She wished there were a way to wipe away the pain and misery they'd suffered.

"I have to confess something to you, Dianne," Faith continued. "I didn't want to come here."

"But why? You know how much I care about you," Dianne said, genuinely hurt that Faith should feel this way.

"I know, but I didn't want to be beholden to another white person."

"But my skin color shouldn't matter. I'm a human being, same as you. A Christian woman, same as you. Color isn't important to me."

"No, I know it isn't, but you have the luxury of feeling that way. Some folks will call you progressive and praise you for your attitude. For me, it's a constant battle. I've always been taught that color does matter—so even *I* don't feel like you do. The color of your skin tells you what's expected of you—where you'll be allowed to go, how folks will treat you. Believe me, Dianne, I don't want color to matter. I don't want it to be an issue between us."

"Then let's not make it one," Dianne said more sternly than she'd meant to sound.

"I hope you'll forgive me, but with the door open I couldn't help but overhear," Koko said as she joined the two women on the porch. "Dianne, you must understand that for you, a white woman, things are different. As Faith said, you have the luxury of taking up whatever feeling or cause you desire. Some will admire your ambitions and others will scorn your beliefs, but it will only be your philosophies they come against. Not you personally—not the color of your skin. People look at me and say, 'Ah, she's Indian. That makes her a heathen child who has no understanding of anything more than chewing hides and raising more heathens.'"

"And for me," Faith declared, "it's, 'Oh, she's Negro. That makes her dim-witted, lazy, and incapable of being educated.' And some will add that I practice black magic and superstitious nonsense too."

Koko nodded knowingly. "It's the same for my people."

For Dianne the discussion was becoming increasingly painful. She knew she was naïve. Knew, too, that her feelings about color were definitely not the thoughts she had heard expressed by so many others. But she honestly didn't want to look at people in the ways Koko and Faith were suggesting.

"I can understand your heart, Faith. I understand not wanting to take another bit of charity or be at the mercy of white people. But you don't have that here. And you *won't* have that here. You are loved simply because you are my friend. And Koko, you know my feelings in this matter. My mother was a very prejudiced woman, sharing many of those beliefs you mentioned. But it's not me. It's not how I feel." Dianne got to her feet.

"I love you both more dearly than any friend I've ever had. Just as dearly as I loved my little sisters. I despise the sorrow you've known because of heartless people, but here on this ranch, we don't have to live as the world does. We can make a change right here. We can raise our children together—share our hopes and dreams together—find a better way, a way that God would have us make."

"That's exactly the conclusion I came to last night," Faith said, smiling. "Remember I was telling you about Hebrews eleven?"

Dianne nodded.

"Well, the last couple of verses in that chapter really caught my attention. After talking about all those wonderful folk in the Bible—all those great men and women of God—it said . . . let me see if I can remember." She paused a moment and closed her eyes. "'And these all, having obtained a good report through faith, received not the promise: God having provided some better thing for us, that they without us should not be made perfect.'"

Dianne shook her head. "I don't think I understand."

"I think it means that our Bible forefathers found their faith commended, but they had only a part of what God promised. It wasn't that God didn't know what He was doing, but He had His own timing for all these things, and because of His timing, we come together in His plan and the promise of Jesus. Folks didn't understand why He promised something and then they died without seeing it come about. We don't always understand why God does things the way He does."

"'For my thoughts are not your thoughts, neither are your ways my ways, saith the Lord,'" Dianne quoted from Isaiah fifty-five. "I know that's true." She smiled. "So many times I have no idea why God allows for the things He does."

"But we must walk in faith," Koko reminded her. "And as Proverbs says, 'Trust in the Lord with all thine heart; and lean not unto thine own understanding.'"

Faith nodded. "Exactly. My understanding used to be that when I found freedom, everything would be different. I would have my promised land, and life would be different. I would be an independent woman. But I know now, that's not the way it is. I thought a great deal about those Hebrews verses, and I see that sometimes God brings others in to fulfill the promise He's given. Maybe that's what He did with me."

"What do you mean?" Dianne asked, eager to understand.

"I had my idea," Faith explained, "of what freedom was. I wasn't about to believe it needed to involve my being dependent on anyone else—especially not any white person. But instead, God has shown me I was just as prejudiced as those who held the color of my skin against me. I was holding your color against you. I know now that God has brought us together in this place to help one another. I feel, like it says in that verse, that God has provided something better—better than I could have ever imagined."

Koko nodded. "I feel the same."

"Me too," Dianne said, reaching out for each woman's hand. "I feel that even though I lost my two sisters on the journey here, God has given me two other sisters to fill that void. You will always be my family—my sisters."

"My sister," Faith said, nodding with a smile.

"Sisters," Koko affirmed.

CHAPTER 7

August 1870

COLE HAD NEVER BEEN MORE MISERABLE IN HIS LIFE. WHAT should have been a nice easy trip west had been fraught with one problem after another. Sickness, bad weather, Indians . . . What else could possibly go wrong?

I should have been home by now, he thought. He prepared his bedroll for sleep but wondered if he'd be able to relax. Lately the threat of attack had been greater than it had ever been before. Everyone was tense, even Daniel Keefer. It was clear a band of Sioux were taunting them—leaving just enough evidence of their existence to let the men of the wagon train know they weren't alone. But why the Sioux had traveled this far west or wanted to continue giving this small band of settlers such grief was beyond Cole.

"I've got a couple of men posted—keeping watch until about three. Can you join me and take over after that?" Keefer asked, walking casually into Cole's camp. He carried his rifle—a sure sign of his worry.

"Sure, Daniel. What's happening out there? Have you managed to figure it out?"

Keefer squatted down by the fire and lowered his voice. "It doesn't look good. That scare we had back in Nebraska still has everyone talking, but I have a feeling this is gonna be much worse. If we can make it another fifty miles west, we should be all right."

"You think they'll just ignore us and let us go along our merry way?"

Keefer raised his face and met Cole's determined stare. "No, I honestly don't, but I figure it doesn't hurt to hope." Cole felt the chill in his words. Keefer's face darkened. "Look, take no chances. If you see or hear anything, alert the rest of us." He stood and looked back down at the fire. "I know they're out there. I just don't know how many." Standing, Keefer rested his hand against Cole's shoulder. "If they attack and anything happens to me, get the train on through to safety." He paused. "And . . . uh . . . let my family know what's happened to me."

Cole nodded, knowing it was futile to argue. There would be an attack. It was just a matter of when and where. This band of warrior Sioux hadn't been following them for nearly a week just to offer them escort.

The camp settled in for the night. The wagons had been drawn together in a tight circle, with all of the livestock inside that perimeter. The smallest of fires had been used for cooking. It wasn't that they could keep the Sioux from knowing their presence on the plains, but rather Daniel told them not to give their attackers any extra benefit. Now nearly all of the travelers were asleep—or trying to do so—and Cole couldn't help but be awash in anxiety for the things that might come. He'd heard too many stories; the memories were still fresh from the tales told at Julesburg. While taking supper one night he'd fallen into a conversation with several townsmen. They were only too happy to relate all of the grisly details of an Indian attack on some railroad men who had been out making repairs to the line.

Cole felt his stomach tighten at the thought of the men whose scalps had been taken and eyes gouged out. Other atrocities had been meted out, but Cole couldn't bring himself to dwell even a moment on them. Not when the same fate might well lie in store for him on the morrow.

He slipped into his bedding, knowing that rest was crucial. He needed to be alert when his turn for guard duty came. Cole tried not to worry or borrow trouble, as his mother would say. He couldn't stop the Indians by fretting. Or by remembering what they'd done to those who'd passed through before them.

If we make it out alive, he told himself, *I'm never crossing this prairie again.* Of course, it was probably silly to have such thoughts. He still had family in Kansas, and the transcontinental railroad was in place to make travel easier. The locomotive couldn't reduce the number of miles between Montana and Kansas, but it could definitely shorten the number of days required for travel.

"I should have spent the money for the train and told Daniel to forget it," he muttered, trying hard to get comfortable. *Then I wouldn't be dealing with cantankerous travelers and hostile Indians.*

He supposed the hostility was understandable. Year after year, the land west of the Mississippi was being deluged by a storm of settlers who were looking to make their dreams come true. It was this very invasion that caused such a feeling of desperation in the various tribes who lived in this region. They saw their hunting grounds disappear, along with the buffalo and other game. The railroad was a nuisance to them. The wagon trains with their hundreds of new settlers, a threat to their very existence. No, it was no wonder they were hostile—even to the point of killing the intruders.

Cole prickled at a sound near his camp. He reached for his revolver, then noticed the slim figure of a man Keefer had hired to help with wagon mending. The young man touched the brim of his hat when Cole continued to stare hard.

"Evenin', Cole."

"Sam." Cole relaxed. "Anything worth reporting?"

"Nah, it's all quiet out there. Maybe too quiet."

Cole nodded. "I'm gonna try to get some shut-eye. Wake me when I need to relieve you."

"Sure thing." The man ambled off toward the west, his rifle leveled at the hip, as if expecting an attack at any moment.

Cole settled down again and sighed. *Oh, Dianne. Why am I here and you're so far away?*

He knew the answer, of course, but still it troubled him deep in his heart. If he died here on the plains, it might be a long time before she ever learned what had happened. He was already over a month delayed from when he'd planned to arrive home. He'd posted a letter from Cheyenne, but that had been weeks earlier, before the constant sickness had slowed their progress to a snail's pace. And then the clouds had unleashed freakish summer storms upon them, deluging them with torrents of rain, leaving the trails horribly impassable. They'd waited nearly two weeks just to progress twenty miles, only to have a bout of cholera hit the train hard.

I should be home. I should be working on the Vandyke ranch, helping Bram build the new house.

He closed his eyes and tried to imagine what the place would look like. Dianne had described her uncle's plan in her last letter. It sounded wonderful. A huge two-story house in a U shape, with quarters in the middle upstairs for guests and two wings— one east and one west—for the two families living there. His family. His and Dianne's. And Bram's family. There would be a large wraparound porch for warm summer nights and a huge stone fireplace for cold winters when they'd remain cooped up until spring.

Dianne was quite excited about the design, having worked

alongside Bram through the winter months helping with the plans.

I should be home helping. I should be with you, Dianne.

Sitting back up, Cole scooted closer to his fire and pulled a small book from his coat pocket. He'd been keeping a journal on the trip since he'd left Topeka. He thought to share some of it with his mother and father but knew he would pore over each detail with Dianne, telling her where he was each night and what had happened in the camp. Now he feared there might not be another chance to tell her of his situation. If the Indians attacked at dawn, as seemed likely, he'd never have a chance to explain if he managed to get killed.

He dug into his other pocket and procured a pencil. Feeling the night chill on his back, he wrote.

Indians—Sioux, we believe—have been following us for nearly a week. We think they'll attack at dawn. All the signs point to it. Dianne, I can't risk dying without writing once again of how much I love you and how very sorry I am for the delay in getting home to you.

You are all I think about, and even now, faced with the chance of death, my only regret is in leaving you—of never seeing you again. I think of you with every waking moment. I long for your touch, your embrace. No matter what happens tomorrow, I pray that you'll somehow be able to read these words and know that I went to my grave loving you.

Cole put the pencil away and yawned. He couldn't keep writing and get enough rest to properly do his guard duty. Instead of replacing the book in his pocket, he stuffed it down inside his boot and eased back onto his blanket.

He could see her smiling face—could remember how her hand felt in his. God just had to get him back to her safely. He'd brought them together, Cole reasoned. Surely He wouldn't stop there. Drifting into a restless sleep, Cole remembered the way she felt in his arms and how very much he wanted to have a chance to share a life with this extraordinary woman.

Oh, God, please get me home. Please give us a miracle.

Sam woke Cole at exactly three. Cole sat up with a start. For a moment he gripped his revolver and scrutinized the young man standing over him. He could barely see him in the dark.

"Sorry . . . didn't mean to scare you, Cole. It's your watch."

Cole calmed and released the gun. Wiping the sleep from his eyes, he got to his feet. "Thanks, Sam. Sorry if I scared *you*. I rarely wake up shooting. I'm usually good about figuring out my targets first. What's the situation?"

The young man shook his head. "Mr. Keefer figures there are at least fifty, maybe more. They're waiting for first light— leastwise that's how Mr. Keefer has it figured."

Cole nodded. "Try to get some sleep. Nothing will happen for at least a couple of hours. No Indian in his right mind is going to try to fight us in the dark."

"Guess not." Sam didn't sound convinced but nevertheless walked off across the camp.

Cole quickly gathered his things, then rounded up Buddy. He saddled the horse in record time, then tied on his gear. Daniel had plans to be ready to fight or flee with the first light. By Cole's best guess that would come in about three hours. Maybe even a little earlier. They needed to be ready.

By five, the camp was starting to stir. A baby cried in one of the wagons. It gave Cole a sickening sensation in his stomach. He could hear other children talking in hushed whispers to their parents. Would any of these little ones live to see another day?

Oh, God, please deliver us from this battle. You know these folks aren't prepared or capable. Our only sin is being here.

Cole rode Buddy around the perimeter of the circled wagons. His keen eyes scanned the horizon for signs of intruders. Daniel suggested the Sioux would slip in early and low, but so far, Cole hadn't seen any signs of them.

"What do you think?" Daniel questioned, riding up on his bay.

"I still think they're waiting for sunrise. I've heard some rustling out there, but I haven't seen anything."

"Well, there's no doubt they're out there."

Cole nodded. "I know."

The next hour seemed to creep by, leaving Cole tense, his shoulder muscles aching and tight. The skies were a mottled blue-lavender just before the sun peeked up above the horizon. Cole scanned the land around him. Maybe they were mistaken. Maybe the Indians had given up the idea of attack. Maybe—

The crack of a rifle being fired split the otherwise silent morning air. Cole felt the air go out from him. He turned Buddy back to the camp and barely made it before the screaming cries of nearly a hundred Sioux warriors descended upon them.

Cole freed Buddy and took cover behind one of the wagons.

"They gave no sign," Cole announced as Daniel Keefer raced up.

"Figures. Well, we were as ready as we were gonna get," the older man said, taking his position. As the Sioux came swooping at them from every direction, the settlers had no choice but to fire.

Cole emptied a box of ammo on the ground. "We're in for the fight of our life!" The words no sooner left his mouth than a bullet ripped into Daniel's shoulder. Blood immediately poured from the wound and his right arm went limp.

Without missing a shot, however, Daniel simply changed arms, firing with the stock against his left shoulder.

Cole heard the screams of children and women coming from

behind him. He turned just in time to see a mounted warrior leap over a wagon tongue and enter the camp. Cole turned and fired at the man, dropping him to the ground.

Cole had no sooner refocused on the attack in front of him when a bullet grazed his arm. A burning sensation traveled down into his fingers. Ignoring it, he continued to fire the rifle, stopping only long enough to reload.

"This is hopeless," Keefer cried just before an arrow pierced the middle of his throat.

Time seemed to stand still after that. Cole saw the despair— the death—in Daniel's eyes. The injured man slumped, trying to speak, as another bullet caught him in the head. Cole couldn't even stop long enough to offer him comfort. In the next second, Cole took two arrows himself, both in the chest. They impacted with a dull thud, stunning Cole enough that he dropped his rifle. He stared down momentarily, dazed at the sight of the protrusions.

He gasped for breath. Stretching, he reached for the rifle. It seemed like it had fallen a hundred feet away. He tried to raise it, but the muscles in his arms and chest refused to work. He felt the rifle slip from his fingers as dizziness overtook him.

Cole closed his eyes. He could smell smoke, hear the Sioux war cries.

"Dianne," he whispered, pulling his revolver from his holster. "Think about Dianne." The thought gave him strength.

He raised the gun and squeezed off two shots before a Sioux bullet grazed his head. Cole was surprised the pain was only minimal. How many hits could he take before his body gave up?

Cole fell back, the revolver in his hands. Daniel Keefer lay dead not a foot away—his open blank eyes staring at Cole.

The world tilted, first left and then right. Cole looked down at his blood-covered shirt. He touched the arrows, marveling at the skill it must have taken to create such accurate weapons. How strange, he thought, to consider that now—at a time like this.

They were completely overrun now. Cole saw a woman cut down with a tomahawk. The man who'd tried to defend her fell at her side, his body riddled with bullets and arrows.

"Dianne," Cole panted, the pain searing his chest. Breathing seemed a pointless labor, but still he would not die.

And then the world went completely silent. Cole was certain this must be the precursor to death. He listened, hoping to hear angels. His mother had once said that heaven was full of angels singing choruses to God. He wanted to hear the music. Closing his eyes, Cole smiled. He could hear it. He could hear the angel songs.

CHAPTER 8

DIANNE STOOD AT THE TOP OF HER FAVORITE HILL. THE long walk had given her much time to think. September was already upon them, and there was no sign of Cole. She searched the trail that would bring Cole to the ranch, but it was empty. Just as it had been the day before and the day before that.

"Where is he, Father?" she prayed aloud. "I'm so worried about him."

Aspens in the valley below rustled whispers on the wind, but they offered no comfort. Dianne pushed back strands of unruly blond hair and tucked them under her wide-brimmed hat.

With her hand to shield her eyes further, she strained to see any sign of life on the hills beyond the ranch. She didn't even see any deer or elk. "Lord, I just want him to come home safe. Please bring him home."

Dianne knew God cared about her and would definitely hear her prayer, but she also knew that His plans were not always hers. Turning back to gaze upon the ranch, Dianne couldn't help but smile. Uncle Bram had worked hard all summer to put his plans into motion for the big house.

To Dianne the new house was reminiscent of a palatial mansion she'd once seen in Memphis. The main portion of the house was already in grand order. Bram had hired extra men from Virginia City to help with construction, and when the livestock didn't require their attention, every hand on the ranch was busy at work on the new house. Dianne had marveled at the transformation.

Wagonload after wagonload of lumber had been brought in from area sawmills, while other supplies were shipped in from the east by train, then transported over the mountains to the ranch. Bram had spared no expense, and the amassed goods were quickly transformed into a house that would rival any eastern society home. Bram had told Dianne he would take great pleasure in putting Koko in such a regal home. She deserved good things, and Dianne agreed. If it weren't for Uncle Bram and Koko, Dianne knew she and her brothers would probably never have made it in Montana Territory.

Sitting down on the browning grass, Dianne let her thoughts wander. Uncle Bram hoped to have the house completed by winter, but in order to do so, he'd had to let other important ranch duties slide. Gus Yegen, his foreman and best friend, had been handling things quite capably, but soon winter would be upon them, and before the snows set in, the herd would have to be driven to winter range.

Thoughts of the herd gave Dianne a real feeling of contentment. The herd had been small when she'd first come here in 1865, but now, five years later, it had grown to a respectable size. Each year, at Gus's direction and insistence, Bram brought in more animals from Texas. Gus had good connections in that southern state, and his friends were only too happy to cut Bram generous deals that profited them both.

Watching the ranch grow had blessed Dianne in a way she couldn't begin to explain. With Faith and Malachi now on hand, they were better equipped than any outfit in the territory. Malachi's blacksmithing talents had brought in neighboring ranchmen and in turn had given the former slave an extra source of income. Bram never begrudged his employee the opportunity to earn money. In fact, he encouraged it, and Dianne had nothing but the highest regard for her uncle's generosity.

"We're all blessed by Malachi's ability," Bram had told her once. "No sense trying to hoard that all to ourselves."

Dianne couldn't have agreed more. The former slave was only now appearing to be comfortable with his role at the ranch, and Uncle Bram's generosity helped to teach both Malachi and Faith that not every white man was out to get what he could from them.

To Dianne's relief, Faith was showing signs of healing. She took great pleasure in helping with the house and the children, and in turn, little Susannah seemed to delight in Faith's company. To Dianne's amazement, Koko never seemed ill at ease with all the attention exchanged between the two. Dianne wondered if she herself would feel as content to give her child over to another woman's care—even Faith's. But Koko seemed to understand the importance of drawing Faith into her little circle of family. In some ways, Koko almost forced her small daughter into the care of the wounded woman. Koko had a way about her that suggested she was purposefully choosing this path in order to see Faith made whole. Her kindness to a woman who until last January had been a total stranger was impressive. Dianne could only hope to emulate such generosity.

The sound of a horse approaching at a rapid pace caught Dianne's attention. She jumped to her feet and wheeled around, wondering—hoping, really, that it might be Cole returning. Instead, she found her brother. Morgan brought the horse to a stop just a few inches from where his sister stood.

"You up here moping?"

"No, just dreaming." She smiled and added, "There's a difference."

"Well, dream no more," he said, thrusting an envelope at her. "He's written."

Dianne's smile broadened. "Truly?" She grasped the envelope, recognizing Cole's scrawled script. She pressed the letter to her breast. "Oh, I'm so happy."

"I kind of figured you would be—that's why I rode as hard as I could to bring it to you." Morgan took off his hat and wiped his brow with the back of his sleeve. "Hope it's good news."

"I'm just happy to have news, but I hope it's good too."

"Well, you gonna read it or just hug it?"

"I kind of figured to read it in private."

Morgan pushed his hat back on and shook his head. "I rode all that way and you're gonna read it in private?" His expression suggested she was completely unjust in her thinking.

She took pity on him. "All right." She opened the letter and sighed at the disappointingly short missive. "'Dearest Dianne,'" she read aloud, "'We're in Cheyenne and I figured to send this out on the mail train. Travel west has been impossibly slow. Sickness has overtaken us on more than one occasion, and the travelers are discouraged. Hope to be home by September, but only if the weather holds and we can avoid Indian trouble. Love, Cole.'"

"That's it?"

Dianne nodded, already rereading the words, as if she might find hidden meaning in the few lines. "That's it."

"Seems hardly worth riding all that way for," Morgan said.

She met his teasing gaze, realizing he was trying to cajole her into a better mood. "I suppose he couldn't write much on the trail. I remember how hard it was. Given his duties, he did well to send this."

"Well, it was posted in early August. I would think he'd be

home any day now, so you'd better lose that dreary look and get a smile back on your face." He remounted and reached down. "Come on. I'll ride you back home."

"That's all right. I'd rather walk. I want to pray and thank God for giving me this much."

Morgan nodded. "I'll see you at the house, then." He rode off, his pace much slower than it had been when he'd approached.

Dianne tucked the letter into her skirt pocket and headed back toward the cabin. Bram hoped to have them in the big house soon, but in some ways Dianne knew she would always miss the little cabin they shared. That house was a true home of love for Dianne. That home had made the losses in her life seem so much less severe.

Dianne was about a quarter of a mile from the house when Faith appeared from her own home and waved. She and Malachi had been in their new place since late in the spring. Malachi especially loved having his very own blacksmith shop, which was just on the other side of the kitchen wall. Smiling and waving, Dianne was pleased when Faith headed out to meet her on the trail.

"I have a letter from Cole," Dianne called out. "It's not much, but it's better than nothing."

"What does he say?"

"That he hopes to be home no later than September. It was posted in August from Cheyenne, so Morgan says he ought to be back any time."

Faith drew near and Dianne could see her smile widen. "That's good news." She paused and halted in front of Dianne. "I have some good news too."

Dianne saw the light of excitement in Faith's expression. "What? Tell me."

Faith giggled like a young girl. "I'm going to have a baby.

I'm terrified and delighted at the same time."

"Oh, Faith. That is wonderful news. I'll bet Malachi is beside himself."

"He's scared too," Faith admitted. "I'm almost afraid to believe it's true."

"When's the baby going to be here?"

"Best as I can figure it should be around the end of April," Faith replied.

Dianne nodded. "That's perfect. We'll have all winter to make wonderful baby clothes. Maybe Morgan and Cole can help Malachi make a cradle and other things you'll need." She pulled Faith into a tight embrace. "I'm so happy for you, Faith. We'll trust God through all of this, and no matter what, I'll take good care of you." She pulled away and met Faith's now sober expression. "I just know this baby will be fine. I feel it deep inside."

Faith nodded. "That's my prayer."

"You are happy here, aren't you, Faith?" Dianne asked.

"Happier than I've ever been in all my life," the older woman admitted. "I know I've said things in the past that might indicate otherwise, but this was a good choice for us. We might not own our land or house, but we are saving money, and someday maybe we'll be able to buy our own spot." She looked off toward the river, where the aspens grew thick. "Someplace real pretty like that."

"I'll bet Uncle Bram will sell you a parcel of land when you're ready. He keeps adding to his own anyway. I think it would be wonderful for you to own your place free and clear, working for yourselves. I know that would mean a lot to you."

Faith met her eyes. "It would be like nothing I've ever known or could hope to know. Dianne, being here has been a blessing we never expected. We'd thought to find you and stay here just long enough to get back on our feet and move on. Didn't want to be beholden to anyone."

"I know."

"But we don't feel beholden now. We both have our jobs and work hard and earn our keep."

"That and then some," Dianne agreed. "You've made life much easier for the rest of us. I for one am blessed."

Faith looked back toward the river. "Heard a fellow call this God's country. I think he just may have been right. I knew God and loved Him before we came here, but now I feel like I live in a little bit of heaven on earth."

Dianne drew a deep breath and lifted her gaze to the mountains beyond the ranch. "I feel the same way—a little bit of heaven."

———————

At dinner that night, Faith made her announcement public. Everyone congratulated her, but Koko actually cried.

"I've prayed hard for this," she said, dabbing her eyes unashamedly. "I'm so happy."

"Well, seems this is a great night for good news," Bram announced. "I wanted to let you all know that we'll be moving into the house at the end of the week. There's still plenty to do, but the main portion of the house is completed. We can keep working to finish the wings as time permits this winter. With the outside structure in place, we can take our time with the interior."

"How exciting!" Dianne exclaimed.

"Since we're sharing good news," Morgan began slowly, "I guess I'll share mine as well."

Everyone turned to look at the young man. He reddened a bit, then cleared his throat nervously. "I'm going to be heading out. I've been accepted to join a group of men who are heading south to survey the land along the Yellowstone River."

Dianne knew her mouth had dropped open, but she couldn't

seem to force it closed. For several moments no one said a word. Finally Bram started the conversation again.

"Well, son, I'm sure happy for you. I know you've wanted to set out on a project like this for some time. I guess this is exactly what you've been waiting for."

"It is, sir."

"Why didn't you say something sooner?" Dianne questioned without thinking. "I thought you'd be here for my wedding and for . . ." She trailed off, uncertain what else she might say. What was she hoping for? She couldn't expect Morgan to spend his whole life here.

Dianne immediately felt guilty. "Forget what I said. I'm happy for you, Morgan, truly I am." She pushed aside her feelings. "When will you be leaving?"

"Right away—tomorrow."

"So soon?" Koko asked, her voice betraying the surprise Dianne felt.

"I know it's short notice, but I just got word on this myself. When I was in town, I met with the men and got their final approval. We'll meet in Bozeman three days from now and head out immediately. The army is giving us an escort."

Dianne nodded. "Well, then, I guess I'll have to give you your Christmas present early." She got up from the table and hurried to her room. Pulling a package from her wardrobe, Dianne returned to the dining table. "Koko helped me make this for you."

Morgan took the package and untied the string that held the edges of the flour sack together. He pulled out the contents and smiled. "A new coat." He held up the soft leather fringed coat and smiled. "I've never seen anything finer. Where'd you get the fleece to line it with?"

"We have our ways," Dianne said, laughing. She tried to avoid showing any emotion but joy. The last thing she wanted was to make Morgan feel guilty for his decision to leave, but deep in her heart she was feeling the loss already. She looked at Koko, who nodded, seeming to understand.

"These ladies could come up with just about anything," Bram said, pushing back from the table. "I can't imagine how they do it, but I'm mighty glad they're so capable."

"You have to be capable in Montana," Dianne said, her voice a bit too somber. "If you aren't, it'll eat you alive."

A week later, Dianne paced the length of the new dining room. "I never thought it would be this big," she declared to Koko and Faith. "It's wonderful."

"It will take some getting used to eating in a real dining room," Faith exclaimed. "I was never allowed to eat there," she murmured as she caressed the backs of the polished oak chairs.

"I've never known such a thing either," Koko said, smiling with great pride, "but I'm happy to give it a try." She gently touched the river rock they'd used to create a large fireplace.

Dianne laughed. "This will become a favorite room to be sure. Some of my best memories are of time spent around the dinner table. That's when we heard stories from Papa and when Mama talked about her plans for the days to come. It was always a nice time." She grinned and added, "Plus, Mama was a wonderful cook and we ate well."

Faith and Koko laughed.

"Well, what do you ladies think?" Bram questioned as he stomped into the room.

"I think it's wonderful, Uncle Bram." Dianne wrapped her arms around the barrel-chested man and stretched up to place a kiss on his cheek. He bent down to receive her offering and smiled. "I never thought it would be so large and lovely. Those were a marvelous surprise," she said pointing to two large floor-to-ceiling windows.

"I'm glad you like it. I plan to have them all over the house. That's why I've laid out places in each room for them. The glass is expensive and pretty hard to get here in one piece, so we'll have to add them as we can afford."

"I think we can wait," Koko said. It was clear she was very proud of her husband and his efforts. "We'll have our hands full just making draperies and curtains for the windows you've already managed to put in."

"Oh, I can just imagine lovely gold damask for this room," Faith said, eyeing the open windows. "We have some material in the storage room that would work just perfect."

"That does sound good," Koko agreed. "We'll have to explore the storage room and see what all there is to use."

"Just don't work yourselves into a lather," Bram said, grinning. He was clearly enjoying their enthusiasm.

"I'm especially fond of the wraparound porches," Dianne added. "And on both the upper and lower levels. It will be so nice in the summer when the days are warm."

"That was the idea. When we have more money, we'll add some real pretty railing and some nice trim," Bram said. He looked as pleased as a young boy at Christmas. "This is gonna be the finest house in the state."

"No doubt it already is," Dianne declared.

Bram's smile broadened as he added, "Oh—I've got another surprise for you."

"Do tell," Dianne said as she looked to Koko and Faith, raising her brows ever so slightly.

"Gus, Levi, and I are taking a string of horses to Bozeman. I thought since you've been working with those animals so closely, you should probably go along and help answer any questions that might come up at the sale. Would you like that?"

Dianne quickly nodded, then realized that Cole was due back any day. "I can't go. Cole might return and I wouldn't be here."

"We won't be gone that long and he'll wait," Bram insisted. "I don't plan to be more than four, maybe five days."

Koko came to her and gently touched her arm. "I think you should go. Bram will need your help, and as he said, Cole will wait."

Dianne nodded. "I suppose you're right. It's just that . . . well . . . I don't want to leave and have this be the time he finally shows up."

"Now, even if that happens," Bram said with a hearty laugh, "I know he'll wait for you. He knows you've been faithful to wait all this time. He won't turn around and head back just because you're in Bozeman."

The next day, Dianne found herself on the trail bound for Bozeman with those very words ringing in her ears. Faithfulness was easy when it came to Cole. Dianne had so long imagined herself with Cole Selby as her husband that any other consideration wasn't an option. And Cole, though he might be delayed a bit, had only shown her loyalty and trust.

Dolly tossed her head as if able to read Dianne's mind. The mount had been a good friend over the years. "Sorry, girl, you've been loyal too." She gave the horse's neck a gentle pat.

Dianne continued to contemplate the meaning of faithfulness and how she could improve on this seemingly small but powerful ideal. God's faithfulness was guaranteed throughout the Scriptures. He promised to be faithful no matter what other people did or didn't do.

"Now faith is the substance of things hoped for, the evidence of things not seen," she recited mentally. The words warmed Dianne's very soul. Could it be that God's faithfulness was based in hope

for His children? Should her faith—her faithfulness—be based in hope?

Dianne shook her head. She felt as if she were on the edge of understanding something very wonderful. What did it all mean? How could she come to a full knowledge of what God was trying to help her learn?

Patience, a voice whispered in her heart. *You must have patience.*

Dianne chuckled. "Not exactly one of my virtues."

"Did you say something?" Bram asked as he rode up alongside his niece.

She shook her head and laughed all the more. "Nothing you don't already know."

CHAPTER 9

BRAM VANDYKE WAS A NO-NONSENSE KIND OF MAN WHO had goals and ambitions for himself and his family. He smiled with approval as he reflected on his growing cattle herd and the exceptional horses he'd managed to acquire for the ranch. When he'd been in Bozeman the week before, he'd been greeted with respect by the town's leading men. They'd heard of his place and of the fine work he was doing. They carefully avoided mention of Bram's wife being Indian, something for which he was grateful. Not because he was ashamed of Koko, but rather because he had no desire to beat those poor men to a pulp.

The men most likely either didn't know about Koko or decided that having Bram on their side was much more beneficial. The community wanted to grow into a powerful town, maybe even steal the title of capital away from Virginia City. The town leaders needed to associate themselves with men like Bram, to rein in his approval. So they offered him their friendship and respect, and for now, Bram took it at face value. If later they proved to be false, he'd deal with that then.

Years ago, he'd never have thought himself capable of putting together this kind of spread. In fact, the few years he'd worked as a cowboy when he'd been a young man had persuaded him that such a career was not for him.

He had taken that confidence with him when he moved from civilization and settled into fur trapping. He liked the freedom and liberties such a life gave him, but then God had gotten ahold of him, drawing him in for a deeper, more meaningful understanding of the Bible, and Bram's entire life had changed.

At age forty-seven, Bram was in the prime of his life, as far as he was concerned. He had a wonderful wife, two beautiful children, and the home he'd always wanted—well, at least it soon would be the home he'd always wanted. He remembered seeing a large, lush plantation when he was a boy. The people who lived there were friends of the family, and the house had left a lasting impression on him. With six large marble columns and three stories of living space, the Hamilton Hills mansion was a monumental achievement in architecture. Bram had determined even then to one day own something just as beautiful.

Easing back in the saddle, Bram again surveyed the land around him. It was all his, for as far as the eye could see. A blessing from the Lord, to be sure. And because the Lord had blessed him, Bram in turn had tried to bless others. It made him feel as though he had finally accomplished the very best in life.

The horse shifted nervously and Bram glanced around to see Levi Sperry. He smiled and waved the young man over. Levi had been with him since just before Dianne and her brothers had come to live with him. He liked the young man, for Levi was industrious and hardworking. He could usually figure out a solution to difficult problems without having to be led by the hand like some of the ranch hands.

"Did you manage to round up the rest of those strays?" Bram questioned. It was almost time to push the herd to winter pasture, and Levi and some of the others had been out all day looking for any cattle that had wandered away from the rest of the animals.

"I have about twenty down in the canyon. I was figuring to see if there were any up there in the trees. Sometimes they get up in there."

"Sure thing. I'll help you look," Bram said, swinging his mount in the direction of the forest. "So have you heard back from Charity and Ben?" The couple had been on the wagon train with Bram's sister and her family. Ben and Charity had taken Levi, who was an orphan, under their wing until they got to Virginia City. Bram had encouraged Levi to ask his former guardians to come to the area and start a church, as Ben was a pastor. It was the final thing missing in his Montana utopia. He even thought he might offer the old homestead up to the pastor and his wife if they should agree to come.

"Nope, haven't had a letter yet. I've sure been praying Ben will say yes."

Bram nodded and gave the horse a bit of free rein. "You and me both."

"Will we build a church for them if they come?"

"Absolutely. You know that piece of land down where the river bends, just to the east?"

Levi nodded.

"Well, I figure that would make a good place. Not too far from some of the other folks in the area. Maybe we'll get a sense of community if we all go to meeting on Sunday mornings."

"We could just spend all day Sunday together," Levi said, moving his horse ahead of Bram's. "Miz Charity once told me that in the old days, they'd sometimes get together at someone's farm—if the area had no regular church. They'd put the word out and get folks from as far as twenty miles away. They would all come to service and bring food for the day. They'd have a big picnic after services and then Ben would speak again after everyone had taken their fill and the children were sleeping in the afternoon sun. Sometimes folks would repent and then they'd do some baptizin' too."

"Well, we could certainly do that," Bram said. "If they want to get started before first snowfall, however, they'd be welcome to hold the meetings in our new house. Oh, and I doubt we'd want to be baptizing anyone this time of year. The Madison is a mite chilly."

Levi grinned and reined back on his horse, cocking his head to one side. "I hear something. I'm betting one of those young bulls found his way in here. I'll scout him out." He urged the horse forward.

Bram brought his own mount to a stop and listened. He heard nothing at first, but then the sound of rustling in the brush made him confident Levi had been right. Maybe there were two or three head wandering around, searching for the last bits of green grass. He nudged his horse with his knees and headed down the path in the opposite direction from Levi. He'd circle around and help.

His mount moved with little urging for several yards, but then he whinnied softly and halted. With nervous little side steps, the animal made it clear to Bram that something was amiss.

He pulled his rifle from the scabbard. It was probably nothing; this horse had always been a little skittish despite his much deserved name—Brimstone. In his early days with Bram, the horse had been almost impossible to break. He was all, as Bram had declared, "hellfire and brimstone." Even now, no one but Bram rode the seventeen-hands-high bay.

Bram squinted to look down the trail in first one direction and then the other. He heard rustling in the undergrowth of the forest but figured it to be the strays. Easing his hold on the reins, Bram started to put the rifle back when the horse grew more agitated.

"Easy, boy. What is it?" He patted the gelding's neck, but the animal wanted no part of it. Tossing his head back and forth, the horse made it clear that he wanted out of this situation.

Bram pulled back on the reins and clicked softly. Brimstone calmed just a bit, but then without warning, the reason for his nervousness became all too clear: a grizzly, perhaps the same bear they'd had trouble with for the last few years, charged out of the woods and headed straight for them. The horse reared wildly, emitting what could only be described as an unpleasant scream. Bram tried to get off a shot, but the horse's unstable back was no place for calculated shooting. Losing his hold on the gelding, Bram fell off backward.

The rifle flew from his hands and landed several feet away. Bram tried unsuccessfully to scramble for the firearm, but it was too late. The grizzly was upon him.

The first searing bite was the worst. Screaming in agony, Bram felt the bear's jaws nearly sever his right leg. He tried to wrench away from the iron grip, but there was no chance of escape. Bram spotted the rifle and stretched to reach it, but the bear readjusted his hold and began shaking Bram from side to side.

Forcing himself to sit up as best he could, Bram began beating the bear's nose with his fists. The grizzly let go of Bram's leg and for a moment just stared at the man. A low growl rumbled from the animal's throat and built into a heinous roar. A dizzying pain traveled up from Bram's leg to his chest. He gripped his chest just as the bear charged again, this time barreling into Bram with a force that felt like a runaway ore cart.

Slamming into the ground, Bram hit his head hard against a rock. As he fought to keep from losing consciousness, Bram heard Levi yelling and firing his gun.

Good, Bram thought as he faded away. *Levi will take care of everything.*

Dianne finished separating the last of the milk and cream, then covered the crocks with clean cloths and tied them securely. Her last order of business was to climb down into the root cellar, taking each crock down to the cool, even temperature of the hand-dug shelter. After delivering the last crock, she was just about to churn some butter when she spotted a rider in the distance. Her heart quickened. Maybe it was Cole.

She shook her head. Cole would never come from that direction. Still, a rider was approaching. Dianne left thoughts of the cream behind and walked to the edge of the barn. Pressing a hand to her forehead, Dianne strained to see who it might be.

He looks to be dragging something behind him. Then she realized the shirtless rider was Levi. What in the world was he doing? He was supposed to be out bringing in the strays.

Dianne waved as he rode closer. She walked past the barn and out to the edge of the fence. "What are you dragging?"

Levi cupped his hand around his mouth. "It's Bram! He's been attacked by a bear!"

Dianne felt the blood drain from her head. For a moment she felt dizzy and reached out to take hold of the fence. They'd been worried about grizzlies for the past few weeks. As the weather had turned cooler and the first snows were on the mountains, they knew the bears would be eating as much as possible to fatten up for their winter hibernation. Bram had even warned the women to carry a gun if they went very far from the house, because there were signs that a rogue bear had been coming in close at night.

"I'll get help!" she called back.

Frantic, Dianne ran first to Faith and Malachi's cabin. Faith seemed startled by Dianne's breathlessness. Panting, Dianne declared, "Uncle Bram's hurt. Levi's bringing him in. We'll need help to get him to bed."

"Be right there. I'll get Malachi." Faith ran toward the black-smith shop while Dianne turned back to the house.

"Koko! Koko!" she called out as she ran into the entryway. There was no sign of her aunt. "Koko, come quickly!"

Dianne ran into the front parlor and then into the dining room. "Koko!"

"Goodness, Dianne, you sound as if the house is on fire. What's wrong?" Koko asked as she came around the corner from the pantry.

"It's Bram." Dianne watched as Koko put her hand to her mouth. The look on her face was one of pure horror. "He's been attacked by a bear. Levi's coming in with him on a travois."

Koko pushed past her niece. Dianne raced after the older woman, but Koko was far quicker and beat her to where Levi was dismounting.

"Oh, Father in heaven, please help my beloved," Koko prayed as she reached down to touch her husband's bloody face.

Dianne touched Levi's bloody arm. "Are you hurt too? What happened?"

"I'm all right. This is his blood. We were rounding up strays in the trees just past the canyon. Bram went one way and I went the other. I heard him holler and came as quick as I could, but he'd already been attacked. I knew I couldn't get him up on my horse, so I threw together a sled with dead branches." He pulled away from Dianne as Malachi approached. "We need to get him to bed. He's almost lost his right leg. I cinched his thigh to slow the blood flow."

"I'll get my healing kit," Koko announced.

Dianne motioned to the three cowboys who'd gathered to see what was going on. "You three run upstairs to the first guest room. Bring the bed downstairs into the small parlor. Hurry."

The men raced for the house as Levi and Malachi unfastened the travois. "Let's get him inside."

Dianne went to the door and held it open. "Take him to the dining room. I'll clear the table." She pushed past them and reached the room only steps ahead of the men. With one sweeping move she pushed back the tablecloth and knocked the candelabra from the table. "Put him here."

Levi and Malachi deposited the bloody body on the table. Dianne grimaced as she forced herself to look at her uncle's leg. Levi had wrapped the leg in his shirt. The blood had soaked through and drenched everything around it. She felt her stomach pitch but forced the contents to remain down.

"Can we save the leg?" She looked to Malachi and then to Levi. Faith entered the room, bringing a large pail of water.

"I think it will take the divine hand of God to save his life," Levi replied matter-of-factly.

A gasp came from the doorway and all turned to see that Koko had returned.

Shaking her head from side to side she cried, "No! He can't die! He can't die!"

Dianne had never witnessed anything so hideous. Bram's leg, although still attached, had been crushed and pulverized by the fierce jaws of the grizzly. He never regained consciousness while they worked on him. This worried Dianne, but she honestly didn't know if it was a bad or good thing.

The day passed into evening and then they all lost track of the hours. Dianne never left Koko's side, and Koko never left Bram, who was now lying motionless in his bed in the parlor.

"I kept dreaming about him getting hurt," Koko said solemnly. She gently wiped Bram's forehead with a cloth.

Dianne nodded. "I remember." She glanced at the clock on the mantel and found it was nearly daybreak. Everyone else had gone to bed. Faith had even taken the children with her back to their cabin, telling Jamie they were on a great adventure. The boy seemed delighted. Especially when Faith allowed him to bring his little bow and arrows that Takes Many Horses had given him.

"I just wish he'd wake up."

Dianne shifted and rubbed her stiff neck. "Mama always told me things were worst at night. When we kids would take sick, she said the fevers would increase with the sunset. She said Grandma always told her the heat of the sun went right into the body."

Koko nodded, never looking away from her husband. "The Real People would say the same thing."

Dianne hadn't heard Koko talk about her Blackfoot relatives in a long time. They called themselves the "Niitsitapi"—the Real People—believing themselves separate and completely different from other tribes and whites. Perhaps speaking of them now would help Koko to think about something other than her husband's injuries.

"Are the Blackfoot a very superstitious people?" Dianne asked.

"By the standards of the white man, I would probably say yes. Although my mother was not given to silly notions. She believed in working with medicine that came from the earth. Healing was something passed down in our family." Koko sat in a chair by the bed and sighed. "I wish my skills were better. I wish I'd listened more attentively."

"You've done much with your healing skills to help the folks around here," Dianne replied softly.

"But I cannot help him," Koko said, her voice filled with resignation.

They fell into silence once again and without meaning to, Dianne drifted to sleep. She didn't awake until she felt someone nudging her shoulder.

Opening bleary eyes, Dianne yawned. "What is it, Koko? Is he worse?"

"No, but someone is at the back door. I don't want to leave Bram."

Dianne nodded, noticing that it had grown quite light. She looked again to the clock above the fireplace. It was already eight-thirty in the morning.

"I'll go see to it." Her body ached as if she'd suddenly aged fifty years. Stretching as she walked, Dianne whispered another prayer for her uncle.

Levi Sperry stood on the other side of the door. In his hands was a large bundle of fur. "I went back and skinned that bear. The boys are butchering him. I thought Miz Koko might like to have a hunk of the meat." He opened the bundle to show her the meat. "Maybe she could make Bram a soup or something."

Dianne smiled. "That was thoughtful, Levi. Come on in and put it on the counter." She led the way into the kitchen and motioned to where he should deposit the gift.

"How is he?"

"Not really any change to report," Dianne said, crossing her arms. She had never felt so tired.

"Billy Joe said he'd heard there was a Confederate doctor who'd settled in these parts, but he wasn't sure exactly where. Somewhere south of here on the Madison. If you want, we could go looking for him."

"No, you men need to be getting ready to drive the cattle up north. We can't afford to be caught in an early snow. Uncle Bram was already starting to worry about such things." Dianne suddenly realized that with her uncle incapacitated, she'd be the most likely one to be in charge. "I'll talk to Gus about it all," she said, thankful that her uncle's foreman was so trustworthy. "He'll help us figure out what's to be done. Is he back yet?" Gus had been up north scouting out the exact location for where they would move the herd.

"Not yet, but it shouldn't be much longer."

"No . . . not much . . . longer."

Dianne felt something inside her break. Like a floodgate that had burst, her eyes welled with tears without warning. Choking back a sob, she tried not to worry about her uncle, about Cole, about herself and Koko and everyone else.

"I'm sorry," she said, turning away from Levi. "I'm trying to be strong, but it's hard."

"Of course it's hard, Miz Dianne. You shouldn't feel guilty for a few tears. Why, I've never known another woman as strong as you, unless it's Miz Charity."

Dianne turned back around and smiled. "I'll take that as a real compliment. I think the world of her. I wish she and Ben were here right now."

Levi nodded. "Me too."

"I wish Cole were here too," Dianne murmured, her tears streaming. She cried softly into her hands, embarrassed that she should break down so completely in front of Levi. "I'm afraid for him. I don't know why he's not come back. His letter said he should have been here by now." She hoped Levi could understand her muffled words.

Levi finally spoke. "I wish he were here too."

Dianne didn't look up to acknowledge him. She was trying too hard to regain control of her emotions. To her surprise, Levi embraced her. The warmth of his touch was her undoing. She cried all the harder.

"I'm sorry, Dianne," Levi whispered against her ear. "I know I'm not the right man for this job, but I care about you. Cole will come back soon, you'll see. And Bram, well . . . he's a tough one. If anyone can survive this, he can."

Dianne cried softly against Levi's shirt.

Levi began stroking her hair and without warning he placed a kiss upon her head. The act sobered Dianne rather quickly. Pulling away, she bit her lip and took charge over her ragged emotions. "Thank you, Levi. For everything you've done. Bram would have surely died if you hadn't been there."

Levi seemed to understand her discomfort. "Well, you let me know if you need anything else. I figured Miz Koko would want to know that bear won't be botherin' anyone else."

Dianne looked at the massive pile of fur and nodded.

Levi began looking uncomfortable and eased back toward the door.

Dianne didn't want to make Levi feel bad for his actions, so she moved forward and took hold of his arm. "Thank you, Levi. Thank you for being here."

He said nothing, as Dianne expected. The words she knew he wanted to say were completely inappropriate. He was still in love with her. That much was clear.

CHAPTER 10

COLE HAD NEVER BEEN IN SUCH PAIN. THERE WASN'T A place on his body that didn't hurt. He wasn't sure why the Sioux had kept him alive, but he knew he wasn't the only one. There were a handful of them. In his conscious moments he'd seen at least two white women and maybe another man, all members of the small wagon train he'd been helping to lead west.

Fever had overtaken him, yet for some reason Cole didn't feel afraid. He figured his death was imminent. Either from the infection in his body or by the hand of the Indians. He tried not to even think of what the Indians had planned for him.

Cole knew they were moving north. He'd figured that out by the course of the sun. Lying on a travois and being dragged along, Cole had watched the sun's passage from left to right, day after day. He had no idea where they were heading or why they were taking him and the others along. Maybe they were heading to Canada, he reasoned, but again his fever-confused mind could not process any reasoning for such a decision on the part of his captors.

An older Sioux woman came to him twice a day and offered him a foul-tasting broth and a bit of pemmican. Cole hardly had strength for chewing, but he forced himself—hoping, praying really, that somehow his efforts would heal his body.

As the days passed, Cole told himself that he was on the mend. His head didn't hurt quite as much and his arm looked better—at least he thought it did. He tried to ignore the red, swollen, oozing flesh where his chest wounds were infected. The old woman who tended him seemed not to be too concerned with them. She did smooth some kind of greasy substance on them, but Cole had no idea why they would try to heal him if they only planned to turn around and kill him.

After what Cole calculated to be three weeks, the tribe stopped for several days along a fairly wide river. He had no idea where they were, but the river seemed to flow east and west. When they'd been attacked, they'd been in central Wyoming Territory, and Cole hadn't been all that familiar with the land. Daniel had been taking a different route than Cole had traveled that first time west. But this area was even more of a mystery. There were more trees here, and there were mountains very close to the west. It actually reminded him a bit of home.

It must be Canada, he thought. But again, there was no way to prove or disprove that idea. He tried to observe the scenery and the people without making it obvious. Moaning, he rolled slowly to his left side, hardly able to move for the pain.

God, he prayed, *if I'm going to die, just let it come quickly and . . . and . . . let Dianne know that I love her. That I didn't leave her on purpose.*

He gazed across the center of the camp, his eyes hooded with lids heavy from sickness. Three men stood in conference not far from where he lay. The first one seemed overly concerned about something. He gestured and pointed in rapid succession. He made a sweeping motion that ended with all three men staring directly at Cole.

Cole forced himself to remain still. Were they plotting his death? Talking about how to finish him off?

One of the other three began a rapid-fire conversation, apparently countering the older man's worries. The third man finally put out his hands and touched each of the other men. He spoke softly, inaudibly for Cole. Not that Cole knew much of the Sioux language. Whatever the third man said, however, seemed to satisfy the other two, and together the three of them went off toward one of the other tepees.

The old woman came to tend to Cole's wounds. She tutted and fussed, speaking without so much as a smile as she applied more grease. She gave Cole the same foul-smelling drink, nearly forcing it down his throat. But this time there was no offer of pemmican. Perhaps their supplies were running low, Cole thought.

The evening came upon them quickly with a brisk cold wind that cut Cole to the bone. He began shivering so hard at one point that he felt like he was banging his head against the ground. To his surprise, one of the three men he'd seen earlier came and placed a buffalo robe over Cole's aching body. He made signs with his hands, then said in very guttural English, "Sleep now."

The next morning there was a dusting of snow on the ground, and by evening the skies had grown heavy with lead-colored clouds. The air smelled of snow and woodsmoke. Cole had seen the young women bringing in wood for fires. It looked as if the Sioux were planning to stay for a while.

Again Cole tried to analyze his surroundings. The mountains were no more than a day to the west—maybe less. A man on horseback would have no trouble reaching them, but a man on foot would be harder pressed. And for a man in his condition, it would probably be suicide to even try.

But I have to try.

The events of that evening made it even more necessary to at least attempt escape. Two of the other prisoners died. Cole didn't know what had brought about their deaths, but they were dragged off to the edge of the camp and mutilated. Cole closed his eyes against the uproar. There seemed to be an anger in the young warriors that demanded attention. The elder Indians remained in control, however. One in particular appeared capable of calming the outrage. It was the same man who'd interceded for Cole.

When it began to snow in earnest that evening, Cole watched as the abandoned bodies were covered in the white blankets provided by God. He wasn't certain, but he thought one of them was a young man who'd been traveling west to join his Mormon fiancée in Utah.

Cole closed his eyes. How many true loves had been separated by this one act of war by the Sioux? He thought of Dianne again and his heart ached with longing and a need to live at least long enough to see her again.

I have to try to escape. I have to live to see her again.

Where lethargy and sickness had left him incapable of making the decision before, Cole now felt a driving need to get back to his home—to Dianne. He knew he was weak, knew it would take an act of God to get him beyond the well-guarded camp. But seeing those angry braves and watching the mutilation of the dead gave Cole a feeling of urgency. He wasn't alive by any desire of the warriors. If they had their way, he'd soon be dead, and then there'd be no hope of seeing Dianne.

I have to try.

That night when the camp was silent, Cole pulled on the heavy buffalo robe and crawled across the camp as quickly as he could manage. His bare stomach and chest made contact with the snow, startling him. He was blessed to still have his trousers and boots on, but even with the buffalo fur, the cold bit at him, freezing his skin. After a time the cold numbed him so that even the little use he had of his muscles began to fade.

There was hardly any light. The moon, shrouded by clouds, offered no help. With each movement, Cole was certain he'd have to stop and wait to be found the next morning. The pain was almost more than he could manage, and his breathing came in heavy gasps.

Cole waited for the sound of the guards who would spot him and either kill him or force him back to the camp. But no one came, and by the time Cole made it to a stand of trees just north of the camp, he was on his feet. There was no strength in his legs, and his head was spinning from the sheer stress of moving. Maybe his head wound had been more serious than he'd known. Fighting the dizziness, Cole picked up a fallen branch and used it as a crude walking stick. It seemed to help a bit, but the pressure of leaning against the stick caused extreme pain in his chest.

For every two or three steps Cole took, he had to rest, either sitting or leaning hard against a tree. The snow fell in heavy wet flakes, but at least there was no wind. Cole prayed the snow would cover any sign of his escape and leave the Sioux clueless as to which direction he'd gone.

"*I* don't even know what direction I'm going," he muttered. He'd started out in the direction he thought was west, but in the darkness, he could have easily gotten turned around. "I could end up in the frozen north for all I know."

When Cole felt he could go no farther, he hunkered down between a couple of dead logs and pulled the buffalo robe close. Panting in the cold, damp air, Cole fought to keep from cough- ing. If he died here, his family and friends might never know what had happened to him. His bones would merely rot away with the fallen trees.

"Oh, Dianne . . . I'm so sorry."

————————

Dianne noted the grim expression on Gus's face and knew the news wasn't good. Bram's leg showed signs of infection with streaks of red now creeping up his thigh. The smell was awful.

"He needs a doctor, doesn't he?" she asked.

"That'd be best," Gus answered. "What do you want me to do? Should I send one of the boys to Ennis or Virginia City?"

"Levi says there's a doctor—well, at least it's rumored the man is a doctor—who lives somewhere down on the Madison. I thought I might ride south along the river and see if I can find his place. If I can't find the man or he's not a doctor, I'll ride on."

"You can't be going off by yourself," Gus said, his tone quite serious. "And most of the boys are bringin' in the herd for the drive. Have you figured a way to get ahold of your brothers?"

"No. Zane's off with the army in the northeastern part of the territory, and Morgan is somewhere south. I have no way of reaching either one of them. I can always send a message to Zane at the fort, but who knows when they'll return and he'd actually have a chance to read it."

"Winter's coming on fast. I figured to move the herd out by the end of the week."

Dianne nodded. "Yes, and that must continue—you've already delayed too long. Uncle Bram wouldn't be pleased with either of us if you didn't stay with the cattle. I'll ask Malachi to go with me. No one is going to bother me with him by my side."

Gus nodded. "I suppose not. Look, if you ain't back when we're ready to leave, do you want me to wait?"

"No," Dianne replied, gazing to where her uncle lay. "If I'm not back soon, I doubt he'll still be alive."

Dianne went quickly to her room and gathered a few things; there was no need to take a lot of supplies. She'd take an extra blanket because she knew the dangers of getting caught in a mountain storm. She'd also wear her heavy coat and pray for clear skies.

Faith came in about the time Dianne was packing some food into a saddlebag. "Where are you heading out to?"

"I was actually just coming to see you about that. Uncle Bram needs a doctor, and we really can't spare any of the ranch hands. I'm going to ride south along the Madison. There's supposed to be a man living down there who's a doctor. I wondered if Malachi could ride with me."

"Of course he can. I'll get him packed. How long will you be gone?"

"I hope no more than a few hours. But if we can't find him, we'll have to try Ennis or Virginia City."

Faith nodded and her brows came together as her expression grew worried. "I don't want to worry you because I've seen the good Lord perform many a miracle, but honestly . . ." Her words trailed off.

Resignation filled Dianne. She'd already come to terms with thoughts of the worst. "I know. He's probably not got much of a chance to make it, but I want to do whatever I can. I owe that much to him."

"I'll get Malachi," Faith whispered. "Then I'll go see how I can best help Koko."

Dianne went to the barn and saddled Dolly, as well as a gentle gray named Toby. Malachi was no horseman, and the gray was as sweet-tempered an animal as lived on the ranch.

She was just leading the two animals from the barn when Faith and Malachi came hurrying toward her.

Malachi eyed the horse with a look of concern. "I ain't much for ridin' a horse, Miz Dianne."

"Toby won't give you a bit of trouble," Dianne encouraged. "Jamie rides him all the time when Uncle Bram . . . well . . . you know. When they went riding." She handed Malachi the reins quickly and turned away so they wouldn't see her tears.

"Faith, I've already talked to Koko," Dianne said as she regained her composure. "I'll do my best to hurry, but there's no telling how long this will take. If the man living on the Madison is a doctor and if he'll come with us, then we might well be back in a few hours."

"If he's any man at all, he'll come with you," Faith replied. "God go with you." She held the reins while Malachi mounted, then handed them over to him.

Dianne took pity on the man. "You'll do just fine, Malachi. Hang on and let Toby do the work."

"Probably be better if'n I ran 'longside," he said with a hint of nervous laughter in his voice.

They moved out and rode to the top of the hill. The day seemed mild, but there was a bite in the air. Dianne didn't like to admit it, but she was certain she smelled snow. She could only pray any storms might hold off until they could get help back to Bram.

Malachi sat rigid in the seat. There was no hope of urging the horses into a gallop given his inability to sit on a saddle with confidence. Dianne sighed. *I should have gone on my own. Malachi is only slowing me down.* But in her heart she knew Gus would never have allowed her to go off exploring without protection. They knew nothing of the man they were in search of. So many people came to the territory to lose themselves in the vast open country and avoid the law.

I'll just have to trust that God already knows our needs, Dianne reasoned, pushing back the urgency that threatened to overwhelm her.

They worked their way down the path and then angled off toward the river. Dianne wondered why a man with the skills of a doctor would sequester himself in the middle of nowhere, but at this point she honestly didn't concern herself with it. If he would come and give her help, he could live in the valley for the rest of his days and Dianne wouldn't care.

The smell of woodsmoke first alerted them to the presence of another human being. Dianne perked up and checked for the wind's direction. Malachi did likewise and pointed.

"Looks to be a-comin' from down there."

Dianne concurred. "Maybe we've found him." She urged her horse forward and picked up the pace. She knew Malachi would have difficulty keeping up, but time was critical and Uncle Bram needed help.

They found a small, crude cabin not thirty yards from the river, sitting on a slight incline. "Hello!" Dianne called out. "Is anyone home?"

"Ya want I should go knock?"

Dianne shook her head and dismounted. "No, you wait here with the horses, if you don't mind." She handed Malachi her reins.

The man seemed almost relieved not to have to dismount. "I'll be watchin'."

Dianne appreciated his protective nature. She knew that no one would cause her harm so long as Malachi had breath in his body. He protected her just like one of her brothers.

"Hello!" she called again, this time making her way to the house.

"What do you want?" a voice called from inside the house. The voice had a decidedly southern drawl.

"I'm looking for a doctor. My uncle's been wounded—badly wounded. He was attacked by a bear and I'm afraid he'll die if I can't get help."

The door opened, and a man looking to be about forty-five, maybe fifty, appeared. He pulled on a coat even as he met Dianne's gaze.

"Ma'am." His eyes were a piercing icy blue and seemed to take in everything around him.

"My name is Dianne Chadwick. I live at the Diamond V ranch upriver from here." He said nothing and his expression remained stoic. "I need a doctor. One of our ranch hands said a doctor had taken up residence along the Madison, in this direction."

The man looked beyond Dianne to where Malachi sat with the horses. "Is that your Negro?"

Dianne looked back to Malachi and shook her head. "Malachi is a free man. He works for my uncle at the Diamond V. My uncle is the one who needs a doctor. He was attacked by a grizzly, and I'm afraid he's going to die if we don't get him some proper attention."

The man's jaw tightened as he continued to stare at Malachi. Dianne felt desperate and put her hand on the man's arm. "Please, if you're a doctor would you come with us? I can pay you."

The man drew a deep breath. "The name is Hezekiah Buford. I hail from Atlanta, Georgia. I was a doctor, but I do not look to practice any longer."

"But why? I'll have to ride twice the distance to find anyone else. Please, my uncle is very ill, and I fear we'll lose him. Please come and at least see if there is anything you can do. I'm afraid at best he'll lose his leg. That's going to require a surgeon."

"I removed many a limb in the war," the man said, his eyes

clouding over, his expression growing distant. "Was your family in the War Between the States?"

Dianne knew her answer would probably validate the man's decision to either stay or come to help. "My father was killed by Union soldiers."

Bufford met her eyes. He had a way of searching her face that made Dianne feel as if he could ascertain the truth merely by study. He nodded. "I'm sorry to hear that, ma'am. Many a good Southern man was lost to those Northern defilers."

"Yes, sir. Please, can you come?"

Bufford squared his shoulders. "I'll get my bag."

CHAPTER 11

HEZEKIAH BUFFORD LOOKED AT BRAM'S INFECTED LEG AND shook his head. "No, ma'am, this is certainly not good. The leg will have to be amputated to even give him a chance of living. I can't give you much hope, however, on that part. He's very ill and the shock of the surgery will likely kill him. I wouldn't expect him to live."

Koko stood on the opposite side of the bed. "He has to live. He has children who need a father and a ranch to work. He loves his life here. He must live."

Bufford eyed her with contempt. "You are of the heathen blood, are you not?"

Koko narrowed her dark eyes. "I am of a Blackfoot mother and white father. So for as much heathen blood as I have, I have equal amounts of white blood."

Bufford shook his head and scratched his stubbly chin. "It doesn't work that way, and the sooner you colored folks learn that, the better."

Though she despised the man's attitude, Dianne quickly moved to intervene. "Please put aside such concerns and do what you must to save his life. If surgery is required, we can set up the dining room. Just tell us what you need."

Faith and Malachi entered the room at that moment. "Can we help?" Faith asked, not realizing what had just transpired.

"I don't work with heathens or darkies," the man replied, looking to Dianne. "If you want my help, you'll get me decent white men. Otherwise, I'm leaving." His icy stare made it clear that he'd not be persuaded to do otherwise.

Koko looked as if she might say something, but Dianne shook her head and took charge. Noting that Jamie was playing in the hallway just outside the parlor, she motioned. "Faith, why don't you and Malachi take the children to your cabin. That way they won't have to be around while the surgery is performed. Koko, we'll need hot water and bandages. We'll need to tear up some flour sacks."

Everyone seemed frozen in place. Dianne looked to each with a silent warning in her expression. Bram needed Bufford, and Bufford would not work without having things his way. Finally Faith nodded, and she and Malachi backed out of the room.

"Come on, Jamie. We're going on an adventure," Faith said as she picked the boy up.

"Going hunting?" Jamie asked.

"Maybe we can hunt around the cabin," Faith said, trying to keep the boy interested. Since his father had been brought in, Jamie had remained close at hand. Taking him now wouldn't be easy, but Dianne knew that Faith understood the importance.

"Maybe you could bring your bow and arrows. The ones your uncle gave you."

Jamie clapped his hands. "I kill Papa's bear."

Dianne watched as Faith handed the boy over to Malachi. "Yes. You can go hunting for bear," she whispered.

Baby Susannah slept in a small cradle across the room. Faith crossed to retrieve the sleeping child. "Koko, you just come on down if you need to nurse her; otherwise I'll give her some sugar water."

Koko nodded, but it was clear her mind was far from the child. Dianne gently touched her aunt. "We'll need lots of bandages. We have to keep the wound clean. Maybe you could fix up some willow tea too. That's done a good job of fighting the fever."

Koko finally nodded, although her stern gaze was fixed on Bufford's unapologetic expression.

"You'll need a hot fire too," the doctor added in a gravelly voice. "And heat a poker. I'll need to cauterize the wound."

Koko finally walked around the bed and stopped momentarily beside Dianne. "I do this only to save his life. His life is more precious than my pride."

Dianne nodded and patted her aunt on the back as she exited the room. Finally Dianne eyed the doctor again. "There aren't many men available to help. The cattle are being rounded up for the move to winter pasture. I'll see who I can find, but you may have to swallow your pride and take help where it can be had. I pray that if you're any kind of a doctor at all, you'll put aside your prejudices in order to save lives."

With that she stalked from the room, trying to contain her anger. She had dealt with her mother's prejudice, but only in part. Dr. Bufford's attitude was clearly the same as her mother's had been. Dianne struggled to understand how people could be so hateful, especially in a time of need.

She rounded up a couple of ranch hands, who were happy to help, eager to see their boss return to work. Everyone loved Bram, and this knowledge only furthered Dianne's willingness to do whatever she could to see him restored to health. They were living a part of her uncle's dream—his desire to see the land tamed and civilized. Had he not been there, none of the rest of them would have been there either.

When she entered the house, she found Koko had already transformed the dining room into an operating theater. The table had been stripped of its lovely cloth once again and in its place an oiled cloth had been spread. The cowboys soon brought Bram's unconscious form to rest upon the fine oak wood. They grimaced at the stench as the doctor uncovered the leg wound once again.

He glanced up to meet Dianne's gaze. "I have no bone saw with me."

"There's a saw in the barn," she replied, forcing the contents of her stomach to remain where they belonged. "It's brand-new—just bought a couple weeks ago."

"Get it."

The time passed quickly after that. Dianne couldn't even remember what happened after one of the cowboys returned with the saw. She stood ready to offer help, but the surgery happened more quickly and with less ceremony than she had anticipated. The doctor cut through the swollen red flesh, using the poker to close any new sources of blood. Next he sawed through the bone and instructed the cowboys to dispose of the leg in a deep grave lest it attract animals.

By the time Dianne could think reasonably again, the procedure was over and she was calmly handing bandages to Dr. Bufford.

"Now what?" she finally forced herself to ask.

"Now we wait," Bufford replied. "We wait and see if he has the strength to pull through. My guess is that he'll be gone by morning."

Dianne hated the finality of his words. How could he so calmly dismiss her uncle's chances at life? She looked to the doorway where Koko stood watching. She'd been obedient to keep clear of the doctor's way.

"Can we move him back to his bed now?" Dianne asked, turning away from her aunt.

"By all means. Make him as comfortable as possible."

The cowboys were summoned again, and Bram was moved to the makeshift bedroom in the front parlor. Dianne's back ached and she stretched, suddenly realizing her apron was stained with blood. Uncle Bram's blood.

She felt weak-kneed. *Lord,* she prayed, *we need a miracle. We need your healing touch on my uncle. Oh, God, we all need him so much. Please help us—please don't take him.*

Dianne hastened to clean up the room and herself. She peeled off the blood-stained apron only to realize blood had soaked through to her dress. She quickly found a clean apron and pulled it on to hide the stains lest they upset her aunt.

Working quickly, Dianne managed to take care of most of the mess before Koko entered the room.

"I hate having that man in our home," Koko said while Bufford was outside cleaning up. Dianne knew, because of the lateness of the hour and the fact that Bram would most likely need further care, they would have to offer him a place to stay for the night.

"I know," she whispered, trying to offer Koko a sympathetic tone, "but we'll have to give him a room."

Koko's expression hardened. "Let him sleep in the barn."

Dianne reached out to touch her aunt. "I would, but we both know he needs to be close to Bram."

"His heart is foul—filled with hate."

Dianne knew the truth of Koko's words. "Still, he's all Uncle Bram has this side of the Lord. We can't possibly know how to best help him. We could never have removed that leg on our own. Maybe God brought him here for the purpose of teaching him about tolerance."

"I've seen many tolerant men who still have no love—no

compassion in their hearts." Koko moved away and picked up the last of the bloody linens. "Dr. Bufford is a man whose past has given him a black spirit. He wouldn't have helped Bram had it not been for you. If I'd gone after his help, he would have let my husband die."

"Perhaps," Dianne replied, knowing her aunt was probably right. "But the important thing is that he did come and he didn't just let him die. Maybe God will soften his heart as he sees how much love we share here in our home."

Koko nodded but said nothing more. Her expression made it clear to Dianne that she found the idea hard to believe. In truth, Dianne knew that men who held as much contempt for others as Dr. Bufford seemed to were not easily persuaded.

Dianne heard Jamie's cries before she saw Faith appear in the kitchen, carrying the boy. "I want to see Papa." Dianne hurried to wash her hands, making sure there was no blood visible to frighten the child.

"I couldn't calm him," Faith announced.

Koko went to her son and took him in her arms. "Did you catch a bear while you were gone?"

Jamie shook his head. His large dark eyes seemed to widen at the question. "No bears. No bears here."

Koko nodded. "Good. We don't want any more bears."

"Want Papa," the boy insisted.

Koko walked with her son to the front parlor. Dianne followed quietly behind, hoping she might offer some solace. "Your papa is sleeping, Jamie. He's very tired."

"Papa hurt." Jamie pointed to where his father slept.

"Yes," Koko said softly. "Papa is hurt."

"Wake up, Papa. Wake up," Jamie called. He looked to his mother. "He sleeping."

Koko bit her lower lip as tears filled her eyes. Dianne wished she might offer comfort to them both. "Yes, he is sleeping, Jamie.

And sleep will help him feel better."

"We play later?" Jamie asked.

Dianne looked at her unconscious uncle and remembered the doctor's negative prognosis. "Maybe," she finally whispered. "Right now we need to pray for your papa and ask God to make him well so that he can play with you soon."

Jamie put his pudgy hands together. "I pray. I pray good. Thank you, God, for the food."

Dianne smiled and even Koko seemed to brighten at this. She tousled her son's hair, then handed him to Dianne. "Why don't you go pray with Jamie while I take care of things here."

Dianne nodded and pulled Jamie into her arms. "So what else should we tell God?" she asked as they walked back to the kitchen, where Faith waited.

Jamie looked into her eyes with such wonder and hope. "Make Papa not sick."

Dianne drew in a deep breath and caught Faith's loving gaze. "Yes," Dianne said. "Make him not sick anymore."

———

Dianne felt that she'd barely drifted off to sleep when Koko roused her. "Come quickly. Bram is dying."

For a moment, Dianne couldn't remember what had happened. *What does she mean, Bram is dying? Why should he—* Then the memories returned. Dianne shot straight up. "I'll be right there." She slipped from the bed and pulled on her heavy robe.

Why, Lord? Why must he die? She'd already reconciled herself to the fact that her uncle would never lead the same productive, active life. She'd even acknowledged that he'd be depressed at the loss of his leg—maybe even angry. But at least she had hoped he'd be alive to enjoy his son and daughter. She could easily help with the ranch, even hire more men to work in Bram's place, but she could never take his place in the hearts of his wife and children.

"Please, God," she whispered as she hurried to the parlor. "Please help us now. Please let Uncle Bram make it through this dark hour."

She entered the parlor as Koko knelt down beside the bed. "I've sent for the doctor, but I know he won't be able to help."

"Nonsense. You don't know that. He might have some way of making things better," Dianne encouraged.

"No," Koko said sadly. "He's not going to live, Dianne. You must tell him good-bye."

Dianne looked at her aunt for a moment. The woman wasn't all that much older than she was, only eight years senior to Dianne's twenty-three years. How could she possibly know this was the end of Bram's life?

"Koko?"

"His breathing is shallow. He's losing this battle, Dianne. We have to let him go." Koko was surprising calm. She lovingly stroked her husband's hand. "We can't keep him—he wants to go."

Dianne sat down beside her uncle's bed and drew his hand to her lips. "I love him so much. I'm just not ready to say good-bye."

Koko nodded. "I don't want to say good-bye either, but it's best this way. He never would have been happy without his leg. He would have withered and died a slow death if he recovered. He would have grown bitter . . . sad. We wouldn't want him that way."

Dianne felt tears slip down her cheeks. The droplets fell upon her uncle's hand. "Oh, Uncle Bram, I love you. You gave me hope when I had nothing left. You helped me to learn about my new life here in Montana. You gave me a home and loved me." Thoughts of Cole flickered through Dianne's thoughts. How she wished he were here to comfort her and help her endure this bleak moment.

Dianne kissed her uncle's still hand again. "I don't want to let you go, but I know God loves you more than even I do. I can give you to Him. I can let you go—as long as I know it's to Him you go."

Dr. Bufford came sleepily into the room. "So he's passing?"

Dianne let go of her uncle and got to her feet. "Can you save him?"

The doctor went to the bed, listened to Bram's heart, checked his breathing, and shook his head. "The night's always worse, but this night will be his last. I'm sorry. Truly, I am."

Dianne nodded. "We'll let you have a few moments alone," she said to Koko. Her aunt said nothing.

"Please come with me, Dr. Bufford. I'd imagine there's still some coffee on the stove."

"No thank you," the man said through a yawn. "I've done all that I can. I'll be leaving first thing in the morning." He moved without any suggestion of emotion or further interest.

Dianne watched him disappear and shook her head. A man was dying, and the only doctor within twenty miles had absolutely no consideration for the loss this family was about to endure.

Bufford stopped at the door. "I know you believe me to lack compassion." He turned and his icy blue-eyed gaze seemed to pierce through to her soul. "And perhaps I do. I saw a lot of men die on the battlefield—a lot of good men who died for senseless reasons. Waste makes me angry and steals away any compassion that I might otherwise exude. Your uncle's death is a tremendous waste—another good man's life is forfeited. I'm sorry for your loss, but I have no desire to make myself a part of it."

He left with that, and his words echoed in Dianne's head. How very calm and collected he was, she thought. He managed to systematically put aside his emotion and turn aside his feelings.

I wish I could do that so easily. Dianne shook her head. No, she didn't really want that. She didn't want to stop feeling or having consideration for those around her. Not when the reasoning was the mere protection of her own heart.

Waiting as long as she could, Dianne slowly made her way back to the parlor.

"Oh, my heart. My love," Koko whispered.

Dianne paused in the doorway and sighed. She could remember Uncle Bram urging her to promise to take care of Koko and the children. The world would never understand the love this family held for one another. Color would blind them—intolerance would leave them without feeling for Koko and her children's loss.

Bram drew a few shallow, ragged breaths, and then silence filled the room. It seemed so sudden—so final. Dianne waited, wondering if he might yet find the strength to go on, but there was no other sound from the loving giant of a man.

Koko lay across her husband and sobbed softly. He was gone. Just like that—her uncle's life had ended.

Walking from the room, Dianne made her way outside. The stars overhead offered brilliant beacons of light. The night greeted her in absolute stillness. Looking back at the ranch house—the dream of her uncle, not yet completed—Dianne suddenly realized that all she could see now belonged to her.

"I want to make certain my family is provided for, and you are the only way to ensure that," Bram had told her long ago. He had explained that Indians couldn't be landowners, so he couldn't will the ranch to Koko. He had petitioned Dianne to take on the ranch and make a home for his family for as long as they needed one. She had agreed, and now the realization of such a matter coming full circle was almost more than she could comprehend. The Diamond V belonged to her—every horse, every building,

the entire herd. They were hers. No one could challenge her if she decided to up and sell the entire thing. No one could stand in her way should she decide to put an end to the cattle business and take up farming. It was all up to her now.

Dianne trembled from the very thought of such responsibility. When she'd agreed to this arrangement, she'd never believed it would ever occur. Bram was supposed to live for a long, long time. He was supposed to be here with them—to raise his children—to teach Jamie how to hunt and fish and ranch.

Now Jamie would grow up without a father. No one would be there for him in the same way that Bram would have been. She knew what it was to lose a father—knew the pain and empty place it made in your heart.

"But I was sixteen," she murmured. "I was old enough to understand that accidents happen. I have my memories of Papa, and no one can take those from me."

Would Jamie remember anything about his father? Would he recall the way his father put him atop his shoulders so the little boy could be a giant? Would Jamie have memories of his father wrestling with him in front of the fire, tickling him and tossing him high in the air as they played?

"It's not fair," she whispered, knowing there was no one to hear. No one but God, and at this moment Dianne wondered seriously if He might be sleeping.

CHAPTER 12

DIANNE RODE ALONG THE WESTERN PERIMETER OF THE ranch, still unable to believe that Bram was truly gone. She thought of all the losses in her life, Cole included, for she had no idea when he might return—or if. Now her uncle's funeral loomed and nothing seemed right.

It was hard to remember those who'd gone before her. When she'd been a little girl and her grandparents had died, she had felt the loss deeply, but nothing compared to the loss of her father, sisters, and mother. She couldn't even be sure Trenton, her oldest brother, was still alive. She hadn't heard from him in a long, long while.

Dianne had ridden Dolly to the top of the hill overlooking the main part of the ranch. There were two large barns, a small cabin used for supplies, several lean-tos, a blacksmith shop and cabin for Malachi and Faith, the bunkhouse, multiple corrals and pens, the old cabin home, and the partially finished dream house Bram had started earlier in the year.

"I'll see to it that the house is finished, Uncle Bram. I know what it meant to you."

Dolly shifted, as if eager to get back to the other horses. Dianne patted the buckskin mare. They'd shared all of the losses coming west. Now they were sharing yet another death.

"How can he be gone, Dolly? How can we go on without him here?"

The chilled morning wind picked up and blew cold down from the snow-capped mountains. Gus and the boys would take the cattle north after the funeral. There was no time to waste, and she prayed they hadn't delayed too long.

Dianne saw Faith step outside her cabin and put her hand to her forehead to shield the sun. She looked directly to the hill where Dianne sat, then waved. Dianne really didn't feel like company, so she waved back but turned Dolly to continue her ride.

I'm more confused now than I've ever been, she had to admit. It would be impossible to sort through the affairs in one conversation with Faith. And though her uncle's passing consumed her, Dianne couldn't help but think of Cole. Sometimes she felt convinced that he'd changed his mind and moved on—that somewhere between Cheyenne and Virginia City, Cole had met another woman.

Images of him with someone else, however, were always blurred by the very real possibility that some sort of calamity had befallen her fiancé. Cole had told her, after all, of the ongoing bouts of sickness and bad weather. Then, too, there were the Indian troubles on the plains. Zane had written her short notes of the conflicts and skirmishes but never in any real detail. No doubt he thought her in need of protection from the truth, when in fact her own imagination was worse than anything Zane could have written. Then, too, the newspapers, when they could be had, were filled with horror stories given in first-person accounts from travelers who'd been assaulted by the "heathen nations."

Just a few years back there had been very graphic stories told about the Fetterman Massacre. Some eighty soldiers went out from their fort to protect woodcutters from Red Cloud and his Cheyenne warriors. Instead, Red Cloud and his men annihilated the entire group—and the things he and his men had done to the soldiers couldn't even be described without crossing the boundaries of propriety. Had Cole's wagon train met up with Red Cloud and the Cheyenne?

"Miz Dianne!" someone called from the next hill. It was Gus Yegen, her uncle's foreman. Her foreman.

She reined back and waited for the man to come to her. Squaring her shoulders, she tried hard to be strong and unemotional. Gus wouldn't appreciate a teary-eyed female, she surmised.

Gus crossed the small valley between them at a gallop, then slowed to a trot and finally a walk for the last twenty feet or so. "I was hoping to find you. Levi said you'd headed up this way."

"I needed the solitude," she admitted. "Sometimes there just seem to be too many folks all together in one place."

Gus pushed back his hat and smiled, causing his gray mustache to lift slightly at the sides. "I reckon I can understand that. I always appreciate ridin' for strays just to enjoy the quiet."

Dianne realized quickly that she had no desire for small talk. Perhaps God had sent Gus her way because he was the very man she needed to talk to.

"I feel lost, Gus."

He sobered. "I figured you might. I just want you to know that I'll be here to help. It ain't the same, I know. I ain't quite ever felt a death like this one. My folks died when I was young, so I don't recollect much about it. I don't let myself get too close to anyone else. Bram just sort of imposed himself on me." Gus grinned. "But in a good way."

"Seems I've done nothing but lose people all my life. At least all of my adult life." She looked Gus in the eye. "What do we do now? I need to know."

Gus nodded and shifted in the saddle. "Well, we go on with life, Miz Dianne. Bram would be the first to tell you that. We have six hundred head of cattle that need to be dealt with 'fore winter sets in. We've got a lot of good folk who want to know that their needs will be provided for. Can you be strong enough to bear that?"

Dianne drew a deep breath and let it out slowly. "I want to make Uncle Bram proud. I know what's expected of me in some ways, but in other ways I'm completely confused. You'll have to teach me—help me to learn."

"Miz Dianne, you've been working on this ranch since you showed up. You know more'n you give yourself credit for."

"Maybe so, but it doesn't feel that way. I feel like there are so many holes in my education."

Gus chuckled. "Guess we've all felt that way at one time or 'nother. I think I'd be more afraid of a man—or woman, for that matter—who thought he knew everything about everything. I reckon either way, you know more than most. Not only that, but you have the respect of the men. You ain't some citified lady with all your doodads and geegaws, having to have things just a certain way. Why, I've seen you standing up to your—up to your—" Gus's face reddened—"well, up to your boots in . . ." He stopped again and shook his head. "Never mind. You know full well what you were standin' in."

Dianne laughed. It was the first time she'd felt like laughing in days. Only Jamie's sweet spirit had kept her from complete despair, and now Gus's comical embarrassment was a blessed relief.

"Yes, I know what I've stepped in and stood in. Around here, there's plenty of piles to choose from."

"Well, the point is, Miz Dianne, you ain't afraid to get your hands dirty and work alongside the rest of us. You wouldn't have had to. You could've showed up with your city upbringin' and refused to be much good to anyone. You could've whined and complained. Believe me, I've seen many a lady dealt a hand like this and not be able to handle it."

"But I love it here. I love the work and the animals. I love the solitude." Dianne thought of all the people who'd come to live on the ranch since she'd first arrived. "I have good friends here . . . and . . . Cole."

"I know you're worried about him and rightly so. It ain't a good time to be traveling through Indian territory. I won't lie and tell you I ain't got my own concerns."

Dianne looked at the older man and felt a sense of relief in his honesty. "I appreciate that, Gus. I wouldn't have it any other way. I know things are grim. I know Cole should have been back here weeks ago. All I can do is pray and hope for the best."

"Well, I know for a fact it ain't for any good reason that boy ain't here yet. He let his honor separate you two, but he's given good time to his pa. He's met any obligation there. Now he needs to be here honoring his promise to you. I'm guessin' that something mighty important is delayin' him."

Dianne looked at Gus long and hard. "But you haven't heard anything?"

"No, ma'am. One of the boys rode back from Virginia City and said there was some talk about Indian troubles along the Yellowstone and south. That's about all I know."

Dianne nodded. "Morgan's down that way as well. Doesn't matter how much I care about folks, I can't control their lives or keep them safe from harm." She smiled. "Guess I need to realize someone bigger than me is in charge."

"Couldn't hurt," Gus answered, matching her smile.

"Ben and Charity are due back before long. Charity wrote

to Levi nearly a month ago to say they were coming. I figured they'd be here by now. It would be nice to have a pastor do Uncle Bram's funeral proper-like."

"I wouldn't worry. He can always speak over the grave later on—if need be."

Dianne nodded. Most folks out here were buried without the luxury of a preacher, but she had hoped it would be different for Uncle Bram. Besides, she longed for Charity's strength to see her through this.

Dianne sighed. "Well, I'll need to go for supplies before we get snowed in. I can probably head out tomorrow after the funeral. Can you spare me a couple of trustworthy men?"

"You betcha. I figured to leave you Levi and Gabe. Those two would give their lives for you any day of the week and twice on Sunday."

Dianne nodded. She knew the truth of Gus's words. "They're good men. I'd give my life for them as well."

"See, that's what makes you a good ranch owner. You love your people—even your cowhands. You care about the land and the stock. There ain't a horse on the place that you don't know from muzzle to tail—you've worked with most of 'em at one point or another."

Dianne drew a deep breath. Gus's confidence in her was finally starting to seep in. It strengthened her to hear this weathered cowhand tell her that she held his respect.

"You'll stay with us, won't you, Gus?"

"I wouldn't think of livin' or workin' anywhere else, Miz Dianne. Fact is, I reckon I figure to settle here permanently—die here too."

Dianne nodded. "Just don't make it too soon, Gus. I need you."

"Now, don't you go frettin', little lady. I got no plans to head to that big roundup yonder. I'm here to help you make this the best ranch in all of the territory. Hard times may yet be a-comin', but we'll face 'em together and you'll see. This big sky country is gonna embrace you and make you a part of all you see."

Dianne gazed around her at the mountains to the east and the river valley below. *I'm already a part of it all,* she realized. *Montana is already a part of me.*

———————

Cole forced himself to keep moving. The wind howled in his ears—or maybe he was hearing the flow of his own blood. Either way, the sound was maddening. Cole longed for quiet, but there was none to be had.

He had no idea how long he'd been on the trail. He would walk until he could walk no farther, then collapse and crawl to whatever shelter he could find. His head seemed somewhat clearer after each rest, and his wounds didn't feel nearly as bad. The only problem was, as his mind began to reason his situation and understand it in full, Cole only managed to feel more anxious. He couldn't help but remember all the times he'd read of settlers or travelers being killed by one thing or another. After all, the wilderness was not the place for the poorly equipped, and Cole definitely fit that category.

"I just wish I had a gun or even a knife," he told himself. But wishing it didn't make it so.

Stumbling in the fading light, Cole lifted his gaze and started at a dark form in the distance. What was it? Animal? Indian?

He shook his head and continued his slow pace toward the object. The shape grew larger and Cole had to blink several times to allow himself to believe the truth of it. It looked to be an abandoned cabin. Probably deserted by some trapper who grew weary of battling the elements and the Indians, Cole surmised.

He pressed on, hurrying in spite of his complete exhaustion and weakness from lack of food. The cabin looked to be no bigger than an oversized room, but to Cole it might as well have been a mansion. At least he'd have decent shelter tonight and maybe even a fire. The thoughts of such comfort motivated him to continue.

The door wasn't much—it barely hung on its sorry excuse for hinges. Cole pushed the barrier back and peered into the darkened room. "Hello?" he called out, just in case there might be a resident.

No one replied.

Entering, Cole gave his eyes a chance to adjust to the dark. There wasn't much of anything in the room, but it didn't matter. Cole closed the door behind him and collapsed. Maybe tomorrow he'd have the energy to explore the cabin's full potential.

———

They buried Bram the next day, but a storm came upon them quickly so there was no time for any real service. The storm also delayed Dianne's trip to town for supplies and the cattle being moved north. With the clearing of the skies came the arrival of Ben and Charity Hammond. Dianne fell into Charity's arms, sobbing out her sorrows and trying her best to explain their misery while Ben listened in.

Before Dianne knew it, Reverend Hammond gathered them all together at the gravesite for a proper funeral. His soft-spoken manner put them all at ease. Dianne didn't know if it mattered to Koko or not, but she liked the idea of having her uncle buried properly, with an honest-to-goodness pastor to speak the final words.

"We are on this earth but a short time," the pastor told them in conclusion. "A mist—a vapor. This life is temporary—the brief stopping place before eternity. Bram Vandyke was a man of honor, as I hear it told. He loved the good Lord, served his fellow man faithfully, and cherished his wife and children.

"In the second book of Corinthians, chapter four, we read, 'While we look not at the things which are seen, but at the things which are not seen: for the things which are seen are temporal; but the things which are not seen are eternal.' As it's been told to me, Bram Vandyke put his eyes on the eternal when the only image he could see was given in the Holy Word. Now he sees in full what the Lord only speaks of in Scripture. Someday we'll all behold the Lord—we'll all give an accounting for our words and deeds. It seems to me that Bram had no need to fear that accounting.

"As for those of us gathered here today, we need to look beyond this temporal situation. We need to remember that this world is only a stopping-over place—a place that cannot hold us—for one day we will follow Brother Bram and join him in the eternal. Let us put our eyes on the eternal rather than this grave."

Dianne appreciated Reverend Hammond's words. They offered comfort in a way that nothing else could. It was easy to forget just how momentary the sorrows of this earth would be. When the brief service was over, Dianne thought about how very much Bram would have approved of this gathering.

Suddenly Jamie cried out, startling them all. "I want my papa!"

Koko handed Susannah to Dianne and lifted her son. "James, your papa had to go away. He has to be with God."

"But I want to play with Papa." He struggled in his mother's arms, and his tears made Dianne's own resolve slip away. She nuzzled the baby's neck to avoid dealing with the weeping boy.

Koko whispered softly to her son, and while Jamie continued to cry, he said nothing more.

I don't want to leave him here either, Dianne thought. *I want to wake up and find this is all a horrible dream. I want to walk out into the kitchen and find Uncle Bram pouring himself a cup of coffee. Just like he did every morning.* But of course that wasn't going to happen. It would never happen again.

This is but a fleeting moment. Just as Ben said. It will pass and we will survive. We will live beyond our tears and pain.

Dianne raised her face and met Gus's compassionate gaze from across the grave. *He thinks I'm strong, but I'm not.* Dianne sighed. She looked at the others; their eyes were fixed on her, as if watching her for direction. *They all think I'm so strong—so capable.* How could she ever manage to convince them that she had nothing left to give? Cole had taken her heart and hopes, and Bram had taken her last connection to her parents—especially her mother.

How can I be strong now?

———————

Cole awoke when light filtered in between the large holes in the wall. He forced his body to respond and got to his feet. Hunger overwhelmed him and pain gnawed at his stomach, back, chest, and head like a hundred tiny animals feasting upon his flesh.

The cabin was sparse. Someone had left a stump as a chair and a crude table, fashioned from four bark-laden logs and an odd assortment of branches. Cole noted an old crate nailed to the wall of the cabin and stepped closer to see what had been left behind. There wasn't much that looked useful. An open tin can held several matches, a few rusty nails, and a stub of a pencil. Cole actually rejoiced over the pencil more than anything else. He still had his journal tucked safely inside his boot. He could write to Dianne and at least record his ordeal. That way if he died . . .

Death had so long dogged his steps that Cole no longer shuddered at the prospect.

"If I die, I die. But at least I might let Dianne know what happened and hope that someone will take my words to her . . . someday."

CHAPTER 13

THE TRIP TO TOWN DID NOTHING TO BOLSTER DIANNE'S spirits. Everything appeared dingy and worn-out. There were more buildings and houses than there were the last time she was in town, but the people seemed caught off guard somehow— almost as if the momentum for civilization had overwhelmed them. There were false-front buildings that pretended to be something more than they were, as well as advertisements boasting all the comforts that could be had in large eastern cities. Somehow Dianne doubted the truth of such claims; after all, they were stuck out here well away from any real connection to the amenities of the East. Of course, there was the transcontinental railroad, completed just the previous year. That now brought goods into Corinne on a regular basis, and the town that had suffered such a poor reputation during the construction of the railroad now achieved a little more recognition and respect.

But Corinne and the railroad were a very long ways away.

Dianne wondered seriously if there might be wisdom in selling off everything and moving away from Montana and its difficult life, but even as the thought came, she pushed it aside. Her uncle had loved this land. He'd lived here for a long time—even before there were towns to offer him more comforts. Surely she could endure whatever hardships befell them, in order to honor him and provide for Koko, Jamie, and Susannah. They'd never be accepted in eastern society. Dianne would be hard-pressed to find any place back East where they could settle and be allowed to live in peace. Besides, Dianne knew they'd never leave the territory—not even if she sold off every inch of land and every animal. Koko would never leave the land where her husband had lived and died.

Settling into her hotel room, Dianne thought of Koko and the children as she prepared for bed. Koko had pretty much sequestered herself away with her little family after Bram's death. Dianne tried to respect and honor her aunt's need for privacy, but in some ways it only served to remind Dianne that everyone had someone—except her.

She crawled into the small bed, pulled the covers up under her chin, and stared at the darkened ceiling. "I don't know what to do, Lord. I don't know where Cole has gone. I don't know how to keep the ranch running. I don't know how to comfort Koko—especially when I can't seem to comfort myself. I wish Cole were here."

There'd been no mail—no letters. Not from Cole nor anyone else. Dianne longed to know what had happened, but even as rumors had abounded in town about stagecoaches and wagon trains being attacked and destroyed by warring Indians, there were no solid answers.

Two doors down the hall, Levi and Gabe shared a room. Dianne smiled at the memory of Levi suggesting they should be closer. He worried over her as if they were an old married couple, and if he had his way about it, they would be just that.

Dianne wished Levi would find someone to love, other than herself. He was a good man, despite having the lowly job of

cowhand. Yet he was a permanent hand, not just a drifter looking for seasonal work on roundups or cattle drives. Now with
Ben and Charity thinking about staying on in the valley, there
was a possibility Levi might even move back in with them, and
then the idea of settling down and finding a wife might become
an even greater possibility.

Dianne had already decided to offer Ben and Charity the old
homestead cabin. There was plenty of room, even if Levi decided
to move in with them. Dianne liked the idea of the preacher and
his wife being so close. Bram had talked about building them a
church and encouraging the community ranchers to gather with
their families, but at this point Dianne didn't have the energy for
such things. There were too many other needs to be considered.
Ben and Charity could just as easily hold services in the cabin,
and the area folks could drive the extra distance to the Diamond
V if they longed for Christian fellowship.

Still, the church was a dream of Uncle Bram's. Maybe there
would be a way to work it all out.

Morning came much too quickly. Sunlight burst through the
open curtains, warming Dianne and forcing her into a conscious
state. She tried not to think of the loneliness she felt at waking
alone. There was no reason to feel so overwhelmed. She'd awakened alone most every day of her life—this day was no different.

She quickly washed up and dressed in her wrinkled riding
outfit. She was hungry and there was work to do. The men
would no doubt be half starved. There was a small café down the
street where they'd eaten a delicious supper the night before. The
owner promised breakfast would be just as grand an affair. Even
though Levi had just packed away a steak, two portions of fried
potatoes, creamed peas and onions, five dinner rolls, and two
pieces of apple pie, he had suggested eating breakfast there three
times before they'd even reached their hotel room the night
before. Dianne wouldn't dare suggest they eat anywhere else.

Stepping into the hall, Dianne found Gabe and Levi already waiting for her. Levi took up her small bag and offered her his arm. "I'm so empty, my stomach is keeping company with my backbone for fear of being forgotten."

Dianne laughed. "How about it, Gabe? Could you manage to put away a little breakfast?"

The young man nodded. "I reckon I'm just about as hungry as Levi. But maybe not quite as much."

"Then we'd best make our way to the café and resolve this situation." Dianne noted they all looked as if they'd slept in their clothes. "I just hope they don't refuse us service for our dowdy looks."

"You look beautiful, Miz Dianne. No doubt about that. Ain't no one gonna be kicking you out of any place," Levi declared, then blushed red at his boldness.

"Why, thank you, Levi. It's kind of you to offer reassurance." Dianne smiled, taking pity on both men. "If they declare me to be too messy, I'll pay for you two to eat and simply wait for you at the livery until you've had your fill."

Gabe laughed and punched Levi in the arm. "See, Miz Dianne cares more about you than you figure. She ain't about to let you starve."

Levi's hue deepened. "Shut up, Gabe. You don't know nothin'."

"I know that you can eat enough for ten men when it suits you. I just hope Miz Dianne brought enough money to pay for your meal."

Dianne laughed and hurried down the hall to avoid causing Levi any further embarrassment.

Breakfast was a grand affair, just as the owner had promised. They ordered the special and grew wide-eyed when the waitress returned with huge plates, each filled with a ham steak some two inches thick, four eggs, and a mound of fried potatoes. She also brought a platter heaped with a pile of biscuits as well as a bowl of steaming redeye gravy.

"This oughta get us started," Levi teased the young red-headed woman. She blushed.

"There's enough food here to see you satisfied, I'm thinkin'," she replied with a quirky, teasing tone. She left them quickly and retrieved a pot of coffee.

Levi held his cup up as if offering her a gift. "Best coffee I've ever had. Drank at least two potfuls last night."

She smiled and filled his cup. "Glad you like it." She batted her eyelashes, then moved on to Gabe and did likewise. Both men seemed completely smitten.

Dianne would have laughed out loud at the spectacle but didn't want to embarrass Gabe and Levi. Instead, she waited for the girl to fill her own coffee cup, then suggested they offer thanks for the food and dig in.

Gabe offered a short prayer, thanking God for their safety and blessings. Dianne couldn't fault him for his simplicity; she knew both men were anxious to dig in.

"There's a couple horses you're gonna want to look at before we head home," Levi said between bites. "A good solid Arabian mare, about seven years old. She's a beauty—some fourteen-and-a-half hands high. Prettiest white I've ever laid eyes on."

"Sounds like she has real possibilities," Dianne said, nodding. "What else?"

"A young buckskin. He's just two years old. He'd need a lot of work, but he's a feisty Spanish Barb, and I'm thinkin' he'd make a great ranch horse—probably a good breeder too."

"Well, I'd like to see them both," Dianne admitted. "It can't ever hurt to improve the stock. What else do we need to take care of?"

"Shouldn't be too much. Me and Levi took the wagon over to the feed store first thing this morning. They're packing our supplies, and we can pick up the rest of the stuff at the mercantile on the way out of town."

Dianne nodded, making a mental note to look for any items that might have escaped their notice on previous trips. "So do you fellas have any requests? Anything special you need that you don't already have?"

"A chessboard would be nice," Gabe said, then acted as if he'd spoken out of turn. "But that's just a luxury and we can do without it."

"Nonsense. You boys will be cooped up all winter on the ranch. You might as well have something you enjoy. I'll look around and see if there's a chessboard to be had in this town."

"Bradley's has one," Gabe offered, looking rather sheepish.

"Good. You go pick it up. Use some of the supply money," Dianne instructed.

"Thanks a bunch, Miz Dianne," Gabe said in such an animated tone that Dianne was reminded of a child at Christmas.

"What about you, Levi? Anything Ben or Charity could use? Maybe something they didn't think to tell me about?"

Levi shook his head. "Can't think of a thing."

He continued wolfing down his food at an alarming rate. Dianne seriously wondered how he could ever manage to eat everything set before him. Already she was slowing down to her final bites, and there was well over three-quarters of the food still sitting on her plate.

Levi motioned at her ham steak. "You gonna eat that?"

Dianne shook her head. "You want it?" The words were scarcely out of her mouth before Levi forked the steak and had it on his plate. Dianne's mouth dropped open and Gabe laughed at Levi's antics.

"You learn fast in the bunkhouse to keep your arm out of the range of Levi's fork," Gabe said, helping himself to more biscuits and gravy.

The waitress returned, made small talk with the boys, then took Dianne's money for the meal. When Dianne saw that Levi had cleared his plate for a second time, she took the opportunity to stand. "You boys needn't hurry on my account." Both men stood quickly, however.

"We're ready, Miz Dianne. I'll go on down to the livery and have those two horses waiting for your inspection," Levi said, grabbing up his hat. "I'll have our horses saddled too."

"And I'll head over to Bradley's and then the feed store," Gabe offered, taking up his brown felt. "I'll drive the wagon on over to the mercantile."

"Good. I'll meet you at the livery, Levi," Dianne instructed. "I just want to see about some fabric for a new dress for Susannah first. Oh, and Gabe, you might pick up a pound of peppermints. That long ride home gets pretty dusty and I'm thinking the treat might just come in handy."

"Yes, ma'am!" Gabe said with noted enthusiasm. Dianne knew he had a sweet tooth and would appreciate the candy.

With the men heading in different directions, Dianne walked slowly down the boardwalk, taking in the sights. There was a lot of bustle and activity. Freighters moved up and down the wide main street at a surprisingly steady pace. All around her folks were preparing for winter and the coming snow.

"Well, if it ain't Dianne Chadwick," a thick female voice sounded from behind her.

Dianne turned around to find Griselda Showalter, an annoying woman she'd met on the wagon train.

"Hello, Mrs. Showalter. How are you?" Dianne asked politely. She had no desire to make small talk with the obnoxious woman—the woman Dianne still held partly responsible for the destruction and death of her mother. In fact, it wasn't until that exact moment, seeing the rotund woman with her graying hair pulled back in its tight little bun, that Dianne realized just how angry she was with Griselda.

"Don't look like the years have been as cruel to you as they have to me," Griselda replied. "Guess some of us are tougher than others. We can take the hard life—while others are meant to have it easy."

"What's that supposed to mean?" Dianne asked without thinking.

"I heard you have a pretty good life now. Living on a fine ranch with servants and plenty," Griselda stated, lifting her chin in a defiant stance. "Some of us ain't had it that easy."

Dianne thought of all the pain and misery she'd known since coming to Montana. She thought about losing her sisters and mother—about losing Bram and not knowing what had happened to Cole. She even thought of her brothers all going their separate ways and of the emptiness their absence had left in her heart. Then memories of the hard work came to mind. Thoughts of all the times she'd worked fifteen-hour days to get things accomplished. Long hours with cold winds and snow in the winter and searing sun and heat in the summer.

"We all heard about the big house being built. Some say your uncle is spending upwards of ten thousand dollars to build that house."

"I suppose you haven't heard that my uncle passed on a few days back. He was attacked by a grizzly bear while enjoying the easy life you speak of," Dianne said sarcastically.

"No need to take that tone with me, girlie. You ain't had to live in the shanties or work with your hands just to eat. You ain't suffered through what the rest of us have."

"You're absolutely right," Dianne said, barely controlling her temper, "and neither have you any knowledge of the life I'm leading or living. Folks really oughtn't talk about what they know nothing about."

"Percy's dead," Griselda said without fanfare or warning.

Dianne bit her lip and calmed her angry nerves. "I'm sorry for that. When did he pass?"

Griselda showed no emotion. "Last winter. He was always a sickly man. Couldn't manage farm life. Couldn't manage much of anything but bookwork. I figured when we came west it would do him in."

"Then why did you force him to come?" Dianne blurted out, realizing too late how cruel her words were.

Griselda shrugged her shoulders. "Hoped it would make a man of him. Instead, it killed him. No surprise there."

Dianne was shocked by her lack of feeling. "So are you and the children still managing the farm?"

"Hardly. We moved back to town. Can't run a farm without a man."

Dianne noted that Gabe was heading back from Bradley's. "I'm sorry, Griselda, but one of our ranch hands is heading to pick up the last of the supplies and I need to help with this. You have my condolences regarding Percy."

She didn't wait for Griselda to say anything more, but the older woman called after her. "Maybe the children and I will ride out to see you sometime. Catch up on old times."

Dianne refused to reply. If she opened her mouth, she knew the only thing that would come out would be harsh and ugly. "Gabe!" she called instead, hurrying to catch up. "Wait for me."

———

It had been a strange experience to revisit the past with Griselda. The woman didn't look a bit healthy. Her once ruddy peach complexion was rather ashen and drawn. Dianne knew life in Montana had taken its toll on the woman who was used to being in charge. No doubt she was unnerved by so much being out of her control—the weather, the land—even Percy's death.

"I'm glad you decided to ride with me a ways," Levi said as he drove the mules down the road. "I have a couple of things I want to talk to you about."

Dianne pushed aside her thoughts and met Levi's sweet boyish expression. He seemed eternally young; even the hard ranch life hadn't robbed him of his joyful expression and charm. "I'm surprised Gabe let you have the wagon. He usually prefers to drive rather than ride." She looked ahead to where Gabe rode.

"I told him it was important, that I needed to talk with you," Levi said, then cleared his throat nervously. "I hope you don't mind."

"Not at all. What did you want to discuss?"

"I'm wondering if you'd thought about what you'd do if Cole doesn't come back."

The comment took her so off guard that Dianne was actually left speechless for several moments. Levi took advantage of the situation to continue.

"I mean, if he doesn't return—if the worst has happened, well . . . what do you think you'll do? You own the ranch now. Everyone knows that and no doubt there are gonna be men come a-courtin' to try and steal the Diamond V from you."

"I have no intention of letting anyone steal anything from me," Dianne replied rather curtly.

"Didn't mean to make you mad, Miz Dianne. It's just that . . . well, I want you to know that I'm here. That I'll see to you and if Cole doesn't come back . . . I'd like you to consider me as a suitor."

Dianne grimaced and looked away. She didn't want to hurt Levi's feelings, but she also had no desire to have this conversation. "Look, Levi. I appreciate your concern, and I thank you for it. I'm not ready, however, to think about the possibility that Cole might not return. I'm not yet ready to believe him . . . gone."

"But there's always that possibility, Miz Dianne."

"Yes," she said, looking past Gabe to the snow-covered mountains. "Yes, there's always that possibility."

The next day, after they'd returned to the ranch, Dianne found herself having a similar conversation with Charity Hammond. Dianne had delivered some of the supplies she'd picked up for the couple and found Charity a welcoming friend.

"You'll never guess who I saw yesterday," Dianne said, sitting down to share company with her friend.

"Well, let's see," Charity said, looking upward as if pondering the matter. "No, I suppose I haven't a clue."

"Griselda Showalter."

"Mercy, I wouldn't have guessed it for all the gold," Charity declared. "How was she? Did you also see Percy?"

"No, Mr. Showalter died last winter—at least that's what Griselda told me. I found myself feeling so angry at her that I could scarcely listen to what she had to say."

"Why are you feeling so angry toward her?"

Dianne lowered her gaze. "I still blame her for the role she played in my mother's death—in her dependence on laudanum. I didn't realize how mad I was about the whole thing until I came face-to-face with her. She was still her harsh, bitter self, and her attitude toward me was that I was nothing more than a snippet of a girl who wasn't entitled to even have an opinion."

"Griselda Showalter doesn't think anyone's entitled to an opinion, except for herself," Charity replied. She put sugar and cups on the table, then went back to the counter for the teapot.

"She said she and the children are living in town. I can't imagine how they're getting by, and frankly I don't really care. They can all sit there and . . . well, they can all sit there."

"Can't be holding it against the little ones. Their mama's the one who doesn't seem to get along with anyone. I thought the children were pretty decent—given what they were exposed to."

"I suppose you're right." Dianne fell silent for a moment, then began again. "Griselda accused me of having it easy—of living the good life while she suffers."

"You probably do have a better life than anything she's been allowed," Charity said, bringing a delicate china teapot to the table.

Dianne admired the ivory piece for a moment, noting the dainty posies painted in reds, oranges, and pinks. She looked up and blurted out, "I've suffered—maybe not in losing a husband or children, but I've suffered. I've lost most of my family, and that should count for something."

Charity took a seat and smiled. "Didn't know you and Griselda were having a contest."

Dianne frowned. "It wasn't a contest. It's just that Griselda thinks I'm out here living an easy life."

"Why do you care what she thinks? You have no respect for the woman, and frankly, she's done nothing to deserve any. Why does it matter what she says or thinks or does?"

Dianne realized Charity was right. "It just hurt, that's all. Uncle Bram's death is so fresh, and I still don't know what's happened to Cole."

"It must be hard for you—waiting and watching. Has there been no other word from your young man?"

"Nothing," Dianne admitted. "I can't pretend I'm not scared half to death for him. Especially after being in town and hearing all the gruesome stories about troubles on the plains—especially in the area where Cole and the wagon train were to pass. There were reports that a wagon train had been attacked somewhere north of Cheyenne. I can't help but worry that it might have been Cole's."

Charity poured a cup of tea for Dianne and one for herself. "And what will you do if it was and he's gone?"

Dianne shook her head. "I don't know." She picked up the

cup and stared at the contents, as if she could read the answer in the tea. "Levi asked me that same question yesterday. I had no more of an answer for him than I have for you."

"It's a very real possibility. One that none of us likes to think about, but one that may very well come to pass."

Dianne swirled the tea and nodded. "I know," she barely whispered. "I keep thinking of Cole . . . wondering what's happened. I vacillate between hoping that rather than be dead at the hand of Indians or because of sickness, he's just run off with another woman." She lifted her gaze to Charity and added, "Then I find myself feeling much kinder toward his death than his unfaithfulness. Isn't that just awful?"

Charity chuckled. "Spoken like a true woman. You've grown up these last six years."

"To be sure. Sometimes I don't even remember that little girl who came west. I was such a child. Do you know I packed satin dancing slippers in my trunk? Mama told us to take what was important to us—what we could fit in our trunks. I still don't know why I took them. I guess there was something in me that found them important, but for the life of me, I don't know what it was."

"Maybe it was your girlish hopes and dreams. Every woman wants to have some beauty in her life. Maybe you thought the slippers would give you that."

"But I have only to step out the door to see beauty," Dianne replied. She put the teacup down and leaned back in her chair. "Maybe it was the simplicity they represented. Maybe it was knowing what was expected of me and being able to live up to those expectations."

"But now all of that has changed," Charity stated more than questioned.

Dianne nodded. "Now I'm responsible for the ranch and a herd of over six hundred head. I have people living here who are dependent upon my actions and my making the right choices."

"But you're just as dependent upon them," Charity replied. "If their choices are poor, you will suffer. If their decisions are good, then you benefit. It's because you're all here together— working as one body. Like the Good Book says, the body needs all its parts to make it work right. You are the head of this ranch, but you need the others to get things done. You aren't alone in this unless you choose to be."

Dianne thought over her words for a moment. Charity always had a way of helping her to see through the darkness. "I suppose you're right. I just didn't figure to be the head of anything. I thought that would fall to my husband."

"Only you don't have a husband."

The words stung, but Dianne knew she needed to hear the truth of them.

"No," she said, drawing a deep breath, "I don't have a husband."

CHAPTER 14

FOR A FEW DAYS LIFE AT THE RANCH SEEMED TO COME together in a slow but orderly fashion. It was almost like a steam train building up speed from a dead stop. Slow methodic movements at first, then more and more fluid action as the time lengthened and distance could be put between themselves and Bram's death.

Gus took the cattle north with a promise to return in a few weeks if the weather held. He wanted to check in on them and make sure everyone was handling things well in Bram's absence. Dianne knew that no amount of checking in would ease her concerns, however. The winter promised to be long and hard, and the first snows were already falling, giving her even more reason to worry.

Her worries proved to be valid when troubles began less than twenty-four hours after Gus headed out.

Koko had shown very little of herself in the passing days. She seldom came to the dinner table, preferring instead to eat in her room with the children. Dianne was just finishing up the breakfast dishes when Koko appeared in the kitchen, her dark eyes sunken, black half-moons hollowing the skin beneath. She was dressed in Blackfoot fashion with a long leather dress. She'd even braided her coal black hair in two thick plaits.

Dianne put her dishtowel aside and smiled. "I was just wondering about you. How are you feeling?"

"I'm all right, but Jamie's sick."

Dianne felt her heart sink. "What's wrong?"

"He's burning up. I've used the last of my willow bark to brew him tea, but I'm going to need more."

"I'll go for it," Dianne said, moving toward the back porch to get her coat. "What do you think is wrong?"

Koko shook her head. "I don't know. He's not hungry and he complains of pain in his head and joints. I don't know if that's just the fever or something else."

Dianne picked up a flour sack and tucked it under her arm. "Where's the best bark?"

"Those trees downstream where we picked the berries last summer should give you the best quality," Koko said, her expression pinched with worry.

Dianne reached out to touch her aunt. They'd had very little chance to talk since Bram had died. "It'll be all right," Dianne declared. "I'll be praying as I go. You pray too, and just care for Jamie. Do you want me to send Faith or Charity over to take care of Susannah?"

Koko nodded. "I'm just afraid, Dianne. What if—"

Dianne shook her head and interrupted what was sure to be a morbid thought. "Don't say it. He'll be fine. Children get sick sometimes. It happens. Don't be afraid."

Koko let out a ragged breath. "It's just so hard."

Dianne hugged her close. "I know, but we love you and we're here for you. All of us. Faith. Charity. Me. Of course the guys care about you too." For a moment Dianne let the silence fall between them. She refused to let go of Koko, but she did pull back enough to meet her gaze. Koko's dark brown eyes seemed to search Dianne's face—almost as if answers could be found there.

"I'll pray," Koko finally said. "Please hurry."

Dianne flew into action. She rushed to find Faith and managed to locate the woman near the chicken house. "Jamie is sick. I'm going to fetch more willow bark. Are you feeling well enough to care for Susannah?" Dianne knew Faith had suffered with some bouts of morning sickness, and she hated to put any extra duties on the woman.

"Of course. I can fix lunch too, if you like."

"That would be good. It may be a long day and even longer night. Let's all eat supper together. I think that would do much to bolster my spirits."

Faith nodded and Dianne hurried off to saddle Dolly. The buckskin mare seemed to understand the urgency. She pranced nervously as Dianne finished with the cinch.

"Hold still, you silly girl. This is important."

The horse calmed, but Dianne knew she was feeling the tension of the moment. Dolly always seemed to know when Dianne was upset.

She gave the mare a gentle rub on the nose. "It'll be all right," she murmured—as much for herself as for Dolly. "It must be all right."

Dianne strapped an ax to the horse's side, then glanced at the wall where they kept two rifles for emergencies. Remembering Uncle Bram's incident with the bear, Dianne took down one of the rifles and checked to make sure it was loaded. She hadn't worried much about such things in the past, but now she felt precautions were very important. And while it was true that Bram had been carrying a gun when the bear attacked and still wasn't able to save himself, Dianne felt better knowing the weapon was at her side.

Dianne mounted and hurried Dolly down the path toward the river and the willows. In her mind she calculated all the possibilities for what could be wrong with Jamie. Children got sick all the time, but they seemed strong, even resilient to things that often caused much worse trouble for adults. On the wagon train, Dianne had seen many a person get sick with the measles, but the children seemed to recover more easily. She prayed for Jamie, all the while hoping it wouldn't be anything as serious as measles.

The frosty morning air left Dianne exhilarated and refreshed. Snow fell in a light swirling pattern, reminding Dianne of downy feathers. There was only a dusting on the ground, but the world had already calmed into that strange insulated silence that always came with snow. Had circumstances been different, she might have stayed out all day just to think and pray. But the situation wouldn't allow for that, as was often the case.

Funny, she thought, it wasn't for a lack of desire that she seemed to spend less and less time in prayer. It was the busyness of life that seemed to keep her from the things she loved.

"I'm sorry, Lord. I'm sorry I allow myself to get caught up in such things, but if I don't take charge and do the work, who will?" She didn't really expect an answer, for in her heart Dianne was convinced that this was the position God had ordained for her. After all, He alone could have kept Bram from dying, but He didn't.

Reaching the willows, Dianne quickly dismounted and pushed such thoughts aside. She tied off Dolly, then unfastened the ax and went to work peeling bark from the trees. A breeze picked up and whipped at her skirt while the river gurgled and danced on the rocks behind her. The earlier silence faded as the sounds of nature came to life. Somewhere to her right, Dianne heard a branch snap.

Holding the ax close, Dianne glanced away from the trees and strained to listen. Dolly acted more skittish than she'd been, moving from side to side as if to see what enemy approached. Dianne saw the rifle in the scabbard on her saddle. She'd been foolish not to take the rifle with her to the trees. Gently lowering the ax to the ground, Dianne crossed the distance as quickly and quietly as she could.

She had barely reached the rifle when she heard a grunt behind her. Whirling with the rifle in hand, she found Takes Many Horses suppressing his amusement.

He pointed to the rifle. "You gonna shoot us?"

Dianne breathed a sigh of relief. "I thought you were a bear."

"That would be Leaping Deer. He makes so much noise we should change his name to Crashing Bear."

Dianne smiled and waited as he whistled for his companions. Three Blackfoot warriors emerged from the thicket of trees and brush. They looked tired, maybe even sick. Sick! The thought brought Jamie back to mind.

"I need willow bark. Jamie is ill and has a high fever," she explained, hurrying back to where she'd dropped the ax. "Can you help me?"

Takes Many Horses and his friends didn't question that she was asking them to do women's work. They pulled out long knives and made short work of the task at hand. Within a few minutes they had more than enough bark.

The Indians retrieved their horses, and together they all made their way back to the ranch house with Dianne. "I know your sister will be glad to see you," Dianne began. "She's been so troubled and overwhelmed in her grief."

"What grief?" Takes Many Horses asked.

Dianne suddenly realized that he'd not heard about Bram. "Bram died. He was attacked by a grizzly, and we couldn't save him." She saw the man's expression tighten. He wasn't one for showing much emotion, but Dianne knew he was very close to Bram. Her uncle had been like a father to him in many ways.

"I'm sorry to just announce it like that," she added. "I know it's not easy to hear."

He shook his head. "I can't believe he's gone. He always dealt fairly with me and with my sister. I never knew a better man."

"I know. He was like a father to me."

They approached the house and Dianne motioned to the entourage. "If you want to put your horses in the corral over there, that would be fine. I've got to get this bark inside," she said, holding up the flour sack.

"I'll take your horse. Tell my sister I'm here and that I'll see her in a few minutes."

Dianne nodded and handed a very nervous Dolly over to Takes Many Horses. "We'll need to stay the night," he said as he turned the horses. "We can sleep in the barn."

He stated this so matter-of-factly that Dianne had no chance to reply. It didn't set well with her, however. There was no reason for Koko's brother and his friends to sleep in the barn when most of the house sat empty. *Maybe I can rectify that later.*

Dianne hurried inside with the bark and called out, "Koko, I'm back."

Her aunt appeared almost instantaneously. "Thank you. He's still the same." She took up the sack and moved to prepare the tea.

Dianne followed her. "Your brother is here. He's come with several friends."

Koko glanced up but never stopped working. "I'm glad he's come. I felt so bad about not being able to let him know about Bram. Did you tell him?"

"Yes. I thought you'd want me to prepare him. I'm sure the news wasn't easy to take."

"No," Koko said, shaking her head. "He loved Bram very much. This will hurt him deeply."

"It's good, then, that he can be here with those who love and care about him." Koko said nothing, but continued working with the bark. Dianne prayed her aunt would find comfort in Takes Many Horses' appearance, but she was beginning to wonder if that would be possible. If her brother became as grieved as Koko was, neither one would be able to help the other.

After supper that night, Dianne went to the barn to do her routine check of the animals. She'd come to love the quiet moments alone with the stock. The men had taken many of the horses up north with the herd. Gus would bring some of them back and leave some of them up north with the ranch hands. Most of the breeding stock were in newly fenced pasture close to the house. They would find the dried grass beneath the snow and even use the snow for moisture, as well as enjoy daily distributions of hay. Winter would not be so difficult for them.

Dianne came to the new white mare they'd purchased. The horse seemed eager for company and trotted up to see what kind of attention Dianne might give. "You're going to be a fine asset, aren't you, girl?" The mare was high-spirited and strong, two very necessary characteristics needed to survive in the territory.

"My sister tells me that you now own the ranch," Takes Many Horses said, surprising Dianne with his sudden appearance.

Dianne turned and met his intense gaze. His dark eyes glistened in the lantern light. "That's right."

"It should belong to Koko and her family."

"I know that," Dianne replied. "And as far as I'm concerned, it does. I wouldn't dream of doing anything with the place without Koko's approval. I think it's foolish that there are laws against allowing her to inherit land."

"The whites don't even recognize them as married. Why would they believe there was anything to inherit?"

"I suppose you're right." The silence fell thick between them. Dianne could see that Takes Many Horses was watching her, almost as if he wanted to ask her something but couldn't.

"Hard times are coming—are here," Takes Many Horses said as he leaned back casually against a pen, "where the Blackfoot and all the other tribes will be forgotten. The Real People talk about it—wonder what to do." He glanced out past Dianne, as if seeing the future play itself out before him.

"There's no hope for changing things. The whites will come and continue pushing the Real People off their land—away from all they love. It happened back East; it will happen here."

Dianne nodded. "Bram often spoke of it. I'm sorry something better can't be done. You know how much I love Koko— it doesn't matter to me that she's part Blackfoot."

"But it matters to the rest of the world," Takes Many Horses replied sadly.

"But it doesn't matter here. Why not stay?" Dianne asked. She brushed off bits of straw from her long wool skirt, then looked up to add, "Koko could use you now. It would be a help to her having you here. You could teach Jamie about the Black-foot, and Suzy too."

"And what else would I do? Be a cowboy? Herd cattle? Cut my hair and dress as a white man, hoping all the while no one would see me for who I really am?"

"But you're just as much white as you are Blackfoot," Dianne protested.

"No, that's where you're wrong." He stepped forward, his expression stern. "My heart is Blackfoot. I'm one of them, even if it costs me my life. I can't be white. Not in my thinking nor in the thinking of your people."

Dianne remembered Dr. Bufford and his attitude about such matters. It hurt, but more than that it angered her deeply that such a thing should be true. Why did skin color matter so much? Weren't people just people?

"I'm sorry," she began. "I shouldn't have said anything. It was wrong to try and impose something on you that you don't want."

"What I want has never mattered much. I want good things for my people—for those I love."

He stepped within inches of Dianne, then stopped. His dark eyes searched her face. She saw the longing there, and it startled her. Was that desire intended for her, or was it merely the passion he felt for the injustice done his ancestors? She trembled.

"Why aren't you married yet?" His voice was a husky whisper.

The words caught Dianne completely off guard. She didn't have time to think up charming excuses, so she simply spoke the truth. "I don't know."

Takes Many Horses smiled. "Did your man run off?"

"In a sense," she said with a shake of her head. "But not truly. He went back to Kansas to help his parents. Then he was working his way back here this summer on a wagon train. I haven't heard from him since he reached Cheyenne. He thought he'd be here by September, but . . . well . . . he didn't return."

"There are bad times on the plains. The Sioux are very unhappy with the railroad."

Dianne smiled. "How do you know about that?"

"The Sioux or the railroad?" he asked in a teasing tone.

"Both."

Takes Many Horses shrugged. "I've been down south hunting. I've talked to many people, both friend and foe. There is a great unhappiness in the tribes because of the railroad. The trains drive the buffalo off and sometimes even kill them. The trains are bringing in more white people every day. The Sioux, Cheyenne, and Arapahoe will fight to take it back. The Blackfoot will help them, if needed. They'll all fight—if the sickness doesn't kill them first."

Dianne could smell the strange collection of greases and oils he'd used on his body, in his hair. She could almost feel his breath upon her face. She felt her throat dry up and could barely speak the words, "What sickness?"

"Smallpox is what Bram called it. The whites have given us blankets that carry the sickness. So many people are sick. Last January many died from the pox, and then the white soldiers came and killed many more up on the Bear River—whites call it the Marias."

Dianne remembered her brother's confession of what had happened there. She had no desire to remember any of the details. She pushed aside the memory. "Sickness is everywhere. Still, I can't imagine the soldiers purposefully giving the Indians smallpox. They would have to concern themselves with it spreading to the whites and even the forts where they live and work."

"They don't concern themselves with anything that is helpful to the Blackfoot or any other tribe. Their way is to take what is not theirs, including the lives of those who interfere with their plans."

"I'm sure it must seem that way, but my brother Zane is a soldier. He only wants peace in the land."

"White man's peace?"

Dianne shrugged and shook her head. "Isn't peace . . . simply peace? No matter the color?"

Takes Many Horses chuckled softly. "You are very young and naïve."

She didn't want to take offense at his words, but they stung nevertheless. She fought to push aside her pride and took a deep breath.

"I hope you always know you're welcome here," she began. "If you change your mind about where you want to live, you have a home here. Oh, and don't sleep in the barn anymore. There is plenty of room in the house, even if it's not finished or filled with furnishings. It will be warmer. Now if you'll excuse me." She edged past the man and headed for the door.

"Wait," he said softly.

Dianne turned to find him watching her. "What?"

Takes Many Horses went to her and reached out to touch a loose strand of hair. Dianne shivered. There was something so savage and refined about him all at the same time. His presence suggested a sense of danger but also afforded her peace.

"You are a special woman. Strong and capable like the Blackfoot women."

Dianne had no idea where this conversation might lead them, but it made her uncomfortable.

"But I honor the fact that you belong to another."

"Thank you," she whispered, uncertain why he should affect her at all when Cole was the only man she ever intended to marry.

"You love him, don't you?" His gaze bored into her, almost willing her to deny it.

"I love him very much. Cole is my life—my hopes—my dreams." She smiled tenderly, not wishing to hurt Takes Many Horses. "And," she said, leaning just the tiniest bit forward, "he doesn't mind that I have no idea how to tan a buffalo hide." She grinned and turned to go.

He chuckled as she walked away. Dianne's smile faded as she headed to the house. She liked Koko's brother and cherished their friendship. He was a man of honor just like Uncle Bram. Dianne worried that his time of freedom would not last long. Changes were coming—like a storm creeping down from the mountains, like an unseen force that would soon threaten them all. The coming storm would not be kind.

———

The sun wasn't yet up when Takes Many Horses mounted his horse and motioned his companions to head north. He tucked his rifle across his lap, knowing he'd miss the soft deerskin scabbard he'd left as a gift for Dianne. He wondered if she'd like the present or if she'd smile in memory of pulling the rifle on him at the river.

He couldn't help but smile himself as he thought of her fierce determination to be strong and undefeated by the land and its elements.

"She should have been Blackfoot," he murmured, turning his horse to join the others. "She should have been mine."

CHAPTER 15

THE PENCIL STUB COLE HAD FOUND IN THE CABIN ALLOWED him to write out the last entry in his journal before succumbing to his hunger, sickness, and the cold. He had no fear of dying . . . only regrets. Regrets that he'd never see Dianne again—never marry her and raise a family. Regrets that he'd die alone in the wilderness and no one would even know to mourn his passing. It seemed so unfair, unjust. He'd managed to slip away from his captors only to die here in some long forgotten trapper's respite.

His last conscious thoughts were of how much time he'd wasted in bitterness and grief. *I should never have taken so much time before proposing to Dianne. I should have married her quickly, and at least then we would have had that time together . . . those memories could comfort me now.*

When Cole next awoke, he was certain he'd be staring into the face of some heavenly being. Would St. Peter really greet him with the keys to heaven? He'd heard the pastor of his parents' church speak of such matters. Or was it Paul who would come with the keys? He tried groggily to clear his mind and remember.

An ancient woman sat beside him. Her skin was a leathery

brown and her snow-white hair had thinned to a fine wisp of covering. She bathed his face with a cloth and spoke in low, soothing tones.

As his eyes adjusted to the light, Cole realized he'd been found once again by the Indians. He gazed about the tepee, wondering if there were others. Two women sat on the opposite side of the lodge, working to mash something in bowls. Perhaps they were preparing a meal, he thought groggily.

"Where am I?" Cole braved the question, hoping one of the three might speak English.

The old woman said something to the other two. One of the other women got to her feet and left the tepee. Perhaps she had gone for help—or at least a translator. She reminded Cole of Koko Vandyke. In fact, he was almost confident these women were Blackfoot. The younger two wore their coal-colored hair parted down the middle and tied off to each side with strips of rawhide. The old woman wore her hair loose, almost as if there weren't enough mass to bother with. The old woman's dress was of coarse wool. It looked as though the color had once been red, but now with time and wear it looked more brown.

The younger woman returned with a stately old man in tow. His silver-white hair suggested advancing years, but his face seemed hardly wrinkled at all. He appeared unimpressed with the old woman's comments. He conversed for several moments, often grunting or making a gesture toward Cole or one of the others in the room. The conversation, good or bad, was obviously about him.

"Do you speak English?" Cole asked, barely able to speak the words. His throat felt so very dry.

The man eyed him for a moment, then said something to the old woman. She nodded and called out to the two women on the opposite side of the tepee.

The old man left and one of the younger women quickly

appeared with a bowl of steaming broth. The smell enticed Cole. He hadn't eaten in days, maybe longer; he'd lost track of how long he'd been on the run.

The old woman helped Cole to sit up just a bit, then offered him the bowl. She saw immediately that he was too weak to hold the bowl by himself, however, and helped him ease the dish to his mouth.

Never had anything tasted so good. Cole felt the warm liquid trickle down his throat and pool in his stomach. The warmth spread throughout his body and with each sip, Cole imagined his strength returning. *There is a gentleness about these people. They want to see me well,* he told himself.

But after a few drinks, he was completely exhausted and waved off any further nourishment or care. His energy gave way to the demand for sleep, and though Cole's mind fought against it, his body had its way and he drifted into dreams.

Cole's recovery came in slow but steady improvements over the days that followed. The old woman seldom left his side, and she nursed him much differently than the Sioux woman had. This woman gently tended his wounds, bathed his body, and helped him to eat. This woman spoke to him, and while he understood very little of what she said, she often offered him a comforting pat on the arm or a smile.

After two weeks, Cole felt more like his old self. He was able to sit up now for several hours a day, and by the end of the third week, he was able to walk around the camp a bit.

He was confident now that the group was Blackfoot. He even managed to draw on memories of words he'd learned at the ranch and converse enough to understand that they were waiting for the hunting party to return before they headed north to better winter seclusion near the Sweet Grass Hills and the Canadian border.

Cole watched the people work around the camp and admired

their spirit. The children laughed and played, chasing after the dogs or each other. Sometimes they would come close to him and watch him. Once in a while one of the children would get brave and rush forward to touch Cole before jumping back to rejoin his companions. Cole imagined in their own way they were counting coup on him, a twist on an old Indian practice. Always the others were quite impressed and would laugh and pound the daring warrior on the back. Cole had to laugh at their antics. They were so pleased and proud of themselves.

It was nearing the fourth week when heavy snows and cold made life in the camp less pleasant. Cole would still sit outside as much as possible, for the dank stench of the tepee was almost more than he could take at times. He'd learned that he was being cared for by the tribe's holy woman and this tepee was her medicine lodge. If he understood correctly, she was a great healer— his own recovery was proof of that.

The women who worked with her didn't live in the lodge. They seemed to come and go, however, as directed by the old woman. Cole thought perhaps they were training for the position of medicine woman. No matter the reason they were in attendance, Cole knew they highly respected their ancient matron.

As Cole's mobility and clarity increased, he thought a lot about what would happen to him and where he would go from here. The Blackfoot didn't seem to want him as prisoner, but neither did they show any desire to send him on his way. Cole was amazed at the care they'd offered. His wounds were pretty much healed, and only a dull ache remained in his chest to remind him that the scars he bore were from recent wounds. Still, with winter bearing down on them in merciless cold and snow, Cole wasn't too inclined to ask for his freedom to leave. He had no idea which direction he'd have to head to find home, and he had no equipment to see him through the bone-chilling temperatures. Since they didn't appear to be a threat to his life, Cole figured to wait things out a bit.

It was on the second day of the desperate winter cold that Cole heard a great deal of whooping and hollering. The children were calling out, from what Cole could understand, that the warriors had returned with the winter provisions.

He knelt at the entrance of the tepee, hoping to avoid being seen, praying that this change would not bode ill for him. He saw the women rush out to greet their men, to boast at the catches of at least two dozen elk and half as many buffalo. The village came to life with an attitude of celebration and victory. The old men came forward to greet the younger men, speaking in words too low for Cole to understand.

Without warning, someone grabbed Cole by the heavy buffalo robe he was wearing and threw him to the ground. It was a young warrior, probably no older than sixteen or seventeen. The boy's eyes shone black with hatred. He called to his friends, and before Cole could even cry for help, he found himself being beaten by the collection of young men.

"Stop!" a voice called out in English. Then in Blackfoot the man added, "*Kai yiwahts?*" Cole recognized the words. They translated, "What troubles you?"

One more kick was delivered to Cole's ribs, causing him to moan. He feared he might throw up.

The boys explained themselves in rapid-fire Blackfoot. Cole heard one declare him to be the enemy, but the man who'd spoken in English denied this.

"Go to your mother's house. You've disgraced yourself," the man spoke in English, then repeated in Blackfoot. The warriors hung their heads and turned like punished puppies to head back to the center of camp.

Cole struggled to stand up, pulling the robe with him. He wanted to thank the man, but just then several of the older men appeared. The one who always appeared to be in charge spoke to the younger English-speaking man. The older man produced Cole's journal—something Cole had figured to be long lost or left behind at the cabin.

The younger man eyed it curiously for several moments, then took it from the other man and opened it. He looked from the journal to Cole. "Does this belong to you?"

"Yes."

"What is your name?"

"Cole Selby."

The man's gaze narrowed. He looked more fierce and his expression aged him. "Where do you come from?"

"I live along the Madison River in the Montana Territory— on a ranch called the Diamond V."

The man nodded. "We'll talk later."

Cole watched the Blackfoot warrior speak momentarily to the older men, then head off across the camp. The warrior had opened his journal again and appeared to be reading it. A feeling of dread came over Cole. What would happen now—now that the younger, more hot-headed men of the tribe had returned? Was it time to run again? And if so, which way should he go?

———

The Blackfoot warrior turned the pages of the white man's journal. He felt he knew the man from his entries. Cole Selby wrote of hard trails and long nights—of cattle stampedes and wagon train sicknesses. But mostly he wrote of how much he missed his woman. His Dianne.

Takes Many Horses closed the journal after reading the final entry. Cole Selby was in a tepee not ten yards away. Dianne's long-lost man. The man who stood between Takes Many Horses and the woman he loved.

He gritted his teeth. How was it that fate had brought them

together? When he'd returned from the hunt, he'd been told that an injured white man was in camp and that he was needed to translate. He'd never dreamed it might be Cole Selby. Yet even as the man had stood after receiving an undeserved beating from the younger men of the camp, Takes Many Horses had known in his heart that this was Dianne's man. He couldn't explain why he knew, but he did.

When he first looked into the eyes of the white man, he saw the man's pain and suffering, but he also saw his determination and fighting spirit. This man had something more to live for than himself. His love and passion for Dianne had kept him alive.

But now Takes Many Horses had this man's life in his hands. If he went back to the council of elders and lied, telling them the journal revealed the man's hatred for the Blackfoot and his plans for killing them, then no doubt Cole would be murdered. With Cole out of the way, Takes Many Horses would be free to return to the ranch, tell Dianne he'd learned the fate of her fiancé, and then perhaps work himself into a position of being the comfort she needed to live beyond her loss.

"He speaks of his love for Dianne as being second only to his love for God," Takes Many Horses muttered. *But how could he put her second to anyone or anything? She is beautiful and strong. She is worth everything and anything a man might own.*

"She would never be second to me," Takes Many Horses said, casting the journal aside. The book fell to the side of his pallet and for several minutes, he could only stare at it.

I have the power to make things the way I would have them be, he thought. *I can remove Cole Selby out of her life forever. I have the ability to make this decision and free her once and for all.*

Takes Many Horses imagined the moment he would tell Dianne of Cole's death. He could see her tears and sorrow. She would be silent, he thought. She would weep silently and be strong as he explained how Cole bravely died. Then she would take herself away and mourn for him in private.

Then he thought of the life Dianne had offered him. *I could live as a white man. I could live as my father did—as Bram did. They were good men, men to be honored. I could live as they did. I have the ability to change my entire future,* he thought. The idea wasn't entirely unappealing. After all, he clearly saw that the life of the Pikuni would soon be altered by the increasing interference of the white man. Men like Cole Selby.

"That's why so many have died," Takes Many Horses muttered, reaching over to retrieve Cole's journal. He could die. Cole Selby was only words away from death.

"Dianne is strong; she could survive the loss. She could live with his death," Takes Many Horses said, still staring at the book.

"But could I?"

CHAPTER 16

COLE WATCHED THE BLACKFOOT MEN SEATED ACROSS FROM him. He'd been called to the lodge of the tribal leader. Here he sat with five Blackfoot men, obvious leaders with the power to determine his future. The one who spoke English sat opposite Cole and seemed to watch him with intense interest.

Cole was offered *nitapi waksin*—"real food," or meat. There was a variety, including a succulent slice of buffalo tongue and a large portion of roasted elk. After they filled up on meat, they passed the *kistapi waksin*—the "nothing foods," which as far as Cole could figure, was anything that wasn't meat. When they'd finished eating, the old man who sat in the center prepared and lit a pipe. A lean younger man who sat next to the old man took the pipe and inhaled. He spoke solemnly after blowing smoke toward the roof of the tepee.

"Oh, Above People, hear us now."

Cole made the words out and wondered at what sounded like a prayer.

"Help us to make good choices. Help us, World Maker, to open our eyes. Pity us." He took another long draw from the pipe and passed it down the row to be smoked from east to west. When they had finished, the old man cleaned out the bowl and put it to one side. Then he turned to his English translator, and they began to question Cole.

"Where were you when you were attacked?"

"We were west of Fort Fetterman, camped on Sage Creek," Cole said, trying his best to remember. "I don't remember much of anything except that a party of Sioux had been following us for several days." He shrugged and added, "We thought they'd lose interest when we camped at the fort, but they continued following us when we moved out. I think we were only a day out—maybe two, I can't remember. They attacked at first light, and before I knew it I had two arrows in my chest. I don't remember what happened next. When I finally woke up, I was being dragged behind a horse on a travois."

The man translated for the elders. Cole watched the play of expression on the faces of the leaders as the story was relayed. The Blackfoot men were dressed in what looked to be their finest clothes. Some of their shirts were beaded and others bore weasel tails. Cole knew from stories he'd heard on the Diamond V that these were special shirts of some importance. Apparently their meeting with him was seen as an event of great significance.

The men stopped talking amongst themselves, and then the interpreter turned to question Cole again. "Where were the Sioux taking you? Did they tell you why they had taken you with them?"

Cole shook his head. He remembered vaguely that there had been other whites with him in the Sioux village. "I don't know why they took us; it came as a surprise to me. Their care wasn't as good as I've received here, but it wasn't all that bad. They fed me and tended my wounds. The other whites died. I don't know if they were killed by the Sioux or if they died from their wounds, but I felt that I had to escape."

"Where were you when you left their camp?"

Cole shook his head. "I have no idea. We traveled north for some time—at least I think we did. We were camped along a river that ran east and west. There were mountains to the west. That's really all I know."

The warrior relayed the information and a great discussion broke out amongst the men. Cole watched and waited, hoping that God would deliver him—praying the Blackfoot would find no fault with him.

Again the conversation waned and the man with shiny black braids turned again to Cole. "Were they making plans for war?"

Cole tried to think of any indication that would suggest such a thing. "I don't think so. There were many women and children—old people too. They seemed more interested in surviving and continuing to move north. I didn't see anything to indicate they were doing anything other than that. They weren't digging in or preparing to fight there."

"But they allowed you to escape," the man replied. "We found their empty camp. They moved out quickly, which was why they didn't come after you."

"Where are we?" Cole braved the question.

"In the territory you call Montana."

Cole perked up. At least he was in the right area. "I desire to go home. My home is on the Madison River in the southwestern region of this territory."

The man eyed him hard for a moment. Cole returned his gaze, wondering what the man was thinking. There was no time to ask, however, as a young boy came into the lodge, shouting. Cole understood enough of the boy's excited declaration to know that soldiers were on their way. And their numbers were great.

Dianne dealt with another Christmas coming and going without Cole by her side. It was hard to maintain hope that he might still be alive. *So much time has passed—so many attacks have taken place. I have to be reasonable.* But she didn't feel reasonable.

The holidays had been particularly difficult with Bram's death so fresh in their minds and hearts. The family had gathered, along with the friends who now lived on the Diamond V, but the celebration held a touch of sorrow as they exchanged their gifts and talked of the new year to come. In the weeks that passed, a gloom seemed to settle over the house and a spirit of despair seemed to touch everyone.

Dianne walked through the unfinished structure that was to one day be her wing of the house.

She held up a lantern to better view the structure. "But there will never be a family without Cole at my side. I can't even imagine it as so," she murmured. The bare skeletal framework had been finished enough to keep out the winter snows and some of the cold, but it would need a great deal of work before it bore any real resemblance to comfortable rooms.

Dianne sighed and leaned against a very crude doorframe. "I can't live in the past. If Cole is dead, then I must go on. I owe it to those who are still living." Dianne thought of her youth and the years she'd spent in Missouri. How simple life had been. She had her friends and her parties and fun. She was spoiled, though at the time she couldn't see it. She despised book learning— hated the hours sitting in school, struggling to memorize dates and perfect her handwriting.

Her father taught her to keep the books for the store, and while that was better than schoolwork and not nearly as taxing to Dianne's mind, she never had any real appreciation for the benefits such a job allowed her.

Those days seemed a thousand years ago. Long before she'd

met Faith and Charity—ages and ages before coming to live with Koko and Uncle Bram.

"I know I must survive, Lord," she began to pray. "I know you have brought me here for a reason, but that reason is far from my understanding."

She moved back toward the finished portion of the second floor. Here she took one of the bedrooms that would one day be given to guests who came to visit. Beyond that room and down the other wing, Koko and her children shared several rooms. It was hard to believe that Susannah was already a year old. The little girl was a handful. She'd begun to walk just a week before Christmas, and now, as Koko said, there would be no holding her back.

Dianne lingered a moment longer, then headed downstairs to the main part of the house. It was late and the lonely silence of the house filled Dianne with a sense of sorrow and regret. At times like this, sleep was hard to find. The longing in her heart overwhelmed everything else—even the need for rest.

Walking quietly through the house, Dianne marveled at the fine woodwork Bram had arranged for, as well as the lovely stone fireplace in the large front gathering room. They had enjoyed a large fire earlier in the evening, but now there were only embers. Nevertheless, Dianne placed the lantern on the mantel and knelt on the floor in front of the hearth. She held out her hands to capture the last bits of heat. The house was growing colder by the minute, but this one last vestige of the fire's warmth seemed to bolster her weary soul.

Dianne whispered a verse from the first chapter of Nahum. "'The Lord is good, a strong hold in the day of trouble; and he knoweth them that trust in him.'" Surely these were days of trouble. Surely no other time called for her trust as much as this moment.

She leaned her head against the warm stones. "I do trust you,

Lord. I'm just not sure where you are leading me—or whether I'll want to be there when I learn the destination. Help me to endure what comes . . . to abandon my fears and think only of the hope I have in you."

At breakfast the next morning, Dianne sat down at her usual place. She couldn't bring herself to take Bram's seat at the head of the table. Neither could Koko. Dianne had encouraged Koko to take her rightful position as head of the family and the ranch, but it wasn't a position Koko wanted.

"It wouldn't be fair to my children," she told Dianne one evening. "They would come to see me in a position of authority, and when the rest of the white world did not also honor that, they would grow angry and confused. I do not wish to see my son grow up bitter and resentful."

But Dianne wondered how the children could help but feel that way as they grew old enough to understand the truth. After all, the day would come when Jamie would face the prejudices Koko feared. He'd one day have to be told that he had no right to the land his father had settled. He'd learn that because Blackfoot blood ran in his veins, he would not even be considered a citizen of the United States. *How could bitterness then be avoided?* Dianne wondered.

Faith served up a fine meal of fried ham and potatoes, and after everyone enjoyed their fill, the men drifted off to their duties. Charity and Faith remained in the dining room, along with Koko and the children. Jamie played quietly in the corner while Susannah nursed at her mother's breast.

"I wondered if we might speak for a few minutes," Dianne said as Charity got to her feet and started clearing the table. "Can you remain a short time?"

"Of course, Dianne," the older woman said, retaking her seat. "What did you wish to discuss?"

Dianne sat down without ceremony and drew a deep breath. "Our future."

Faith looked intrigued, while Koko appeared to be lost in thought.

"Dealing with the future is a business I'm well familiar with," Charity laughed. "'Cept we look more into the eternal future."

Dianne and Faith both chuckled, but Koko looked at Dianne, her dark eyes searching Dianne's face. "What do you have in mind?" she asked softly.

"Well, I wanted to ask that very question of you, Koko," Dianne began. "We have a ranch to run, and we have some decisions to make before spring rolls around." Dianne paused and lowered her voice as if in respect for the dead. "I know Bram has only been gone a short time, but he'd be the first one to tell us that life out here stops for no man. Not Uncle Bram—not Cole Selby."

The mention of Cole's name sobered every face at the table. Koko's expression grew sympathetic. "I'm sorry," she whispered. "I haven't even stopped to think of how his absence has hurt you."

"I won't lie to you, my dearest friends. I'm terrified that he's dead and at the same time know that if he's not dead, he's changed his mind about us and hasn't had the guts or gumption to tell me." Her words were frank, almost rehearsed, but Dianne knew she had to keep her momentum going or she might well give way to emotion.

"Cole should have been home last September. There have been multiple reports of wagon trains attacked and destroyed by Indians. I have to allow for the fact that Cole may have met with a fate such as this. It's a very real possibility."

"We have to have hope," Faith said softly.

"Yes," Charity agreed. "And faith that God has Cole in His care."

Dianne appreciated their words, but she'd already told herself all of this. "I know, but here again, decisions have to be made. Gus has agreed to stay on. He has no desire to go anywhere else or work for anyone else. That's definitely to our benefit, agreed?"

Koko nodded and shifted the now sleeping baby. "Most definitely. Bram had great confidence in Gus. He would always consult Gus about important matters. He said Gus was the best man for the job and knew much about ranching."

"The herd is growing every year. Gus thinks next year we'll be able to sell off quite a few steers to the army. That will increase our revenue and allow us to hire workers to finish the house. I know this place was important to Uncle Bram. It was his dream, and I'd like to see it finished. Beyond that, Gus said we should look to expanding the bunkhouse and taking on a few more year-round workers. I figure Gus knows best about these things, and I'm inclined to heed his requests."

"I agree," Faith said, putting in her thoughts. "Malachi says that man knows more about horses and cattle than a human being ought to know. I'm glad he's staying on. As for me and Malachi, well, you know our intentions. We want to stay on and make a home here. We are pleased to be a part of the Diamond V. Pleased to have jobs we enjoy. I like cooking for the men. I can even keep meals for everyone here at the house—'course, that's up to you and Koko. I don't want either one of you to feel like I'm stepping out of line. If you'll let me, though, I'd be happy to keep everyone fed."

Dianne looked to Koko. "Does that meet with your approval?"

"Certainly. I have nothing but praise for Faith. She saved my Susannah from death when I was too sick to care for her, and Jamie adores her." She looked to Faith and actually smiled. "I love you like a sister."

"I feel the same way. Not many places in this world where a

Negro would be welcome to sit at the same table as white folks. You've all made me feel as though the color of my skin doesn't matter."

"To us, it doesn't," Charity agreed. "I'm pleased to be a part of an establishment where people are judged by their actions rather than their skin color or education or even gender. I look at you three and feel a deep pride—almost like a mama. I knew Dianne when she was just a slip of girl who didn't even know how to thread a needle. I've watched you all work together and pray together, and I'm proud to be a part of this family and this ranch. Ben and I feel it's important to stay and put down roots—establish a church right here in the valley. I'm here to help in whatever way I can." She paused. "I guess I'm best with a needle, so if you'd allow me, I'd be happy to do the mending and sewing for the ranch. I know we'll probably all need to pitch in on it from time to time, but I'm still pretty quick with my work, despite my rheumatism."

Dianne laughed. "I'll bet you are."

"Dianne's gotten very good at her sewing," Koko put in. "When she first came here she was very capable, but over the years she's really learned to master her skills."

"I'm better with a horse, though." Dianne couldn't help but make this statement. Truth be told, she'd rather be outside working with the livestock on any given day, rather than sewing or cooking. She was pleased that her friends were volunteering for the jobs they loved the best.

"Our herd of horses has grown considerably. Gus has given me good ideas for breeding stronger, more efficient animals. The army is always in need of good horseflesh, and Gus believes we can make a good amount of money in rounding up wild horses and bringing them in to break. I think he's absolutely right. Gus even has a couple of friends he'd like to bring up here to help. They're the best in horse-breaking, as far as Gus is concerned."

"So you will work with the horses and cattle," Koko said thoughtfully.

Dianne shrugged. "Guess so. I can also keep the books. Uncle Bram taught me about that early on—right after he found out I kept books for Papa." She smiled. "Uncle Bram didn't care for bookkeeping any more than I did, but at least it was something I could do to help."

"Where does that leave me?" Koko asked.

Dianne smiled. "Where would you like it to leave you? There's still plenty to be done, and you hold some very valuable skills that none of the rest of us can boast."

Koko shook her head. "I don't know how I can be much good to anyone."

Jamie came to his mother and put his head against her. "You're good, Mama." He patted her hand and repeated the words. The action nearly brought tears to Dianne's eyes. She hadn't stopped to think how much or how little Jamie might be hearing.

"Yes, you are a good mama," Dianne said softly. "You're also very gifted in leatherwork, something the rest of us aren't that experienced with. You make many valuable products for the ranch, and if you choose, you could go on making them."

Koko nodded. "I like working with the hides. I'd be happy to continue with that. I also like to garden and can the fruit and vegetables we grow. So when spring comes, I could plant the garden and can our food."

"I help plant too," Jamie said in a very serious manner.

Dianne smiled, realizing how neatly God had ordered this gathering. "See there? We each have these great skills—needed skills. We make quite a grand collection of workers."

"I'll say!" Gus drawled as he came into the dining room from the kitchen.

"Gus! When did you get back?"

"Just now. I rode a storm across the valley and barely beat it in."

"How bad of a storm?" Dianne questioned. "Do we need to make provision?"

"I don't think we need to do anything more than we've already prepared for. I think we'll be just fine nestled up here. Probably snow—maybe heavy, but nothing we can't handle, eh, ladies?" The weathered cowboy grinned and winked. His confidence bolstered Dianne once again.

"Absolutely," she said, nodding. "We can do all things through Christ."

Koko nodded, stroking the head of her boy with one hand and cradling her daughter with the other. "Yes, all things through Christ."

"That's where the strength is," Charity added. "We get our strength for all things through the Lord."

Gus laughed. "Ain't nothin' can drag us down. We're workin' for God hisself and ain't no one able to go interferin' with that."

Dianne drew a deep breath and felt a warmth spread through her. *Yes,* she thought, *my Father will give me strength to go on. Together, we'll make this work.*

CHAPTER 17

Denver
March 1871

PORTIA MCGUIRE PATTED HER GLOVED HAND AGAINST HER chocolate brown hair. The train travel west from Kansas City to Denver had left her feeling fatigued and dirty, but time was of the essence in reaching her destination. Especially since the telegram she'd received said her mother's health was failing.

The Clarkston Sanitarium was said to be a fine institution for the terminally ill. Portia sincerely hoped this was true, as her mother was one of its newer residents.

The carriage slowed as it turned onto the hospital grounds, allowing Portia her first real view of the place. The two-story brick structure seemed unimpressive, but the well-manicured lawn and gardens of spring flowers were impressive. Spring had come early to Denver this year. In fact, during her journey west, Portia had been greatly impressed by the warmth and beauty she'd found along the way. Back East, especially in Boston, they were still experiencing an unseasonably cold spring.

The driver brought the carriage to a halt, then opened the door for Portia. "Here we are, ma'am." He offered his assistance, and Portia alighted from the conveyance, clinging to his arm. She pressed a coin into his hand, then smoothed out the wrinkles in her black traveling suit.

How she hated black. It was such a dull color unless done up in a fashionably low-cut evening gown. But black was expected of her as a widow, and Angus had only been dead for little more than two months. Her mother would expect nothing less than the grieving widow.

Portia made her way to the whitewashed front doors and was surprised when a short elderly man opened the door before she could even ring the bell or knock.

"Good afternoon, madam," he said with a refined English accent. "How may I assist you?"

She handed him her calling card. "I'm here to visit my mother, Mary Brady. She was recently admitted."

"Come this way," he instructed, leading her to a small wood-paneled office.

A stern-looking older man peered up from his desk. Gold-framed glasses hung precariously on the end of his nose. He took the card offered by the butler and nodded. "Ah, Mrs. McGuire. Please be seated. I am Dr. Wadsworth."

Portia hated his condescending tone but graciously smiled and lowered herself to a red leather chair opposite the desk.

"As you know, your mother is gravely ill," the man began. "Her condition is such that there is very little we can do."

"What has been done for her?" Portia asked, feeling very frightened by the man's tone. She knew the asylum was for the terminally ill, but she'd really not allowed herself to believe this was the case for her mother.

"Surgery was performed, and that was when the tumor was discovered. I'm afraid there's nothing more we can do for her."

"Can I have her moved—taken back East where the hospitals are better equipped to deal with this kind of thing?"

The man's face pinched as he frowned. "Mrs. McGuire, our medical facilities here in Denver are quite capable of handling this situation. Your mother is beyond any help that even the eastern hospitals might afford her. She has a cancer, and it's spread considerably further than we'd anticipated. She is dying and probably has less than a month to live."

Portia felt as though the man had slapped her in the face. How could this be true? Only a few weeks ago her mother had come to Denver to set up housekeeping in preparation for her husband's retirement from the army. Samson Brady didn't even know his wife was ill, much less dying.

"Is she awake—able to communicate?" Portia asked numbly.

The man withdrew his glasses and put her card aside on his desk. "Yes. I am certain your company will be most welcomed. I'll have a nurse take you to her." He nodded to the still waiting butler. The man quickly exited the room and Portia got to her feet.

"I want her to have the best care. Money is of no importance," she told the doctor.

He offered the first hint of a smile. "I'll have her moved to a private room later this afternoon, in that case."

"Thank you. I'll come to settle with you after I visit with her."

A middle-aged woman dressed in white and black appeared at the door. She wore a strange white bonnet on her head and a perpetual frown on her face. It seemed that everyone in this institution was unhappy.

"Yes, Doctor?"

"Escort Mrs. McGuire to see her mother, Mrs. Mary Brady, in D Ward."

"Very well," the woman replied in a voice that suggested it was an imposition.

Portia thanked the doctor and followed the woman out the

door and up a flight of carpeted stairs. "Do you work with my mother?"

The nurse looked at Portia and answered in a tight-lipped manner, "No. I am an administrative nurse. I do not work directly with the patients."

"So you have no knowledge of my mother?"

"Only that she's terminally ill. None of the patients on D Ward are long for this world."

Portia swallowed hard and tried not to show any emotion. This woman would certainly show no compassion for her tears. They reached the top of the stairs and moved to the left. Passing several open doors, Portia could see people dressed in white sitting by windows or in beds. Some rooms seemed bright with sunlight and others were darker with the draperies pulled. She couldn't help but think that this was a sorry way to end one's life.

"This is D Ward. Your mother is in the bed at the end of this row." She motioned down the left side.

Portia didn't bother to thank the woman but instead moved across the room to find her mother. The last bed revealed a shriveled, pale version of the woman she'd known in her youth.

"Mama?"

The woman opened her eyes and a look of recognition crossed her features. "Portia. You've come."

"How could I not?"

As an only child, Portia knew it was her duty to be at her mother's side, but as a beloved only child, Portia desired to simply be with her mother in her time of need. Her mother had been Portia's only friend in life.

"How are you feeling, Mama?"

The woman, not yet fifty years old, struggled to sit. She looked exhausted, and even with Portia's help, she seemed unable to accomplish this simple feat. She paled even more, and the look in her eyes let Portia know the pain was great.

"I'm not so good. I'm sorry," her mother apologized.

Portia nodded and helped her mother ease back onto her pillow. "I've asked them to take better care of you. They plan to move you to a private room later today."

"One with a window, I hope."

Portia had no idea if a window were in the plans, but she would definitely demand it. After all, if she was going to pay a small fortune, the least they could do was give her mother a window.

"How did this happen, Mama?" Portia asked, pulling up a chair to sit beside her mother's bed.

"I had pain in my gut," her mother said. "It hurt a great deal and only got worse. It's something I can barely tolerate now." She grimaced.

"Do they give you anything for it?"

"No. I was afraid to take anything for fear I wouldn't be awake when you arrived."

"Oh, Mama. You need medicine. They can help to ease the suffering."

"I'm dying, you know," her mother said matter-of-factly.

Portia pushed down her emotions. "Yes, they told me. I still don't understand why this has happened, but I want to make you as comfortable as possible and do whatever you need me to do."

"I need you to let your father know the truth. I couldn't just telegraph him. It's not the kind of news you give that way."

"Are you suggesting I go to Fort Ellis and tell him in person?" Portia asked in disbelief. "You want me to go to Montana Territory?"

"I would like that very much. I know it's a long trip and there are problems with the Indians, but he must know. Wait until I'm gone, then go to him."

Portia nodded, though she had no intention of keeping her promise. She'd never had much use for her father. He was a career army man and seldom had time for his little daughter. He'd wanted a son and made no attempt to hide his disappointment in the dark-haired beauty. Never mind that men from far and wide coveted time with Portia. Her exotic features and trim hourglass figure brought her many compliments—but not from her father.

"I want you to promise me," Mary Brady whispered.

Portia bit her lip. She could lie to the rest of the world, but her mother was the one person with whom she couldn't be false.

"He should be at your side. Why did he send you here alone? Because of the army—that's why. The army has always been more important to him. He never cared enough to be with us when we needed him."

"Don't say such things. Your father cares very much."

Portia started to say something, then held her tongue. Her mother was dying; there was no sense in arguing with her. Especially since Portia could never change her mind.

Hoping her mother would forget the request, Portia began to talk about her travels west. "The trains were incessantly slow. And then crossing Kansas was humid and unbearable, but all the way I kept telling myself I'd soon see you. I've missed you so much, Mama."

"I'm sorry to meet again under these circumstances. Sorry, too, for your own loss. I learned only shortly before leaving Montana that your husband had died."

Portia frowned. Her mother sounded so weak—so exhausted. "Don't concern yourself with it, Mama." She glanced around the room at the other patients, most of whom were sleeping soundly. *The sleep of the dead,* Portia thought. "I should go and let you rest. I can come back later after they've moved you and you've rested."

Her mother closed her eyes. "No. Please don't leave. I know my time is coming soon."

Portia reached out and took hold of her mother's hand. "I love you. You know that, don't you?"

Mama nodded and opened her eyes. "I know that. That's why I'm asking you to help me. It's the last thing I'll ever ask of you, Portia. Please go to your father for me. Please go to him and . . ." Her face tightened, and the expression left little doubt as to the intensity of her pain. "Please, Portia."

Portia squared her shoulders. She had no desire to ever see her father again, but if it offered her mother comfort in her final hours, then Portia would acquiesce. She gently squeezed her mother's hand. "I'll go to him, Mama. I'll do as you ask."

"Thank you. I knew you would." She closed her eyes again, but her breathing was still heavy.

"I'm going to ask the doctor to bring you something for the pain," Portia declared, getting to her feet. "You must let them help you now. I'm here and I won't leave until the end."

"Very well, Portia. Bring the medicine."

———————

"Faith, you're as big as a barn," Dianne teased. "That baby must be a big one."

Faith patted her rounded abdomen. "Malachi says it's a boy. I'm just praying it's a healthy baby—healthy and strong."

Dianne put her arm around Faith's shoulders. "He will be. I just know he will be absolutely perfect. You'll see."

Faith nodded. "That's my prayer—my hope."

Dianne released her and went back to the table, where an assortment of tiny baby clothes was spread. Some were Jamie's and Susannah's and some were new little outfits that the women had been helping to sew throughout the winter.

"I think you'll have enough here to dress three babies," Dianne said, holding up a baby quilt that Charity had finished only that morning. "My, but Charity does the nicest work. I wish I could make such pretty things."

Faith lovingly ran her hand atop the quilt. "She's gifted, all right."

Dianne sighed and replaced the blanket on the table. "I'll box these up and have one of the boys take them to your cabin." She felt a pang of longing as she began to stack the little outfits.

Little by little Dianne had resigned herself to Cole's absence becoming a permanent arrangement, but the pain was still acute and the baby clothes only served to remind her of what she didn't have—and probably never would.

———

Dianne found solace in working with the horses. Learning to watch each animal to gauge its mood and understand how best to handle it, Dianne was able to forget about her own troubles. She made her way to the training corral in the afternoon and reached for a halter, thinking about how surprised Cole would be at her ability. She couldn't help but remember their first encounters and how little she'd known about animals.

"Are you going riding?" Levi asked.

Dianne startled at the sound of his voice. "I thought I would. I figured I'd take Jack and ride the mean out of him." The black stallion had refused to calm and be useful, and because of that Bram had gelded him. But it hadn't helped that much. Still, Dianne couldn't give up on him. He was a beautiful animal and she didn't want to lose him.

Levi laughed. "Guess I won't see you back until summer, then. There's still a lot of mean in that horse."

"I know, but it won't work itself out."

"Why don't you let me saddle him for you? Jack can still get a little feisty when first approached."

"I'll be just fine, Levi. Don't worry about me." She smiled

his way but saw the look of worry on his face. "Truly, Levi. I can manage."

"I know you're having a hard time. I just want you to know that I care. I'm not trying to overstep my place here. I'm your friend."

Dianne nodded. "I know that, Levi. I appreciate it . . . honestly I do. It's just going to take time."

"I'll always be here for you."

She nodded again and left to retrieve the gelding. Jack seemed to understand her mood and stood as still as stone as she saddled him. His silky black mane, warmed by the sun, felt good to her touch. She stroked the horse for several minutes, then led him out the gate. Dianne walked him for several yards before stopping to mount him. He'd been exercised a little that morning, but now she'd give him a good hard ride—hopefully wearing him out enough that he'd tolerate Malachi shoeing him later that day.

She mounted, stroked his mane for a few moments, then gently nudged him with her knees. Clicking to him at the same time, she put the gelding into motion. Jack fought the reins for a few moments but soon settled down. As he calmed, Dianne picked up the pace and before long they were traveling at a full gallop across the grassy ridge west of the ranch.

Dianne didn't go to her typical perch atop the road that led down to the ranch. She wanted to ride and forget all about her life and her sorrows. She wanted to ride and think only of the moment.

The winter had passed more quickly than she'd expected, and already Gus was making plans to retrieve the herd. The spring was warming up nicely, and while there might yet be another snow or two, Gus felt confident that the worst was behind them. Dianne had already decided she'd go to help with the roundup. It would do her good to focus on something other than the ranch. Even Koko was recovering from her grief. The spring had brought her a new resolve to live in a way that would make Bram proud.

Dianne couldn't be happier about this, but she hated the fact that she was the only one who still seemed to be drifting along without aim. *I have to put this aside,* she thought. *I have to be content with my life and what is expected of me.*

Without warning Jack let out a whinny and reared. Dianne hadn't been paying attention—a mistake, to be sure—and went flying off backward. Crashing against the rocky ground, Dianne hit hard, her left arm and hip bearing much of the impact. The pain was searing. Jack skittered away, whinnying and bucking as if something were after him. Thoughts of another grizzly or perhaps a wolf gave Dianne a start, but the pain in her side was too intense to allow her to flee. If something had spooked Jack, she'd just have to face it head on.

Dianne moaned as she slowly got up. She stood gingerly, testing her left leg and assessing her injuries. There was pain in her hip, but otherwise everything seemed solid. Stretching her arm out, Dianne grimaced as white streaks of pain shot through her arm and up to her shoulder. It was broken—no doubt about it.

Holding her arm close to her body, Dianne tried to figure out where the gelding had taken himself off to. She walked a few feet to a mound of rocks and boulders and tried to climb for a better view, but it was impossible to work her way up very high without the use of both arms. Giving up, she stretched her neck to see as far as she could. There in the valley below, Jack was still running—probably heading back to the ranch, even though he was still more wild than tame.

"Once he gets there and they see I've been thrown," Dianne said to herself, "they'll come for me. I might as well start back down."

She inched off the rocks and because the pain was so much worse when the arm was allowed to dangle down, Dianne figured it would be wise to make a sling. She surveyed her outfit and decided the very full riding petticoat was probably the easiest to tear. She lifted the material to her mouth, holding it with her teeth and pulling with her good arm. The material gave way easily.

Dianne had never realized how many things required the use of both hands. She was sorely frustrated by her inability to master simple skills that ordinarily were of no importance. Now, even her attempt to secure her arm was a practice in futility.

"I knew better than to give Jack his head. If I'd been paying attention, this never would have happened," she muttered.

Eventually Dianne managed to work the ends of the material into a knot. With this done, she slipped the loop around her neck and under her left arm. It was a little tight, but better that than loose and hanging down too low. Having accomplished this, Dianne realized she was almost dizzy from the pain and exertion. She steadied herself, closing her eyes momentarily until the spell passed.

Looking heavenward, she shook her head. "Well, Lord, you certainly have your hands full with me."

Heading down the hillside, Dianne looked to the mountains and the grandeur they offered. The day was lovely with a lemony sun, pale blue skies, and only a hint of wispy clouds. Had she not been injured, it would have been perfect. Spring was always lovely in the mountains, and while it was still chilly, Dianne found it a pleasure to be outside.

"Lord, I need to count my blessings, I guess." The walk was jarring every injured portion of her body, but Dianne pressed on. There was no sense waiting around for rescue when she knew she could meet them halfway.

She remembered Charity Hammond once saying that a

person could get through just about anything if they put their mind to praising God instead of complaining. Dianne had tried this on more than one occasion and knew it worked. It was just hard to praise when she hurt so much.

"Lord, I am grateful that the accident wasn't worse. I could have been killed, and that would have left a lot of folks in a bad way. I thank you for watching over me and not allowing the accident to be any worse than this." She went on thanking God for one thing or another—forcing her mind from the pain and the long walk home.

It wasn't long before Dianne heard her name being called. Apparently there was more than one person coming to her aid, for several people called to her.

"I'm here!" she called, easing onto a convenient rock. The pain was robbing her of energy. "I'm here!"

She looked to the skies once again. "Thank you, Lord," she whispered, knowing her focus on God had helped her get through the worst of it.

————————

Koko finished setting Dianne's arm and offered her a cup of tea. "This will ease the pain. Drink it and then try to get some sleep."

"Thank you." Dianne drank the entire cup without pausing. She hadn't realized how thirsty she'd become. But more so, she wanted whatever help she could have to eliminate the pain.

Handing the cup back to her aunt, Dianne eased back into her bed. "I'm sorry to be such a bother."

Koko shook her head. "You've been so strong for the rest of us; it's time you let us do something for you. You aren't indestructible, you know."

Dianne chuckled despite the pain. "I guess I learned that lesson today—the hard way."

Koko nodded. "Dianne, I'm blessed to call you family. I know I would have died along with Bram had it not been for your love and kindness. Now you have to let us help you. Faith and Charity and I can be your hands and feet. You need to rest, and you won't get well unless you listen and obey."

Dianne grinned. "You know me pretty well. I was just thinking how tomorrow or the next day I needed to go visit Jack."

"Oh no you don't. No more riding for you—not until this arm heals up."

Gus peered in through the open door. "How's our girl?"

"She has a broken arm, but otherwise she's doing well," Koko told him. "I'm trying to get her to rest, however, so make your visit short. You know how she can be. She's just like Bram."

"That she is—ornery through and through," Gus agreed.

Koko nodded in agreement and then left them, taking up the goods she'd used in ministering to Dianne.

"I'll be brief, I promise." Gus came closer to Dianne's bed and offered her a sympathetic grin. "Guess you're broke in now. A real horsewoman."

Dianne thought he sounded almost proud. "Yes, well, I certainly learned a valuable lesson about paying attention. I knew better, but I let my mind wander."

"That black wasn't one to be daydreamin' with. I think you're gonna have to stay away from him."

"Maybe for now, but I want another chance at him. I have to have it," she said, sleepiness overtaking her. She yawned and added, "It's important to me, Gus."

The Texan nodded and stroked his chin. "Guess you won't be able to make the roundup now."

"Don't you dare say that," Dianne declared. "I'll be there. You'll see. I may not be able to sit on a horse, but I'll come in the wagon with Malachi. I can help with something—cooking or—"

"Whoa, now," Gus interrupted. "Let's get you on the mend first, and then we'll talk about the roundup. I shouldn't have said anything."

Dianne appreciated his concern but wasn't about to back down from her stand. "I'll be there, Gus. You'll see. And I'll ride Jack again as well. He and I have a long future together. I just know it."

"Well, he ain't gonna have much of a future at all if Levi sees him causing you more grief. I thought we'd have to tie that boy up to keep him from puttin' a bullet in ol' Jack's head."

The thought alarmed Dianne. "Tell Levi that if he cares one whit about me, he'll take good care of Jack so that I can ride him when I'm well. We don't shoot those who show spirit around here. Uncle Bram always told me you have to be tougher than the land to live here. I am tougher than the land—tougher than that black too. I'll show all of you."

Gus laughed and slapped his hat against his leg. "By golly, little girl, I'll bet you do just that."

CHAPTER 18

Colorado Territory
March 1871

TRENTON CHADWICK SCRATCHED HIS STUBBLY CHIN. HE hadn't had a bath in four days, nor had he been able to shave, and his face itched something awful as the start of a beard formed. Years in the company of Jerry Wilson and his little brother, Sam, had seasoned Trenton to long stretches between personal grooming.

"You gonna just sit there all day scratchin' your face?" Sam Wilson asked, throwing a dirt clod at Trenton.

"What do you expect me to do?" Trenton asked. "Jerry said to wait here and that's what I'm doing."

Sam laughed. "Just like a good boy. You better do what we say. We saved your sorry neck from the hangman and you owe us your life."

And well Trenton knew it. Sam and Jerry, along with the other members of the Wilson gang, never failed to remind Trenton of the night they broke him out of jail. Trenton had been falsely accused of being a part of the Wilson gang's bank job where three men had died in the crossfire. Trenton had been elsewhere and certainly not a part of the gang, but because of the company he'd kept, he'd been associated with the gang. They were planning to execute Trenton, so he felt there'd been no choice but to accept Jerry's offer to rejoin the sorry lot. Of course, Jerry didn't exactly ask him to rejoin but rather forced the issue. Jerry was always one for forcing issues.

"Come on, Sam. We'll take the bank," Jerry said, finally returning from his reconnaissance ride into the small Colorado town. "Mark, you and Chadwick post a watch just to the south of the bank. I figure that's our best route of escape."

Of late, the Wilson gang consisted of only the four of them. Some of the others had come and gone, including the Swede, who had been a particular favorite of Jerry's. Mainly because the Swede knew how to use explosive material and didn't tend to blow up entire buildings like Jerry and Sam did.

Trenton went to his horse and mounted. The years of his association with the Wilsons hung on him like an old unwanted garment that had long since worn out its usefulness. Trenton had gone along with their forced companionship because at the time, sitting in that jail and knowing they were about to hang him, Trenton saw no other way to survive. God certainly hadn't cared about his survival. But now, years later, Trenton had wearied of the game. He didn't have the heart of a bank robber or killer, yet that was the life imposed upon him.

The gang moved out in the early morning light. Trenton felt his heart begin to pound like it had on all the other occasions they'd robbed banks. Jerry Wilson used to watch Trenton like a hawk, but over the last year or so, he'd eased up his vigil, realizing that Trenton was in too deep to merely walk away and hope for the best. His face was on a *Wanted* poster, same as Jerry's.

The town was barely big enough to have a bank, but Jerry had heard that some local rancher had deposited a large amount of money. That rumor was good enough for Jerry, but Trenton thought it rather lame. How could they be sure the money would even be there? Worse still, how could they be sure it wasn't just a trick to trap the gang? After all, the Wilson brothers had been terrorizing banks all around the Denver area.

Trenton felt for the gun on his hip. It was little comfort. Mark motioned him to a position on the far edge of town, yet still close enough to see the bank, while the wiry man moved in for a closer view. Trenton was glad to be left behind. Being out here, away from the actual robbery, Trenton could distance himself from what was happening—at least he tried to. Sometimes Jerry insisted he come into the bank. Those were the times Trenton hated the most. Especially if someone was wounded or killed. Trenton knew he had no power to stop Jerry, but he felt guilty for simply going along with the man. He could remember the face of every person he'd encountered during these robberies; the terror on their faces burned in Trenton's memory. *I caused that terror,* he'd remind himself from time to time. *I'm no better than Jerry.* And those were times Trenton found a bottle of whiskey a better companion than any human soul. He remembered his old friend Henry and finally understood why the man drank—even though it certainly would mean his death. Those moments of blissful ignorance—even ignorance brought on by a drunken stupor—were better than remembering.

There were very few people out and about in the town. Trenton felt a wave of nausea come upon him. He usually got weak in the stomach when the tension mounted. He was just about to search his pockets for a peppermint when shots rang out. Thoughts of more innocent lives being lost worsened his condition. He might have lost his breakfast right then had Jerry not come running from the bank.

Sam was holding the horses, as Jerry figured this job was small enough for one man. But Jerry had apparently underestimated the situation. Three gunmen emerged from the bank, raining lead as they came. Jerry fell first and then Sam. Their attackers fired on them without mercy. There was no doubt they were dead.

Mark turned his horse and headed back toward Trenton at an accelerating pace. "Get out of here, Chadwick!" he yelled.

By now, Trenton could see that the three gunmen were mounting horses and heading after them. It was all the encouragement he needed to heed Mark's warning. Turning his horse, he put his heels into the animal's side and flew from the scene in a rage of hooves, dust, and sheer terror.

He passed Mark without effort, knowing his mount was the better of the two. The last bit of shared money Jerry had given him had gone into improving his horse situation. Apparently it had been the best possible choice.

Mark cried out just as Trenton passed him. The hairs on the back of Trenton's neck crawled as if infected with lice. He hunkered down against the horse's neck but couldn't avoid the bullet that grazed his arm. There was no time to react. Trenton knew his life depended on escape. He urged the horse to go faster and did his best to stay low.

He never had a chance to look back, so he never knew if Mark had been killed or taken prisoner. Trenton only knew the urgency to save his own life. He had no lost love for any of the Wilson gang.

The thought struck him as he ducked in and out of pine trees: *I'm free. I'm really free. Jerry and Sam are dead. I can change my name and move off to Montana with Dianne. If she's still there. If I manage to stay alive.*

A bullet whizzed past his head, letting Trenton know that the men were still in pursuit. He knew the area well enough and figured his best chance might actually be to take cover in Denver. The city was growing every day with miners coming west to try their luck and railroad officials looking to prosper their lines with expansions to those hard-to-reach mining towns. It would be easy to lose himself in the bustle of that city—of this, Trenton was certain.

Working his way deeper into the trees, Trenton felt fairly confident that he could lose the posse. He knew of a cave where the gang had camped several weeks ago and thought maybe he could make his way back there momentarily, then change his course and head into Denver. If the gunmen thought his destination was the wilderness of the territory, rather than civilization, Trenton just might make his escape.

After ten minutes of silence, Trenton slowed his horse and tried to regain his bearings. He looked at his arm and saw that the wound wasn't too bad. Once he found the trail to the old hideout, his confidence returned. A surge of excitement filled his heart. He could almost imagine coming face-to-face again with his family. Almost.

He maneuvered the horse down the side of a ravine, remembering that the trail would soon dead-end. The steepness didn't seem to bother the horse. The gelding handled the transition with the same surefootedness that had brought them this far. Overhead, Trenton could hear voices. He wasn't at all sure how far away the men were, but it motivated him to hurry the horse through the narrow canyon and across the icy waters of the small mountain river.

Trenton feared they might figure out what he'd done, but there was no choice but to keep moving. If they caught him, they'd kill him. Maybe not here, but surely on a gallows.

———————

Portia read to her mother from the Denver newspaper. She knew her mother enjoyed being informed about the events of the world, and the reading helped Portia forget that her mother was growing weaker by the minute.

At least the doctor had agreed to increase her dose of laudanum. The pain seemed so much stronger now than it had a week ago, when Portia had arrived. The doctor said she might linger like this for weeks, although he'd assured Portia death was imminent.

"Well, it appears the Langford silver mine has pulled out a record load of silver," Portia voiced as she scanned the story. "'Ned Langford, son of the wealthy silver baron R. E. Langford, reported from his apartment at the Bradbury Hotel that the Little Maribelle mine shows no signs of slowing in production.'" There was a sketch of a smiling Mr. Langford, who looked to be somewhere around Portia's own age of twenty-seven. He seemed very appealing, and Portia began to see possibilities for making the man's acquaintance. After all, she was a woman of means and he was a wealthy man.

She put the paper aside and considered how she might just happen to run into the man. A smile crossed her face. His hotel, of course. She could move from her establishment on Tenth Street and make her residence the Bradbury Hotel. A plan began to formulate in her mind.

Her gaze traveled back to her mother. The woman's eyes were closed, but her uneven breathing proved that she was still alive. It seemed cruel that anyone should have to linger and suffer so much pain. Portia looked toward the open door. *Why do they ignore her here?* Privacy was a wonderful thing, but her mother was all alone. No one cared if her mother continued in this sorry state. No one.

Except for me, she thought.

Portia looked to the door again, then slowly got to her feet and walked over to close it. Leaning back against the frame, she closed her eyes. It simply couldn't be allowed to go on.

————

As the sun lowered behind the Rockies, Trenton began to relax. Either the men had given up on him or they'd made camp. Either way, Trenton wasn't waiting around to find out. Gingerly, he lifted the makeshift bandage on his arm. The bleeding had stopped and the wound looked clean. Two very good things. Taking a strip of cloth, Trenton bound his arm and changed clothes. No sense showing up in Denver in a bloody shirt.

Leading the horse out of the canyon, Trenton headed toward Denver. There wasn't a single sound except the rush of the river. He pressed on, crossing the water once again and hurrying with a sense of urgency up the ravine and toward the back roads he knew so well. Jerry and his gang hadn't limited themselves to pulling bank jobs—after all, folks were constantly bringing in ore from the silver and gold mines in the area. Highwaymen lurked in all parts of the mountains—eagerly waiting their chance to strike it rich.

That was how Trenton had met Ned Langford only a few months back—on this very road. Ned had been most unfortunate to be making his way from Central City to Denver. He wasn't escorting a load of ore, but rather he was in a hurry to make a train to Kansas City. He hadn't been paying attention to the road, and when Jerry and Sam assaulted him, the man was theirs for the picking. Jerry forced Ned from his horse and without even giving the man a chance, hit him over the head with the butt of his pistol and emptied his pockets.

Trenton had been posted to keep watch down the road, but seeing Jerry act in such a fashion distracted him from his duty. He rode back to the robbery, dismounted as the other mounted, and firmly told Jerry he was going to tend the man lest he die.

"You just go ahead and do that, Chadwick. Oh, and be sure and tell him who you are when he wakes up." Jerry's raucous laughter still rang in Trenton's ears.

He took care of Ned long enough to rouse him from his

unconscious state and get him back to his horse. Ned indeed asked for the name of his rescuer, but Trenton refused, reminding the man there wasn't time for such things. Trenton led the wounded man back to Denver, leaving him with a doctor before disappearing into the less desirable parts of town.

Trenton thought himself free and clear of any other encounters with Mr. Langford, but without much ado at all, he ran into Ned on his way to a poker game. Ned instantly recognized him.

"My champion," he declared enthusiastically. He took hold of Trenton's hand and shook it so hard and long that Trenton felt as though they were experiencing an earthquake.

Thoughts of Ned gave birth to an idea. Trenton knew from the local newspapers that Ned was back in town with a record load of silver. He'd seen the article just that morning—just before they'd headed off to the bank.

"Ned would be happy to help me," Trenton reasoned aloud. "After all, I'll tell him the same thing happened to me." The idea took wings. "I'll tell him I was robbed and they shot me as I escaped." He smiled. It was perfect. Ned would take him in and treat him to a fine meal and a good bed. And with any luck at all, maybe even a round of poker or two, which Ned, of course, would stake . . . and lose.

CHAPTER 19

"I'M SORRY FOR YOUR LOSS," DR. WADSWORTH STATED AS Mary Brady's coffin was lowered into a plot on the sanitarium grounds.

Portia looked up, her eyes brimming with tears. The wispy black veil blew gently in the unseasonably warm breeze. "Thank you."

"I know this is a most difficult time, but you might want to consider creating a memorial in your mother's name. Perhaps a nice statue or a new garden for the grounds. Many of our patients leave endowments to the hospital."

Portia hated the man for his greed. After all, her mother wasn't even cold in the ground and here he was with his hand out for all he could get. "I'll think about it," she said, reaching under the veil to dab her eyes with a handkerchief.

"Sorry about your mother, Mrs. McGuire," the pastor who'd been notified by Dr. Wadsworth said in mock sincerity. He was playing a part, nothing more. Portia had seen it a hundred times.

"Thank you, Reverend. Now if you'll both excuse me, I'd like to go back to my hotel to rest. This day has been most trying."

"You will come back for your mother's things?" Dr. Wadsworth asked. The man's beady eyes almost glowed in anticipation of having another chance to work Portia over for funds.

"Yes," she replied, shifting her open umbrella to block the man from view. "I'll come back tomorrow." She told the lie without regret. She had no intention of ever laying eyes on the institution again—much less Dr. Wadsworth.

Stupid man, she thought as she allowed her driver to assist her into the closed carriage. It would be unmercifully hot inside, she knew, but it was better than being viewed by those simpering ninnies who only wanted her money.

She'd worked hard for her fortune, and she wasn't about to turn it over to the likes of greedy men like Wadsworth and Reverend What's-His-Name. She strained for a moment to put a name with the rotund, hairy man, but her memory failed.

Settling back in her finely upholstered leather coach, Portia began to relax, allowing her tears to fall. The only person she had ever truly loved was dead. Her mother had been her confidante and friend—her only real friend. Portia could tell her mother anything without fear of judgment or condemnation. Her mother never criticized Portia's choices—never called her unreasonable in her spending.

Thoughts of Angus McGuire's ugly sentiments regarding Portia's spending came to mind. The penny-pinching Scotsman had been ruthless in his disregard of her feelings. Never mind that Portia had to live in that awful dank, cold country. Scotland held no appeal for Portia, except that her husband owned a healthy portion of it, and because of this ownership, he was quite wealthy.

Was wealthy.

Now she was the wealthy one.

Angus's death in January had been unexpected by everyone. The man had been as healthy and robust as a man could be one day, and the next he was dead. Dead as dead could be. His passing had brought great wails of sorrow from the household staff, but surely those outcries didn't begin to equal the caterwauling that took place when the widowed Mrs. McGuire announced that everything Angus owned was being sold at an auction.

The housekeeper, Odara Grant, had been particularly nasty about the entire matter. Odara had been with Angus since he was a lad, and she thought him sorely abused by his young wife. She didn't care at all that Portia hated the country and its cold. She felt that Portia owed it to Angus to see that his estate continued to grow, especially since Portia was carrying Angus's child.

Portia frowned. Losing the baby wasn't something she liked to think about. The miscarriage had come shortly after Mrs. Grant's harshest dressing down, and Portia hadn't bothered to restrain herself from pointing out to the angry old woman that the miscarriage was entirely her fault. Mrs. Grant had been aghast at Portia's accusations, but amazingly enough, the doctor had agreed with the young widow, and the old woman had been devastated. Portia could hear her wailing throughout the massive estate. It actually rivaled the wind blowing down from the hills.

Portia smiled in satisfaction. Yes, the doctor had made a convincing argument, and the old woman was never the same. It was fascinating what could be had for a little gold. Portia often wondered what was said in the wake of the doctor's sudden departure for Spain.

But even with that satisfying memory, Portia felt overwhelmed by her mother's passing. Troubled, too, by the promise she'd made to deliver the news to her father in the Montana Territory. She could lie to anyone else—break promises without concern—but she wouldn't lie to her mother. She couldn't. If she even dared to do such a thing, she feared her mother might well come back from the grave and haunt her.

She sighed and sniffed back a new onslaught of tears. *Why*

did Mother have to get sick? Why now? Portia had come back to the United States with the sole intent of finding her mother. She had planned to whisk her away on a trip to Europe. Her mother deserved a good time. She had never been abroad—never owned more than three dresses at a time. No, Mary Brady had lived from post to post following the husband she promised to love and obey till death.

Now death had taken her from the world—from Portia.

Portia stared out the carriage window at the passing city. The people here thought themselves quite metropolitan, but the idea was laughable. Portia had lived in the really great cities—London, Paris, Vienna. Married at sixteen to a man whose most desperate desire, second only to having Portia, was to avoid the War Between the States, Portia had been taken abroad to live.

William Travers had been only four years his bride's senior, but to Portia he seemed decades older and wiser. He had been handsome—almost too handsome. He was the kind of man that made everyone take notice. His honey-gold curls and well-defined features had brought looks of approval from both men and women. Only those close to him ever came to realize that his beauty ran only skin deep.

Billy hadn't been a man given to searches for knowledge or intellectual feasts. He hadn't any desire for college or an education that could prove useful in matters of real life. Billy wanted to have fun, and he wanted to have it with his beautiful Portia.

At sixteen, Portia had been completely overwhelmed by his courtship. They had met while her father had been briefly stationed near Kansas City. Their engagement was quick to follow, despite her father's protests. Billy's family thought Portia witty and gracious. They enjoyed having an intelligent daughter-in-law and honestly believed that Portia's ambitious nature could help motivate their son to greater things.

But Portia had never aspired to be Billy's inspiration. She

laughed now, even thinking of it. *Billy was a simpleton. He'd sleep until noon if I'd let him. The only thing that drove him was the promise of a good time.*

Well, she'd certainly proven to be that, and more. Right up until the day that freight wagon had run Billy over in the street.

The carriage hit the same hole it always hit when approaching the Bradbury Hotel, and Portia forced herself back into the reality of the moment. She dabbed her eyes one last time before the driver opened her door.

He helped her down with a gentleness reserved for old ladies and babies. "Thank you, Dougal." The man had been with her only a few days, but already she thought him a first-class servant. "I won't be going out again. Feel free to retire for the evening."

"Thank you, ma'am," he said, tipping his top hat.

Portia smoothed her black bombazine skirt, sweltering from the sheer weight of the material. She could hardly wait to reach her suite, where she'd have the liberty of disrobing and slipping into something light and breezy.

"Mourning is for the ancient," she muttered. "The ancient and the hopeless. Neither of which I am."

———

It hadn't been hard to find Ned Langford. Most everyone knew where he was residing from the newspaper article. Trenton, however, had already known the Bradbury was Ned's favorite hotel in Denver. He knew, too, that the man had a permanent arrangement with the hotel and had rented out the largest suite the hotel could offer.

"I'm glad you came to me," Ned had said when Trenton showed up at his hotel door. "Now I have the chance to return the favor you did me—although you are far from death's door. However, under my poor care, you just might get there yet."

Trenton had laughed. He enjoyed Ned's sense of humor and

banter. Time under Ned's care had already done Trenton good. It had also given the bearded stubble on his face a couple days to grow out. It altered his appearance nicely—so, too, the expensive clothes Ned had bought him. Trenton wasn't sure there would be any decent *Wanted* posters of him—the only ones he'd seen were poorly drawn after his escape from Missouri, but he didn't want to take any risk of being noticed or recognized.

Now sitting across from Ned and enjoying a wealth of fabulous food for lunch, Trenton tried to forget the past and look to his future.

"Pity those fellows shooting you. Probably same old boys that took me down."

Trenton nodded. "I'm sure they had something to do with it." That much was true. Trenton was trying hard to turn over a new leaf. He figured the fact that he'd managed to elude the posse was proof enough that God truly hadn't forgotten him. Nevertheless, his relationship with the Almighty was on rocky footing, and Trenton wasn't entirely convinced that the relationship could be salvaged. Mainly because he wasn't certain God could forgive a man with a past as horrible as his.

"Well, I want to help you in whatever way I can. Of course you may stay with me as long as you like. I have the two bedrooms in the suite, so there's no sense in the one going to waste. I thought perhaps my father would venture west when we struck the mother lode, but he wired to say he's unable to leave Baltimore."

"I'm just grateful for the help, Ned. I've got absolutely nothing to my name—except my horse and saddle—and gun."

"Well, don't give it a second thought, old man. I certainly can afford to see to us both—especially while you recover. Say, after that arm mends, what do you think about coming to work for me?"

Trenton was rather stunned by the offer. He knew it would

probably be wise to lay low for a while and then get out of the territory altogether. "I kind of figured to go to Montana after I recovered. My sister lives there and she's been after me to come for a visit."

"You could always visit her later," Ned said, stabbing a large piece of iced melon.

"Well, the thing is, I've been rather bad about keeping her informed of my whereabouts. I haven't written her in several years."

"Goodness—years? Why would you let so much time pass by?"

Trenton pushed at the concoction of vegetables on his plate. "I guess I'm just inconsiderate. Time got away from me. One day it was 1865 and the war was finally over, and the next thing I knew it was April 1871. What can I say? I'm a thoughtless man."

Ned laughed as though Trenton had told a great joke. "My mother writes me off as dead if I don't send her a note at least twice a month. I once asked her how in the world I was supposed to get anything accomplished at the mine or here in Denver when I had to constantly stop business in order to drop her a line. She told me she didn't care—that it was my duty as the only son to keep my mother informed of my health and general circumstances. So my secretary jots off a note every two weeks like clockwork, and when Mother's missives arrive, I give them a quick perusal and pass them on for his crafty answer."

"And she doesn't realize it's not your handwriting in the letter?" Trenton asked. He always managed to get caught up in Ned's stories, in spite of himself.

"Mother's eyesight is poor and she's much too vain to wear reading glasses. She just has one of the house girls read her the letter. It works out quite well and everyone is happy," Ned said, bobbing his head a bit from side to side. "It's all a matter of properly running one's affairs. Otherwise, your affairs will run you."

Trenton knew that to be true. It seemed his affairs had always been running him in one way or another.

"Say, there's a gentlemen's game tonight; would you care to play a few hands?" Ned questioned. "I know you could no doubt make back more than you lost in that robbery. I'll stake you fifty dollars, and I'll bet before midnight you'll have tripled it."

Trenton laughed. "By midnight, I could have ten times that—if I'm playing with the right gentlemen."

Ned leaned forward. "These are very wealthy gold and silver barons—rivals in the business, don't you know. I'd love to see them taken for all they're worth. Say, if you'll split the earnings with me, I'll spot you five hundred dollars."

Trenton leaned back and grinned, a lock of sandy-colored hair falling across his left brow. "I think I could probably accommodate you. Of course, I'll have to get better clothes than these to wear."

Ned laughed and crooked his head toward the door of his bedroom. "You're about my size, I'd say. Take what you need."

———————

Portia McGuire watched Ned Langford from across the room. He seemed such a jovial man. The man who sat opposite him was quite handsome, but not nearly so gay. In fact, he seemed quite serious, almost stoic at times. He had smiled just a few moments ago, and Portia had thought him even more handsome than before. But Ned Langford was wealthy, and that was far more important than looks.

As Ned eased back in his chair, Portia got a better look at his features. He didn't look much older than thirty—maybe thirty-five. His mousy brown hair and mustache were unremarkable, just as was his face. His nose seemed a bit too small—his eyes too far apart. His lips were very full, so much so that Portia almost grimaced at the thought of kissing them.

Still, she was a woman of means and if she was to remain that way, she would need a constant source to feed the pot. Angus had been right that she was horrible with money. Money seemed to slip through her fingers without effort. But Portia liked the things money could buy. Gowns from Paris, furs and jewels. Trips abroad and fancy hotels and dinners. Those were the things that made life worth living.

Ned laughed again. It was rather a high-pitched braying sound, no doubt somehow related to his undersized nose. Portia noted again that his friend remained much more serious. She made a note to find out who Ned Langford's companion might be. After all, it was possible the man was even more wealthy than Ned.

"Luncheon is served," the waiter told her as he placed a silver-domed plate before her. He pulled back the lid to reveal a succulent slice of pork roast smothered in a currant sauce. Portia's mouth watered. She'd skipped breakfast and now her hunger was catching up to her.

"Thank you," she said softly.

Cutting into the meat, she couldn't help but continue her surveillance of Ned Langford. The man was worth millions—at least that's what she'd learned. He was the only son of a million-aire father, and while there were two younger sisters to consider, it was rumored Ned would inherit the better portion of his father's vast earnings.

The idea of owning silver mines appealed to Portia. Not as much as if they'd been gold, but if the one couldn't be had, the other was certainly the next best thing.

Billy's money had come from old stuffy lines of New England textile mill people, while Angus had built his fortune one bank note at a time. The miserly Scot had hoarded away his fortune, forcing Portia to use her remaining money from Billy in order to maintain her desired standard of living. But once Angus was gone, there was no one to stop Portia from doing as she pleased with his money. Still, she wasn't about to be caught in another bad situation like before. She would use Angus's money sparingly—at least until she had a sure source of income elsewhere.

If she could somehow entice Mr. Langford, for instance, there would probably never be any reason to worry. Silver was a valuable commodity and Colorado seemed to be brimming with the stuff.

Ned Langford laughed and held up his glass to his companion. Portia tried not to be too obvious in her observation, but she couldn't help but wonder what the two men were toasting as the more serious man touched his glass to Ned's.

Perhaps they've struck some great financial arrangement— the marriage of two great fortunes. Perhaps Ned Langford has just found a way to further his ledger balance and he's celebrating in grand style with a good friend.

Portia's imagination ran rampant. *Whatever the occasion,* she mused, *I want to celebrate too.*

———

Dianne forced her left arm to extend. She did this small bit of exercise at least a hundred times a day. She could feel the arm stiffen up on her otherwise, and the thought that she might lose even a small amount of usage was more than she could tolerate.

The arm was healing nicely. In fact, Koko figured the setting to be exact and that the bone was knitting perfectly.

"I still don't think you need to be planning on going to the roundup," Koko said, her tone stern. "Besides, Faith's baby is due almost any day. You don't want to miss that."

Dianne was truly torn. She'd had her heart so set on going to the roundup that the birth of Faith's child really hadn't entered her mind. "I suppose you're right, but I feel I should be there.

It's important. It's the first roundup without Uncle Bram."

Koko sobered and nodded. "Yes, I know. I thought of that as well."

"I just want everything to go as best it can," Dianne said, stretching her arm out again. "I want to do right by you and the children."

"You've done right by us over and over. I cannot imagine anyone else being so loving or generous."

"Bah," Dianne said, getting to her feet. She watched Suzy toddle around the kitchen floor, occasionally plopping down on her bottom, then getting up to do it again. "How could I ever deny this little darlin'," Dianne drawled in Gus Yegen fashion.

Koko laughed and went back to sewing the moccasins she'd been working on since morning. "That little darlin', as you so sweetly put it, was into the flour and sugar sacks this morning. I had quite a mess to clean up while you were out there watching Levi work with Jack."

"Well, she can make all the messes she wants," Dianne said, wishing she could just reach down and pick up her little cousin. It was so infuriating to be unable to do the things she'd always done before. Simple things like brushing her hair—tying her bootlaces—were now considered carefully by degree of difficulty. Most required some form of assistance, and for the independent woman that Dianne prided herself on being, it was quite maddening.

But, in all honesty, the broken arm had taken Dianne's mind off of Cole. Well, not entirely, but since there were other things to worry over and concern herself with, Dianne found that thoughts of Cole didn't grieve her quite as much as they used to. It was more bittersweet now. More like a tender dream that faded a little bit with each passing day.

Dianne watched the baby and felt her heart nearly break. *But I don't want the dream to fade,* she whispered in the depths of her heart. She knelt and Susannah immediately made her way to Dianne. With her right arm, Dianne scooped Susannah close and nuzzled her neck.

I won't let the dream fade.

I can't let it die.

CHAPTER 20

PORTIA DRESSED HER HAIR IN A GENTLE UPSWEPT MASS, then pulled on a new hat of black-dyed straw and feathers. A short veil was attached in a wispy sweep, but the material was light enough to see through clearly. That was important, Portia told herself, for today she intended to encounter the elusive Mr. Langford, and she wanted him to see her face without hindrance.

She studied her reflection in the mirror for a moment. The black gown hugged her frame in a fashionable manner, yet made clear her mourning status. She despised the color but loved the way the gown hung. Knowing that a woman in black would always solicit sympathy, Portia didn't mind missing out on the colorful gowns she'd seen only the day before when she'd purchased the bonnet. There would be plenty of time for bringing color back into her wardrobe. Black would work to her advantage, so she would wear it a while longer.

Tying the hat securely, Portia nodded in satisfaction. She picked up her handbag and then headed downstairs to enjoy breakfast in the dining room. With any luck at all, Mr. Langford would be having his own meal.

The Bradbury Hotel was a completely modern affair with over a hundred rooms and a restaurant that boasted a European chef. The walls of the dining room were dark red with gold trim, and overhead were a dozen crystal chandeliers that spoke of the city's prosperity and love of beautiful furnishings. The tables were of the finest oak, with beautifully embroidered linen coverings that matched the walls.

Portia had eaten in many fine establishments both in America and abroad, and she had to admit, to her great surprise, that the food at the Bradbury was superb. She actually looked forward to her meal as much as to furthering her plans.

"Good morning, Mrs. McGuire." The hotel employee, dressed from head to tail in black and white, had served her on the previous day. "Would you care for a table by the window?"

Portia glanced across the room and noted that Ned Langford and his friend were seated near the back. She shook her head. "Mr. Reems, is it?" He nodded. "I'm in mourning and would rather be over there," she said, glancing in the general vicinity of Ned's table. "That way I wouldn't be forced to endure unwelcome advances or attention."

"Of course. Please forgive me." Reems seemed genuinely upset that he should have suggested such a thing. He motioned her to follow as he led her to a table beyond her true destination. "Now, if anyone bothers you at all, simply signal me and I'll come to your aid."

"That's very kind of you, Mr. Reems," Portia said, her voice as smooth as the surface of a mountain lake.

Portia's plan played itself out in perfect order. As she came up just behind the stranger who shared Langford's table, she put her hand to her throat and made eye contact with Ned. Reems continued moving forward, clearly having no idea of Portia's designs.

"Oh my," she said, taking another couple of steps so she might be well within Ned's reach.

"Are you quite all right, ma'am?" Ned said, getting to his feet rather quickly.

Portia feigned dizziness. "I think I'm going to faint," she said, closing her eyes. She began to collapse, not even opening her eyes to ensure that Ned would catch her.

She felt the warmth of his embrace before hitting the floor. Opening her eyes through fluttering lashes, she was appalled to find herself staring into the face of Ned's companion.

"Oh my," she said again, pushing away. Her shock and dismay at being held by anyone other than the wealthy silver baron worked well to her advantage. "I do apologize. I'm afraid I've interrupted your meal."

Reems was at her side. "Are you quite all right, Mrs. McGuire? I could have something sent up to your room if you wish to retire."

She shook her head as she composed herself, then looked to Ned. "I'm afraid it's just that . . . well . . ." She paused and took out a handkerchief. "It's just that life has been very hard for me. I recently lost my husband . . . and now my mother has passed on as well." She raised the cloth to her eyes and pretended to wipe away tears that didn't exist.

"What a tragedy," Ned said, reaching out to steady Portia. He looked to Mr. Reems and motioned to his table. "Bring Mrs. . . ." He turned to her and shook his head. "I'm afraid I didn't quite catch your name."

"McGuire," Portia said softly. "Portia McGuire."

"Bring Mrs. McGuire a glass of cold water." Ned pulled out a chair while continuing to hold on to Portia's arm. "Here, please sit down. I wouldn't want you fainting again." Reems went running to do Ned's bidding.

Portia did as she was instructed, turning her attention to Ned and then to the stranger. "I do apologize for the interruption.

I'm certain to be right as rain in a moment. I don't wish to impose."

"Nonsense," Ned said in that way that assured Portia he was already being drawn to her charms. "Are you alone?"

"Yes, quite. I've lost everyone now." She sniffed as though she might well break into tears again.

"Then that settles it. Please remain here and share breakfast with us. You don't mind, do you, Trenton?" Ned asked, looking to his companion. Before the man could respond, however, Ned interjected. "Oh, where are my manners? I should introduce myself. I'm Ned Langford, and this is Trenton Chadwick."

Portia held up her gloved hand, but Trenton ignored it. Instead, he gave her a look that might have intimidated a lesser woman. "Mrs. McGuire."

Ned, however, took hold of her hand and held it for a moment longer than necessary. "I'm very pleased to make your acquaintance. Why don't you tell us what brought you to Denver?"

Portia nodded and accepted the goblet of water Mr. Reems placed in front of her.

"Are you quite all right, Mrs. McGuire? Are you certain I can't have something sent up to your room? Are these gentlemen bothering you?" He sounded very protective of Portia, and she rather liked the way he made such a fuss.

She smiled reassuringly. "No. I'm feeling much better now. Mr. Langford has graciously seen to that." Reems looked notably relieved.

"I'll just be over at the door should you need anything. Anything at all."

"Thank you. You're very kind, Mr. Reems. I shall have to mention such graciousness to your supervisor." The man's face reddened before he hurried away.

Portia took up the glass of water and sipped it slowly. Mr.

Reems and his seemingly undying devotion might well come in handy at a later date. Putting that thought aside, she cast a quick glance at Trenton from beneath partially lowered lashes. She would have to be careful of this man. He wore the look of one well familiar with the ways of the world, while Ned seemed completely oblivious. This Trenton Chadwick could put an end to her plans before they'd even begun.

She rested the goblet on the table. "As I mentioned, my mother recently passed away," she said with a sigh. "She was here at the Clarkston Sanitarium—a hospital for women. She had only been in town a couple of months. You see, my father is in the army at Fort Ellis in Montana Territory." The Chadwick fellow seemed to perk up at the mention of Montana. Portia made a mental note to keep this in mind as she continued.

"My mother had moved here to set up housekeeping prior to his retirement from the army, but alas, God needed her more." Portia let her voice become quite soft. "She was ill for only a few weeks, but it was a cancer and it . . . it . . ." By now both men were leaning toward her, just as she had anticipated. "It stole her away from me." She cried softly into her handkerchief while Ned patted her arm in a consoling manner.

"There now," he said, "you mustn't overgrieve yourself. I'm sure she's at peace. But what of your father? Have you sent him word?"

Portia lowered the cloth. "No. He was away and couldn't be reached. Fighting Indians, don't you know? I'm so afraid he might very well lie dead—butchered by heathen savages," she lied. "My mother was so looking forward to his retirement. She had great plans for their life here in Denver. Then it was all stolen from her." Portia sniffed into her handkerchief. "She made me promise to take word to Father, but I fear that may well be impossible."

"But why?" Ned asked.

"Well, I'm alone, as you can see. I can hardly travel all the way to the Montana Territory alone. Why, the thought positively gives me the vapors."

The waiter came and served Ned and Trenton's breakfast. Portia started to get up, but Ned reached to keep her from leaving. "Please stay." He turned to the waiter. "Bring her the same thing and be quick about it." The man nodded and hurried back to the kitchen while Portia repositioned herself.

She noticed that the Chadwick man dug into his food as though she'd already vacated the table. *Such rudeness,* she thought. *I've given him my best performance and still he acts as though I have the plague.*

She turned back to Ned and smiled weakly. "Some people have no notion of how difficult it is to be a woman on your own. Why, I nearly died of fright on the train. I had to come all the way across America, and it's such a huge expanse of country. I simply had no idea."

The waiter returned in record time to place a plate containing an arrangement of fruit, toast, and eggs before Portia. The eggs were covered in hollandaise sauce—her favorite. She smiled her gratitude at Ned. "You must at least let me pay for breakfast. I'm quite well off and assure you I can manage it."

There, she thought, *let him think you know nothing about his financial means. That should help your cause considerably.*

"My dear woman, I wouldn't dream of it. I'm a man of means myself. I will happily pay this bill. It isn't often I am allowed the privilege of a beautiful woman's company. I realize you are in mourning, Mrs. McGuire, so I hope I haven't offended you with my boldness."

Portia lowered her gaze as if embarrassed. "Not at all, Mr. Langford. We are, after all, only human."

"And fate has smiled so sweetly upon me this day," Ned added, unable to take his gaze from her. "I feel this is a remarkable meeting—almost as if something wonderful were about to happen. How about you, Trenton? Don't you feel the same?"

"I feel like a cup of coffee, that's what I feel," Trenton replied, waving the waiter over with his cup.

Portia lowered her head and contemplated the situation. Apparently the two men were somehow intricately connected. They were apparently good friends, but good friends could be separated under the right circumstances. She lifted her face and met Mr. Chadwick's eyes. He narrowed them as he scrutinized her. She smiled.

Mr. Chadwick was going to be a problem, but certainly he was no match for her.

Trenton didn't know exactly what it was about the McGuire woman, but he didn't trust her. Her manners were impeccable, and she genuinely seemed not to realize who Ned was or how much he was worth, but still she rubbed Trenton the wrong way.

For one thing, he thought as he applied a generous amount of jam to his toast, she hadn't really been in a faint. He'd caught his mother once or twice when she'd passed out cold, and she had been as limp as a wet towel. Portia McGuire had been nearly rigid when Trenton had caught her in his arms. He was fairly confident the entire spell had been staged.

"Isn't that right, Trenton?"

Trenton looked up from his plate. "What? I'm afraid I was lost in my thoughts."

Ned chuckled. "I was just telling Mrs. McGuire that you have family in Montana and you plan to go north very soon."

Trenton didn't like the thought of where this might be leading, but he couldn't deny the truth of it. "Yes. I have family in Montana."

"I was just thinking, Trent ol' boy, we could escort Mrs. McGuire and take her to Fort Ellis. As she's just explained, the fort is not far from Bozeman, and I know you mentioned that town before. Perhaps we could make our way north and serve both purposes."

"I didn't know you had any plans to go north, Ned," Trenton said almost sarcastically. There was no possibility that he would allow himself to become entangled with this woman.

Ned's grin widened. "Well, now, I didn't realize there would be any ladies fair who needed rescuing."

Portia laughed ever so slightly. "I hardly need rescuing."

"There, you see. She doesn't need rescuing," Trenton said, staring hard at Portia. He willed her to protest, but she only lowered her gaze and remained silent.

"But of course she needs us. You can hardly go into Indian country without an escort," Ned declared. "Chadwick, you've read the papers. There's been one account after another. Think of the long distance she'll have to cover and the threat to her well-being."

"If she fears Indian attacks, perhaps she should stay away from the places where the Indians live," Trenton said matter-of-factly.

"Oh, I don't fear the red man as much as trying to make my way around a military post. Soldiers can be so crude and disrespectful," Portia expressed. "Indians only murder you."

Trenton had to admit she played the part well. But he was still convinced it was only a part. On the other hand, how could she have possibly known that by appealing to Ned Langford, and inadvertently Trenton, she could get help in her travels north? She couldn't have had any knowledge of his family connections in Montana.

"Come on, Trenton. I'll handle the travel expenses and get you both to your destinations. I'd enjoy seeing the north country. Maybe even do a little hunting. I understand some of the most marvelous moose and elk to be had are in that territory."

"Oh, as I said, I can pay," Portia argued. "My husband was a man of some means in Scotland. I have plenty of income and would be happy to pay."

Ned laughed. "I'm part owner of one of the most productive silver mines in all of the West. I hardly need a lovely lady—a lady who has lost her most beloved mother and husband—to pay for my well-being." He glanced at his pocket watch. "Oh dear, the time is getting away from me. What say we meet here again at supper. Six-thirty?"

Trenton hoped the woman would decline and simply disappear from their lives. Instead she nodded. "I'd like that very much."

He turned and looked at Trenton. "Six-thirty?"

Trenton wasn't about to let Ned meet the woman alone. "I'll be here," he muttered and followed it with a long drink of coffee. He watched Portia McGuire over the rim of the cup as she pushed back from the table.

"I'm afraid I'm feeling poorly again. I should retire to my room. Please allow me to pay for breakfast."

"Nonsense," Ned declared. "The bill has already been taken care of—they know to charge my table to the room."

"Well, thank you," she said with what seemed great sincerity. Then she turned to Trenton. "And thank you for your gallant efforts to keep me from further harm when I fainted."

Trenton got to his feet. "You're welcome," he managed to say without sounding too sarcastic.

"Perhaps you should accompany Mrs. McGuire to her room," Ned suggested to Trenton. "After all, she isn't feeling well."

Portia put up her hand in protest. "Now I must decline. It would hardly look appropriate to have a gentleman escorting me to my hotel room. Remember, the Bible says we must all be above reproach and even the appearance of evil should be avoided."

Trenton was taken somewhat aback by her declaration. Maybe he'd misjudged her after all.

————————

Dianne would have preferred to deal with Cole's absence by busying herself with all manner of work. But with one arm incapacitated, her ability to accomplish much of anything was questionable. So in the days of her recovery, Dianne found the opportunity to read quite a bit. The only trouble was, there weren't that many books to read, and she'd never been much for reading.

She found the Bible a comfort most of the time, but then there were moments when her thoughts were plagued with the hopelessness of her situation, and even God's Word offered no solace. She might have borne even this with some graciousness if not for the fact that everyone around her seemed completely content with his situation, while hers seemed impossible.

"Things can't get any worse," she muttered as she struggled to wipe down the counter.

Levi came to the back entrance of the kitchen and peeked his head in. "I have those supplies from town," he said. "Where do you want them?"

Dianne thought for a moment. If her arm hadn't been broken, she might actually have helped Levi with his duties. "I guess you can put the bulk of it in the storage room. I know Faith said we needed more sugar, so you might just bring a bag in here, and I'll let her know where it is. Oh, and leave some coffee here as well."

He nodded and turned to go. "I almost forgot." He dug into his coat pocket. "You had a couple of letters. Well, actually one. One's for Cole."

Dianne's heart began to pound. A letter? Could Cole have written? She went to Levi quickly and took the letters in hand.

She looked at the first and noted it was from Morgan. The second one was from the Selbys, addressed to their son. "Thank you," she managed to say before hurrying from the room.

Her heart was in her throat as she went into the front room and took a seat. Surely if Cole were able to write, he would have at least kept in touch with his parents. Even if he'd forsaken the idea of marrying Dianne, he would have written his family.

Putting Morgan's letter aside, Dianne made the decision to open the letter from Cole's parents. After all, they would need to know the truth—if the truth could be learned.

Dianne struggled one-handed to open the envelope. She pushed the single sheet of paper open and scanned the lines.

Dearest son,
You haven't written since leaving, and we wanted very much to know of your safe arrival.

The rest of the letter blurred before Dianne's eyes. It almost seemed as if the letter, pleading for correspondence and assurance of safety, was a confirmation of Cole's demise. He hadn't written his parents since leaving Kansas. The letter mentioned his promise to post a note upon his arrival in Virginia City, but excused it, supposing that the post might have been destroyed by Indians.

Dianne hugged the letter to her breast. *He's dead, isn't he, Lord? My Cole is dead.*

CHAPTER 21

"Look, Ned, you don't even know her. She could be lying, for all you know." Trenton had tried for over a week to reason with his friend, but to no avail.

"You can't possibly understand. I'm in love with her."

Trenton nearly dropped the glass he held. "You're what?" His tone was incredulous.

Ned shook his head and put aside the ledger he'd been working on. "She's everything I've ever wanted in a woman. Beautiful, kind, gracious, generous. That's really all I need to know."

"That's not all you need to know. At least check into her story." Trenton had thought for days that his friend should hire someone to collect information on the young widow. "Find out if her mother really died in the Clarkston Sanitarium like she said. Find out who her husband was and if he's really dead. Better yet, find out if she was ever really married."

"Gracious, Chadwick, but you're a doubting soul. Where would you be if I'd taken that attitude with you? I'm hardly in the habit of investigating my choices of friends. What if I'd awakened after my attack and thought you to be one of my attackers instead of my salvation?"

Trenton instantly felt a wave of guilt. It was true. He didn't deserve a place in the life of this gentleman, given his past. But maybe that was why he felt so intensely regarding Portia McGuire.

"But love, Ned? How can you honestly believe yourself in love with the woman?" Trenton tossed back the remaining contents of his glass, then put it aside. He crossed the room to where Ned had begun to pace.

"Trenton, when I look at her, my heart begins to pound and my breath is suddenly stolen from me."

Trenton laughed, trying hard to lessen the severity of his earlier tone. "Sounds like something to see the doctor about."

"I've never met a woman like her, Trenton." Ned's words seemed accentuated with each step. He walked to the hotel window of their suite and gazed out into the night. "She makes me feel alive. I care about where she is and what she's doing. I can't help but wonder if at this very moment perhaps she's gazing out her window as well. And maybe, just maybe, she's thinking of me." He turned and shrugged. "I can't help it. I'm in love."

"But she's just recently widowed," Trenton said, trying a different approach. "And as you've pointed out on other occasions, she's a woman of some decorum and breeding—despite her father being in the army. But that aside, she isn't going to consider giving her heart to anyone so soon after losing her husband."

"Yes, but the loss of her mother has sent her seeking comfort," Ned said, as though going through the logic of solving a very difficult mathematical equation. "She was used to the comfort her husband could offer. Therefore, it seems reasonable that she seek male companionship and solace now. I cannot deny her that, nor can I expect her to hold to some silly tradition of rules that says she must suffer and linger in her widowhood until enough time has passed. That would be cruel."

Trenton shook his head and tried yet another tactic. "But what if she plans to stay in Bozeman with her father?"

"She won't. She hates her father."

"How do you know this?"

Ned shrugged. "She told me so. She told me he was seldom a part of their lives. She mentioned it just yesterday when we ran across each other in the hotel lobby."

Trenton had no idea Ned had been left alone with Portia McGuire. He knew Ned was a man full grown, but he somehow felt responsible for keeping him from harm. "I just think it would be wise to know a little bit more about her before we go traipsing off to the wilds of Montana. But more than this, I think you should definitely give strong consideration to who she is and what she believes in before you let your heart carry you away."

"You are certainly no romantic, Chadwick," Ned declared with a frown. "Haven't you ever been in love?"

"I haven't had time for love."

"Well, neither had I, until now. I can tell you this, ol' boy, we're missing out on a very fine arrangement."

Trenton realized the conversation was going nowhere and quickly changed the topic. "So when have you and Mrs. McGuire planned for us to leave?"

Ned smiled. "As soon as possible. We'll take the stage to Cheyenne and then enjoy the train to Utah. After that, we'll again take the stage and journey to Virginia City."

"Sounds like you've got it all planned out. I doubt you need me to come along."

Ned laughed. "But of course I need you there. It wouldn't look fitting for me to travel alone with Mrs. McGuire. And frankly, you know me to be a man of action, therefore I went to work immediately on planning the arrangements. I've already purchased your ticket for the stage to Cheyenne. No sense in heading out blind."

"But that's what you're doing with Portia McGuire."

Ned came and slapped Trenton on the back. "Oh, Trent, you must learn to relax and have fun. Find some nice young woman and fall in love. You'll see. It's just the thing to change a man's perspective."

Trenton eyed his friend seriously. He didn't know why he cared about Ned. He should have just told him he'd make his own way to Montana and let it be done. After all, Trenton had a good horse and saddle, guns, and a nice wad of earnings from his gaming nights. He really didn't need Ned—not to accomplish getting to Montana.

Still, he cringed every time he thought of Portia McGuire getting Ned alone. Given the state of mind the poor man was in, he'd no doubt go proposing before the week was out, and where would that leave any of them?

"So what's the plan at Virginia City?" Trenton finally asked, feeling defeat overcome him.

"Well, first we'll find out where that uncle of yours lives. After all, you said it was supposed to be somewhere near Virginia City. Then we can get directions to Bozeman and Fort Ellis."

"All right."

Ned poured them both another drink. "Don't sound so resigned, Trenton. This is all going to work out very well. You'll see."

————

Cole knew the Blackfoot were more than a little frustrated by the recent turn of events. For the last six months they'd been on the run from an army of soldiers who seemed to doggedly pursue no matter which direction they went. The Blackfoot were more cunning and capable, however. They knew the territory and how to navigate secret passages that eluded the soldiers.

The Blackfoot man who spoke English often visited with

Cole in the evenings. He called himself White Tongue, telling Cole it was a name given him by his tribal members. It wasn't, however, his real name. Cole had asked about his real name, but White Tongue seemed to feel it unimportant. What did seem important to the man was his unusual interest in Cole and his life on the ranch. Cole in turn had learned from the man that the Blackfoot hoped to trade Cole back to the whites for the return of one of their chiefs.

"If they will give us Mountain Fire," White Tongue told him, "we will hand you over."

"Who is this Mountain Fire?" Cole asked. He'd tried hard to be patient with his plight, but he was constantly looking for a means of escape. Unfortunately, the Blackfoot seemed to anticipate this and kept him under continual guard.

"He's a powerful holy man. We need him in order to have victory over our enemies. He keeps us from defeat and harm."

"Only the true God can do that," Cole interjected.

White Tongue looked at him oddly. "How can you believe in your God when He didn't keep you from falling into the hands of the Sioux? You were nearly killed by them, and now you're here with our people."

Cole wondered if the man's heart would be open to hearing the truth. He had come to like White Tongue in spite of this captivity, and he honestly wished the man might come to know God.

"Knowing God—believing in Him—doesn't mean we will never encounter harm," Cole said honestly.

"Then why believe in Him? If His power is so limited—if He is not strong enough to keep you from the hands of your enemy—then what good is He?"

Cole picked up some pemmican and ate it slowly while he pondered White Tongue's question. "I don't serve God only in times of prosperity and safety. I trust Him to know what is best for me. Sometimes others interfere with God's plans—sometimes I do—but it's never a matter of God not being strong enough or powerful. It's a matter of choice. God gives man a choice. You may choose to believe in Him and follow His ways, or you may deny Him and go along your own path. Either way, you can't ignore Him and do nothing."

White Tongue seemed to consider this for a moment. "My sister believes in your God. She has suffered greatly. I do not see that her God cares."

Cole leaned back, nodding. "Sometimes it's hard. Like now—with me here. All I truly want is to be back home so I can marry my girl and raise a family. I want to ranch and learn what I need to know to be productive and useful. Instead, I'm here learning the ways of your people. I don't know why God would put me in this situation, but here I am."

"And you do not question Him for this?"

Cole chuckled. "Of course I question Him. I've asked Him about a million times why this happened."

"And what does He tell you?"

Cole could see the interest in the warrior's eyes. "He tells me to trust Him. To wait patiently."

"Bah! Those are the actions of women. A man must be in charge of his world. He must be a leader—strong, fearless."

"But without God, it would all be meaningless," Cole declared. "Jesus came into this world as a baby, not in charge and certainly not strong or fearless. He came to show us that the way to God is through Him. If we turn from our wickedness and accept that Jesus is the way, we can have eternal life."

"But a life of eternity as someone's prisoner? What kind of life is that?" White Tongue asked.

"My life here is temporal, at best," Cole declared, and for the first time in months he began to understand something that had eluded him. These troubles truly were light and momentary afflictions. He would live or die and then be gone, and only the things he did for God would remain. It was all about the way in which he looked at life—at his life.

"The Bible says we're just a mist—a vapor. We're here one day and gone the next. My heart's desire is to live a life worthy of God's praise. I want to hear Him say that I did my job well," Cole admitted.

"What job do you speak of?"

Cole shrugged. "The job of serving Him."

A commotion arose outside the tent, and White Tongue quickly jumped to his feet. "I'll be back. Stay here."

Cole wondered if this might be his chance to escape. As if reading his mind, White Tongue turned at the opening to the tepee. "Don't even try to leave. There are those in this camp who would just as soon the Sioux had killed you." With that he left.

Cole went to the opening and peered out to see what was happening. A group of men had gathered, and with them came women and children. Cole listened to the excited declaration of one young man. He understood most of what was said, enough to know that something had gone wrong in the negotiations with the army. Apparently two of the party had been killed and the others had barely escaped. They feared the army was going to follow and might have even hired a scout to follow them back to the camp.

Cole shook his head. No doubt this meant they would pack up and be on the move within the next hour. Every time they moved, he felt certain it took him farther and farther from Dianne.

Cole went back to his place in the lodge and wondered what he should do. It seemed like a good time to run, but White Tongue was the kind of man who would pursue him for the sake of pride, if nothing else.

Nearly half an hour later Cole looked up as White Tongue

came through the door. "What's going on?" he asked, hoping the news might be better than he'd understood it to be.

"I'm sure you heard most of it. Your Blackfoot is good," the man replied.

Cole shrugged. "I'd still like to hear it from you."

"Two of our warriors were killed. The soldiers are on their way. We'll break camp and head west."

Cole sighed. "I suppose you'll bind me."

White Tongue shook his head. "No. I think you're an honorable man. I believe you'll come with me and do what I tell you to do."

Cole jumped to his feet. "What are you talking about?"

"You're going with me. We're breaking into several groups. The people will come together on the Bear River."

"The Bear?"

White Tongue nodded. "You call it the Marias."

"Ah, yes," Cole said. "Are we far?"

White Tongue ignored the question and motioned to the buffalo robe Cole had carried with him since the Sioux. "Gather your things. We leave in a few minutes."

A sense of excitement ran through Cole like a prairie fire. The Marias was quite a ways north of the Madison Valley, but nevertheless, Cole knew he could find his way home—if he got that close.

He began to reason in his mind how he might get the upper hand with his Indian companion. White Tongue was a powerful warrior, well muscled and highly trained. He wouldn't suffer defeat easily.

"Come," White Tongue commanded when he returned. "I have horses waiting."

Cole whispered a prayer and followed the warrior to a small but broad-chested Indian pony. All around them was an organized chaos of women and children, elderly and animals. The warriors appeared to have gone—at least most of them. Cole knew the men would probably try to draw the soldiers away from the village in order to give the others more time to break camp. What few warriors remained were busy with instructing those around them.

"It's never easy to run," White Tongue said, looking back with an expression of regret. "But it has come to be a way of life."

Cole mounted the horse without waiting to be instructed. He looked to White Tongue for further instruction, but there was none. The man simply jumped upon his horse's back and jerked his head to the left. "We go this way."

They rode fast and hard for miles. Cole admired the endurance of the ponies and of the warrior. It was the New Grass Moon, April to the whites, and the chill of winter was still upon Montana. As the sun moved to the west, Cole wondered if they would make camp—and if they would meet up with any of the others.

White Tongue didn't seem inclined to slow their progress, much less to speak, so Cole remained silent. In the back of his mind, however, a plan began to take form. He didn't like the idea of harming the Blackfoot man, but if need be, Cole would do what he had to do. He would do anything necessary to finally get home to Dianne. He had waited long enough.

CHAPTER 22

IT WAS LATE WHEN TAKES MANY HORSES FINALLY STOPPED beside a river. "We'll camp here tonight," he told Cole. He watched the white man survey the area, as if trying to figure out how an escape might best be accomplished. If the situation had been other than it was, Takes Many Horses might have let the matter play out, just to see what the man chose to do.

The Blackfoot warrior dismounted. "Let's make a fire, and then I have something very important to tell you. I'll take care of the horses; you gather wood."

Cole Selby eyed him curiously, then dismounted. He left the pony with the man, then went toward the river, where the brush was quite thick.

Takes Many Horses watched him for a moment, wondering if Cole would be stupid enough to make a run for it. Hopefully not. The man seemed reasonably intelligent. He'd have to know that it would be almost impossible to get far from the camp on foot. He'd also have to believe that Takes Many Horses would come after him.

Contemplating these things, Takes Many Horses cared for

the ponies. He couldn't help but wonder how Cole would take the news he was about to share. For months he'd tried to negotiate Cole's release without seeming too interested in the man. He didn't want to arouse suspicions that Cole meant more to him than any other white man. Otherwise, there could be all sorts of trouble.

The council, however, wouldn't hear Takes Many Horses' arguments that it was bad medicine to keep Cole. They were confident Cole would be their best chance of getting the army to release Mountain Fire. Now two more of the Real People were dead at the hands of the white seizers, and the rest of the people were on the run. Bad medicine indeed.

He sighed. It seemed so pointless some days. It was almost as if Takes Many Horses could see the end of the Blackfoot nation. He'd heard of men who spoke of prophecies and dreams. Perhaps he had been given a vision of things to come. But even if this was true, what could he do about it?

Takes Many Horses kicked at the riverbank. He often wondered if the best thing would be to take Dianne Chadwick up on her offer to live at the ranch. Live as a white man, taking up his father's heritage instead of his mother's. It could solve many problems in his life. He could hide away there—work for Dianne . . . love her from afar.

He knew, however, he could never do that. It wouldn't be honorable. Not feeling as he did about her. It would be torturous to see her with Selby day in and day out. To watch them produce a family, grow more deeply in love.

He walked away from the ponies and gathered a few small branches and broke them into neat stacks, then positioned them for a small fire. He'd managed to get a nice blaze going by the time Cole returned with the extra fuel. "That should get us through the night. We won't stay here for long," Takes Many Horses instructed.

"Why?" Cole asked. He deposited an armful of wood by the fire.

"The soldiers may yet be following us. I can't say for certain. We'll sleep for a few hours and then head out."

"What's this river?" Cole asked, taking a seat by the fire.

"The Big River, or Missouri, as your people call it."

"How is it you know so much about my people? Where did you learn about them—learn English?"

Takes Many Horses retrieved the leather pouches he'd brought and withdrew bags of pemmican. He handed one to Cole. Then he reached back into the bag and withdrew Cole's journal.

"I believe this belongs to you."

Cole's left brow raised. His expression turned to one of disbelief. "I figured this to be forever lost. At best, I figured you probably destroyed it." He turned the book over in his hands as if willing himself to accept it as real.

"I read it," Takes Many Horses admitted. "I read it several times, in fact."

Cole nodded and looked up from the book. "It still doesn't answer my question. How is it that you speak such good English, White Tongue?"

"My father was a white man," he replied. He noted the look of surprise on Cole's face. "Does that shock you?"

"You don't look white."

Takes Many Horses chuckled and settled down beside the fire with his pemmican. "Which is exactly why I don't attempt to live as a white. As a half-blood, I'd never be accepted. Besides the fact that I find greater understanding and acceptance living as a Blackfoot, I also prefer the life. At least I did."

"Things have changed greatly," Cole admitted. "I never thought I'd live to see the day we'd have a railroad that stretched from one end of the country to the other."

"Yes, things have changed, and not always for the better. I know the time is coming soon that my people will be imprisoned on reservations without hope of living free. Your nation doesn't even see us as citizens—we aren't even human as far as they are concerned. They'd just as soon kill us off with the buffalo. We're just one more animal to be rid of."

"I've never felt that way, and I'd be willing to bet there are a lot of folks who don't. I know a lot of good white folks. Mr. Vandyke, for instance. He's a good man—married to a Blackfoot woman."

The Indian smiled. "I know. Koko is my sister. I am called Takes Many Horses." The words came out so matter-of-factly that he hardly realized he'd said them.

Cole's mouth dropped open and for several minutes he said nothing. Takes Many Horses ate pemmican and contemplated what to say next. He wondered if Cole had any idea how he felt about Dianne.

"I've heard many things about you," Cole finally said. He looked as though he'd been punched in the gut. "Your sister and my fiancée think quite highly of you."

"And I think very highly of them."

Cole shook his head. "If you knew who I was, why did you let them keep me prisoner all these months?"

"It seemed the better thing to do. At first, I encouraged the council to let you go, but the leaders were convinced you could be exchanged for our holy man. I tried to explain that it would look good in the eyes of the government if you were released— that keeping you was bad medicine—but they wouldn't hear me. As time wore on I ran out of excuses to use without making it seem that I had a special interest."

"So what happens now?" The excitement in Cole's voice was evident.

"I traded all my ponies, except these two, to obtain your freedom. Now we go home."

"How long will it take? When will we arrive?"

Takes Many Horses laughed. "It will take at least a week, and that depends on how deep the rivers are and if they're flooded with mountain snows. And of course we have to be able to avoid the army, who would just as soon see me dead, or other tribes, who would be hostile to letting you go."

"I just can't believe it. I mean . . . I was sitting here wondering how I might escape." He looked at Takes Many Horses and laughed. "I was trying to figure out how to overpower you."

The warrior grinned. "You couldn't have fought me and won."

"Well, now we'll never know."

Takes Many Horses sobered. "Dianne loves you a great deal."

"How is she? Has she changed much? Have you seen her recently?" The rapid-fire questions only served to cut Takes Many Horses more deeply than the journal had. He knew this man cherished Dianne as much as he did.

"She is well. She misses you and has feared for you," Takes Many Horses said. "I won't lie. I have strong feelings for her myself. Had your accounts in that book showed anything less than the strongest of faithful love, I would have let you die."

"Would you have really let that happen?"

Takes Many Horses assessed his heart and knew he probably wouldn't have killed Cole himself, but he doubted he would have stood in the way of it happening. "I don't know what would have happened. I wouldn't have seen Dianne hurt more than she already has been."

"Hurt? What do you mean? What has happened?"

Takes Many Horses spent the next hour explaining all that had happened over the months since Cole's capture.

"I can't believe Bram is dead. It won't be the same without

him," Cole said, shaking his head.

"Dianne now owns the ranch. She has a great deal of responsibility for one so young."

Cole nodded. "Yes, but she puts her trust in God. She takes her strength from Him."

"I know. She has told me so on many occasions. I suppose that's why our talk earlier today was of such interest to me. I know the Christian way; I've heard Bram talk about it many times. It just seems that it's a hard life—harder than going on without God."

Cole leaned over and put more wood on the fire. He poked at the pieces with a long branch, then settled back down before answering. "I've often heard folks talk that way. I've talked that way myself, truth be told. I had a hard time trusting God, because God didn't seem to care about the things that were important to me."

"What changed your mind?"

Cole chuckled. "That's easy. Dianne. Dianne changed my mind. She helped me see that my bitterness and anger weren't serving anyone, except maybe the devil. Dianne helped me realize there is real power in forgiveness—both being forgiven and in forgiving. There's also freedom. A real freedom that no one can take from you—not the soldiers or sickness or anything else."

Takes Many Horses looked away. "We need to sleep." He stretched out with his robe.

"Who can sleep? How can you sleep knowing we're on our way back to . . ." He let his words trail off.

"To Dianne?" Takes Many Horses murmured, the pain of his loss so strong that he could barely breathe.

"Sorry," Cole whispered. "I didn't think of how it might make you feel. Look, I appreciate what you've done for me. I know it couldn't have been easy, especially since you love her so much."

Takes Many Horses was surprised that Cole would so blatantly declare the truth. The warrior thought of Dianne—her wavy golden hair . . . her blue eyes . . . her gentle smile. "It's because I love her that I had no other choice," he said, his voice breaking slightly. He hoped Selby would ignore it in his excitement. There was no sense in the two men becoming rivals or enemies because of this woman. Takes Many Horses knew how Dianne felt about this man. He wouldn't interfere.

————

Portia McGuire ignored the discomfort of the stage. The dust was impossible and so, too, the constant jarring of the rutted road. Nevertheless, she remained completely at ease, as though this were nothing more strenuous than a Sunday outing. To help herself along, she tried to focus on Ned Langford. "So tell me about your family," she cooed.

"Well," Ned began, "the family estate is in Baltimore, but my father had a passion for the wild West. When he came out here, he was immediately captivated by the mining industry. He saw the sense of getting involved to broaden his holdings. He bought into several ventures and the rest is . . . well . . . the stuff of newspaper articles."

Portia fanned herself and laughed lightly. "How very true. I saw in the paper only the day before we left that your holdings were nearly the largest in Colorado."

"There are a few who have it over us, but not to worry. The Little Maribelle hasn't yet revealed all of her secrets. I'm convinced she's got a lot more to give."

"How exciting." She looked to Trenton, who sat beside Ned. His seeming disinterest didn't stop him from watching her, and that made Portia feel very uncomfortable. This Trenton Chadwick fellow was nothing like Ned. He didn't have the manners or breeding, and it was obvious that he made his way by living on the gambling earnings he won.

"So, Mr. Chadwick, are you anticipating the reunion with your family?"

Trenton narrowed his eyes. "It will be good to see them again."

"What caused you to be separated?" she asked, hoping to learn more about the man. She'd already made some inquiries into his past, but so far her information had been limited. She would have asked Ned, but the Chadwick fellow would never give her time alone with the man. He followed Langford around like some kind of guard.

"I would have to say the war separated us, ma'am," Trenton replied. He looked out the stage window as if to dismiss her further questions.

"What of you, Mrs. McGuire?" Ned asked. "Tell us of your family."

"Well, there is precious little to tell. My father was of course involved in the War Between the States. As the concerns of war came upon us, he was very preoccupied with his duties as a soldier. My mother, however, was concerned that I should not be exposed to such violence, so she was happy for me to marry and live abroad."

"In Scotland?" Ned questioned.

"No," Portia said, shaking her head. She fanned herself furiously, as the air in the stage seemed quite stifling. "I married a young man when I was but sixteen. As he had no desire to serve in the war, he took me abroad, where we traveled extensively. Were you in the war, Mr. Langford?"

"No, I did not serve. My father bought my way out. I can't say I'm overly proud of this, but it eased his mind to know his only son would be safe from the war."

"But of course," Portia said, patting his arm gently with her gloved hand. "You did the honorable thing."

Ned seemed to puff up at this. Portia thought it almost comical. Men were always delighted to be thought of as noble or honorable. She'd learned at a very young age how to advance their egos.

"What of you, Mr. Chadwick? Did you serve?"

"No," Trenton said, without giving her any other explanation.

"Well, I'm blessed to have you both here, so I cannot help but be glad that you were both spared the horrors of such things. I've heard terrible stories from those who did fight." She gave a ladylike shudder. "Awful to even think of." She paused for a moment, then smiled. "Life in Europe was quite different from life in America. I sometimes miss it very much."

"Did you remain abroad throughout the war?" Ned asked softly.

"Yes. My poor husband was killed when a freight wagon ran him over early one morning. They supposed it was the liquor that put my dear Billy into such a stupor. He had no idea what was happening until it was too late. He was very troubled by the circumstances of his life. He'd learned that two good friends had been killed in the war. It caused him to drink heavily. I suppose to forget."

Ned nodded sympathetically. "No doubt that is true. I'm quite sorry. You've known much sorrow in your young life."

"I was only twenty when he died. The war was still going on in the States, so I remained in London. I took a small house just outside of town and mourned my poor Billy. I was blessed that he left me so well endowed, for the expenses of a single woman are surprisingly many."

"Did you meet your second husband in London?" Ned's question was innocent enough, but Portia felt a slight tightening in her chest at memories of Angus.

"No, I was on a trip with friends. I met Angus in Edinburgh.

We encountered one another at the party of a dear friend. He was very kind and gentle of spirit." She paused, hoping the effect would be that she was lost in her memories of the dear man. She needn't tell either one of them that it was Angus's bank account that honestly drew her to the ugly little Scot.

"I don't wish to pain you in the telling of this tale," Ned said kindly.

"Oh, it's a pleasure to remember Angus," she lied. "I know I shall always have pleasant memories of both Angus and Billy. They were dear, dear men, and I've been so blessed to have known love not once, but twice."

Trenton coughed and Portia could tell it was due to disbelief rather than the dust. He eyed her with contempt, almost as if he knew the truth about her. But that was impossible, she told herself. Still, he made her uncomfortable. She truly hated people like Chadwick, people who seemed to be able to see beyond her facade. They made her feel cheap and dirty—as if she were somehow harming or offending them personally.

"Angus and I eventually married and remained in Scotland. He had a large estate, and I was quite happy there." She thought of the incessant stench of sheep dung and the long stretches of misty days and repressed a frown.

"Well, perhaps Montana will see you happy again," Ned said with great enthusiasm. "I've heard it's a marvelous land with everything a man or woman could ask for. Of course, there is some taming left to do. But that's true of any territory west of the Mississippi."

"I'm afraid I could never abide the loneliness and isolation," Portia declared. "I love the city. The bustle and the excitement make me feel alive. And, of course, I need friends. Friends, I've learned, help any grief to seem greatly lessened."

"So you have no plans to remain in Bozeman?" Trenton asked dryly.

She eyed him carefully. "No. My father will no doubt wish me gone as soon as he hears the news about Mother. He has no lost love for me, nor I for him."

"I'm sure you're mistaken. He couldn't help but love a daughter as beautiful and perfect as you," Ned interjected.

Portia smiled. "That's so very kind of you to say, but truthfully, we have always been at odds. I would chastise him for deserting us—leaving my mother so very lonely. He would tell me it was not my place to reprove him for any action he might deem worthy."

"I can understand that," Trenton said. It was the first time he'd volunteered any comment at all.

Portia frowned. "Had you lived in such a manner, you might well have believed it your place to strive toward making things right." She took out her handkerchief and pressed it under the veil to her eyes. "No doubt you always honored your father—respected him in every way."

"Now, now, Chadwick. You've upset her. You mustn't be so hard on her."

Trenton shrugged. "I suppose the truth is hard to deal with."

She hated his smug tone. "Mr. Chadwick, I would suggest that unless you personally experience the pain of another, you are hardly in a position to judge them for their response. My mother and I endured a great deal of pain because of my father's choices. It seemed only right that he should know the misery he had caused."

"But it accomplished nothing by your own admission," Trenton declared. "Rebellious natures seldom do. You've already suggested that you spent a lifetime trying to convince him of his wrongdoings. Why do you suppose showing up at the fort with the news that your mother died is going to change him now?"

Portia felt slapped by the question, and for the first time in a very long while, she felt words escape her. Instead of responding, she pretended to weep into her cloth.

"Oh, now look, Chadwick. You've gone and upset her. We need to remember her position. She's just lost her mother, and this on the heels of losing her husband. We must handle Mrs. McGuire with great care."

Portia looked beyond the handkerchief to see Trenton roll his eyes and pull his wide-brimmed hat down over his eyes.

"I'm gonna get some shut-eye," he said in disgust.

The only other passenger on the stage, an ancient old woman who sat beside Portia, began snoring. The noise was no more disruptive to Portia, however, than the tone of Trenton Chadwick's voice. She would have to be very careful around this man. He had the eyes of someone who had been betrayed and knew too much. His demeanor screamed danger.

Yes, she thought, *I'll have to be very careful around Mr. Chadwick.*

CHAPTER 23

DIANNE LOVED ROUNDUP TIME. THE AIR WAS FULL OF THE musky scent of cattle, dust, and dung, but she didn't care. It was all wonderful. There was an energy and excitement in roundup that wasn't found any other time of the year. This year even promised to hold some entertainment for the cowhands and ranchers. There were plans to show off some of the cowboys' finer skills with demonstrations of roping and bronco busting. Gus seemed particularly pleased, but Dianne wasn't sure if it was because he was reliving his days as a youth or because of the herd's good turnout.

"We've got a lot of twin births this year. That's a good omen," he said as they shared breakfast.

Dianne looked out across the field. The mothering up had been fairly easy, and today they would start branding. She was even pleased to see that two other local ranchers had joined in the event, bringing their wives along with their crew.

"Mrs. Farley from the Lazy MW says they've had a very productive year as well. She actually seems more knowledgeable about such matters than her husband. She's out there directing her crew as if she were in charge."

Gus laughed. "I think she's just the kind of woman who doesn't cotton to lettin' someone else run things. Her man's a good one, seems to take her in stride. I ain't sure I could be the same way."

Dianne grinned. "Are you giving me a warning, Gus?"

He appeared embarrassed. "Now, don't go puttin' words in my mouth, Miz Dianne. You know I think highly of you."

"Yes, but you also know I consult you on everything related to running this ranch. What if I were to just up and get bossy about things? Get out there like Mrs. Farley and try to tell you what to do."

"Well, frankly, I have to admit the little lady knows her business. As I hear it told, she grew up on a ranch down in Kansas. She knows a sight more than her man, which is probably why he tolerates it. He was a farmer." Gus crammed in a mouthful of sourdough biscuit, then chased it down with a swig of hot coffee. He wiped off his mouth with the back of his sleeve and continued. "They got all excited about homesteading up this way when they saw some sketches of the area. Don't rightly know that a few picture drawings would send me traveling a thousand miles from home, but they seem happy. Their place is just about ten miles from our northwest boundary post."

"They seem nice," Dianne said, watching Maggie Farley handle a rope as well as any of the men.

"That other couple—the one that brought their young'uns— they don't know a whole lot about nothing, but they have the heart for it. I've been trying to share a thing or two with the man. His name is Clark Vandercamp and her name is Hilda."

"I can't imagine bringing children to a roundup," Dianne commented, looking across the camp to where Hilda sat fixing the hair of her oldest daughter.

"Oh, roundup is a great time for the community to gather. I

remember times in Texas when folks would come from hundreds of miles. Roundup might last weeks into a month—just depended on how big a territory you had to cover. I remember bein' in the saddle eighteen hours a day—sleepin' there too."

Dianne grinned. She loved it when Gus talked about his days in Texas.

"Always wanted to be a wagon boss. Spent my time as a circle rider, horse wrangler, even a rough-string rider."

"What's that?" Dianne asked, finishing the last of her meal.

"Ah, that's a man who's brought on to ride the really mean horses—the bad ones. You put them all in one string."

"A rough string," Dianne said, nodding. "Makes sense. Guess you'd have to put Jack in that group." She flexed her arm. It was pretty much mended, although it still felt stiff. She was blessed that Gus had put off roundup until the latter part of April. His decision had proven to be very wise, when a surprise snow delivered a foot of icy whiteness only a week and a half earlier. The break had given Dianne's arm extra time to heal, and by the time they headed out, she actually felt confident sitting atop Dolly. The only real problem was that she longed to participate—to get in there and help with the roping and cutting, but she was wise enough to recognize her limitations.

"How's the arm?" Gus asked, seeing her rub the muscles.

Dianne grinned. "Feels almost as good as new."

"I've had more busted on me from ridin' mean ol' broncs like Jack than I care to remember. You were lucky, little lady."

"Well, you always said a fellow didn't know what he was made of unless he got out there and gave it his best."

"I said that about fellas. Not ladies."

Dianne laughed and gathered up her dishes. She poured out the remains of her coffee. The stuff was strong enough to walk away on its own. "Wish you boys would be a little more liberal with the water when you're making coffee."

Gus shook his head. "Been my experience most folks make it too weak. If I can't stand a spoon in it, I don't wanna drink it. Never did cotton to milkin' it down either." He got to his feet and handed his dishes over to Dianne. "Although I can tolerate a little sugar." He grinned. "Always did have a sweet tooth." He looked off to where the boys were already preparing to brand. "Well, the work won't do itself." He tied on his neckerchief and gave Dianne one last nod.

Dianne watched him walk away, wishing she could join him in branding the calves. Just last year she'd finally gotten the hang of roping. She'd gotten pretty good with a lariat, if she did say so herself. But she'd promised to be good, and she intended to keep her word.

"I can see you're itching to get in there and work with the boys."

Dianne smiled at Boris Masters. He was an older man who'd been hired on to cook for the outfit. He'd worked off and on at the Diamond V, and Dianne had always liked him. He took the dishes from Dianne and plunged them into steaming, sudsy water.

"It's hard to just watch," she admitted. "I see those other women helping and it just seems unfair."

"Those other gals ain't nursin' a broken arm," Boris said in an authoritative voice.

"I know. I know," she said in an exasperated tone. "No one is about to let me forget it either." She gave him a quick smile and added, "Breakfast was great. You make one fine trail cook."

Boris's ears turned red and Dianne realized she'd embarrassed him. Turning, she called back to him, "You'll make some woman a fine husband."

She heard the man sputter and cough, as though the comment were impossible to comprehend. Dianne chuckled to herself, remembering Gus's tales that Boris was courting some

Sunday school teacher in Bozeman. If it got serious, she'd have to let Boris know that they'd be more than open to the idea of yet another woman on the Diamond V.

Dianne took her place at the back of the wagon Gus had set up for her. She watched as the men got to work. The fires had been going since before dawn and the brands were heated and ready to go. She felt sorry for the new babies that had to be branded, but at the same time she felt a pride she couldn't explain. These were Diamond V cattle—Uncle Bram's livestock. It made her happy to see them so marked.

The ropers were on their horses and working to single out the babies for the morning's work. Gabe Presley, who'd been with the ranch for nearly three years, threw his rope and started the morning's affairs. He heeled the calf quickly and dragged it from the circle by its back legs over toward the branding fires.

"Diamond V," he called out, indicating the brand to use. This done, he turned the calf over to the flankers, who went to work to keep the calf down.

Dianne was fascinated as one man grabbed the calf at the flank and foreleg, then finished rolling the animal to its side. Once down, the man grabbed the top foreleg, while the other flanker took the top hind leg and stretched it out behind the calf. They made it look so easy. The calf bawled, causing its mama to become quite disturbed. Dianne felt sorry for both of them. They couldn't understand what was happening.

Levi, the iron man, came forward with the brand. Dianne knew from talking to Gus that branding was a very precise job. Too little pressure and the brand wouldn't be deep enough to peel and leave a good mark. Too much pressure, especially with the more detailed Diamond V brand, and the mark would often be blotched or run together.

"You don't need a heavy hand to lay a brand," Gus had told her. Watching as Levi applied the iron, Dianne could see that he was very comfortable with his job. Years under Gus's tutelage had made Levi quite good at his job.

The morning continued in like fashion. Calves were mothered up, then pulled from the circle to be branded with the appropriate markings, then passed on to the next round of workers. By lunchtime, dozens of babies had been branded, inspected, and in some cases castrated. It was all a very orderly, busy affair.

———

The roundup weather held in a grand fashion without spilling even a drop of rain on the crew. There was no sign of Indian or animal that might want to attack, and only two cowboys endured injury, and even those were minor. On the last day before they were to head back to their own ranches, a party had been planned. It was during this time that the boys would show off their talents. Dianne chose a good place to stand and cheer on the participants as the festivities got started.

"I'm sure glad we finally had a chance to meet," Maggie Farley said as she took a place beside Dianne. "We'd heard about you last summer when we moved in, but there wasn't much time to come visiting."

Dianne offered the redheaded woman a smile. "I'm glad we could spend time getting to know each other."

Maggie pushed back a lock of errant hair and tucked it up under her wide-brimmed hat. "My husband tells me you're the owner of the Diamond V. Pardon my saying so, but you seem a mite young to be handling an outfit this big."

Dianne tensed at the woman's comment, then realized it was probably curiosity rather than criticism that drove the woman's question. "The ranch belonged to my uncle. He was killed last year by a grizzly bear."

"I'd heard that. Heard he left a squaw wife and children behind. Did they go back to their people?"

"They're with me. I'm their people," Dianne said more severely than she'd intended.

Maggie Farley's eyes widened. "I didn't mean no offense. It's just, well, in Kansas that kind of thing wasn't looked upon favorably."

"Neither is it accepted here. That's why I own the ranch now instead of my aunt."

Maggie nodded. "Whitson—he's my husband"—she spoke as if Dianne wouldn't remember this—"he said your intended was overdue. Have you had word yet?"

Dianne had no desire to discuss Cole's absence, but she didn't want to appear offended by Maggie's remark about Koko. "No. We've heard nothing."

"That's what's hard about being up here. We've only been here for a year and a half, but it's hard getting word from home. I don't hear from my ma but maybe once or twice a year." She shook her head. "Gets pretty lonely out here."

"It can, that's for sure."

"There's not another woman around my place to even talk to. God hasn't seen fit to bless us with babies, so I don't even have that comfort."

Dianne felt sorry for the woman. "The Diamond V's not that far and we have several women there, but . . ." She fell silent, wondering how she could explain that she wouldn't tolerate prejudice. She decided rather than make it personal, she'd speak of it in a more general way. "Some people have no tolerance for folks who aren't white. My aunt, as you mentioned, is part Blackfoot, but she also had a white father. One of my dear friends is a former slave."

"A slave? Truly?" Maggie asked.

Dianne smiled. "Truly. Faith is dearer to me than most. She's been a good friend through the years, and I wouldn't trade anything for the friendship we share."

"Well, I'll be. I never thought about a white person being able to be friends with a black. Never figured they'd have anything in common."

"Have you ever known a black person?" Dianne asked gently.

"No," the older woman said, shaking her head, "I've never known one personally. Heard they were strange—practice black magic and put curses on white folks." She looked rather embarrassed to have mentioned that and added, "But like I said, I've never experienced it firsthand."

Dianne smiled again. It seemed Maggie was trying to be sociable and tolerant, in spite of her beliefs. "A lot of what you've heard is stories told out of ignorance. We're all Christian folks at the Diamond V—well, most of us. Either way, we wouldn't tolerate black magic. You should come by sometime and get to know Faith. I find that worries about such things are easily dealt with when folks give themselves a chance to familiarize themselves with what they don't understand."

"We aren't that far," Maggie said, crossing her arms thoughtfully. "I'll have to see if Whitson can spare the time. Of course, it would have to be later, in the summer. We don't have near the critters you do to care for, but we'll have our hands full. It's just us and the two hired men."

"Why don't you come around the Fourth of July? We always enjoy a grand celebration. You could bring your hired men and stay a day or two. We have plenty of room to put you up, and you'd have a real chance then to get to know some of the folks at the ranch. We've also got a blacksmith and shop, so if you needed some smithy work done, Malachi would be happy to work it in."

Maggie smiled and met Dianne's eyes with a steady gaze. "I'd like that. I'd like that a great deal. I'd like to meet your friend too. I think in a country like this, a person ought not to turn her nose up at friendship. I'll talk to Whitson before we leave and let you know what he says."

"We also have church every Sunday."

"With a real preacher?" Maggie questioned.

"Yes. Reverend Hammond gives a powerful sermon. His wife, Charity, is good to lead the singing and to listen to the troubles of those around her. I know you'd enjoy meeting her."

"Is she . . . well . . . not that it matters," Maggie stammered. "I just wondered if she used to be a slave too."

Dianne grinned. "No. She's just as white as you and I, but she thinks the color of a person's skin ought not to matter. After all, the Bible says God doesn't look on man's outward appearance but at the heart."

"Do tell. Isn't that a wonder?" Maggie said, seeming genuinely enthralled. "Well, I'm gonna tell Whitson about this. I just know he'll be interested to hear it all."

It was a beginning, Dianne thought. At least the woman hadn't run off in the other direction. Everything comes by little steps, Dianne reasoned as she turned her attention back to the men and their games.

———

With roundup over and the herd headed to summer range, Dianne thought the ranch had never looked more welcoming. She rode with the other hands, confident on her faithful Dolly instead of a more rambunctious horse. She loved the way the valley and mountains had started to green up. The garden plot to the back of the barn had already been worked up. Dianne couldn't help but notice the size had doubled from just a few years past.

Plans for finishing the house started churning in her head. She would see to it that Koko's wing was finished off first and then start on her own. Koko had mentioned wanting some delicate print material to make curtains for Susannah's room. Dianne would have to make a list and then go to town and see what could be had. For her own room she thought maybe something in a dark green damask would look nice at the windows.

"I'll take your horse for you, Miz Dianne," Gabe said as they halted near the corral fence.

"Thanks. I think all I want is a good hot bath and plenty of soap. I've got half of Montana to wash off," Dianne said, mindless of talking about such a delicate matter as a lady's bath.

Gabe nodded. "I figure to take me a dip in the river. It'll be cold, but it'll feel good."

Dianne much preferred her idea of cleaning up to Gabe's. She knew, however, a lot of the cowhands would follow suit. It saved time from having to heat water, and several of the boys were headed into town, where they'd probably have a nice hot bath and shave before enjoying whatever entertainment could be had.

Making her way to the house, Dianne pulled off her brown hat and smacked it against her side several times to rid it of all the dust. No doubt it would take a heap more than that, she thought. Even her mouth tasted gritty from the trail ride. No wonder so many of the boys spit. She laughed at the thought of taking up the bad habit.

She caught her reflection in one of the windows as she made her way to the back door. "What a sight," she moaned. She looked as though she'd been years on the trail instead of just a couple of weeks. Her hair was mostly matted against her head, with stray strands falling in disorder down the sides.

She hung up her hat and coat on the back porch, then checked her boots so as not to drag in mud or manure. She looked forward to seeing Koko and checking in on Faith, but the bath had to come first. She wouldn't have imposed herself on anyone in this state. She had just started for the back stairs when someone called out.

"You been wallowing in a mud pit?"

She looked up in surprise to find Takes Many Horses. Somehow the man always had a way of turning up when he was least expected. Dianne put her hands on her hips. "Very funny. I'll have you know I've been out on the roundup. Something you could help with if you chose to stay around and make yourself useful."

He laughed. "I've been busy."

Dianne wanted only to dismiss the man and head to her room, but he seemed so happy, it was almost contagious.

"What have you been busy with?" she asked in spite of herself.

"I've had my own roundup, you could say."

Dianne eyed him curiously, cocking her head to one side and narrowing her gaze. "And just what have you been rounding up?"

"Something you lost." His grin broadened and he winked. "Something you'll want to have back."

Dianne strained to think of what he could possibly be talking about. She had lost a fine pair of riding gloves, but she seriously doubted he had any knowledge of that.

"I don't know what you could possibly be talking about."

Takes Many Horses took hold of her arm. "Then come see for yourself."

He pulled her through the kitchen and past the dining room and sitting room until they stood in the front entryway. "There," he said, pointing toward the front sitting room.

Dianne gazed into the small room and saw nothing amiss. "What are you talking about?"

Dianne looked around the warrior and froze in place. Cole stepped out from the doorway that led to the large gathering room. The look on his face was one she would remember until her dying day. There was such joy—such hope in that expression.

"Cole." Her voice barely croaked the word.

He stepped forward and Dianne did likewise. "I thought you were dead," she whispered.

He nodded. "I thought so too."

She reached up to touch his face. He was warm . . . alive. A sob caught in her throat as she reached up to take hold of him. "I . . . oh . . . Cole." She fell into his arms, feeling the despair of long months fade away.

They embraced, holding each other as if they would never again allow anything to separate them. Dianne felt her heart pounding in her ears, blocking out all sound. *He's here! He's here!* Her thoughts tumbled over each other. *What happened to keep him so long? How did Koko's brother find him?*

Does he still love me?

CHAPTER 24

EVERYONE REJOICED AT COLE'S RETURN. A VERY PREGNANT Faith insisted on creating a celebration supper, and they all pelted Cole and Takes Many Horses with questions while enjoying her fine fare.

"How did you recognize Cole?" Koko asked her brother as dessert was served.

As the conversation swirled around her, Dianne wondered what Cole had endured at the hands of the Sioux. Had his encounter with the Indians added that new harder look to his face—the loss of his boyish charm? Of course, Cole had always been on the serious side, she recalled. He'd always seemed angry when they were coming west on the wagon train. But even then, despite the anger, there'd been a gentleness to him. Just as there was now.

"It seems to me," Koko was saying, "Cole passed into true manhood on this journey."

"There's always one event in the life of a man that changes everything," Gus said knowingly.

Dianne could scarcely eat for all the excitement, but the

warm apple pie sent a marvelous aroma into the air, making her instantly agree to the piece Faith offered. Still, she drew Takes Many Horses back to Koko's original question. "But how did you find Cole? How did you recognize him?"

"When I returned from hunting," he began, "the council told me of this white man they had found. They knew he'd been taken by the Sioux, because the buffalo robe had Sioux markings. He had been seriously wounded, and his injuries were not healing properly. He had a high fever and was near death when a hunting party found him. They asked me to speak to him because they wanted to know who he was and why the Sioux had kept him alive."

"So why had they kept you alive?" Gus asked, completely caught up in Cole's story.

Cole shrugged. "I'm still not sure; it certainly wasn't their usual way. They took four or five of us from the wagon train. At least two died, and I don't know what happened to the others. I was so sick while with the Sioux, I don't remember a great deal. They treated me decent enough. I suppose if I had to guess, they were planning to trade me, just like the Blackfoot thought to do."

"Is that why you were so delayed in returning Cole to us?" Dianne asked.

Takes Many Horses met her eyes. His expression seemed almost pained, but he quickly covered it by looking back to his dessert. Dianne wondered what was going on inside his head but decided against questioning him here in front of the others.

"Yes, our people planned to trade him. They were working on negotiating with the army, explaining that they'd found a wounded white man of some importance. Of course, they didn't know if the man was really important or not, but they were very impressed with Cole because he carried a book with him and in it he'd written a great deal. They'd seen important men with these kinds of books in the past and figured he might be someone who could help us."

"They were always good to me," Cole added. He sat next to Dianne and slipped his hand in hers to give it a reassuring squeeze. "They kept me under guard but fed me well and treated my wounds. I have no complaints, except that they kept me so long."

Takes Many Horses shrugged. "I tried to get them to release you. They wouldn't hear me. They were convinced that because they had the attention of the white seizers, they would make their trade for our holy man."

"What happened?" Dianne asked. She felt so blessed to have Cole back, but it all seemed so unreal. She had pretty much convinced herself that Cole was dead, and then just as she was beginning to accept his death, here he came back into her life.

"I'm not sure, but apparently the soldiers got tired of negotiating. They killed two of our men, then sent the third man back to explain that they were coming to wipe out the village and take any whites they found. It was then that I was finally able to convince the leaders to let Cole go."

"But you didn't answer our question," Koko interjected. "How did you know it was Cole? I don't remember you ever meeting him."

"I hadn't met him before, but I knew the name. I've talked to Dianne enough about him." Dianne felt her cheeks grow warm as Takes Many Horses stared directly at her. His expression almost challenged her to deny his words, but she had no desire to refute his statement.

"Then," he continued, turning his attention back to his apple pie, "I read Cole's journal. If I had doubts about remembering his name correctly, they were all put aside with that. He spoke of his life here at the Diamond V and of . . . Dianne."

Koko nodded. "I see." She shook her head and turned to

look at Cole. "It's a miracle that you survived. There have been so many losses—so much pain because of the warring between the two peoples. I hope you can find it in your heart to forgive."

"I already have," Cole said softly. "I knew God had a plan even in my being taken. I knew He had a plan in the length of time and all the frustration it caused me. I'm troubled by all the hate that exists between Indians and whites, but I know it won't be easily resolved."

"Hard times are coming—are here even now," Takes Many Horses murmured.

"Yes. It will only get worse. I even fear for what it will mean to us here," Cole replied. "We're so isolated; if the Blackfoot or any other tribe wanted to attack, we'd have very little defense."

"The Blackfoot won't attack," Koko threw out. "They know I live here—that Bram lived here. Bram was good to them, and they honor that."

"Things will change. Old agreements will be forgotten in the fight to survive."

Dianne heard the sadness in Cole's voice. It was true. Things were changing faster than she cared to admit. Every time she managed to get ahold of a newspaper she saw signs of the progress made in the territory. And with each step toward "civilization," the Indians generally suffered.

Dianne no longer wanted to dwell on the sorrow of it all. "Faith, supper was wonderful. The pie was especially good." Though, looking down at the crumbs on her plate, Dianne realized she had barely tasted it in her excitement.

Faith struggled to her feet. "I'm so glad to have Cole home. I'm mighty glad I could be the one to cook supper for him."

"It was perfect, Faith," Cole said, nodding. "Glad you're back among us. You too, Malachi. I'll always remember what a great help you were to folks on the wagon train—despite the way they treated you."

Malachi nodded but said nothing. Faith began clearing the dishes, but Koko got to her feet and waved her off. "I'll take care of cleaning up. Dianne and Cole have plenty to talk about, and I will be happy for the time to talk with my brother."

"I need to get back down and let the boys know what we'll be doing tomorrow," Gus said, pushing back from the table. "Cole, I'll look forward to talking to you later."

"Me too. I'll find you tomorrow."

Gus made his way to the kitchen door, carrying several plates with him. "I might as well help out on the way."

Everyone began going their separate ways, leaving Dianne and Cole time to be alone. Dianne got to her feet, then turned, holding on to the back of the chair. "Would you like to take a walk?"

Cole smiled and nodded. "I've wanted that for longer than I can say."

They walked in silence to the front door. Dianne took her shawl from a peg, then took down Uncle Bram's holster and revolver.

"We might need this. You can never tell what varmint might decide to wreak havoc." Cole nodded and strapped the gun on. It was plenty loose, but he managed to cinch it up enough to keep it from falling off his hips.

Dianne handed him a hat. "This is one Morgan left behind. You can have it."

Cole took it from her, studied it for a moment, then planted it on his head.

"I'm going to have to get to town and buy a new hat—after I earn some money." He shook his head. "I've lost everything."

"Not everything," Dianne said, shaking her head. "You haven't lost me."

They walked out into the chilled evening air, down the lane that led toward Dianne's favorite hill. They held hands, each seeming at a loss for words. Dianne wondered if Cole's time with the Indians had changed him—changed the way he felt about her and life on the Diamond V. Would he tell her now that he'd had enough of the barbaric West—that he planned to head back to Kansas?

"I know this must be hard for you," Dianne finally said, her voice barely a whisper. "It's been hard for me too." She stopped and looked up into his eyes. "If you've changed your mind—you need to say so now."

Cole looked down at her for a moment, then pulled her close. "You are all I thought of. You and God. I wouldn't have survived those first few days if I hadn't been determined to see you again. Even when I thought I was about to die, leaving you was my only regret." He paused and studied her face. "I haven't changed my mind."

Dianne relished the feel of his arms around her, but she knew they needed to talk this matter through. She pulled back, breaking his hold. "I know you lost all of your possessions in the attack. I even know about the money, because I overheard you talking to Gus about it."

"That was money to help us start a new life—a married life."

"With Uncle Bram dead, I own the ranch," she said matter-of-factly. It was difficult to see, even in the moonlight, but Dianne imagined that Cole's jaw had tightened. "Cole, I don't want to see us separated any longer—especially by things that shouldn't matter. I need you, and I want to be your wife. Please don't let your pride keep us apart."

"What are you talking about?"

She turned away. She feared she might start to cry, and it was so important that she remain strong. "I know you've lost your personal possessions, but Cole, everything I have is yours. You don't need to worry about saving up money for new clothes—we'll just go to town and buy them. You don't have to worry about restoring your fortune before we can marry, because I have more fortune than either of us will ever need. In the long run, you'll earn every cent you make on this ranch—it has a way of demanding your all," she said softly. "Just don't put off the wedding . . . please."

"What gives you any idea I would want to put off getting married?" He took her by the shoulders and turned her back to face him. "Dianne, I wasn't suggesting that at all. I was just talking back there. I didn't mean to scare you."

Dianne reached up to touch his face. "But I know the pride of a man. My brothers were very prideful—needing to have things a certain way. I know you want to do it all on your own. I don't blame you, but I also don't want to see that come between us."

"I don't intend to let anything come between us. In fact, I wanted to tell you that I plan to ride into town tomorrow or the next day and bring back the preacher."

Dianne laughed. "Oh no you won't. I'm not letting you out of my sight for even a moment. Besides, Reverend Hammond is living right here now, and he can marry us. He and Charity have been away, but they're due back tomorrow. I'll talk to them first thing. I want to get married right away before something sours the whole thing."

"Like what?"

"Who can tell? Forest fire, floods, Indian attacks, bandits . . ."

Cole chuckled. "If God brought me this far, do you really suppose He'd let something happen to ruin this now?"

She looked down and sobered. "I don't want to take a chance."

He put a finger under her chin and raised her face to meet his eyes again. "God's already worked this out, Dianne. You mustn't fear. It wouldn't be trusting Him if we started second-guessing everything every time one of us needed to go some-where."

"I just don't want to lose you again."

"You've never lost me."

Tears welled in Dianne's eyes. "It was so hard. You said you'd be home in September."

"I know."

"I was absolutely horrified when I heard you tell what you've been through. I can't imagine being the same person after all of that. You even look different."

"I'm not the same," he admitted. "But the differences aren't all bad. In fact, I think they make me a better man, and that in turn will make me a better husband. Besides, you look different too."

Dianne hadn't considered this. "Are you displeased?"

Cole chuckled. "Hardly. You grew up while I was gone. You're a beautiful woman—my woman."

Dianne's nerves felt raw with emotion. "So where do we go from here? Will you have a problem marrying me and running this ranch? Will you honor my word to Bram and allow Koko and her children to remain here—to help run the place?"

"This is their home. I wouldn't think of putting them from it, and if Koko wants a say in the decision-making, I'm all for it, but I think Gus probably knows better than any of the rest of us. Bram probably should have left the ranch to him."

Dianne couldn't help but laugh. "I've often thought the same thing."

"But Bram probably saw the same thing in you that I do: determination, honesty, intelligence, and a willingness to learn."

Dianne smiled at his compliments. "I love you, you know."

Cole laughed. "I'm certainly glad to hear it. Especially since you keep demanding we marry right away."

"I guess I just have so many unanswered questions in my

mind," Dianne began. "But then again, I feel like the only important questions *have* been answered. You're here and suddenly the rest no longer seems important."

Cole stroked her cheek, letting his fingers work into her hair to let loose the pins. "I've always loved your hair. Even when you were a little girl on the wagon train."

Dianne laughed. "I wasn't such a little girl. I was sixteen years old."

He shook his head and continued stroking her hair. "Seems like a hundred years ago."

Dianne hugged him close. "Yes. Yes, it does." She wanted nothing but to go on holding Cole. To forget about the sorrows of the past year—to focus only on how wonderful it felt to be in his arms again. She might have gone on embracing him for a long, long while, but Cole broke it off this time. He pulled her along behind him and headed back toward the house.

"It's getting late," he said as she caught up. "I know you're tired, and there will be plenty of time for this later."

Dianne gripped his arm tight. "So will you talk to Ben about marrying us—or should I?"

Cole laughed and the sound filled the otherwise silent night. "Someday I'm going to tell our children about how you forced me into marriage. Couldn't even let the dust settle on my boots after being stolen by Indians before you had me off arranging for the preacher."

"And I'll tell our children how you fought Indians and bad weather and death itself to get back home to me."

Cole stopped at this. They'd almost reached the house, but Dianne could see that he had something more to say. "I would have walked through hell itself to get back to you."

"I think you probably did," she whispered.

"Dianne, the days to come won't be easy. I want you to know that here and now, although I figure you probably already know it even better than I do. There are going to be more Indian wars, more killing. We're not in a good place, no matter what Koko says. There are plenty of tribes besides Blackfoot. Most would just as soon see us struck from the earth."

"I know. And if not the Indians, I know the odds are against us with the weather and the land. . . . But, Cole, I'm not afraid anymore. The worst that could happen was losing you. Now you're here and the rest seems so unimportant."

"But it is important and we have to be prepared."

She nodded, knowing he was right. It seemed a good time to hand the reins over to him. "Whatever you and Gus decide is fine by me. Just let us know what we need to do and we'll do it. I want everyone to be as safe as possible. We've grown into quite a family here, and I'd like to keep everyone safe and healthy."

Cole nodded and they continued walking until they'd reached the porch. "I'm going to go on down to the bunkhouse and talk to Gus." He grinned and pulled her close once again. "But not before I have what I really came out here for."

Dianne knew he would kiss her, and for the moment she thought her heart might actually stop beating. She lifted her lips to meet his and melted against him as the warmth of that kiss spread throughout her body. This was all she wanted—all she needed.

Takes Many Horses watched the couple kiss from the shadows near the side of the great house. A tightness in his chest spread fire through his body. There was a dull ache that wouldn't leave him, even as Cole walked away from Dianne and headed down to where the rest of the ranch hands lived.

Dianne watched him go, lingering on the porch for some time. Takes Many Horses knew it was a mistake, but he couldn't help going to her. He was drawn, just as a moth to the flame.

"It's good to see you happy again," he offered, hoping he wouldn't startle her.

"It's good to be happy again," Dianne replied. "I didn't hear you coming. I must have been lost in my thoughts."

No doubt. Would that you could lose your thoughts over me the same way. He looked up at her. "It's of no matter."

"I want to thank you again for what you did. I know you didn't have to risk your life to save Cole, but I'm so grateful that you did."

He could hear her voice break. He couldn't—wouldn't lie to her. "I know how much he means to you. How could I not move heaven and earth to put you two back together?"

"Still, I know it cost you. I'd like to make it up to you," Dianne said, taking a step closer. Takes Many Horses could see her better now. The glow from the front room window shed light on her image. Her hair was loose, flowing free down her back. He longed to reach out and touch the silken strands. He longed to have her kiss him the way she'd just kissed Cole Selby.

He shook off the thoughts and stepped backward. "I should go."

"Wait, please." She reached out to take hold of his arm. "I want you to know how grateful I am. Koko said you traded all of your ponies for Cole. I want you to pick out ten of our best horses and take them with you."

He cringed and pulled away quickly. Her touch was driving him mad. "I'm glad you have your man back. He's a good man. He'll be good to my sister and to you. There's no need for me to take your horses. I'll probably have no use for them in the days to come anyway."

"Cole says bad times are coming. Especially for the Indians. I wish you'd reconsider and stay with us."

"I cannot do that, Stands Tall Woman." He kept a tight hold

on his emotions. "I am Blackfoot. The Real People are my people."

"But you may get killed." He heard the worry in her tone,
and it touched him deeply. A part of her did care about him, but
not in the way he wished she cared.

"I was born Blackfoot, and I will die Blackfoot," he whispered. "For me, there is no other choice. Just as there is only one
path for you—that of wife to Cole Selby." The words pained
him, but he knew they had to be said—not for her, but for him.
Somehow he had to convince himself that she was better off
here—better off with Cole. Somehow.

CHAPTER 25

DIANNE SHIFTED NERVOUSLY AS KOKO DID UP HER BUTTONS. "I didn't think this day would ever come," Dianne chattered. "I thought I'd die an old maid. Oh, Koko, do you think this dress is all right? Do you think Cole will like it?"

Koko laughed and stepped away to scrutinize the ivory wedding dress. "It's perfect. So much better than the blue material we had thought to use at first. You are positively radiant. Never has there been a more beautiful bride. Here, see for yourself."

Dianne turned to take in the view from her bedroom mirror. She gasped at the sight of herself. "Oh, it's lovely."

The soft cotton cloth wasn't anything special in and of itself. It was nothing more than a simple bolt of ivory material until Faith and Koko worked their skills upon it. Dianne marveled at the sweeping flow of the skirt, the fitted, pin-tucked bodice with its delicate embroidery work. It was perfect.

She touched the high collar. The lace gracing the edge had been created by hand thanks to Faith's diligence. They had found the perfect pattern for the lace in a *Godey's Lady's Book* Dianne's friend Sally had given Dianne when she was preparing to leave

Missouri. Faith, never having attempted such a feat before, had pored over the instructions and began to work out the details. The evidence of her capable skills now swirled in a delicate pattern at Dianne's neck.

Tears formed in her eyes. There had been a time when she'd honestly thought there would never be an opportunity to wear the lovely creation.

"I'm so happy," she whispered.

Koko touched her hand. "I know, and I'm happy too. I wish Bram could be here to give you away."

Dianne nodded. "I do too, but I know Gus felt very honored to be given the job."

"If you hadn't been in such a hurry, you could have had Zane or Morgan give you away."

"I doubt that. Zane's regiment isn't even at the fort, and I have no idea where Morgan has gotten off to. No, it's better this way. I wish they could be here, but I'm not about to wait until they return."

Koko smiled and it lit up her entire face. Dianne marveled at the lovely woman. Koko had dressed in a dark burgundy gown with fitted sleeves and a pleated band at the waist. The skirt was fuller than the fashion dictates of the day, but it certainly wasn't one of the wide bell-shaped monstrosities of the 1860s. Sometimes when she and Koko were looking for something helpful in the old copies of *Godey's,* they would laugh and laugh at the wasteful fashions.

"Imagine," Koko had said, shaking her head, "twenty yards of silk for one dress."

It did seem outrageous, especially here in the middle of Montana, where the most important thing about clothing was functionality instead of fashion.

"I'm glad we made this dress in such a reasonable manner," Dianne said, turning back to the mirror. "I'll get lots of use out of it. Especially if we dye it like you talked about."

"I think it's lovely as it is. Wear it this way for a time and then dye it. It will be like having a completely new gown," Koko said, bringing the new bonnet they'd made for the occasion.

Charity had given over one of her straw bonnets, and Koko had used ribbon and lace to decorate it into a stylish wedding piece. She helped to fit it onto Dianne's carefully styled hair. Faith, although miserable in her latter days of pregnancy, had insisted on dressing Dianne's hair. The result was both elegant and simple.

Dianne looked into the mirror and guided the bonnet over the piled curls. "I feel so blessed. I could cry."

"Well, don't do that. You don't want Cole to think you're sad about this."

Dianne grinned. "He knows better than that. He already teases me about pushing him into this ceremony."

Koko laughed and handed Dianne a handkerchief. "Keep this just in case." She went to the bedroom door and opened it. "Now, if you're ready . . ."

Dianne looked at the open door. She would walk out of this room for the last time as a single woman. When next she returned, Cole would be with her and they would be husband and wife. A nervous trembling coursed through her. *Mrs. Cole Selby. I'll be Mrs. Cole Selby.*

Cole waited impatiently in the parlor for the wedding to begin. Reverend Hammond leaned over with a grin. "You're looking a bit green, Mr. Selby. Are you sure you aren't coming down with something?"

Charity overheard the comment and giggled. "Now, Ben. Don't you go picking on the poor boy. He's been through a great deal just to get this far."

Cole tried to concentrate on her amused words, but his mind

raced with thoughts. Were they doing the right thing, rushing ahead like this? Maybe they needed more time. After all, so much had happened. Maybe he wasn't the same man she loved. He looked up and caught sight of Takes Many Horses. He wore his very best clothing—a long deerskin shirt with beaded designs on the shoulder and neckline. Fringed buckskin hung from the sleeves, as did weasel tails. The shirt extended nearly to the top of the warrior's knees. Below, he wore tanned leather leggings that were also beaded and fringed. His coal black hair had been carefully parted and braided, and on his feet were new beaded moccasins, compliments of Koko.

Cole knew the man was in love with Dianne. He saw the haunted expression every time Takes Many Horses glanced her way. But Cole also knew the man was honorable, that he valued his honor too much to steal a few moments of pleasure. If Cole were to leave again for any extended amount of time, Takes Many Horses would be his first choice to guard and protect Dianne. That was the reason he'd asked the man to stand with him as best man at the wedding.

Takes Many Horses came forward and greeted Cole with a smile. "She's bound to look better than when she got back from the roundup."

"She looked perfect that day. There was absolutely nothing wrong with her."

Charity laughed. "Love is blind, Takes Many Horses. Didn't you know that?"

The man sobered and nodded. "Sometimes it must be."

Just then Koko appeared in the doorway. *She looks very fashionable,* Cole thought. *She could easily pass for a white woman.* Koko looked directly at him and smiled—almost as if she could read his mind.

Behind her came Dianne on the arm of Gus Yegen. She took his breath away. She had on a pretty dress to be sure, but it was the radiance of her face that held Cole's attention. He didn't want to look away even for a minute.

They quietly assembled, with Charity taking her place beside Faith and Malachi in the front row. Gus stood rock rigid between Cole and Dianne. If Cole didn't know better, he'd think Gus was actually her pa. He couldn't have been prouder.

"Who gives this woman to wed this man?" Ben asked.

"I do," Gus replied. He handed Dianne over to Cole, then surprised them all by planting a kiss on Dianne's cheek. "You're getting a fine little gal here," he told Cole. "You do right by her or you'll hear it from me."

Cole nodded, amazed that this rugged Texan could hold so much love for Dianne. "I promise you, I will."

They turned back to hear the words Ben shared. He spoke of the responsibility of marriage and of the life they would share. Cole barely heard the words. They seemed nonsensical and unnecessary. *Just say we're married,* he thought. *Just say the final words and I'll know she's mine forever.*

And finally the words came. "I now pronounce you man and wife. You may kiss your bride."

Cole pulled Dianne into his arms. "Happily," he whispered against Dianne's lips.

He lost himself in the kiss, cherishing the moment and the way Dianne seemed oblivious to the people who watched them. He might have gone on kissing her forever had Faith not cried out.

"It's the baby!" Faith said, then groaned and shut her eyes in concentration. "I'm sure sorry, Dianne. I thought it would wait," she said when the contraction ended.

Dianne pulled away from her husband. "We should get you upstairs to a room where you can lie down."

"No, I want to go back to my place," Faith asserted.

Malachi quickly lifted her in his arms.

There was a bustling of activity, and before Cole knew what had happened, Dianne was swept along with the others fussing over Faith.

Dianne pulled off her wedding bonnet and motioned to Charity. "Please run to my room and bring me back my brown calico. It's hanging in the wardrobe."

Charity never questioned that her friend was leaving her own wedding to assist in Faith's birthing. In fact, the thought only crossed Dianne's mind for a moment. Cole will understand, she told herself. Babies wait for no one.

Dianne went ahead of Malachi to the small cabin. She hurried to open the front door, then went in to open the bedroom door as well. Dianne pulled down the covers on the bed and motioned Malachi to deposit Faith. He lowered her, but Faith waved him away.

"Just let me sit a spell," she told him. "The pain's not so bad now."

"We women will take care of her now. You get some water on to boil and make a good strong pot of coffee as well. There's no telling how long this will take." Malachi backed out of the room, looking rather lost. "Don't worry, Malachi," Dianne said as she started to close the door and offered a comforting smile. "This time will be different. You'll see." She prayed her feelings on the matter were correct. *Please, Lord, let it be perfect this time.*

Dianne felt like an old hand at deliveries. She'd assisted with Koko's two babies and numerous calves and colts. Nothing was more rewarding or more frustrating.

"When did the pain start?" Dianne asked Faith.

"Early this morning, but it wasn't strong. I figured I had plenty of time. Didn't get bad until about the time Preacher Hammond started in on the service." She fumbled with a band that hooked just above her bulging stomach to cinch her blouse.

"Here, let me help you get out of your clothes," Dianne said, pushing Faith's hands aside in order to undo the belt. When Dianne began working the buttons on the oversized blouse, Faith took over.

"I can manage," she declared, looking to Dianne with a sober expression. She took to unfastening the buttons, all the while keeping her eyes on Dianne. "I wish I had your faith."

"Nonsense. You have your own—it's even your namesake." She smiled and began to unfasten her own cuffs. "You'll see. It will be all right."

Charity soon arrived with Dianne's dress. "Koko said she'd be here directly. She's going to change and then she'll come with her birthing bag."

Dianne nodded and took up the brown dress. "Please help me get out of this," she said, turning her back to Charity.

"I'm sure sorry about this, Dianne. It's your wedding day and you didn't even get to eat the cake we made," Faith said, struggling to get out of the blouse.

"Bah, don't worry about it. I'm honored that Baby Montgomery has decided to make his or her appearance today," Dianne said, stripping off the lovely ivory gown.

"Goodness, don't apologize," Charity threw in. "This just makes the day that much more special. The cake will wait. Unless, of course, the men decide to eat it without us, in which case we'll bake another one."

Faith laughed. "I can just see them sitting around looking at that cake—asking themselves what they should do—if they dare go ahead and cut a piece." The three women laughed together at this.

Dianne pulled on her dress, grateful that it buttoned in front. She cinched it with an apron, then went to work rolling up her sleeves just as Koko came through the door. "I told Gus and Cole they would have to take care of the children," she announced.

"You should have seen their faces."

"Probably because they're worried they won't get any cake," Dianne teased.

Koko looked at her oddly but said nothing. She went instead to help Charity get Faith into a nightgown.

The women worked together as if they'd been a team for a long, long time. With Faith standing beside the bed, they pulled a cotton nightgown over her head. The contractions soon gripped Faith again, and this time a gush of water came with the pain.

"What fortune to have you out of the bed," Charity declared. "Now you won't have to worry about drying out the mattress or changing your gown again." Dianne smiled. Charity was always the practical one.

They finally got Faith back to bed, and Koko quickly checked to see the progress of the baby. "The baby is down pretty far. If the contractions come steady and strong, it shouldn't take too long."

The afternoon passed quickly as the women chatted about the baby to come and how Dianne would probably be having children of her own this time next year.

"And miss roundup?" Dianne teased as she put a cold cloth to Faith's forehead.

"I can just see it now," Koko laughed. "She'll be bearing down in the back of the wagon, yelling for someone to let her see how many calves are being branded."

"Probably stamp the Diamond V on the poor baby's rump before he makes it back to the ranch," Charity teased.

Even Faith smiled at this, in spite of her almost constant pain. Dianne held her right hand, while Charity had the left.

"All right, Faith, the baby is very close," Koko announced.

"What if . . . what about . . . the cord," Faith gasped out.

"We're watching for that," Dianne assured. "Koko has her

knife ready just in case. Rest in the Lord, Faith. No matter what, He's already seen tomorrow."

Charity agreed. "Remember not even a sparrow falls but what the Lord doesn't know it. He's here with you right now. He won't leave you even for a moment."

"Push hard, Faith," Koko interjected. "Push . . . come on."

Dianne and Charity helped Faith to lean forward. Dianne knew Faith's pain was intense, but she knew the woman's fear was even stronger than the pain.

"All right, stop pushing. Hold it right there," Koko declared in an authoritative voice that left no room for argument.

Dianne watched as she gently rotated the baby's now delivered head, slipping the cord to one side as she did so. Faith, ever determined to do the right thing, froze in place, barely even breathing. Sweat beaded on her lip as she bit down on a piece of leather.

Koko smiled. "All right, push again. Let's get this baby born."

The baby's lusty cries filled the room. Faith fell back against her pillow, tears streaming down her face. "It's a good sound. A good sound."

Dianne nodded. "Look, Faith, it's a baby girl. You have a daughter!"

Faith looked up as Koko held the screaming child for her to see.

"What will you call her?" Koko asked.

Faith smiled and reached out to touch her daughter's head. "Mercy," she whispered. "Because God has been merciful."

Dianne nodded, wiping tears from her own eyes. "Indeed, He has been."

It was later, nearly midnight, by the time Dianne made her way to the small cabin where she and Cole had agreed to spend their wedding night. The cabin was actually one built as a storehouse during the early days of the ranch, but Charity and Koko had surprised Dianne by putting it together as a little honey-moon cabin.

Dianne wondered if Cole had completely given up on her. It was their wedding night, after all, and she'd run off to help her friend deliver a baby. She smiled. No, he'd understand.

As she approached the cabin, she saw him silhouetted in the open doorway. A soft light glowed from the room behind him. She began to tremble.

"How . . . did you know . . . I was coming?" she asked, feeling suddenly nervous.

"Just knew it," he replied, stepping forward. "Figured I'd carry you over the threshold—not for luck—just because I can't wait to get you in my arms again."

"Don't you even want to know about the baby?" she questioned as he lifted her up.

He nuzzled her neck, then kissed her nose. "Not now. You can tell me all about it tomorrow. Tonight belongs to us."

Dianne sighed and wrapped her arms around Cole's neck. It was the night she'd thought would never come—the night she would begin her new life as Mrs. Cole Selby.

CHAPTER 26

"I CAN'T BELIEVE THE TROUBLE WE'VE BEEN FORCED TO endure," Portia said in a sweet but clearly irritated tone.

Trenton was tired of the woman's complaining. Tired, too, of the things she did to lengthen the journey. When they'd reached Cheyenne, she'd forced a week's delay in order to, as she said it, "regain her composure." Trenton reminded her and Ned both that they were vulnerable to Indian attack out here on the plains, but neither one seemed overly worried. Cheyenne was, after all, a fair-sized settlement.

After a week of watching Portia simper over Ned, flattering him with every type of false adoration she could, Trenton was relieved when the woman finally announced she was ready to move on.

Of course, now it was May and the heat on the train was most unbearable. Not only this, but there had been stops in Laramie due to trouble on the tracks, then another delay in two other towns much smaller than Laramie or Cheyenne.

By the time they reached Corinne, Utah, Portia's company was wearing on Trenton like a bad summer cold. The woman was clearly up to more than traveling to Bozeman. She had her sights on Ned as husband material, and it was apparent that Ned was going to be more than happy to accommodate the woman.

Corinne, affectionately called a hell-on-wheels town from its days during the scurry to build the transcontinental railroad, was not an appealing little place. Pulling into the town in the dead of night, Trenton noted the place fairly crawled with all manner of two-legged vermin.

Named after a Union Pacific land agent's daughter, Corinne hadn't grown much past the tent-and-tarpaper grading camp that it had been upon its birth. Still, it was the main point of entry into the Montana Territory—unless of course one had the money to take a steamer up the Missouri River.

Trenton couldn't help but remember back to a time when that had been his plan. Now, here in the town ambitiously proposed as the "Chicago of the Rocky Mountains," Trenton wished only to move on. Perhaps it was because of the seediness, but it could just as easily be comments whispered by Portia that this seemed to be exactly his kind of town. He was rapidly coming to the place where he'd just as soon forget both Portia and Ned and take his horse and go ahead on his own.

Money talked in small towns, and Ned quickly arranged for accommodations at one of the sleeping establishments. Ned worried incessantly about Portia, however.

"I don't think it's safe to leave her alone," he said as Trenton returned from arranging for his horse with the railroad office.

"I think Mrs. McGuire is more than capable of seeing to herself," Trenton said with a yawn. He plopped down on the bed he would share with Ned. Pulling off his boots, he yawned again. "I'm sure even Corinne's prestigious population has to sleep sometime."

"But she's alone," Ned argued.

"She's right next door," Trenton replied, throwing his boots to the end of the bed.

"I intend to propose," Ned said matter-of-factly. "I want to marry her—hopefully before we return from Bozeman."

Trenton shook his head and shrugged out of his coat. "Ned, I wish you'd listen to reason. You know nothing about this woman."

"I know what I need to know—that she's wonderful," Ned replied quite seriously. He began undressing, but his mind was clearly on Portia. "I cannot imagine my life without her. I would die for that woman."

"You very well may die if you marry that woman. She's already lost two husbands."

Ned looked horrified. "You can hardly blame her for that."

"I wonder."

Trenton finished undressing and slipped into bed. Ned soon followed suit, turning down the lamp before pulling up the covers. The two men didn't say another word, but all night Trenton wrestled with dreams of Portia McGuire and Ned Langford.

———

Portia paced the small space of her room, which she found deplorable. Even the offer of additional money had not bettered their situation. The hotel clerk had merely shrugged and suggested she look elsewhere if she was dissatisfied.

"Dissatified! That's putting it mildly."

The entire trip had been an exercise in drudgery. If not for the incredibly wealthy Mr. Langford, Portia might very well have given up her promise and headed back East. Her father hardly deserved such personal notification.

Portia touched a cool cloth to her neck. The lawn nightgown was light enough, but the room was terribly stuffy, despite the open window.

"I must devise a plan to encourage the elusive Mr. Langford to propose," she muttered. "I know the man is interested—I know he wants nothing more than to know me better. Perhaps he's put off by the widow's weeds." She glanced to the black gown that hung on the back of her door.

"Maybe it's time for a change." After all, she'd been in black for the past four months. "Maybe I'll go shopping tomorrow and see if I can find something more suitable. Perhaps that will entice Mr. Langford."

Again she couldn't help but think of her strongest opposition: Mr. Chadwick. He was definitely a thorn in her side. If she could only rid herself of that man, she was certain to be able to bring old Ned into line. Chadwick was a mystery, but one that she hoped to solve soon. In Cheyenne she'd sent several telegraphs for information. All replies would be waiting for her in Virginia City, but she would have to be sure to give them enough time to check into Chadwick and get back to her.

"I believe another delay is in order," she said to herself.

Portia began to contemplate how she might slow their progress just enough to get the information she needed. Once she got the goods on Chadwick, she could easily manipulate him—controlling the situation in any way she chose.

"I could be ill," she said. "After all, this place is enough to make a person sick."

She despised the shoddy workmanship of her room, the lack of color or design. It was like a box and nothing more. A box with a window and a bed. If she were to remain in Corinne for long, she would have to have a better room. That would absolutely be necessary. On the morrow she would nose around and see if a boardinghouse with better facilities might be available. If so, she could easily delay their trip by a week, maybe two.

———————

Three weeks! It had taken three weeks to get from Corinne to Virginia City. Trenton could hardly contain his anger at the thought of it. Mrs. McGuire had once again fallen ill and insisted they remain in Corinne until she regained her strength. She told Ned it was the heat and her own weak constitution. Tearfully she had encouraged him to abandon her, to which Trenton had quickly agreed, but Ned would hear nothing of it.

Then there had been difficulties securing a place on a stage bound for Virginia City. Trenton had threatened to leave on his horse, but Ned had begged him to reconsider. He'd even offered Trenton money to stay.

In the end, Trenton stayed, but not for money or because his heart went out to the sickly Mrs. McGuire. No, he stayed because, quite frankly, he was caught up in the game. He felt almost as if he were reading a novel, and the only way to learn the ending was to continue through the parts he hated the most.

Virginia City was welcome civilization after Corinne. There were plenty of buildings to suggest a significant population, but it became very evident that the town had suffered loss.

"The gold ain't panning out like it used to," the livery owner told him when Trenton went to check his horse. He'd asked the old man why the town seemed strangely quiet.

"We still get a good holler up on Saturday night," the man said, "but we've lost many a good man. They all wander off to where the next strike promises fortune and fame."

Trenton nodded. "I'm sure." He glanced around the livery. "Do you have wagons or buggies for rent?"

"Nah, no real use for that," the old man said, then spit a stream of tobacco out the side of his mouth. "Don't rent horses neither."

"Well, I have a bit of a problem," Trenton said, scratching his stubbly chin. "How would a person go about getting transportation?"

"To where?"

Trenton chuckled. "I'm not exactly sure. I'm the nephew of Bram Vandyke. The name's Trenton Chadwick. I heard Uncle Bram had a ranch up this way on the Madison River. I was hoping to go see him. I have my mount, of course, but I have two friends who are afoot."

The old man eyed Trenton suspiciously. "You say you're Bram Vandyke's nephew?"

Trenton nodded. "I don't really know anything about him, though. Uncle Bram came out this way many years ago. I don't have much to go on, I know, but I was hoping maybe someone here in Virginia City would know him."

"Most folks in Virginia City would know him. Well . . . they knew him. He's passed on now."

"What?" Trenton felt his heart sink. "But my family came out here to live with him. My sister and two brothers, Zane and Morgan."

"I know your brothers well. Your sister too—quite a horsewoman. Seems to me your ma died sometime back."

Trenton nodded, remembering Dianne's long-ago letter explaining just that. "She died in '64."

The man appeared to relax, almost as if he'd been testing Trenton. "Your sister owns the Diamond V now—that was your uncle's ranch. She's quite a little pistol. Knows a good piece of horseflesh when she sees it and isn't afraid to work right alongside the boys."

Trenton laughed. "I can't imagine. She was sixteen when I saw her last." The memory pained him. They'd once been so very close. Then he'd driven a wedge between them by deserting the family. Thoughts of the past welled up inside. Maybe she'd blame him for everything. Maybe she wouldn't want to see him.

"Your sister married a couple months back. A feller named Selby. He appears to be a good man—honest fella. Saw 'im in town a few weeks past. As I heard it told, Selby was taken by the Indians while trying to make his way west. Savages robbed him of everything, so he had to restock hisself."

Dianne had married. The thought comforted Trenton, who had always worried about his little sister's welfare. After learning about their mother's death, Trenton had almost given up his way of life to go find his family. The cards were stacked against him, however. Nothing ever went well for him for too long.

"I can't imagine her married. She was just a girl when I saw her last. But I guess that has been—" he mentally did the math—"seven years." He shook his head. Dianne would be a woman full grown by now. He almost laughed out loud. In his thoughts of her she was still that sweet young girl who was always giving her opinion.

"How can I find her now?" he asked the man.

"The ranch is about twenty-five miles east and north. Maybe a little more. You can follow the main freight road, then there's a turnoff that will take you down toward the Madison. Diamond V is a big spread. Can't rightly say how big it is, although I heard tell they added on to their acreage just last year."

"And there's no wagons or horses to rent?" Trenton asked again, hoping the man would relent now that the man knew who he was.

"No, not a thing. Fact be told, your sister came in here a few weeks back and bought up most of the extra stock I had. At least the decent stock. I don't like to keep many horses around—the cost ain't worth it. Most folks know I'm not here for such things and don't come looking to me for it. I mostly board other folks' animals and keep the freight horses."

Trenton nodded. "Would there be someone I could maybe hire to take a message to the ranch? Perhaps my sister could come with transportation."

"Now, there's a right good idea. I'm sure one of the boys

around here would be mighty happy to do that. You'd have to pay 'em, of course, maybe even lend them your mount, but you could prob'ly have word back in a couple days."

Trenton didn't like the idea of lending his horse to anyone, but he was sure that if he lost the animal, Ned would buy him a new one.

"Well, point me in the direction of a reliable young man—not some no-account," Trenton said.

The man grinned. "I know just the one."

————

"I suppose if all we can do is wait," Ned began rather slowly, "then that is what we must do."

"It shouldn't be more than a day or two. Nothing like the weeks we've already endured," Trenton said with a sarcastic glance at Portia.

"A day or two is certainly fine," Portia said, her tone lacking emotion.

Trenton never failed to be amazed at the young woman and her many faces. Sometimes she was the pouting, simpering belle of the ball, and other times, like now, she played the part of fragile, stoic widow.

"Of course you're right, Portia," Ned said, reaching over to pat her hand. "I suppose I'm just overly anxious to speak with your father."

She smiled at this and then looked at Trenton with an expression that suggested triumph. *So he's proposed. Why else would he talk freely of wanting to speak to her father?* The thought of Ned marrying the conniving widow sickened Trenton. *He's a grown man . . . let him make his own way. If she's in it for his money, he'll soon know that.*

Trenton could tell by the way she studied him that Portia was hoping he'd reveal understanding of Ned's statement, but instead he played dumb. Why give her any satisfaction?

Trenton toyed with his coffee cup, then motioned the woman who'd served them to come fill it up again. Ned, however, got to his feet. "I'm going to step outside and smoke a cigar. I shouldn't be long."

Trenton figured Portia would offer to join him, suggesting they take a long stroll or some other such nonsense. Apparently Ned thought she might too, because he waited for a moment looking directly at her.

Instead of paying him much attention, Portia pointed to her coffee cup. "I'd like another serving. Also, please bring me some cream."

The woman poured the coffee while nodding. "I'll be right back with it."

"Well, then, I'm off," Ned said, again sounding as though he expected Portia or Trenton to stop him—or join him.

The woman returned as Ned walked to the door. Trenton was irritated that Portia had chosen to remain behind. He supposed he'd be forced to answer some stupid question about his sister or the ranch. Questions he really had no answers for.

"I suppose you wonder why I stayed here," Portia said, her voice smooth, charming.

"No, not really. I can't say as I care," Trenton replied before taking a drink.

"You probably should," she said, leaning closer. "I intend to marry Ned." Her tone changed, as did the countenance of her once emotionless face. Now pinched, almost severe in her anger, Portia's expression reminded Trenton of his mother when she would lecture him about sneaking out in the middle of the night.

"I do not brook fools, Mr. Chadwick," she said very slowly. "You are a fool if you think to try and stop this wedding."

Trenton remained unmoved. He matched her stare with his own gaze of contempt. "You hardly worry me, Mrs. McGuire."

"Then that is your mistake, Mr. Chadwick," she spoke with emphasis on his name. "I am not a woman to be toyed with. I'm not some simpleton you may push around or force your will upon. You would do well to see me for what I am."

"A snake in the grass?" Trenton asked with a mischievous grin. "I figured that out a long time ago."

She sat up straighter, rigid and tight. Her face went nearly blank again as she recomposed herself. "Stay out of my way, Chadwick. I mean it. Stay out of my way, or I'll make you sorry you didn't."

Trenton laughed. "And what do you propose to do if I don't?"

Her smile was bone-chilling. "Whatever it takes, Trenton dear. Whatever it takes."

CHAPTER 27

"I CAN'T BELIEVE HE'S REALLY HERE," DIANNE SAID AS SHE rode beside Cole on the way to Virginia City. Trenton had been a ghostly memory relegated to the past these last few years. She would think of him from time to time, dust off the images of their childhood, and remember the closeness they'd shared. Then just as quickly as the thoughts had come, she would put them away.

"I wonder what his circumstance is," Cole replied. "His message really didn't give us much to go on."

"Well, he's with friends who are trying to get to Fort Ellis. We know that much." She'd brought two extra horses and a wagon, not really knowing what all was needed. Trenton had only mentioned that he had his own mount, but that the woman and man traveling with him were without transportation. Dianne had no idea how much baggage they would be transporting or whether they could sit a horse, but either way they should have things under control. Cole had even seen fit to bring Gabe and Levi along to drive the wagon and handle the luggage and anything else they would need to bring to the ranch.

"Still, it seems kind of strange that he just suddenly shows up," Cole said.

Dianne smiled as he reined back on Jack. Cole had taken to riding the black in hopes of bringing him in step. The horse did a little side stepping out of orneriness, then settled back into line.

"It is odd," she said, "especially since he never bothered to write these last few years to tell me where he was or what he was doing. But I have to say I'm happy to be seeing him again."

Cole met her gaze. He looked worried, Dianne thought. She wasn't sure why he should be so uneasy, but then again, she had to admit to her own apprehension. What would it be like to see Trenton after all these years? And who were the man and woman traveling with him? Had he married? Was the woman his wife?

They topped the hill that finally allowed them to look down on Virginia City. She pushed aside her worries and smiled at her husband. "I'm sure it'll be all right. I've prayed so long for this, I can't see how it could be a bad thing."

Virginia City had calmed considerably over the years since gold was first found in Alder's Gulch. As territorial capital, it boasted nearly nine hundred citizens, but that was a far cry from the thousands who had flooded the city in the early 1860s.

Dianne had been surprised at how quickly a town could empty of people when she'd first gone back after its mass desertion. Still, the place held a kind of charm in spite of its worn appearance. There was a great deal of civic pride, and new fraternal orders, social clubs, and even a theater group had been formed in the years since the town first enjoyed its stampede. Of the people who chose to remain in Virginia City, nearly a third were Chinese who came to clean up in the gold fields after the whites deserted their claims. Dianne found the Chinese to be a most unusual people. Their manner of dress alone was fascinating; at times the women wore the most beautiful outfits of silk and cording. Dianne wouldn't have minded having such a garment herself.

They made their way to the hotel Trenton had noted in his letter. Dianne wondered if she would recognize her brother after all this time. When they'd parted company so long ago, there was still enough boy in him that he wore a look of innocence and youth. Dianne was certain that would be gone.

A man stepped out from the hotel door and watched them as they approached. His face was shadowed by the black hat he wore. He watched her for a moment, then raised his head, revealing a weary expression. Dianne instantly saw that it was Trenton. He wore the look of a man who'd seen more of life than he cared to. But it was his eyes that haunted her the most. They seemed so sad.

Cole and Dianne stopped their mounts in front of the hotel. "Trenton?" Dianne called as she dismounted.

The man stepped forward. "Look at you. You're all grown up."

Dianne grinned. "So are you, big brother." She grabbed him and hugged him tightly. "Why haven't you written me all these years? I should have Cole take you out back for all the grief and worry I've suffered over you." She felt unexpected tears come to her eyes and pulled away. "Are you all right?" she whispered.

Trenton smiled, but it didn't quite seem genuine. "I'm as right as the day is long, little sister."

"Well, around here you'll find the days last a sight longer than down Missouri way," Cole interjected. Cole handed the reins over to Levi. "Take 'em on down to the livery and get them watered and fed. We'll head back out in an hour." Levi took the reins and he and Gabe started down the street.

Cole turned back and Dianne made the introductions. "Trenton, this is my husband, Cole Selby. We were just married this last April."

The two men seemed to size each other up, then Trenton smiled again and shook Cole's extended hand. "Treat her right," Trenton said in greeting.

Cole seemed unaffected by the command. "Wouldn't dream of doing it any other way."

Dianne looked around for Trenton's friends. "Where are the others? Are they here at the hotel?"

Trenton frowned. "They've gone for a walk. Should be back soon."

"I hope so," Cole replied. "We intend to load up and head right back. With the extra light, we needn't wait until tomorrow, and the road's good, so the horses won't have to strain through mud."

Dianne agreed. "That's why we left the ranch as soon as we could. We wanted to get you back to the ranch, where we could give you decent food and shelter."

"I'll be glad for that," Trenton replied. "Been living out of saddlebags for too long." He looked past Dianne and scowled. "Here they come."

Dianne turned to look but couldn't get over the tone of obvious contempt. "Who are they, Trenton?"

"That's a friend of mine, Ned Langford. He's the son of a wealthy silver mine owner. The woman is, as best I can tell, a gold digger who's trying at every turn to hook her fingers into Ned's fortune."

"Why do you say that?" Dianne questioned as Cole stepped closer to her, as if to protect her.

Trenton shook his head. "I can't really say for sure what it's all about. Guess we can talk about it on the ride home. The point is, I just don't trust her. I don't think any of you should."

"Why, Trenton," the woman said in a silky voice, "do tell me this is your sister."

"Dianne, this is Mrs. Portia McGuire and Mr. Ned Langford." He turned from her to his friends. "My sister, Dianne Chadwick . . . I mean Selby."

Dianne sized up the woman as she drew near. Her exotic features seemed pinched in the strong June sun, yet she was very beautiful. Portia's dark brown eyes seemed to take in everything at once. She looked at Cole and smiled rather enticingly. "And you are?"

"Cole Selby." His reply was short and curt.

"My sister's husband," Trenton added.

Portia shifted her parasol and extended her gloved hand. Dianne thought a wide-brimmed cowboy hat would have served the woman better than her flimsy blue parasol but said nothing.

"Mrs. McGuire, we are pleased to meet you," Dianne finally said, reaching out to take hold of Portia's hand so that Cole wouldn't have to.

Portia looked rather disappointed but only smiled. "Mrs. Selby, it's good of you to extend hospitality to strangers."

Dianne could see why Trenton felt uneasy about the woman. There was something about this woman that smelled phony. "Well, the real hospitality will have to wait until we're back at the ranch, I'm afraid."

"And we plan to head back there as soon as the horses are rested up—probably in less than an hour," Cole stated for all to hear.

Ned Langford finally joined in the conversation. "I'm Ned Langford, Mr. Selby. Good to meet you." He turned to Dianne and tipped his hat. "Mrs. Selby, I'm delighted to finally meet you."

Dianne smiled. The man seemed very sincere in his greeting. "Our pleasure. But Cole is right. We haven't a great deal of time. It's quite a journey home, and we need you all to gather your things."

"I'd rather we wait until tomorrow," Portia said in a pout.

She turned to Ned and spoke again. "Could we not stay just one more day? I'm very tired of traveling."

"No, we can't wait another day," Trenton said, his voice edged with anger. "My sister and her husband have come all this way to help us out. We'll go when they tell us to go."

Ned seemed in agreement but offered Portia comfort. "I'm sorry, my dear. I know you're tired, but I'm sure Trenton is right. The Selbys have been gracious to come all this way to offer us transportation. We shouldn't delay them."

Portia looked at Dianne and let her gaze travel the length of her body. Dianne knew her riding outfit was old and well-worn. She hadn't come here, however, hoping for fashion approval or critique. Hoping to head off any comment, Dianne smiled. "You'll want to dress more appropriately, Mrs. McGuire. There's nothing between here and home but miles of wild country. You won't be all that comfortable in silk."

Portia touched the collar of her gown and then looked to Ned. "I don't have the constitution to ride twenty-five miles on horseback."

Dianne heard her husband give a brief snort before saying, "That won't be a problem, ma'am. We've got a wagon. You can ride in it. We'll spend the night at the halfway point."

———

Later, as they made their way up the freight road for home, Dianne rode in close step beside her brother. "She's a very determined woman," Dianne murmured. "I'll give you that."

"She's obnoxious," Trenton replied. "The woman has been nothing but grief since she passed by our table and pretended to faint."

"She did what?" Dianne asked, all the time watching Portia McGuire as she struggled to maintain her seat in the bouncing wagon.

"We're having breakfast at a hotel back in Denver. She comes by the table and grabs at her throat and then faints. I had to catch her for fear of her landing in my lap."

"Oh my," Dianne said, stifling a giggle. "I'll bet that was quite the scene."

"She gave us some sad song about her mother dying and being a widow. I suppose it was all true, but still, she's working Ned like a faro dealer. She knows the cards he's holding, and she wants them all."

"Is that why she's traveling with you—to get to him?"

Trenton shook his head. "We've actually accompanied her. She has business in Bozeman—at Fort Ellis, actually. Her mother passed on, as I mentioned, and she's here to bring word to her father, who happens to be a soldier at the fort."

Dianne's mind traveled back in time. "How sad. It's hard to lose a mother."

"I'm sorry I wasn't here for you, Dianne. I know it couldn't have been easy losing the girls and then Ma. Seems I've always let you down."

"Nonsense," Dianne said, pushing aside her sorrow. "A man has to do what he feels is necessary. I do have a question for you, however."

He eyed her with a raised brow. "What is it?"

"Did you ever feel that you managed to avenge Pa's death?"

Trenton shook his head. "No. I managed to make a mess of that as well. I might as well tell you, I've done things you wouldn't approve of. I've not lived a good life at times."

"The past doesn't matter. What matters is that you're here. How long will you stay?"

Trenton looked ahead to where the wagon jostled down the road about a quarter mile ahead of them. "I'd like to stay on—at least for a time. I don't rightly know what I'm good at and what

I'm not. I know that may sound foolish, given that I'm twenty-six years old."

"We all have to find our way, Trenton. You may find you take to ranching. You're more than welcome to live here as long as you like. In fact, if you take to it well enough and want to start your own place, you can either homestead land nearby or we'll deed you part of ours."

"That's mighty generous. How does your husband feel about this?"

"Cole completely agrees. I wouldn't have offered if not. You see," Dianne slowed her horse, "the ranch really should belong to Koko and her children. But because she's of Indian blood, the laws in the territory are rather strange. Uncle Bram was told different things by different lawyers and finally decided he'd add my name to the deed, and the property would come to me to keep Koko from being put off the land on some technicality. However, I had to pledge to always give his family a home—which of course was not an issue."

"I see," Trenton replied, wiping his forehead with the back of his sleeve. This pushed his hat back, giving Dianne a better view of his face. She was surprised to see a thin scar on his right jawline.

"What happened to give you that scar?" she asked.

"Knife in the hands of the wrong person."

She looked at her brother. "I feel that you're keeping things from me."

"Like I said, I haven't lived the kind of life a person feels free to talk about. Let's just let it go at that." They rode in silence for several minutes before Trenton added, "I do have some ranch experience. I worked on a place in Texas for a time. Seems I have the balance and endurance for breaking horses." He grinned. "Would that be useful to you?"

Dianne laughed. "I think we could probably stand having

another wrangler around. Especially one with that kind of talent."

Trenton laughed. "It's been a while—might take some getting used to."

Dianne nodded. "You can take all the time you like."

Up ahead, the wagon had come to a stop, and it appeared that Mrs. McGuire was in need of a moment's privacy. Trenton frowned and Dianne could tell he held much disdain for the woman.

"I'm sorry about having her here."

Dianne turned to her brother. "She's a part of what brought you home, so I won't complain."

"She's got a mean streak. You need to be warned."

Dianne laughed out loud. "I've been through blizzards and bear attacks, deaths and births. I've dealt with Indians and ranch hands, prejudices of every kind, and loneliness that ate my soul raw. I think I can handle Mrs. McGuire."

"I hope you're right," he replied, pulling back on the reins to stop his horse.

Dianne did likewise and turned to her brother. "Everything will work out, you'll see. God has a plan even in bringing Mrs. McGuire to the Diamond V."

CHAPTER 28

PORTIA HAD TO ADMIT THE DIAMOND V WAS AN IMPRESSIVE ranch. The house itself boasted some very modern designs and was a far cry from the log cabin structure she'd expected to find. After enjoying a tour of the house and immediate grounds, she had settled into a nice guest room near the top of the stairs. The room, she'd learned, had once been inhabited by Dianne Selby.

"I enjoyed this room very much when I used it for my own," Dianne had told her that first night. "Since then, however, my husband has worked to finish a few of the other rooms, and we now have our bedroom down the hall."

Portia was impressed with the delicate rose wallpaper in the room. It complemented the intricate design of the bed quilt and the draperies. The bed itself was of a fine quality wood, boasting the softest down-filled mattress she had ever known. Her first night had been quite pleasant—probably the first truly good sleep she'd had since taking off on this northern excursion. The nights that followed, however, had Portia awake half the night, plotting and planning how she might get close to Dianne Selby. After all, the woman and her husband owned this massive estate, complete with livestock and workers. There had to be a great deal of money involved.

But these people were a strange bunch. Dianne Selby seemed just as difficult to handle as her brother. What was it about this family that caused such distrust and apprehension?

"It's certainly a challenge," Portia told herself as she finished putting the final touches on her hair. One thing she had definitely decided: she would have to hire a girl to travel with her and see to her clothes and hair. The idea of constantly seeking help from hotel maids or housekeepers in order to adjust her corset or button up her gowns was a great irritation to Portia. Even here at the Diamond V, it seemed that most of the work was done by the family and a few others. Besides, house staff could often be paid to share information about their employers.

"I should encourage Mrs. Selby to get some regular staff in the house. It must be a drudgery having to keep things clean."

Of course, there was the Indian woman. Dianne had introduced her as her aunt. Portia shuddered at the thought of mixing blood in the family. The Chadwicks' uncle must have been a heathen, she decided, for what other reason could possess a man to marry such a woman?

There was also a black woman—Faith. Yes, that was her name. Portia had made the mistake of presuming she was a house servant, but then the woman actually sat down to luncheon with them. It so stunned Portia that she nearly commented, but Mrs. Selby saved her the trouble.

"Faith is a good friend of mine. We met on the wagon train west. She and her husband run a blacksmith shop here on the ranch."

Portia pretended the information didn't bother her, but it did. She looked down and smoothed the dark green gown. Ned had been surprised when she'd rid herself of the black, but it was a pleasant surprise by his own account. Portia particularly liked

this gown because the neckline scooped rather low, compliment-
ing her more feminine qualities.

"Well, I might as well go among them," she told herself and
headed for the door. "After all, if I'm to accomplish anything, I
must learn what I can." She smiled at the delicious bits of news
she had already managed to gather on Trenton Chadwick. The
telegraphed replies she'd picked up in Virginia City had given
her new thoughts regarding how to deal with him. *That man
should no longer prove to be a problem. I seriously doubt he'd want his
sister to know what an unsavory past he's known.*

"Portia!" Ned declared as she descended the stairs, "I feared
you might be ill."

Portia smiled sweetly. "No, I'm feeling much better. The rest
here has done wonders for me. I'm sure I'll be up to traveling by
the end of the week." She took hold of his arm and allowed him
to escort her to breakfast.

Dianne looked up from where she poured coffee into her
husband's cup. "Good morning, Mrs. McGuire. How did you
sleep?"

"Quite well, thank you." She allowed Ned to help her sit.
The breakfast looked amazingly good. There were platters of
fried potatoes, scrambled eggs, and stacks of bacon strips on her
end of the table. At the other end there appeared to be biscuits,
gravy, and a bowl of cinnamon apples. Portia found the mixed
aroma quite appealing.

Dianne finished pouring coffee, offering Portia her choice
between the dark heady brew and a lighter tea. "I'd love some
tea. I'm particularly fond of the spicy Oriental blends."

"This is a wonderful mix that my aunt created. I think you'll
enjoy it." Dianne went to the sideboard and changed out the
pots. Pouring the tea, she smiled, but Portia thought her stance
rather rigid.

Portia noted this morning that Faith and her husband were

absent. Mrs. Vandyke and her children were seated on the opposite side of the table, while Mr. and Mrs. Hammond were seated to Portia's left. Together with Ned and Trenton, there were ten people gathered round the table.

"Ben, would you offer the blessing?" Cole asked as he had every morning meal they'd shared. The entire ritual caused Portia a great deal of discomfort. Angus had been a very religious man, and it had nearly driven her mad.

"Amen," she heard the folks repeat in unison.

She opened her eyes and smiled. "It's so good to be among Christian folk again," she said, taking the platter of eggs offered her by Charity Hammond.

"Poor child, were you long traveling to get here?"

She nodded and accepted the platter. "It was truly a misery. Had Ned, I mean Mr. Langford, and Mr. Chadwick not helped me in my ordeal, I might never have made it this far." Mr. and Mrs. Hammond hadn't been present when Portia arrived, so the older woman hadn't heard Portia's tales of woe.

The food was passed around in an orderly fashion, and when everyone had taken what they wanted, the meal began. Portia nibbled on a biscuit, trying hard to give the appearance of disinterest when in fact she was starved. She'd played ill the last few days, hoping to gain a little more time before heading to Fort Ellis. She wanted very much to know if there was anything at the Diamond V that could benefit her more than Ned could.

"Your ranch is lovely, Mrs. Selby. I've been quite amazed at the flowers and garden, as well as the beautiful horses."

Dianne looked up from near the end of the table. "Thank you," she replied. "Not one of us could do it without the other. Running a ranch takes a team of people all willing to pull their weight."

Portia wondered if the woman were being snide in her remark, but there was no edge to her voice that might suggest it.

"Since you're feeling better," Mrs. Selby began again, "I thought maybe you'd like a real tour of the ranch—on horseback."

Portia had just picked up her cup to sip her tea. She paused thoughtfully. "That sounds wonderful. Ned, would you be able to join us?" She didn't even bother with the pretense of formality.

Ned, who couldn't keep his gaze from her, nodded enthusiastically. "I would love to accompany you both."

"I'll be along as well," Cole interjected, then added, "What about you, Trenton? Care to make the ride?"

Trenton looked to Cole and then to Portia. He grinned. "I suppose I could be persuaded."

"Wonderful!" Dianne went back to eating, as did Cole, but Trenton held Portia's gaze, leaving her most uncomfortable. Why did he have to constantly interfere in her life? Portia wanted to say something—hint at her findings and how she could condemn him in the eyes of his family—but she knew that was a card to hold until later. *I can bear up under this,* she reminded herself. *The goal is in sight, and soon I'll be the wife of Ned Langford. At least for a little while.*

———

Within the week many of the same party that had shared a meal around the Diamond V breakfast table found themselves east of Bozeman. Dianne had been convinced that accompanying Ned and Portia would be a wise choice. Neither of them was familiar with the area, and the last thing she wanted was for them to lose their way. Trenton had agreed to come because of the possibility of seeing Zane again, and Charity and Ben wanted to visit with the area pastors.

Dianne leaned closer to Cole as they waited for a post runner to find Sergeant Samson Brady and Corporal Zane Chadwick.

"What do you suppose Mrs. McGuire's father is really like?" she whispered over her shoulder.

"I hope he's nothing like his daughter. Otherwise I pity the men he commands."

Dianne giggled and looked into her husband's eyes. "Perhaps I should become spoiled like Mrs. McGuire. Would you fret over me if I lounged in bed until noon?" She batted her eyelashes.

Cole grinned. "I'd fret over you if you lounged in bed until six. That woman is an absolute pain in the neck."

Trenton came over about that time. "I heard the words *pain in the neck*. You must be discussing our dear Portia."

Dianne shook her head. "It's so hard to have Christian charity when she acts so completely uncharitable. She insults my friends and family at every turn."

"Not to mention the way she insults you personally," Trenton threw in.

"That's for sure," Cole said. "I thought I was going to have to have words with her the other night when she made that comment about your cooking."

Dianne shrugged. "I can bear my own insults. It's when she demeans Koko or Faith or the babies for the color of their skin or suggests that the ranch hands are stealing from us when things go missing that I see red."

"I'd count the silver after she goes," Trenton said snidely. "She seems to have a real hunger for it."

"Does Ned truly intend to marry her?" Dianne asked her brother.

"I'm afraid so. I've tried to talk sense into him, but he won't hear it. He's already wired his father and told him that they'll be married here and come back East as soon as she settles matters with her own father. Portia wants to have a wedding trip to New York before they return to Denver and settle back in to the silver mining business."

"Maybe it will all work out," Dianne said, not really believing it. Portia McGuire was a selfish woman who had little regard for others. Watching her now as she waited for her father's appearance, Dianne prayed for the grace to accept the frustrating woman and treat her kindly.

Dianne saw Zane first. He looked good—lean and tall in his uniform. He'd regained the title of corporal, and from letters she'd had from him, she knew he figured he might be promoted soon. Beside him, a man with graying black hair and dark eyes wore the stripes of a sergeant and the cynical look of one who was about to encounter a well-known enemy.

The man stopped as he reached Portia. Eyeing her without a smile, he spoke. "Daughter."

"Hello, Father," Portia snapped back. "I thought you were retiring from all this nonsense."

"And I thought you were happily occupied in Scotland."

"My husband died," she said, the hate evident in her voice. "Not that I suppose you would care."

"Your mother isn't here. I figured you'd know that. She's in Denver setting up house for us."

Portia sneered. "No, she's not. She died at the end of March. She had cancer—there was nothing they could do."

Dianne nearly gasped at the heartless manner in which Portia delivered the news. The man's face paled considerably. Everyone was so stunned they froze in place, staring at the widower.

"This can't be true," Sergeant Brady said in a hoarse voice.

"Do you know any other reason I would come to this wretched country?" She narrowed her eyes and shifted her parasol. "Mother made me promise to come and tell you in person. So now I have."

"Now, Portia dear," Ned began, reaching out to pat her arm in a comforting manner, "you're just overwrought. The heat of the day is upon you, and the trip here was quite long."

"I'm fine," she said, her tone guarded. She continued to glare at her father as though she could further hurt him.

The man turned to go, then stopped. Looking back at his daughter, he said, "I suppose I should thank you."

"You needn't bother. I didn't do it for you—I did it for her."

Ned couldn't help himself at this point. Dianne watched as he maneuvered himself between Portia and her father. "Sir, I would like to ask for your daughter's hand in marriage. I know it's not the most appropriate time or place, but I love her."

Brady looked up and shook his head. "Then I pity you. You're welcome to her, but she'll never love you. She's incapable of love. Has been all her life."

"That's not true, old man," Portia cried, pushing Ned aside. "I loved my mother. She was the only one who ever truly loved me. I loved her and would gladly have seen you in her place, dying a slow, painful death. Just like the one you inflicted upon us all of our lives."

Brady turned to walk away. "Like I said, you're welcome to her."

Portia waited until her father was gone to break into tears. Ned looked up apologetically. "If you don't mind, I'd like to drive her back to Bozeman. She needs to rest, and I can get us rooms at the hotel there."

"Go ahead," Cole replied. "We have our mounts."

Ned nodded and encircled Portia with his arm. "Come along, my dear. The sun is too much for you."

When they'd gone, Zane looked to Dianne as if for explanation. Dianne shook her head. "Don't ask. There's no reasonable explanation for what you just witnessed here."

"Who was she?"

"Sergeant Brady's daughter," Dianne replied. "But of course, you already realize that. She came north with Trenton and Mr. Langford."

"Trenton?" Zane looked at the remaining three people. Recognition touched his eyes. "I was so taken by that display, I didn't even recognize you."

Trenton stepped forward and the brothers embraced. "Good to see you, Zane. Have you had word from Morgan?"

"I had a brief note. He's gotten himself involved in some exploration team that plans to go south along the Yellowstone. They'll be here in August. Plan to come here on the chance they can talk old Major Baker out of an army escort. I haven't had a chance to write him back."

"Maybe he'll come through the Madison Valley," Dianne said hopefully.

"No, I don't think that's the plan. Didn't sound like it, leastwise. You can read the letter if you want. I left it in my quarters."

"Can you get away from the fort?" Cole asked. "We'd like to take you to dinner in town."

"I might be able to wrangle that. I'll see if I can borrow a horse. It's too hot to ride double and much too hot to hike three miles."

Cole nodded. "We'll wait for you here. See what you can do."

Zane smiled. "It'll be good to sit and jaw with you. Especially you, Trent. It's been seven years—you had to have lived a lot in that time."

Trenton frowned. "Probably too much."

———————

They passed the evening in pleasant conversation about the state of the world and of the past they'd been unable to share. Trenton was limited with his dialogue. He talked of ranch work in Texas and of meeting and helping an old man in Missouri. Cole listened to the stories, realizing that his wife's brother was uncomfortable discussing his past. He couldn't help but wonder why. By the time Zane left to return to his post, the brothers had made plans to meet up at the ranch and have a real time of reunion.

The next morning at breakfast, Cole helped Dianne into her chair and leaned down to whisper. "Are you all right?" She'd been so quiet in their hotel room that morning—almost as if she, too, were trying to put all the pieces into place where Trenton was concerned.

"I'm tired," she admitted but looked up to smile. "As I recall, someone kept me awake much too late last night."

Cole grinned and leaned back down to whisper, "I like keeping you awake."

He watched his wife's cheeks flush red as he sat down beside her. He was about to make a further statement when Trenton came to join them. Charity and Ben weren't far behind.

"Good morning, my dears," Charity said as she allowed Ben to seat her. "You all look very fine this morning."

"Dianne's tired," Cole commented with a winning smile. He groaned softly as his wife planted her boot heel in his shin. Charity never had a chance to reply because Ned and Portia entered the restaurant in a burst of energy and laughter.

"You may congratulate us, old man," Ned said as he approached Trenton. "We were just married."

Portia smiled at them with a complete look of victory. "Yes," she said, extending her hand. "It's all legal now."

CHAPTER 29

December 1875

DIANNE STOOD ON THE FRONT PORCH, HER HAND SETTLED gently atop her extended abdomen. She would have a baby in a matter of weeks, maybe days. It was an exciting time for the Selbys—for all on the Diamond V. The expected first baby for Cole and Dianne gave great joy to those who shared their lives, but no more so than to the parents, who had waited for four long years to conceive.

Dianne was scared, as was to be expected. She had been present at Koko's birthings of Jamie and Susannah, and she had shared in Faith's deliveries of Mercy and Daniel, born just a year ago on the Fourth of July. But this was different. This was her own child. And she knew firsthand that childbirth was difficult. Susannah had nearly died being born prematurely, and Mercy had the cord around her neck, though Koko had aptly dealt with that. Daniel, too, had been a difficult delivery. He had a larger head than most and had troubled Faith something fierce in the birthing.

Still, Dianne tried not to worry. But on days like today when the winter air was biting and held the scent of snow, Dianne couldn't help but think of her mother. She had died close to Christmas back in '64. She would have delivered a baby any day, but she wandered away in a drug-induced stupor, fearful that her children, who'd actually died on the trail, were out there some-where—alive—waiting for her to find them. The memory pained Dianne every time she thought of it. She had been her mother's caretaker, and Dianne had failed to keep her safe. For years she'd tried to deal with the guilt. She'd given it to God over and over but still couldn't shake the nagging feeling that she was to blame.

Dianne leaned against the railing and sighed. This was the happiest time of her life, but the hints of sorrow were enough to drape shadows over her joy. She had lived in the Montana Ter-ritory for over ten years, and in that time she had witnessed a tremendous growth and development for the territory. New people were moving in at an alarming rate. Copper mines were added to those of silver and gold, and with money to be made, crowds were bound to gather.

Still, the land was hard and unforgiving. Mistakes were sel-dom easy to overcome and were dealt in the details of life and death. Winters varied from mild to fierce. There were years they lost cattle to blizzards and sub-zero temperatures and years where they were blessed with few predators and multiple births. The cattle herd, thanks to Gus's capable direction, had grown to just over a thousand head. They helped to supply beef to the area forts and often sold to other ranchers who were looking to better their lines. Gus continued to bring in new additions from down south, but all in all, the herd was advancing nicely. The horses of the Diamond V were also earning a great reputation. Dianne found herself constantly dealing with ranchers and army officials who requested new mounts or strings of good cattle horses. The business was quite lucrative, and she and Cole had talked of hir-ing on additional help to wrangle.

In spite of this boon to their ranching economy, however, Indian troubles were all around them. Over the last few years the government had gotten serious about restricting the use of liquor, and prohibition had come in full to the Indians. Of course, enforcing the law against liquor use was difficult due to the number of whiskey peddlers and the great love of firewater among the Blackfoot people and other tribes.

The Blackfoot Wars, as some had come to call the conflicts with that particular tribe of people, were settling down. There were even rumors—wishful thinking most likely—that an agreement between the Blackfoot and the government was soon to be signed. In 1874 Congress reduced the Blackfoot lands, stating that they had grossly overestimated the number of actual residents. Dianne saw it as nothing more than a ploy to further cheat the Real People out of their land. When Little Plume, a chief who did not take to liquor himself, became chief over the tribe, working closely with two other leaders, White Calf and Generous Woman, the white people hoped this would mean peace. The conflict with the Sioux, however, was unaffected.

With gold discovered in the Black Hills, the Sioux had found themselves displaced once again, with a frightful inpouring of whites to the Dakota hills. The names of leaders like Crazy Horse and Sitting Bull were often discussed among army folk. Zane had speculated that a major conflict was bound to come upon them and soon. The Indians already positioned in the Montana Territory were resentful of the newcomers, as they'd always been. It was no different that these tribes were suffering the same grievances that plagued the Blackfoot, Assiniboine, Kutenai, and Gros Ventre. The tribes that had always lived on these northwest plains and mountain regions did not wish to share their heritage with the Sioux, Cree, Shoshone, and Arapahoe. But still they came, just as the whites came.

Dianne felt sorry for the tribes, but not sorry enough to leave the land. She felt confident that a means could be established for the two groups to live together peaceably, but the government did not see it that way. Unfortunately, neither did most of the newcomers.

Towns were springing up everywhere, and with them came more politicians and government. Dianne didn't mind the civilizing of the West. What she hated was that the newcomers were demanding to make it over in the image of the East. But if the eastern dudes wished to continue eating their large steaks and lamb chops, they would have to leave room for ranchers to raise their animals. Already there was talk of fencing and registering ranches and limiting free range. Cole and Gus talked about the issue often, and Dianne could see the flurry of conflicts that stood just beyond their door.

"You feeling all right?"

Dianne turned and saw that Zane had come to check on her. "Yes, I'm fine. Just thinking about all the strife and how much the territory has changed."

He came to join her. He looked handsome in his uniform of blue. Dianne noted the dark red neckerchief. Most of the men in the western army wore scarves of some sort to keep out the dust—especially during storms, when the wind blew harsh against their faces. Still, Dianne knew the army hadn't regulated these scarves. Zane wore a scarf to match the unit of men he once again commanded. He was mighty proud of having regained his sergeant stripes.

"Your men will be glad to have you back, but I shall miss you," Dianne said, leaning over to hug her brother. "I wish you could stay until Christmas. That's just a week and a half away."

"I know, but there are others who'd like to share Christmas elsewhere, and I'm trying to be a considerate man." He grinned, but it was hard to see his mouth under his newly acquired lip hair.

Dianne hadn't gotten used to his mustache. It was very thick and gave him the look of one much older than his twenty-nine years. "Twenty-nine."

"What?"

Dianne shook her head. "I was just realizing that you're twenty-nine years old."

"I'll be thirty next June," he admitted. "Seems like a real milestone in the life of a person."

"Do you ever think of marrying?"

"If the right woman came along, I might. So far I haven't found that woman. She'd have to understand army life and be willing to move about and endure the worries of an army wife."

"So you plan to stay in the army?" She felt a twinge of disappointment even in asking. She'd always held hope in the back of her mind that he might come and stay with them and take on some of the ranching—just as Trenton had done.

"I like the army well enough. I don't like the constant conflict with the Indians, but someone has to help keep the peace. That's my focus. Keeping the peace."

"But keeping that peace requires you to kill people. I know that goes against everything you stand for."

Zane looked thoughtful. "I feel compelled to consider the better good of the masses. I don't like to see the Indians hurt, you know that. But the whites will come and continue to come. They won't be stopped. Immigrants are flooding into the nation by the thousands. They want the land of milk and honey—well, they just want the land. Most can't own property in their native lands."

"Still, to come here and impose themselves upon us. We were born here."

"We were and our parents were, but not our grandparents. Ma's Dutch folks were no different than the Dutch immigrants coming now. They come with a dream to live a new life—to make a better way. The English are coming, the Germans, the Swedes . . . anyone who has a dream sees America as the place for that dream to come true."

"And the price is to rob the Indians of their land—their way of life."

"You're thinking of the discussion on that new Indian law, aren't you?"

"For lawmakers to sit in the capitol and declare that all Indians must be on their reservations by the end of next month or be considered hostile seems harsh."

Zane nodded. "I know. But there has to be order. If the Indians don't return to their reservations and set up their lives there, they'll make war on the whites who come into the land, and we'll be forced to get in the middle of it."

"To kill the Indians, you mean," Dianne stated more than asked.

"To keep the peace," Zane said, his voice touched with sorrow.

———

Dianne undressed for bed, pulling on a very full flannel gown. She loved being with child, but she also looked forward to returning to her slim figure and old clothes. She wasn't very fond of sack-style dresses that tied above the swell of her stomach, nor the oversized blouses and drawstring-type shirtwaists. She'd be happy to once again cinch her waist with a belt.

Sitting down at her dressing table, Dianne pulled the pins from her hair. The gold mass fell below her waist in a wave. With long, determined strokes, Dianne began brushing her hair. She relished this quiet time of night when she was alone to think. Cole would soon be up, and they would talk for a while in bed. He would then read to her from the Bible, and they would pray before going to sleep. She realized, as the baby's time neared, that some of their most precious time together was the time they simply talked and shared their hearts.

Dianne felt the baby move and smiled. It was a good feeling. The baby moved less and less these days, and Koko assured her that meant the birth would be soon. Dianne could feel that the child had moved lower. It was hard now to walk, and sometimes the baby caused pain in her hip joint. Koko thought it to be because the baby was pressing on the blood flow. Dianne only knew that the baby was making him- or herself well known.

"We'll have to settle on a name soon," she murmured. She and Cole had been thinking for some time of what they would like to call the baby. Dianne had been partial to the name Martha, until Cole had brought her the book *Little Women* by Louisa May Alcott. Now she really liked the name Louisa May, as well as Amy, from one of the characters in the story. She thought the name Amy Selby sounded quite nice for a girl.

For a boy, they'd already discussed several possibilities. Cole was partial to the name Lucas, and Dianne had to admit she liked it. They could call him Luke. Other names discussed were William and Michael. John Selby also had a nice ring to it, as did Walter, but Dianne felt that Lucas would probably win out over the others.

Cole wanted very much for their first child to be a boy. Dianne honestly didn't care whether it was a boy or a girl, but she wanted to please Cole and therefore hoped the baby would be of the male persuasion.

"As long as he's healthy and strong," she whispered. "I don't care otherwise."

She finished with her hair and had just crawled into bed when Cole opened the door to the room. "The wind's picked up," he said, smiling at her. "I hope that brother of yours had the good sense to ride at a quick pace back to the fort. I think a snow may be on his heels."

"He's smart; I'm sure he's seen worse."

"No doubt." Cole deposited his jacket on a chair near the door and began unfastening the buttons on his vest. "So how are you feeling this evening, Mrs. Selby?"

"Tired but good. I'm anxious for the baby to come. I was just thinking again about names."

"And what did you come up with?" he asked, casting the vest over the jacket.

"I think if it's a boy we should go with Lucas. The more I try the name, the more I like it. It's strong and has ties to the Bible. I liked your idea of using my maiden name for his middle name, so Lucas Chadwick Selby should suit him just fine."

"And if it's a girl?" Cole unfastened the few buttons on his shirt and pulled it off over his head. "There's always that possibility."

Dianne nodded. "I think I'm stuck on Amy. I just love that name. It's all your fault for bringing home that delightful book."

"As I recall, I brought you two delightful books. *Little Women* and *Les Misérables*. Were there no perfect names in the latter?"

"None that I cared for," Dianne admitted, thinking back on the characters. "I was deeply moved by the story, however. I think you'd like it very much. Funny," she said, rubbing her abdomen, "I never really liked to read until moving here. In the evening, after work is done, reading has become a wonderful pastime."

Cole finished undressing and slipped into bed beside his wife. Dianne snuggled into his arms and sighed. She loved being here more than anyplace else in the world.

"Hmm," Cole murmured. "You're nice and warm."

"And you're strong and make me feel safe," Dianne whispered.

"I'll always keep you safe, my love."

"But bad times are coming. Zane said as much when he first

told us of the government's decision to round up all the Indians."

"I know, but we can't worry about it. We need to bide our time and see what happens."

"What about Takes Many Horses?" Dianne asked, leaning up to see her husband's face. "He's out there somewhere. At least I hope he's still alive. No one, not even Koko, has heard from him in all these years. Just that one visit in '73. Now 1875 is nearly gone, and there's still been no word. And a lot has happened with the Blackfoot tribe in the meanwhile."

"If he's dead, he's beyond our worry. If he's alive, he knows he's welcome here," Cole said thoughtfully. "My guess is that he's alive and well. He's a fighter and a good man. I think he's still out there somewhere."

"Then why doesn't he come for a visit? I know Koko pines for him. She loves him so and worries about him."

Cole shook his head. "I don't know, Dianne. But George is his own man. He'll come and go at his will, not our desire."

"Do you suppose he's on the reservation with the Blackfoot?"

"I don't know. I can't see a man like that penned up on a reservation, but then again, I can't see any of those men penned up like that. If he feels it's for the betterment of his people, he might go."

"If he doesn't go, the order says they may be considered hostile. Zane says that means they can be killed without question."

Cole's expression was loving. He caressed her cheek, warming her from the outside in. "He's in God's hands, sweetheart. We can stew and fret over him all we want, and it simply will not change what's going on. I'm not pleased with the government's new order. But I can't change it either. If the Indians, no matter the tribe, choose to make a stand and fight the soldiers, then I can only imagine the outcome."

Dianne settled back against her husband. "So much has

changed. New people and ranches are springing up everywhere. Gus is worried about the sheep people and farmers who want to fence everything off. Towns are forming, and that means more rules and more troubles."

"I know, but things will always change. Wouldn't be alive without change. Even here," he said, gently touching her swollen stomach. "Change."

"It will be so different. You and me—parents. I sometimes wonder if I'll be any good at it."

Cole chuckled. "You are good at everything you set your hand to. Mothering will come naturally, I know. I remember you with your little sisters."

"They weren't infants. I helped a bit when they were young, but I never had to care for them as babies. I just worry that I won't know the right things to do—that I'll miss something and won't keep him safe." Dianne trembled at the thought of somehow failing to care for her baby, as she had failed with her mother.

"You've had a hand in helping with Koko's children and Faith's. I doubt very seriously you'll have any trouble with our babies. I do have a suggestion, however. This place is growing fast. The cattle and horses are bringing us a nice income, and there's no reason it won't continue to get better.

"The boys and I have plans to finish the construction on the remaining unfinished portions of the house over the next few months. It's going to be larger than ever, and I think we ought to consider getting a regular housekeeper and maybe a cook and a couple of other girls to help out."

"Do you really think we need that kind of help? I mean, Koko and I are pretty capable."

"I know you are, but Koko wants to school little James, and that takes a good deal of time. These children will need more and more schooling. I think we may even have to form our own school right here on the ranch. After all, I doubt other schools are going to take in Indian or black children."

"Charity has already offered to do this," Dianne said, her fears passing away as her excitement grew. "She believes she can teach the children everything they'll need for their primary work. We'll just need to get some primers and other books for her to use."

Cole nodded. "I should have known you'd have this all worked out."

"Well, with Ben running the church in their cabin, it seems natural that Charity could run a school."

"That's another thing we need to think about. With all the folks in the valley now, we really should build a church. Maybe somewhere to the north."

"That'd be nice," Dianne agreed. "I've always invited the other families when we're at roundup, but driving all the way here from their ranches isn't all that convenient."

Cole pulled her close and sighed. "Not much in this country is convenient, but we'll make it work. Because that's what taming the land is all about. We'll make this work too. I think we need to look at all the good around us. We have some good neighbors, new doctors, and stores. It's a whole lot easier to get supplies ordered with the telegraph system in place and freight roads so easy to pass over. With the train running regularly across the country and talk of new tracks being put in across Montana, well, we should see things become a little easier every day."

"But the Blackfoot won't," she sighed, laying her cheek against his chest. "None of the Indians will see an easier day, and that breaks my heart."

"I know," Cole whispered, "but all we can do is trust God for the outcome. He's already seen the future—He knows what's coming. He knows."

CHAPTER 30

DIANNE EXPERIENCED THE FIRST PAINS OF LABOR EARLY ON the morning of December 22. She hadn't really known what to expect. Koko had told her how it felt, as had Faith, but Dianne's labor seemed completely different. An ache in her lower back woke her that morning, but it wasn't all that different from the other backaches she'd known during the latter months of her pregnancy.

"You're moving kind of slow today," Cole said as he dressed.

"I'm stiff and sore. This baby is no doubt eager to be born." She massaged the small of her back and sighed.

Cole came and put his arms around Dianne. Leaning down, he whispered against her ear, "I'm eager too. I think this is the best Christmas present we've ever had."

Dianne smiled. "Maybe he'll be born on Christmas."

"Maybe *she* will be," Cole countered.

They laughed at their little game. For weeks they'd pondered and explored each possibility, always concluding that no matter what God gave them, they'd be happy and blessed by this new life.

Dianne began to dress, feeling great frustration in her inability to do the simple tasks that used to be easy. "I tire so quickly. It just doesn't seem fair. I can stay in the saddle nearly as long as Gus. I can rope and shoot, work the roundup . . . but carrying another human being is just a little more than I seem capable of."

Cole finished with his own clothes and came to Dianne. "Here, let me help. What can I do?" She pointed to her gown and he immediately took it in hand.

"I'm the size of Dolly," she bemoaned.

"No you aren't," Cole chided as he helped her into the dress. "You're beautiful, and soon you'll back to your old size and feel more like yourself. In the meanwhile, every time I look at you, I'm just reminded of how much I love you."

Dianne turned in his arms. He seemed to understand her need for reassurance, and she loved him for it. He kissed her gently on the forehead and then the lips. Dianne melted against him in the warmth and contentment of true love.

"Thank you for helping me," she said, doing her best to ignore the nagging pain in her back.

Later that morning Dianne stood by the kitchen table, helping Koko prepare a wild turkey for the smokehouse. She rubbed at the powerful ache in her back until finally Koko commented.

"Are you hurting?"

Dianne nodded. "Usually the stiffness leaves by now, but this is much stronger."

Koko clapped her hands and Suzy, sitting in a chair next to the table, did likewise. "It's the baby," Koko declared.

"The baby? You mean I'm having him now?" Dianne asked in horror.

"You are probably in labor. Back labor. My mother spoke of having it with my brother. I've never experienced it, but she said most all of her pain started in her back and was strongest there."

"I don't feel bad otherwise," Dianne said, getting excited at the prospect of finally delivering her child.

"We will just prepare for the arrival and wait until the pains are stronger. Oh, Dianne, I'm so very happy this day has come." Koko hugged her close and giggled. "It's so exciting—like knowing a secret."

Dianne couldn't help but giggle in turn. She felt like a little girl on Christmas Day. Well, it was three days before, but it felt the same.

By afternoon, Dianne was notably miserable. The baby had pushed low, making her uncomfortable standing or sitting. Koko wanted her to go to bed, but Dianne knew she'd have plenty of time there. By evening, however, she was reconsidering. When Cole returned from working with a couple of green-broke geldings and heard what was going on, he gave his wife no choice.

"You're going to bed," he declared and lifted her into his arms.

When Koko finally decided to check Dianne's progress she wasn't at all pleased. "The baby is breech," she concluded.

"Can we turn him?" Dianne questioned, already used to referring to the child as male.

"I don't think so. Not now. He's too low," Koko said, sitting beside Dianne on the bed. "Breech deliveries are never easy."

"What should we do?"

"I think it would be good to have a doctor. Dr. Bufford isn't so far away. We could send one of the men for him. I think he'd come without reservation because it's you."

Dianne suddenly felt afraid. Afraid for her baby—afraid for herself. "Do whatever you think is best." Just then a deep, immobilizing pain spread from her back to her abdomen. Dianne couldn't help but moan out loud and double to her side. "Whatever you do, you'd better be quick. I don't know how much longer this little guy's going to wait."

Koko stood and nodded. "I'll get Charity or Faith to come

and sit with you. I'll talk to Cole and let him know what's happening. He may even want to sit with you himself."

"Cole knows exactly where Bufford's place is. He may want to ride for him. If he does . . . tell him . . . I'll be fine and that it's all right . . . for him to go," Dianne said, panting against the pain.

"I'll tell him."

Koko left the room and suddenly Dianne felt very alone. *Oh, Lord,* she prayed, *I'm so afraid. Please save me and my baby. Please don't let us die.* She hated feeling so fearful—so alone. She knew her family was all around her—knew that God was with her as well.

"What's this I hear?" Cole asked, coming into the room and quickly crossing to her side. "Is my son giving you a hard time?"

"So you finally are ready to concede that it's a boy?" Dianne questioned, trying to sound jovial so as not to worry her husband.

"I'm ready to do whatever it takes to get that baby born. Including going for Dr. Bufford. Are you sure you don't want me to send someone else?"

"I'd love for you to be here, but I also know it's going to be hard to find his place in the dark. You know your way around here better than most. I trust you to bring him," Dianne answered, the pain subsiding.

"Then that's what I'll do." He kissed her on the forehead. "Dianne?"

She looked up to meet his eyes. "Yes?"

"I love you. Remember that and take strength from it. I love you more than life itself, and I am absolutely confident that everything will be all right."

She saw the truth of it in his face. He did believe, and because he did, she began to trust it to be true as well. "I love you too," she said as another pain came upon her. "Please hurry."

Koko came into the room just as Cole exited. Faith was close on her heels and came around the bed to take hold of Dianne's hand.

"So it's to be like this," she said with a smile. "The best things in life come hard, don't they?"

Dianne knew Faith understood the fear and the thoughts that poured through her mind. "Cole says everything will be all right."

Faith nodded. "I feel the same. Charity too. We've been praying and we both have a great peace. You just rest in His care, Dianne. This is going to be a wonderful day."

The twenty-second blended into the twenty-third of December and it was nearly four in the morning before Cole and Hezekiah Bufford came bounding into the room. Bufford took charge immediately, ordering everyone to go with exception to Koko.

Cole waved to Dianne from the door, but in her state of pain, she didn't attempt to return the wave. She saw Faith lead Cole away and knew the older woman would be able to say and do the right things to comfort his mind.

"Have you ever helped in a breech birth?" Bufford asked Koko.

"No," she admitted. "Only with animals."

"Well, the concept is somewhat the same. You have to get the baby out before the body clamps down on the neck. See, the normal birth allows for the largest part of the body to be delivered first—which is the head. But in a breech birth, the body thinks the baby's bottom is the biggest thing to come. If I had some forceps, I probably wouldn't give it much thought, but I can't boast a pair, so we'll just have to do this the best we can."

"You can save him, can't you?" Dianne asked, tears threatening to spill. She eased up on her elbows to better see his face. The action took all of her strength.

Dr. Bufford smiled. It was one of the only times she'd ever seen the man smile. "I believe I can deliver this child in good order, but you'll have to be brave and strong, and you'll have to trust me."

Dianne fell back against her pillow. "I do trust you, Dr. Bufford."

Dianne heard her son's first cries three hours later and knew her trust had been well placed. "Thank you, Father," she breathed as Koko made the announcement.

"You have a son, and he's perfectly healthy."

Dianne nodded sleepily. "I knew it'd be a boy. I just knew it."

"Congratulations, Mrs. Selby. You did just fine and so did he," Dr. Bufford declared.

Dianne couldn't contain a yawn. "Where's Cole? Somebody needs to let him know."

"I'll tell him as soon as I get the baby cleaned up," Koko said. She crossed the room to Dianne's dressing table, where they'd already prepared warm water and towels.

Dr. Bufford finished his work, and with the tenderness of a father, he pulled the covers up to warm Dianne's chilled body. "Are you feeling better now?" he asked.

"I am. Much better. Thank you for coming. I don't know what we would have done without you."

Koko brought the baby to Dianne's arms. "Here he is, Mama. He's anxious to be with you. You take him, and I'll go find his papa."

Dianne looked into her son's eyes for the first time. They were the darkest blue. He seemed so alert, so interested in seeing her. "Oh my," Dianne said, shaking her head, "he's so tiny." She laughed. "He didn't feel tiny a few minutes ago, but now he seems so little."

"I'm guessing around six-and-a-half pounds," Bufford said.

"If you have a scale around here, you could certainly weigh him and see."

"I honestly don't care," Dianne replied. "I'm just so glad he's here."

"I'm glad I could lend a hand."

"You should probably take a room and sleep for a time," Dianne said as Dr. Bufford swayed a bit on his feet.

To her surprise he nodded. "I'd like to do just that. It would make me feel better to stick around for a while and just make sure you have no complications."

Dianne tensed. "Are you afraid something is wrong?"

He shook his head and reached down to place his hand upon her shoulder. "Not at all, my child. It just makes me feel better to watch over my patients for a few hours."

"Here he is!" Koko announced, bringing a sleepy-eyed Cole into the room.

"Well?" he asked. "Boy or girl?"

Dianne laughed. "You mean to tell me you didn't let him know about his son?"

"A boy! Yippee!" Cole gave a holler, coming fully awake. "I have a son!"

"I think they could have heard that in Virginia City," Dianne declared as the baby began to cry. "At least we know there's nothing wrong with Luke's ears."

"Lucas Chadwick Selby," Cole said, coming to her side. She held the baby up to him and with a hesitant glance in return, Cole reached out to take him. "Kinda little, isn't he?"

"He'll grow soon enough," Koko said, coming to stand beside him. "He'll be big as his papa before you know it. Out there breaking horses and riding the roundup."

Dianne yawned and closed her eyes. She could picture Lucas as a small child riding on the back of his own horse. He would look just like a miniature Cole, with cocoa brown hair and dark eyes. No doubt he would love the land, just as his father did. Just as she did.

————

Dianne awoke with a start. Had it all been a dream? She felt her stomach and realized the relative flatness. It wasn't a dream. She'd had the baby and he was healthy and safe. She closed her eyes again. *Thank you, Lord. Thank you so much.*

The wind moaned softly, rattling her windows. Dianne glanced toward the open draperies and realized it was snowing. Somehow it all seemed fitting.

"So you're finally awake."

Dianne looked to the door, where Dr. Bufford stood peering in. "I just now opened my eyes. I've never been more tired."

"You had a hard time of it. Wears a body out." He came into the room and reached for her wrist. "I just want to check your pulse." He smiled. "Feels strong and steady. Always a good sign."

"Where's the baby? Where's Luke?"

"With his proud father. He'll be wanting you soon enough, though. Koko fixed him up with a sugar-teat for the time being, but he'll need to be put to your breast soon."

Dianne felt her cheeks warm at the comment. "I want to thank you again for coming," she said, quickly changing the subject. "I know you don't care for the way things are here. I know you've avoided coming to our parties or to church."

"I have only the highest respect and admiration for you, Mrs. Selby," Bufford said, stroking his bearded chin. He looked tired and Dianne wondered if he'd managed to sleep. "I was happy to come and lend a hand."

"Can you sit for a moment?"

He pulled up a chair and eased into it. "My knees are bothering me something fierce," he admitted. "The cold weather always does it. I suppose I'll always be a Southerner at heart."

"I see it's snowing. How long has that been going on?"

"It started just a little after the birth. Looks like it'll be going on for some time."

"You will stay with us, won't you? We'd love to have you for the holidays. I know you're all alone out there, and we'll have plenty of food and festivities." She paused, seeing him stiffen. "I know you're uncomfortable with people of color, but these are good folks, Dr. Bufford. They would give you the shirt off their back or their last bit of food. They are truly kind people, and I know we'd all be honored to have you here to celebrate the birth of Jesus."

For several moments he said nothing. Instead he stared at his hands as if weighing the situation. "I haven't celebrated anything in a long, long while."

"Please, just do this as a favor to me. I know I don't have a right to ask, but I truly want you to be here with us."

"I'll stay," he said, looking past her to the window. His voice sounded hard, almost irritated. Had she gone too far?

"Please forgive me if I said the wrong thing. It wasn't my desire to make you feel uncomfortable but rather to make you feel welcome. You've made your beliefs known, but we have no room for prejudice here. We must all live together or surely we would die." Dianne said without censoring her thoughts. She hadn't meant to be so bold, but the words were out before she could stop them.

Bufford's eyes narrowed, but there was no hint of anger. "I had a good life when I was your age. We had a wonderful home in Atlanta, Georgia. That was a fine city, if ever there was one. I had a lovely wife who played the piano and served marvelous dinner parties for our friends. We had three fine children. Two sons and a little daughter. She was our delight, for she came in our mature years—a surprise, you might say."

"And then the war came?" Dianne asked softly.

"Yes."

The single word spoke volumes. The pain was so evident in Bufford's expression that Dianne hesitated to continue. Something inside her, however, caused her to press for answers. "What happened to them—to your family? Why are you here alone?"

"My sons enlisted. My wife and I, along with our daughter, stayed in Atlanta to roll bandages, tend the sick, and keep the home fires burning. After all, we were going to lick the Yankees by Christmas. I did my duties around Atlanta, working at the hospital and continuing to aid the sick, and my wife rallied support and donations for the troops and their families." He shook his head.

"My first boy fell in a battle near Great Falls, Virginia, that July of '61. He was just a child, not quite yet twenty. He'd been so proud to serve—to sustain and defend our way of life, our rights."

Dianne watched as Bufford folded his hands and lowered his face. He almost looked to be praying. Her heart went out to him as he continued, his voice edged with deep sorrow.

"Our second boy died from wounds he received, also in Virginia. It was near Philmont in November of '62. He had an arm completely blown off. They just couldn't save him."

"I'm sorry. I can't imagine the pain of losing a child."

Bufford opened his eyes and looked hard at Dianne. "But you will have that possibility now. You live here in the middle of heathen country, and the Indians are not at all happy with the whites these days. You look down on me for my prejudiced ways, but in all honesty, you will have to face the truth sooner or later. The Indian is just as prejudiced toward you. They don't care for your manner of life or the belief systems you hold to be true. I know you to be a Christian woman, Mrs. Selby. Well, your Indian folk are certainly not of the Christian persuasion. Oh, of course your aunt, who was raised with a white father, as

I understand it, has accepted our ways, but that won't account for an entire nation of savages. I've seen the effects of war, and I've no desire to relive it. I've honestly given thought to pulling out to head to more civilized realms."

"There's danger to be had wherever you go," Dianne said, quoting something she'd heard Cole say at least a dozen times.

"True enough, but no sense in just sitting by and letting it come to you. Like I did."

"How so?"

"I watched my wife and daughter die when Atlanta went under siege. They were already sick—they'd contracted dysentery and no matter what remedy I tried, they couldn't seem to recover. I'd wanted to move them from Atlanta when I heard the soldiers were coming, but there was no chance. They died within hours of each other." His eyes glazed over. "You wonder at my bitterness, but you see, there's nothing left me. Hope deserted me the day God took away my beloved wife and little daughter. And for what?" He looked directly at Dianne, and the raw hatred of all he'd known was there for her to see. Dianne cringed.

"I lost my family so a bunch of darkies could go free. So a bunch of illiterate heathens could share the same rights and freedoms that I had? Those people weren't even Americans. They were brought to this country, albeit against their will, from Africa. What gave them the right to make such a demand as freedom?"

"I don't recall that they made the demand," Dianne said. "Of course, I was just a girl when the entire matter began, but as I remember, there were other elements to the War Between the States. States' rights, for instance. South Carolina left the Union because they wanted to have their own say over what happened in their state. My father used to joke that South Carolina threatened to leave the Union every time the wind changed directions."

Bufford actually bore a hint of a smile at this. "Well, we Southerners tend to feel strongly about our beliefs."

"Apparently Northerners felt no different," Dianne replied with a sigh. "It just seems to me that there were other matters to be resolved."

"Bah, those things could have been overcome. Everything would have been different if slavery hadn't been on the agenda." His anger was evident, but Dianne felt no fear. The man was clearly wounded—just as wounded and near death as the loved ones he'd lost.

"Dr. Bufford," she said, reaching out to touch his arm, "my loved ones had nothing to do with the death of your family members. You may blame the slaves and their desire to be free, but I believe you would be wrong to do so. Would your wife have wanted you to live out your life like this—with such hatred and scorn for others?"

He looked taken aback by her words. His blue eyes widened as he let the words sink in. "My family had no desire to see the war come or the slaves set free."

"I've no doubt they would have rather the war not come, but honestly, Dr. Bufford, would you rather have had slavery continue? You just don't seem like the kind of man who would support such an institution. Did you have slaves?"

"Certainly not. We were not a wealthy family by any means. We could not afford servants."

"Would you have had them if you could have afforded them?" she asked, not at all certain why she felt compelled to keep pushing the matter.

Bufford got up and walked to the window. He stood with his back to her for a very long time. So long, in fact, that Dianne was almost positive he would never answer her question. Just when she thought to ask him to send Koko with the baby, he turned.

"No, Mrs. Selby. I wouldn't have had slaves in my possession. However, I didn't think it right to tell other free men what they could and couldn't do. I saw no reason to deny them their laborers because my conscience wouldn't make the same choice."

"My brother Zane told me something a while back. He quoted a statesman from Ireland named Edmund Burke. Mr. Burke said, 'The only thing necessary for evil to triumph is for good men to do nothing.' I cannot stand by and allow evil to continue simply because I would not choose to partake in it myself. It's a little like saying I would willingly allow my ranch foreman to kill anyone he chooses so long as he leaves the workers of the Diamond V alone. Evil is still evil, even when I choose not to participate in it. I didn't realize the implications then, as I said, for I was quite young and uneducated. The biggest concern I had was whether I'd get to share Sunday afternoon with my friends."

Bufford seemed to be hearing her words, but his gaze was fixed somewhere over her head. Dianne wondered if it might not be better to just let the matter drop. After all, she could hardly expect to persuade a man who'd been through so much sorrow and grief. *Then again,* she thought, *I've known just as much sorrow. Just as much loss. Maybe not a child of my own or a husband, but the pain is just as real.*

"I cannot blame the slaves or the Southern patriots or the Northern defenders of the Union," she said softly. "I blame things like hatred and bigotry. I place responsibility on those who deny the truth—who refuse to heed God's word and warning."

"After my wife and daughter died," Bufford began as he walked back to the chair beside Dianne's bed, "I enlisted. I went with the Confederate soldiers by sneaking out beyond the siege lines. I hoped to make a difference—to save lives that might otherwise have been lost, like my sons'.

"I still believed in my oath to save lives. I still believed I could make things better—to ease the misery of my fellowman." He leaned against the chair back and shook his head. "But in truth, I could do very little. Good men died despite my efforts. War is not a pretty sight, Mrs. Selby."

"I know that well enough. I lived in New Madrid, a town that witnessed battles and skirmishes. My father was killed in a small fight—right on the street outside his store. I watched him bleed to death, and no one could help him. He was innocent— he bore no weapons, nor did he desire his sons to bear arms. We were Southern by way of our family heritage, but my father held strong beliefs about preserving the Union. About doing whatever it took so that when everything was said and done, he could still live with the choices he'd made."

Bufford closed his eyes and shook his head again. "Some choices can never be lived with. Some choices must be expunged in death."

———

Dianne was still considering Bufford's words even as they celebrated Christmas two days later. Every time she looked into the eyes of her newborn son, she couldn't help but feel a tremor of fear. Would the Indian Wars be settled by the time he'd grown to be a man? And even if they had, would there be other wars for him to participate in?

Bufford seemed to be enjoying the holidays. He ate like a man long starved of decent food and appeared to bear no ill will toward Faith or Malachi or their children. He had seemed to make a peace of sorts with Koko. They talked of healing, and while Dianne had not included herself in the conversation, she often heard comments by each one that seemed to be approved of or respected by the other.

Koko even gave Dr. Bufford a new pair of leather gloves. This had been her primary gift to most everyone on the ranch that year, and Dianne was touched that she'd found it in her heart to share her efforts with a man who had at one time been so rude toward her.

Perhaps he is allowing God to heal his wounded heart, Dianne thought as she nestled Lucas in her arms. Perhaps in time the good doctor would be able to put the war behind him and let go of his ghosts.

———

"He sure can raise a ruckus," Trenton said, looking at his squalling nephew.

Dianne laughed and finished changing her son into dry clothes. "He's hungry. He's no different than most of the men around here. When his stomach's empty, he fusses until he gets fed."

Trenton shook his head. "Awfully small. Is he . . . well . . . are they supposed to be that small?"

Dianne looked at her brother and tilted her head to one side. "And what size would you suggest they be when they're born?"

Trenton felt a rush of embarrassment. "I don't know. He just seems small."

Dianne shook her head. "He's just right. Someday he'll grow as big as his uncle Trenton and papa, but for now, he's just perfect."

Trenton nodded. "I reckon he is." He felt overcome by the happiness and peace he'd known these last few years. "Dianne, thanks for asking me to stay."

She seemed surprised by his change of topics. Lifting Luke into her arms, she said, "You were always welcome here—long before you came."

"I know, but you could have sent me packing. I mean, I let you down when you needed me most. I should have gone west with you and Mama. If I had, the girls might not have—"

"Stop," Dianne said firmly. She shifted Luke in her arms and held up her hand as if to ward off anything more Trenton might say. "I had enough guilt for all of us. Mama was in my care when she wandered off. The girls were more or less my responsibility when they were taken from us. I could blame myself, but it wouldn't change things. I've had to fight this a long, long time, so I know. Please don't allow yourself to be caught in that trap."

"I've just never been the man I should have been. I know I've let everyone down. The past is . . . well, it's too awful to talk about."

"Then don't," Dianne said, moving to where he stood. "There's nothing to be gained by dwelling on what we should have done. I know you're sorry for your wrongdoing. I know you've repented of anything that you should have. I was there when Ben baptized you, so I know you've made things right with the Lord. Don't be dragged back down by 'should-haves.' It won't do you any good."

Trenton saw the truth of it in her eyes. "You're right. I guess I'm just afraid it will all catch up with me."

"Well, if it does," Dianne said softly, "we'll simply deal with it then. But for now, we lay the past to rest and look to the future."

Trenton nodded. It had been easy to give up gambling and drinking, but giving up the despair of his wasted years was something he hadn't quite figured out how to do. Dianne might feel confident of being able to deal with his past, but she had no idea what his past represented. *If she did, she probably wouldn't want me here. If she knew what I was capable of, she'd tell me to leave.*

CHAPTER 31

THAT YEAR THE MADISON VALLEY EXPERIENCED A MILD
winter without too much peril or loss of animal life. Life on the
Diamond V passed in ease and comfort, but it wasn't to be so for
other areas of the territory. To the east and south the winter was
hard, with snows and low temperatures that threatened to destroy
everything they touched. Across the northern plains native people moved with guarded caution to avoid being caught by blizzards or the government. With the ultimatum that all Indians be
on their reservations by the thirty-first of January, tempers flared
and conflict could be found at every turn. A kind of cat-and-
mouse chase was on, and no one could really hope to win.

Rumors told of conflicts to the east. The Sioux and Cheyenne, who refused to return to their reservations, or who simply
hadn't heard the requirement due to poor communications, were
immediately considered to be in violation of the order. War was
declared on February 1, 1876, and the army prepared to deal
with what they perceived as a direct defiance to the U.S. government's authority.

Dianne received word from Zane sometime in February that

he would move out with soldiers from Fort Ellis to go to the aid of Fort Pease. Dianne knew the fort was somewhere near the mouth of the Big Horn River. Her brother had no idea of when they might return to the Bozeman area but assured her they would be fine and that she shouldn't worry.

So despite her joy over being a mother and the blessings they'd enjoyed that winter, Dianne couldn't help but worry about Zane. He was thrown into the middle of this entire war—not necessarily of his own doing, but certainly of his own free will.

A letter from Morgan came near the middle of March. He told of joining up with a group of men who desired to explore the regions to the southeast of the Madison Valley and the Diamond V. Dianne had read in the papers that the government had set aside land for a national park. Apparently the territory was in need of mapping and exploration, and Morgan intended to enjoy a time later that year doing just that.

"He sounds very happy," Dianne said as she shared the letter with Faith. The ladies had joined together to work on their various mending and handcraft projects—a habit they had come to call their Tuesday morning sewing circle. Their children were busy playing or working all around them.

"He's been up to Canada and all across the northern parts of Montana. He says there's a great deal of beauty to the northwest of us—a range of high peaks and deep mountain lakes."

"Sure sounds pretty," Faith said, glancing over the masculine scrawl.

"Will he come here before going south?" Charity asked.

"I hope so," Dianne said, rocking Luke's cradle with her foot while continuing to stitch on the large blue-and-white quilt she and Koko were making for one of the guest rooms. "It would be nice to see him and sit down and hear what he's been doing all this time. The letters are always so brief and so far between."

"At least you've had word," Koko murmured.

"I know." Dianne immediately felt guilty for complaining. "I've worried over Takes Many Horses, just as you have. I can't help but wonder if, with the government's declaration of war on the nonreservation Indians, he's caught up in that." She paused long enough to meet her aunt's gaze. "I pray for him daily."

"I know that much has been settled with the tribe, but I don't see George," she said, using her brother's Christian name, "sitting within a fenced boundary, never roaming the mountains or valleys at will. He'd never be happy that way. Then, too, what happens when the game plays out and hunting is poor? How will the people survive? Government beef?"

"I've wondered the same. I know George cares a great deal about the welfare of the Blackfoot. I'd like to believe he'd involve himself with the council and help lead the people in wisdom."

"My uncle is very brave," Jamie declared. He'd been working quietly in the corner on his schoolwork, but mention of Takes Many Horses gave him reason to chime in.

Dianne smiled at the boy's fierce pride in an uncle he barely knew. "He's one of the bravest men I know," she agreed.

Jamie nodded solemnly. "He's very strong too."

Koko pulled her son close. "He is a strong and good man. But he also learned his book lessons and so, too, must you."

"I'm hungry," Jamie protested.

"Me too," Susannah whined from where she sat at her mother's feet.

Soon the room resounded with chants from Faith's children as well. Faith looked at the clock. "Well, it is almost noon. I should have been paying better attention. Good thing the men are off to roundup, or I'd be hearing from them as well." She put aside her mending and got to her feet.

"I'm sure we can have a fine dinner momentarily," Dianne declared, peeking at her son before putting her quilting needle away. "While he's asleep, I'll come and help you," she told Faith.

"I can lend a hand as well," Charity said, moving a little more slowly than the others. Her joints were stiff and sore most days, and today was no exception. Still, the woman managed to continue to do beautiful stitching.

"Faith and I can manage," Dianne said gently. "But I'd be obliged if you would keep an eye on Luke. No doubt he'll wake up wailing and half starved before I finish."

They chuckled at this. Luke seemed to have a voracious appetite, something evidenced in his chubby body.

"I'd be happy to care for Luke," Charity said, easing back into her chair. "Nothing makes a body feel more useful."

With the promise of something to eat, the children calmed and Faith and Dianne left the others to see to fulfilling their pledge.

"I'm pretty sure I'm going to have another baby," Faith told Dianne when they were alone.

"How wonderful!" Dianne gave her friend a quick hug, then pulled back to look at her trim waist. "When?"

"Near the end of October, as best as I can figure."

Dianne reached up into the cupboard and pulled down two jars of canned green beans. "I'm so happy for you, Faith. I love that we have so many children here at the ranch. We seem just like our own little town."

"It's a good life—hard, but good," Faith agreed. "Malachi is happier than I've ever known him. He loves working with his hands, and now that he can read pretty well, he feels he can stand his own ground with some of the other men."

"We do have a good life here. I sometimes get caught up worrying about things to come, then Cole reminds me that either I trust the good Lord to work out the details or I don't. I can't bring myself to say that I don't trust Him, so I always have to back down in my worries."

Faith sliced bread for sandwiches. "I've never known such peace. This valley just has a way of bringing peace to a body."

Dianne laughed and poured the beans into a pot to heat on the stove. "This valley brings a little bit of everything to a body. I know with the good times come hard times, but still I love it. I wouldn't want to be anywhere else in the world."

Faith looked up and met her eyes. "Me either. Wouldn't want to raise my babies anywhere but here."

"I can't help but wonder about the Indians," Dianne said, taking up some side meat to cut in with the beans.

"No sense worrying. The government will do what it wants, when it wants. I've known that firsthand. You can never tell what the course of action will be. Things may smooth out and be peaceful. Then again, we may see a hard, long war ahead. Either way, we can't forfeit the peace we have for what might come."

Dianne nodded. Faith was right, of course. Still, it was a fearful thing to ponder. Especially with her baby in the next room. When it had been her own welfare to consider, or even that of her adult friends, Dianne had felt certain they could face most anything. But now she had a baby, and along with her son there were four other children to consider. An Indian war or even a small skirmish could leave them all dead. She shuddered at the thought.

———

Zane Chadwick showed up near the end of the month. The men were still on roundup, so seeing him was a welcome relief to all of the women, who'd had little news of what was going on in the world.

"What have you been doing?" Dianne asked as she picked up Luke and brought him for Zane to see.

"He's a handsome boy," Zane said, reaching out to take the baby.

His action surprised Dianne. Zane handled the child with a familiarity that suggested practice. "How is it that you know how to hold a baby?"

"There are women at the fort," he said, smiling at his nephew. "I've done my share of baby handling."

Dianne laughed, as did Koko. "Well, brother of mine, you seem to manage the job quite well. I just might slip away for a ride and leave you to tend the baby."

Zane grinned. "Wouldn't hurt my feelings none."

Dianne couldn't believe his comfort with her son, but instead of taking him up on his word, Dianne sat down beside him. "Did you manage to get the folks from Fort Pease to safety?"

Zane nodded but continued to watch the baby. "They didn't want to go. They figured to stay on and fight off any attackers, but we held our ground and moved out everything but one cannon, a dog that managed to give us the slip, and the flag. The United States flag still flies over the fort."

"So will you be home for a time now? Cole said we'll probably be coming up to Bozeman in a month or so. I'd love to have some time with you there."

"We'll be gone. That's the reason I decided to ride over and see you now. We're heading back out again. There's more trouble in the East. The Sioux and Cheyenne are causing more grief than the army knows how to handle. We've had folks killed and travelers attacked. The army feels it has to make a stand and push the Indians back to their reservations."

"Have you had any word from my brother?" Koko asked.

Zane looked up and his face reddened. It was as though he'd forgotten her presence—or at least her heritage. "No, I've not encountered any Blackfoot tribes at all. I think most have gone to their reservations—the rest have traveled on up into Canada. We've got our hands full here and can't very well go chasing after them."

"Have most of the tribes complied with the order to be on their reservations?" Dianne asked.

Zane shrugged. "It's hard to tell in some cases. The Indian agents report in, but they can't get accurate counts. They try to tie in the counts with food distribution, but it doesn't always work well. I've heard rumors that tell of a great many marauding tribes, but it could just be rumors.

"For instance, a while back we heard that the Sioux and Cheyenne had amassed some two thousand warriors. That seems hard to believe, but because folks are being killed and property is being destroyed, we have to check into it."

Luke began to fuss and Zane shifted the baby to his shoulder. Dianne smiled as her son calmed and nuzzled against her brother's neck. "I hope it won't lead to an all-out war," she said quietly.

"We're expecting it to, unfortunately."

Dianne felt a hopelessness in his statement. She wanted so much to believe that war could be averted. "But can't something else be done? Some other agreement?"

"Too many agreements have already passed between the government and the Indians. They don't believe in our agreements anymore, and frankly, who can blame them?" He patted Luke gently on the back and added, "That's not to say that the tribes haven't been to blame for their share of conflicts. The Sioux are convinced if they fight hard enough, their enemy will be defeated. What they can't see is that they are limited in their numbers, where our numbers are definitely superior. Our methods of war are superior as well."

"So you will fight?" Koko asked.

Dianne remembered the horrors she'd heard Zane describe when he'd witnessed the massacre on the Marias River six years ago. She looked at her brother, seeing the conflict in his expression. He lowered his eyes and took Luke from his shoulder. After studying the baby for just a moment, Zane handed the boy to Dianne.

"I'll do what I have to do—to keep him safe. To protect all of you." He looked to his aunt. "I know you've always enjoyed safety because of your brother and the connection you have to your people, but it won't stop what's coming, and if the Sioux attack here, they won't care if you are part Blackfoot. They'll only want you to die."

Dianne swallowed hard and pulled Luke close. The thought of the ranch being vulnerable to attack was not one she allowed herself to consider very often. It terrified her. Cole had even asked her to stop reading the newspaper accounts of conflicts across the West. He believed the stories to be sensationalized and exaggerated, but here Zane was telling her otherwise—telling her that her fears were very real.

"Do you believe we'll be attacked here?" Dianne finally found the courage to ask.

Zane met her eyes and she could see the concern in his expression. "I think we all must be very careful—prepared for the worst. Hopefully I'll have a chance to talk to Cole before I have to leave. You did say he was due back any day, right?"

Dianne nodded. "With new people coming all the time and the herd growing larger, roundup takes longer. I expect him, however, any day."

"Good. I'll stay on a bit—I can do that much. I'll talk to Cole about precautions you can take—just in case."

Dianne felt a chill run down her spine. Precautions—just in case. The words caused a deep dread to settle over her. It was as if the end of the world loomed just on the horizon.

"When will you have to leave?"

"I need to report by the twenty-eighth," Zane admitted. "We're waiting on some of Colonel Gibbon's troops. Word has it they're coming south from Helena. Should be at the fort within days if the wet weather doesn't hold them up. I heard it was exceedingly muddy up that way."

"Then what?" Dianne asked, almost afraid to know.

"Then we march out—hopefully on the first of April."

"And where are you headed?"

"East," Zane replied. "To find the Sioux and Cheyenne and force them back to their reservations."

———————

Cole washed his neck and face with water from the river. It was icy from the snowmelt but it felt wonderful.

"Sure glad you're gettin' the hang of this job," Gus said as he walked up, leading his horse. "Not sure how many more years I'll be good for this kind of thing."

Cole laughed. "You'll be out there riding the herd long after the rest of us are dead and gone." He knew the older man had at least twenty years on him, maybe twenty-five.

"I seriously doubt that, my boy."

The grizzled cowboy took off his hat and knelt down by the river's edge. He splashed water all over his face and head, then plopped his hat back on his head, letting the water rivulets snake down his neck and into his shirt.

"So did you manage to get things straightened out with those cowboys from the Bar S?" Cole asked. There had been some trouble at the branding and a declaration from the smaller outfit that the Diamond V was stealing their cattle.

"I explained the situation and showed them the brands. They're still convinced several calves were motherin' up to our mama cows because their own mamas had been killed. I assured them it weren't the case. Sometimes it's hard to just take bad news like a man and leave well enough alone."

"We could go have a talk with the owner of the outfit. I

don't know the fellow, but I'm willing to try and smooth ruffled feathers."

"It'll pass. Leave well enough alone," Gus suggested. "Once they get back to their outfit, it'll come clear to them."

"I hope so. We have enough trouble around here from the Indians. Don't need to be starting up bad relations with the neighbors."

"There's bound to be more trouble as time goes on. They fight over cows in Texas like drunks on a Saturday night. Down that way you have to worry about the Mexicans comin' in to steal cattle and taking them back over the border. You think you got it bad here with folks tryin' to change brands and make them over for their own—down south they get downright *loco*. They'll add a bar or swirl, tack on a circle or horseshoe, all to change the brand. I pity the cow that has to wear a Mexican brand."

Cole shook his head and wondered if they'd really have to start looking out for such things. The country had been so free of that kind of worry. Oh, the occasional head or two were taken, usually by Indians, but to imagine people going out of their way to steal heads of cattle for their own stock . . . well, it just wasn't something Cole wanted to deal with at this point.

"There's other problems too. I heard tell a big sheep outfit is moving in just south of us. Sheep are bad news. They'll eat the grass out at the root. Leave us with nothing for range feed." Gus shook his head. "I see the day comin' when we'll be fencing everything in as far as the eye can see."

Cole couldn't help but laugh at that thought. "It'll take a whole heap of rail to fence in Montana."

Gus wiped his wet face with the back of his shirt sleeve. "Yup, but some folks won't have it any other way. Mark my words, the times are changin'. Sheep and fences, farmers and rustlers. It's all come a-courtin'."

CHAPTER 32

COLE HAD STILL NOT RETURNED BY THE TWENTY-SIXTH, and Zane felt it imperative he get back to the fort.

"Look," he told Dianne as he mounted his horse, "stay close to the house. Don't go off for long rides. Keep plenty of water and food close at hand and use a bell or something else you can clang to get everyone's attention in case you need to bring everyone up to the main house. It couldn't even hurt to have an outrider or two keeping watch. Someone on a fast horse with a keen eye for movement, in case the Indians decide to attack."

"I'll do my best," she told Zane. She glanced over her shoulder to see Koko wipe away a tear. The tension of the Indian conflicts was causing her a great deal of concern about her brother.

"You may run into Cole," Dianne said, meeting her brother's serious expression. "If you do, share this information again—just in case I somehow forget."

Zane nodded. "I'll be in touch. Try not to worry."

He pulled the reins hard to the right and kicked into the horse's sides. "Haw!" he called, pushing the horse into an immediate gallop down the muddy drive.

It had rained off and on all night—much needed moisture, but not at the best of times. Rain would make it harder to move the cattle. Rain would delay Cole further.

The day after Zane had gone, Dianne felt a restlessness that she couldn't explain. She thought about all the instructions Zane had left and considered what they might do to make themselves safe from attack. She had it in mind to call a meeting that night and have all of the remaining ranch hands and other residents join together for supper. She reasoned it would be easier to discuss the matter in full with everyone around the same table.

If only Cole were here to lead it. I'd much rather this be his decision, she thought. But there simply wasn't time to wait. Zane implied that the need was immediate—that danger could be just over the next ridge.

Thoughts like that caused Dianne to worry that perhaps Cole and the others had met with harm. After all, they would be out there all alone, well away from help or other people. Only those folks who shared in roundup would be present, and if a band of Indians could take on and destroy a wagon train with a few hundred people, they'd have no trouble with twenty or thirty cowhands.

Leaving Koko to watch over Lucas, Dianne decided to take a short walk around the immediate area and assess what needed to be done. She would heed Zane's warning not to go far, but she felt the desperate need to do something other than merely wait for trouble to come to her. Taking up a rifle, Dianne walked out onto the front porch and gazed down the long lane toward her beloved hilltop perch. There was no one there to indicate any problem or the return of her men. She sighed and stepped from the porch, heading toward the first barn.

In the corral outside, there were two wild horses. One of the men had been working with them throughout the winter. They would soon be tame enough to begin breaking in earnest. They were good, strong ponies, and Dianne looked forward to seeing how they reacted to training. She felt confident they would make good cow horses.

In the distance beyond Faith and Malachi's cabin, Dianne's eye caught sight of movement. She froze in place, doing her best to listen first before she reacted. It might only be an animal—a deer or elk—even a grizzly. She put her hand to her forehead, hoping to shield the sun and give herself a better view.

The image of a man crouching in the brush startled her. She knew if she could see him, he could probably see her as well. Dianne pulled the rifle in front of her and wondered what she should do. She didn't want to alarm the others, but neither did she want to leave them without warning. Just as she moved toward the house, however, the man got up and darted back into the trees.

"Indians," she murmured. She began to tremble and her breathing quickened. Had the Sioux come to attack? The man was clearly an Indian, but she hadn't gotten a good enough look to tell if he were Sioux or some other tribe.

She moved slowly backward, hoping she might get another glimpse of the man. By the time she made it to the porch, however, she'd seen nothing. Leaning against the post, her rifle still ready, Dianne pondered the situation. She couldn't very well go out there to investigate, and if the woods were full of Sioux warriors, there was no time to warn anyone and get them into the house.

Then movement once again caught her eye. The wind picked up ever so slightly, rustling the trees and brush in the direction she'd seen the Indian. She held her breath and leaned forward. Much to her relief a somewhat familiar sight came to her eyes.

"Takes Many Horses," she breathed and immediately relaxed

her hold on the rifle. He waved from across the field. Dianne waved in return and watched as he turned to motion to someone.

From their hiding place, three other Blackfoot warriors emerged—one of them the man she'd seen just moments earlier. As they drew near, Dianne could see that they were all very dirty and they looked very tired. Takes Many Horses approached her first, smiling in his lazy manner as if they'd parted company only the day before.

He stopped about eight feet away. "Stands Tall Woman, your ears and eyes do you proud."

"We've been very worried about you," Dianne said in greeting. "You're welcome here—you and your friends. Come around back where you can wash up, then I'll feed you all."

He watched her for a moment. "Where is your man?"

"Roundup. I figured you already knew that. You surely have watched the ranch and seen that most of the men are gone."

"Yes. We saw, too, that the white soldier was here."

"My brother Zane."

Takes Many Horses nodded. "Is he looking for us?"

Dianne shook her head. "Not at all. He's headed off to pursue the Sioux and Cheyenne and return them to their reservations." She paused and bit her lip. There were a hundred questions she longed to ask him.

"We are renegades," Takes Many Horses said matter-of-factly. "The soldiers are after us—at least they were."

"So you have left the reservation? Will you return?"

He shook his head and gave a pretense of dusting off his flannel shirt. "No. I will not live as a caged animal. I will die a free man."

"George!" Koko declared as she came out the door, Lucas in her arms. She handed the fussy baby to Dianne and rushed to embrace her brother. "I've been so worried. Where have you been? Why haven't you written me or come to see us?"

He held his sister for a moment, but his gaze was ever fixed on Dianne. "I'm sorry to have worried you, but there was much trouble."

Koko pulled away and noted his friends. "You're very warm and you look tired. All of you look tired." She felt her brother's face and grimaced. "Are you ill?"

"We've been traveling without much rest. We tried to hunt, but the game is far to the south. Now we're heading back north. Canada."

"So you won't go to the reservation?"

The man met his sister's gaze. Dianne saw the defiance in his expression but also noted the pain in his eyes. "No."

"Well, come inside. We can discuss this later."

"Stands Tall Woman says we must wash up first," Takes Many Horses said in a teasing manner.

Koko nodded. "It would be best. You smell as bad as . . ." She grinned. "Well, you smell bad. Come. I'll get you soap and towels." Koko turned to her brother's companions and spoke in Pikuni. Dianne easily translated the words in her mind and waited as the trio moved off with Koko.

George started to follow, then stopped. Looking up to where Dianne stood on the porch, he asked, "Is this your child?"

Dianne held her son up for the warrior to better view. "Yes. This is Lucas—Luke. He was born just before Christmas."

"You should put him in a cradleboard. It would be much easier to get work done with him on your back or propped up beside you."

She smiled. "I enjoy the feel of him in my arms. I couldn't stand to lose that." She nuzzled the baby and kissed his neck.

"You are a good mother—I can tell by the way he is calmed by your touch."

"Mostly he's hungry," Dianne said, "as you no doubt are. Go

wash up. We can talk about him later."

Takes Many Horses stood fixed for several moments, his gaze fixed on her, before he finally nodded and followed after the others. Dianne felt troubled by his scrutiny. Cole knew of the Indian's love for her, but he also had told Dianne that the man's honor was stronger still. She felt safe enough with Koko's brother, but there was something of his pain—something of the longing that he hid away just below the surface of his conscious thought—that gave Dianne a feeling of discomfort. It was rather like watching her uncle suffer after the bear attack. There was nothing she could do to ease his suffering. Nothing.

At noon they sat down to an abundant table of food, but the Indians seemed to have little appetite. Dianne tried not to worry or fuss over them; in fact, she kept her place near the opposite end of the table while Koko plied her brother with questions. Dianne tried not to seem too eager for their comments or answers. She tried too not to worry that they looked flushed, even feverish.

Excusing herself, Dianne went upstairs to nurse Luke and put him to bed for a nap. She cherished this quiet time alone with her baby. It seemed to her to be the very best time of the day, next to her evenings with Cole.

Lucas nursed greedily, making smacking, gurgling sounds as he ate. He watched his mother with dark blue eyes that seemed wise and intelligent. Dianne thought he looked as though he had many things to speak on, but then his lids grew heavy and he settled into a deep sleep. Apparently his declarations could wait for another day.

Dianne smoothed back his soft brown hair. Luke made her feel so very different. She thought of the times when she'd been a girl playing dolls. Though she had known the first stirrings of love for her doll babies, her feelings for Luke were something so fierce they were almost frightening.

Dianne got up and put the baby in his cradle. She stood watching her son for several minutes, not at all eager to leave him. He was so vulnerable—so helpless. Baby animals were able to do much for themselves when they were born, but not so baby humans.

"We're all vulnerable," she whispered, thinking of the troubled times about her.

Dianne crossed to the window and looked out across the valley. Thick, dark clouds were moving in from the south. No doubt it would rain again. She could only pray that Cole would hasten the drive and make his way back to her soon.

"Some days are just so hard," she said aloud. "I look at the work ahead and know I can never rise to the responsibility. Other times, I feel completely confused by what's expected of me." She looked heavenward. "Lord, what is expected of me?"

She was thankful Cole assumed the responsibilities of heading up the family, but some of the ranch hands still looked to her for approval and direction. Gus listened to Cole and respected him greatly, but Gus still honored her with discussions and asked for her opinion. Maybe he was just being nice, but Dianne felt he truly wanted to know what she thought.

Cole said it was because she was a natural at ranching. Dianne didn't know how natural it was. She felt there were certainly enough times when common sense eluded her and she failed at her tasks. She'd been thrown from many a horse and had gotten herself into more than one bad situation with equipment and gear.

"But you have a heart for this business," Cole had told her in his most serious tone. "Ranching is in your blood. Your uncle picked wisely when he set you up to help run this place."

Dianne rubbed the back of her neck and yawned. A nap sounded like a wonderful idea right now. There was really nothing pressing, and if she remained up here, Koko would have time alone with her brother.

Sitting on the edge of her bed, Dianne slipped off her shoes and stretched atop the covers. Closing her eyes, she whispered yet another prayer for her husband's safety, but this time she added a prayer for Takes Many Horses and his friends.

"I will not live as a caged animal. I will die a free man." The words resounded in her head. She'd always known it would be that way—so had Koko.

"Oh, God, you alone know tomorrow. Please, Father, please direct our steps. The path is rocky and strewn with obstacles. I know we'll not be able to survive save by your mercy."

"Dianne! Wake up!" Charity stood over Dianne and shook her gently but with a firm determination that suggested something was wrong.

"What is it?" Dianne struggled to sit. She rubbed the sleep from her eyes and glanced at the cradle. Luke was still asleep. "Is something wrong?"

"Yes. Oh, it's terrible," Charity said. Dianne could see the fear in her eyes.

"What is it?"

"Smallpox."

That single word had been known to strike terror in the hearts of entire communities. Dianne scooted to the edge of the bed. "Smallpox? Where?"

"Here. The Indians. Takes Many Horses and his friends. Koko just figured it out. Two of the Indians are already showing signs of the pox. The other two have the fever. In fact, they've had it for days. The pox will soon be marking them as well."

Dianne was sickened by the news. She buried her face in her

hands. *How can this be, Lord? Why would you allow this pestilence to come our way?*

"We'll have to be cautious," Dianne said, finally looking up at her friend. "What's to be done?"

"Quarantine," Charity said. "At least I'm certain that's required to keep others from getting sick. We need a doctor to be certain about the pox."

Dianne nodded. "You've not been around the Indians much, have you?"

Charity shook her head. "No, I just found out about this when Koko sent me to tell you. I was helping Ben with some notes for his Sunday service."

"Good." Dianne struggled to think clearly. "We need to get word to the others—to Faith and Malachi. They need to stay away from the house. Everyone needs to stay away. Koko and her children have been very close to Takes Many Horses and his friends. Jamie sat beside his uncle at lunch, and Susannah was on and off his lap. They've no doubt had a good exposure to the sickness."

"What about you?"

Dianne shook her head. "We've maintained a good distance. I sat at the opposite end of the table, then came up here with Luke. I don't know how bad this might get," she said, looking to her friend, "but I know the time to act is now."

"I'll go tell Faith and Malachi the situation. I'll tell them from a distance, just in case," Charity declared.

"Good, then come back here if you would, and watch Luke. I'll ride for Dr. Bufford and see if he can help us."

"You're going to leave?"

Dianne jumped up, unfastening her skirt as she did. "I'll be back as quick as I can. I'll take Pepper. He can manage the distance in a short time." She took up an altered pair of Cole's trousers and pulled them on. She started to take hold of a wide full skirt she often threw over the top of these, then stopped. "I'll just go like this." She took up a long jacket and slipped into the sleeves.

"Get the word out," she told Charity as she hurried to pull on her boots. "I'll be back as fast as I can."

Dianne was uncertain whether Hezekiah Bufford would be any help to them or not. After all, the only ones who were sick at this point were Indians. Still, she couldn't sit by and do nothing. If anyone would help them, it would be him.

Dianne pressed Pepper to race across the hilltop road. They ignored the pelting spring rain that started in a gentle sprinkle. By the time she neared Bufford's place, the rain came as a downpour and she struggled to keep her seat, while Pepper worked to keep his footing.

She saw the doctor's cabin and much to her relief spied his horse in the lean-to out back. Dianne barely brought Pepper to a stop before jumping from his back. She dropped the reins, knowing the horse was used to being ground-tied. She prayed the storm wouldn't spook him into running off.

"Dr. Bufford!" Dianne pounded her gloved fists against the door.

The man came quickly, barely containing his surprise at her appearance. "Mrs. Selby. It's not fit weather for you to be out there." He pulled her inside and closed the door. "What in the world prompted you to get out in this weather?" He noticed her method of dress and frowned even more.

"I think we have smallpox at the ranch," she said, dripping water onto the doctor's well-worn rag rug.

"Smallpox? Are you sure?"

"That's why I've come to you," she said, taking a deep breath before continuing. "Koko's brother showed up today with a couple of friends. They appeared tired, even feverish, but I didn't see signs of the pox. Koko did, however."

"So they're heathens?"

Dianne lowered her head and prayed for the right words. "They're very sick. Not only that," she said as she looked back up, "I'm afraid for the others. For my son. Please, can you come and help us? At least tell us for sure if it's smallpox, and if it is, show us how to help them."

Bufford stood fixed in place for a moment. He seemed to be considering her words. Turning rather quickly, he pulled on his coat. "I'll come, but I don't know that I can do much to help. If it is smallpox, then we may be looking at a long spell of sickness as it passes from person to person."

"Will everyone get it?"

Bufford took up his bag. "Hard to tell. Disease never acts in a predictable manner. Indians have had it much worse with the smallpox. Might be they'll take it and nobody else will suffer. We won't know for weeks."

"Weeks?" Dianne asked, her voice edged with fear. "But what about the men? They've not returned from roundup, but they will. They should be home any day."

He shook his head. "We need to keep them on the other side of the quarantine line. That's very important, Mrs. Selby. Otherwise we might just have an epidemic on our hands. Do you understand?"

Dianne nodded. "I suppose I do."

Cole could only remember one other time when he'd been happier to see the Diamond V ranch, and that had been when Takes Many Horses had brought him to safety after the Sioux had nearly killed him. Now, sitting atop his horse, reading the word *QUARANTINE* on a crude sign across the lane leading to his home, Cole's disappointment was turning to anger.

"Who posted this? Is this some kind of joke?" He turned to Gus and the other boys.

"What's it mean, Cole?" Gabe asked from behind.

"It means there's sickness here," Gus answered before Cole could speak. "It means we'd best find out what's going on before we cross the line."

Just then a rider approached from the direction of the house. Cole's eyes adjusted to the sun and he could make out the figure of his wife as she rode up the lane. She halted a good ten yards away.

"I'm so glad to see you, but you must keep your distance. We're under quarantine. We have smallpox."

Cole noted the fear in her voice. "How? What happened?"

"Takes Many Horses and a couple of his friends showed up about ten days ago. They fell ill almost immediately. Dr. Bufford came and he's done what he could, but we've already lost two of them."

"Takes Many Horses?" Cole questioned.

"No, he's still alive, but very sick. Dr. Bufford doesn't expect him to live."

"What do we need to do?" Gus asked.

"Dr. Bufford said you could go around the long way and stay down at the bunkhouse, but you need to keep away from the house. Faith and Malachi can give you more information about the way they've been helping us." She paused and Cole heard her voice break. "I'm so sorry about this. I know you're all tired and have worked hard."

Cole wanted only to jump from the horse and go to her—to hold her in his arms and tell her that everything would be all right.

"How's Luke and the others?"

Dianne wiped at her tears. "So far, we're all fine."

"And you're going to stay that way," Cole said, trying his best to assure her. "You do what the doc says. He'll have the best idea of how to keep you healthy."

Dianne nodded. "I know. It's just so hard. I've missed you all so much and now this. I don't know if Takes Many Horses will live or die. I just know that I'm very, very afraid."

Cole looked to the men. They seemed sympathetic to his plight, but Gus shook his head. "You can't go in there," he said firmly. "I won't let you."

"Neither will I," Trenton said, coming up beside his brother-in-law. "It wouldn't be right."

Cole met Trenton's narrowed eyes. For just a moment Cole thought of defying them all. It wasn't fair that Dianne should have to bear this alone. She'd already had to endure so much on her own. Why this? Why now?

"I know how you feel," Trenton said softly. "I think everyone here feels the same. But it won't help her at all if we all go gettin' sick. Think of the sorrow she'd have at havin' to bury one of us—or all of us."

Cole realized Trenton's logic, but his desire to help Dianne—to bear this for her—was almost more than he could stand.

"Don't you worry about a thing. We'll keep a good eye on Cole for you," Gus called across the distance. "We're gonna head around to the bunkhouse, little lady. If you need anything at all, send a message. I'll talk to Miz Faith and Malachi and see what else is to be done."

"Thank you, Gus."

Cole couldn't find the strength to turn from his wife. He wanted to look strong, to be reasonable. "I'll be close," he finally said. "If you need me, I'll be there. Quarantine or no."

"Stay away, Cole," she said, barely loud enough for them to hear. "All of you, stay away. I couldn't bear to lose you."

CHAPTER 33

DIANNE HATED BEING ISOLATED IN HER WING OF THE HOUSE, but Dr. Bufford thought it better that she not help care for the sick. Koko, however, insisted on working beside the doctor, giving whatever care she could to her brother and his one remaining companion, Runs Too Far.

Smallpox was a hideous disease; Dianne already knew this quite well. She'd heard horror stories from wagon train travels and from others who had dealt with the sickness. Even Zane had talked of the times he'd encountered the disease in Indian camps. Apparently there were varying degrees to the illness. Some people took smallpox so hard that they were covered in pustules and died within days. Others with lighter cases recovered much more quickly. In any case they were marked for life with the telltale pox marks. So far, Zane had managed to avoid getting sick himself, so Dianne hoped fervently that she and the others might also remain well. It seemed for all of his exposure he would have had a very good chance of succumbing to the disease, but even Dr. Bufford had to admit he'd been around smallpox on many occasions and had yet to take ill himself.

Shortly after midnight, Dianne finally managed to get Luke to bed. It was as if the turmoil affected his ability to rest. He'd been fussy for two days running, and all Dianne could think about was whether he was coming down sick. She checked him one last time as she covered him. His skin was dry and cool. No sign of fever. It was too early for him to begin teething, so Dianne prayed it was nothing more than a colicky stomach.

Luke settled into sleep, his baby lips sucking at the air for a moment. He looked so sweet—so peaceful. Dianne breathed a sigh of relief at his contentment. She had just begun to undress when a knock came on her door. She couldn't imagine who it might be.

"Yes?" she called.

"It's Dr. Bufford." She opened the door and he continued, "You must come. Your aunt has collapsed from exhaustion and Runs Too Far has died. I need to bury him as soon as possible, and while I didn't want you working with the sick, I now have no choice."

Dianne nodded, pulling the door closed behind her. "We can have Charity take care of Luke. What of Takes Many Horses?"

"He's not good. I don't expect him to make it. The pox is covering most of his body, and his breathing is so labored he can't hope to keep fluid from building in the lungs. He's not even strong enough to cough."

They walked to the stairs and Bufford reached out to take hold of Dianne's shoulder. "I wouldn't have come for you, but your aunt begged me to. I don't know if she's coming down with smallpox or if it's just the long hours she's worked to keep the others alive."

"What are you trying to say?" Dianne asked, looking up to meet the doctor's stern expression.

"I'm saying you may come down sick. You may contract smallpox."

Dianne continued down the stairs and Bufford quickly caught up with her. "Did you hear what I said?"

Dianne nodded. Her heart was torn. She wanted to stay alive and healthy for her husband and son, but she felt compelled to care for Koko and her children—and if necessary, Takes Many Horses. "I promised my uncle that I would take care of them. I know she'd do the same for me."

"I kind of figured you'd feel that way, but I wanted to let you know just how bad this can be."

Dianne reached the bottom of the stairs and turned to the older man. "I know you probably think it foolish to trade a white life for that of a Blackfoot, but if that's what is required, then I'll do what I must. I love my family, Dr. Bufford. I love all of them. Lucas and Cole, as well as Koko and Takes Many Horses. If they need me, then I must put aside my fears. I must do what is required of me. Just as you have. As you've pointed out to me, you've managed to remain healthy all these years, and you've dealt with the pox many times." She looked at him as if daring him to contradict her.

"Very well. Your aunt is in the small room just off the kitchen. I believe the children are there as well."

"Thank you. I'll come find you after I see to her."

"I'll be digging a grave for Runs Too Far," he said matter-of-factly. "Gotta bury them quickly to keep from spreading the disease. I'll be burning the linens and blankets as well. Sorry for the waste. After that, I'll come check on Takes Many Horses; of course, he'll probably be dead by then."

Dianne tried not to believe they might yet need a grave for Koko's brother as well. She wasn't yet ready to let him go. He'd been such a strange part of her life, and the thought of losing him was more than she wanted to consider.

"I'll go get Charity, then I'll tend my aunt. I'm going to

suggest Charity take the children to her cabin. Will that be all right?"

Bufford nodded. "I suppose so. Tell her to keep the Indian children away from your son."

"Dr. Bufford, I've told you before that—"

He held up his hand. "I wasn't saying that out of a prejudiced heart, but rather a doctor's reasoning. Those children have been exposed to this illness; your son has not. If she can keep them separate, we'll limit the exposure the baby has to the pox."

Dianne calmed and realized she'd misjudged him. "I'm sorry. I shouldn't have reacted that way. I'll do as you say."

Dianne went and woke Ben and Charity. She explained the situation quickly and after the couple prayed with her for her health and safety, they followed her back to the house.

"Luke is asleep in his cradle. I suppose you'll have to feed him milk. I don't want him around me until I'm sure I won't take sick."

"I'll see to him—don't you worry about a thing," Charity said.

"Ben, if you want to come with me, I'll help you get Jamie and Suzy."

Ben nodded, suppressing a yawn. He followed Dianne to the kitchen and waited until she was able to rouse the children and bring them out. She carried Susannah to Ben and turned to find a sleepy-eyed Jamie standing behind her.

"Mama's sick, isn't she?" he asked.

"Yes, I suppose she is. We don't know if it's the pox or if she's just been working too hard. I want you and your sister to stay with Pastor Ben and Miz Charity. They will take good care of you. I'll try to let you know how your mama is doing, all right?"

Jamie seemed a little more awake now and nodded. "I can stay and help."

Dianne tousled his hair and shook her head. "No. That

would only worry your mama. She'll feel better knowing you and Susannah are safe from the sickness."

"Come along now, Jamie," Ben said gently. "I have some cookies we can nibble before we go back to sleep."

Jamie seemed quite open to this idea and followed Ben from the house just as Charity came down the back stairs with Luke wrapped in blankets. Dianne longed to see her son—to touch him one more time, but instead she nodded to Charity and turned away so she wouldn't see the tears beginning to form.

"Thank you, Charity. I'll rest easier knowing he's safely with you."

Dianne went quickly to Koko's room. The storage room was large and roomy, but with one bed and two pallets, the space had been eaten up. Now with the children gone, Dianne gathered the bedding and put it to one side, again giving the room a more spacious feel. *I might well need this bedding for myself,* she thought and she draped it over the edge of the food shelves. *It might be wise to make my bed here with Koko.*

Dianne was relieved to find Koko already sleeping. She touched her hand lightly to her aunt's forehead and found it warm—maybe feverish. The possibility was great, and only time would tell whether Koko would have to endure the pox.

"Oh, God, please put an end to this sickness. Let there be no more cases. Let the sick recover."

Seeing that Koko slept easily, Dianne made her way back through the kitchen and to the small sitting room they'd used for nursing the ill. Takes Many Horses was alone—a shadow of the man he'd once been. The sickness had ravaged his body, leaving so many pustules he was almost white from the covering. He struggled to breathe, but otherwise he was completely still.

Dianne approached him quietly, tears once again forming in her eyes. He had been a handsome man, full of life and strength.

Now he was reduced to this. Barely alive—completely oblivious to his circumstance.

She took up a washcloth and dipped it into the basin of cool water. Touching it to Takes Many Horses' forehead, she was startled when he opened his eyes.

"Stands Tall Woman?"

"Yes, I'm here. You should be sleeping—not talking."

"I'm alone," he said, closing his eyes.

She noted the empty bed where Runs Too Far had most likely been only an hour before. "Your friends have passed on," she admitted, then continued carefully blotting his face with the cold cloth.

"I will die," he said, his voice resolved.

"No!" she declared, halting her ministering. "You don't have to die."

He shook his head. "At least I'm not on the reservation."

Dianne sat down beside him. She hadn't meant to be so stern. She softened her voice. "No, you're safe here."

He fell silent, and Dianne was certain he'd fallen back into his sickness-induced sleep. She tried not to be appalled by the pustules that covered the warrior's face and body. He couldn't help the condition of his body.

"You know that I love you," he said without opening his eyes.

The words startled her, more because she'd thought he was asleep. "Yes," she whispered.

He opened his eyes and looked into her face. "I've loved you since that first day when you—" he gasped for air—"stood tall against us."

"You shouldn't talk. You need your strength to recover."

He shook his head. "I won't recover. I'll die as my friends did. Not as a warrior, but at least as a . . . a . . . free man."

"You might not die," Dianne said, dabbing the cloth to his

neck. "You must at least try to fight the sickness and live. Koko needs you to live. She may well have the pox herself."

"I'd like to live, but life will never be the same." He drew a ragged breath. "The Blackfoot ways are gone—or will be soon."

"I know," Dianne whispered. "But you always have a home here."

"Can your God forgive me . . . even now?"

Her eyes widened. "God can forgive you anytime—any-place."

"But my life . . . my deeds were not always good."

Dianne smiled. "Nor were mine. I still make mistakes."

"But I've taken lives. Can God forgive that?"

She stood and rinsed the cloth before answering. "Yes, Takes Many Horses, God can forgive that. If you are repentant and truly sorry for what you've done, God will forgive it. God looks into the heart of a man—He'll know if you are sincere."

She came back to his bed and put the cloth upon his brow. "Do you wish to ask forgiveness?"

"I don't know how," he replied.

"I could help you to pray," she said, her hope growing. "I could pray the words aloud, and you could pray them silently so as to save your energy and breath."

"Then we should pray," he said, closing his eyes. He struggled to breathe, the raspy sound growing worse.

Dianne knelt beside the bed and took hold of his hand. She began to pray aloud, conscious of every breath the man took. *I know he'll probably die,* she prayed silently, *but God, he's reaching out to you. He needs to make his peace.*

"Dear Father," she said aloud, "I know I've done many wrong things—you know what they are." She paused, giving Takes Many Horses time to consider the words and pray them for himself. She continued the prayer, ever mindful of the sick man's breathing.

"Please forgive me for the wrong I've done—for the lies and deceit, for taking what didn't belong to me—for taking lives." She prayed the words for Takes Many Horses, hoping he would make them his own. The warrior said nothing, but his breathing evened and became less labored.

Dianne couldn't help but open her eyes, fearful that he was passing from the earth even as she prayed. But instead of finding him nearly dead, she was encouraged by his more peaceful, rhythmic breathing.

Oh, Father, please heal him, she prayed. *He's so important to this family. It would hurt so much to lose him. Please restore his strength and give him the ability to recover from this sickness.*

An hour or two later, Dr. Bufford listened to the warrior's heartbeat. "I actually think he's doing better. He may have turned a corner on this."

Dianne tried not to get her hopes up. "What about Koko?"

"I'm afraid she's contracted the disease," he said, shaking his head. "All we can do is wait it out and hope for the best. If no one else comes down sick, we're still looking at a few more weeks of quarantine."

She sat down hard, still unable to imagine living even longer without her husband, brother, and the others. "Were you able to get Runs Too Far buried?"

"Yes. I managed it. I buried him near the others. As I mentioned, we'll need to burn all the linens—the mattresses too."

Dianne nodded. "That's fine. Whatever we must do to keep this from spreading." She got to her feet and readjusted her apron. "I'll care for my aunt. There's no sense in both of us losing sleep. I can check in here as well."

Dr. Bufford rubbed his bearded chin and nodded. "Very well. Come get me if things get worse."

Dianne sighed. "Things are already worse," she murmured, thinking of Koko.

She went to her aunt and was surprised to find her awake. The fever was already causing her to feel chilled and achy. Dianne tried to compensate with a fresh blanket.

"Are the children still sleeping? Are they well?"

Dianne nodded. "Yes. They seem fine. No fevers. I sent them with Charity and Ben. They'll keep them at the cabin."

"Good," Koko said in relief. "I hoped you would move them to another place. I don't want them near me while I'm sick."

"It's already been seen to," Dianne said, hoping this thought would offer comfort. "Takes Many Horses is doing better. Dr. Bufford said he may actually recover."

"Can I be moved to his room? I'd like to be near him."

Dianne could see no reason why this wouldn't be acceptable. Since Koko already had the pox, it wasn't as if they would risk spreading it further. "Let me see if Dr. Bufford has destroyed the mattress yet. If he has, I'll need to move this one to that room. You'll have to sit on a chair in the sickroom while I work. All right?"

"That's fine. I'm strong enough to sit. I can even walk to the room with your help."

"All right." Dianne got to her feet. "Let me go check the bed first."

"Wait, please." Koko's voice sounded urgent.

Dianne turned. She could see the fear in Koko's eyes. Reaching out, she took hold of her aunt's hand. "What is it? Are you in pain?"

"No, it's the children."

"They're fine. I already told you."

"No," Koko said, shaking her head from side to side. "If I die—"

"You won't," Dianne asserted, not wanting to hear anything more on the matter.

"Please," Koko whispered. "Please hear me."

Dianne braced herself and sat down beside the sick woman. "All right. I'm listening."

"I know how this sickness can be. Remember, I watched the others die. You must promise me that if I die, you'll take care of Jamie and Susannah."

Dianne would never have considered doing things any other way. "But of course I will."

"I just need to know that they'll be safe—that they won't have to go to the reservation."

"Oh, Koko, I would never let Jamie and Susannah be taken from us. They belong here. This is their land—their home. I will fight for them every step of the way."

Koko's expression softened as relief spread to her features. "Thank you. I knew what you would say, but I needed to hear it. I needed to know."

Dianne could well understand. If the roles were reversed and she were the sick one instead of Koko, Dianne would want to know that Luke was well cared for.

"You rest now. We're going to need you to be strong in order to fight this illness."

Dianne left Koko, her thoughts traveling in a hundred different directions. There seemed no end in sight for ridding themselves of smallpox, and now Dianne was taking on the job of nursing the sick—leaving herself vulnerable to catching the disease as well.

"Oh, God," she prayed, leaning against the back door of the kitchen, "please help us. Please deliver us."

———

Gus, Cole, and Trenton headed back to the ranch from Virginia City. Cole wasn't at all happy with the information he'd picked up in town, but it was hard to know what was merely rumor and what was truth.

"I heard that three ranches to the east, down on the Yellowstone, were burned out, but no one has any confirmation of this," Cole said, trying to figure out what was to be done about the news. "The man I talked to said it was done by Sioux raiding parties."

"Could be," Gus replied. "Hard to tell if it's true or not."

"The man at the newspaper said that since they moved the capital to Helena, their information isn't as reliable as it had been," Trenton said. "I'm guessin' there's a lot of speculation going around. Fear spreads like wildfire."

Cole nodded. "I know that well enough. I just can't figure out what we need to do. I'd load up the family and take them to safety if I knew where safety was."

"You'll probably just have to ride this one out," Gus said, sounding fatherly in his manner. "You'll have to do what you can to make your own place as safe as possible."

"I'd gladly do that if we weren't restricted by the quarantine," Cole replied.

"We've got a good perimeter watch going," Trenton threw in. "I think we're doing the best we can. There haven't been any signs of Indians, so I think we're pretty safe."

Cole sighed. "I suppose so. I just feel like there oughta be something more we should do."

"Guess we could pray," Gus said off-handedly. "Seems like the thing to do, anyhow."

"I've been praying, Gus. I've been praying my boots off," Cole replied. "I've been praying for healing from the sickness, for safety from rampaging Indians, and for the general protection of all the folks I love and care about. I don't know what else to pray for."

"Patience," Trenton said with a grin. "I think we all need patience."

CHAPTER 34

Koko suffered only a mild case of the pox. She wasn't nearly as sick or covered with pustules as her brother and his friends had been. Dr. Bufford said this was a very good sign, and he believed she would mend very quickly.

Takes Many Horses' recovery was slow but steady. His once-smooth brown skin now bore the mark of his disease, but he'd started to fill out again and didn't look nearly as bad as he had.

"I'll leave here soon," Takes Many Horses told the women as Dianne helped Koko pull a shawl around her shoulders. She paused and looked to where he stood by the window.

"Where will you go?" Dianne asked.

"North. I will go north. You probably won't see me again."

"George, sit down and speak with me. I want to talk about this," Koko admonished.

Dianne straightened and took up a few articles of clothing that she intended to wash. "I'll be outside at the washtub," she said, leaving them to their discussion. She had no idea if Koko would be any more successful in convincing her brother to stay on the Diamond V than she had been. She knew Koko's brother was restless. Knew, too, that his heart was torn. His companions were gone and his own health was so newly recovered that his body was still weak. He didn't feel like a man at this point. It would probably take leaving—heading off on his own—to help him regain his confidence and peace of mind.

Dr. Bufford crossed from the barn to where Dianne had set up her washing. "Well, I think we can safely say that no one else need worry about the pox. Your aunt's case was very mild, and she's nearly recovered. I'd say in another week we can lift the quarantine."

"I'm so glad." She felt her shoulders slump as the relief overtook her. "I've prayed so hard for this day."

"Your strength saw you through, Mrs. Selby. No doubt about it."

"God saw me through, Dr. Bufford. He brought you to come help. He kept the sickness from spreading, and He saved the people I love."

Bufford took off his hat and scratched his chin. "I suppose it would be appropriate to credit Him at least with the latter."

She smiled. "It would be right to credit Him with all. Remember, God sees even when a sparrow falls. He's been with us all along."

Bufford cleared his throat and looked away. "I'll be leaving as soon as we lift the quarantine. It's nearly May, and it would do me good to air out the cabin and bring in some supplies."

"I plan to pay you a good sum," Dianne said, putting one of Bufford's shirts to the washboard. "You've gone above and beyond neighborly kindness or even good doctoring. You've been a blessing to us, and I plan to bless you in return."

"You needn't worry about that. I told you before that it wasn't my intention to continue practicing as a doctor."

"Yes, but you also mentioned that your sorrow and loss during the war kept you from feeling that you were accomplishing anything good with your medical skills. That's not the case any-more, and I think it's time you reconsidered. This valley could use another doctor. There are hundreds of new families in the areas surrounding us. They aren't going to just go away, but they will get sick and need treatment. I'd like it very much if you would think about this."

Bufford toyed with his hat. "I'll consider it, but don't get your hopes up."

Dianne didn't want to embarrass the man, but she couldn't help adding, "I appreciate that you put aside your personal feel-ings toward the Indians. I know my aunt would probably be dead—her brother too—had it not been for your training and wisdom."

"I suppose my mind, while not completely altered in its thinking, has come to accept that we're facing a new day. I don't know that I can deal with people of different colors and not feel strange about the situation, but you have taught me something of tolerance."

She met his eyes and smiled. "I'm so glad. These are good people. I'm certain they would be happy to be your friend."

Bufford motioned to the house. "I need to go check on my patients."

She let him go, noting his face had reddened somewhat at her suggestion. Most people made changes a little at a time. At least that was her observance. Of course, there were those like her family who pulled up stakes to come west—who endured a great deal of change in a short while. She supposed it was just a matter of personalities and needs.

"I need to say something to you."

Dianne straightened and found Takes Many Horses standing at the corner of the house. He'd apparently come from the back door and followed the smoke to where she stood working with the laundry.

"Are you feeling well enough to be out here?" she asked, leaving her scrubbing momentarily to retrieve wood. She wanted to keep the water hot in order to assure that all the disease was cooked out of the clothing she washed. Throwing more wood into the fire under her caldron, Dianne straightened and met the man's fixed gaze. "What did you want to say?"

"I want to apologize."

"For what?"

"For speaking of my love for you," he replied. "It was wrong of me and dishonoring to your husband."

Dianne nodded. "I accept your apology. You are a man of honor."

"My apology doesn't mean that my words weren't true, but I know you are happy with Cole, and that makes my heart sing. If you are happy, then I can leave and live out my days without regret."

She was rather taken aback by his statement. "Do you remember when we prayed?"

Takes Many Horses nodded. He continued staring at her.

"Did you pray? Did you understand about God's mercy for you? His love of you?"

"I understood," he replied, his voice low and husky. "Why do you ask?"

"I want to go my way and live my days without regret as well," Dianne said firmly. "I want to know that I did everything I could to convince you that God's love for you was more powerful than anything you could do or had already done."

He came closer, stopping only inches away. For a moment, she thought he might try to embrace her, but again he held himself in restraint. "I am grateful for that night and the prayers you offered. My soul is at peace. I do not pretend to understand everything about God and His mercy. In fact, at times He does not seem very merciful."

Dianne nodded. "I know," she managed with some difficulty, then bit her lower lip as if to keep from saying something more.

"I will travel with the one true God," he stated softly. "I will trust Him for my days. Does that make you happy, Stands Tall Woman?"

She nodded, unable to pretend it didn't. "I'm glad to know that I'll see you again. If not in this world, then in the next. You are my friend, and you will always be my friend—from now until the end of time."

He smiled and it warmed her heart. "I give you my pledge of friendship," he said. "I will honor it always."

———

The day after the quarantine was lifted, Hezekiah Bufford headed back to his cabin. His pockets were a bit better lined, thanks to Dianne's generosity, and he had smoked hams slung on both sides of his mount—an extra thank-you from Koko.

Takes Many Horses left the same morning. He hadn't said a word to anyone. Without so much as a farewell, he simply vanished—taking his companions' weapons. Dianne was rather hurt by his disappearance.

"He could have at least said good-bye," she told Koko as she cleaned the kitchen.

Her aunt looked at her sympathetically. "It hurt him to go—to leave you."

"To leave me? What about you and the children? I've never seen a man so happy to play with little ones."

Koko smiled, but there was a bittersweet tone to her voice. "Jamie wanted to go with him—to be Blackfoot like his uncle. But my brother spoke with him and then Jamie seemed happy to stay behind."

"What did George say to him?"

"He told him that he was now the man of our family. That

he had a responsibility to take care of me and his sister. That he had two women in his lodge, and that required much bravery and great strength."

"I can well imagine Jamie is just about to bust a button regarding such matters."

"He was very proud and even more excited when George gave him his Blackfoot name."

Dianne finished wiping the counter and turned. "What name did he give him?"

"The translation is Little Man Waits," Koko said with a smile. "Jamie was very pleased."

"I can well imagine." Dianne tried the name on for herself. "Little Man Waits." She nodded. "Yes, I like it very much. We'll have to celebrate."

That night, after the last of the bedding had been burned or washed, Dianne allowed herself the luxury of a hot bath. Cole had helped her by carrying gallons of hot water to the tub upstairs.

"Stay as long as you want," he told her. "I'll see to Luke."

Dianne barely breathed words of thanks before her husband pulled the door closed. Shedding her dressing gown, Dianne sank into the hot water and sighed as it came up over her shoulders. She edged down farther and let her hair soak up water. She felt as though she were washing away the last couple of months and all its misery.

"Mmm," she sighed. Nothing had ever felt better.

Dianne lost track of the time. She let her mind wander, remembering times when she'd been a girl—back before the war had come and her family had split apart. She remembered a picnic they'd all shared by some pond. The day had been warm and lovely. Trenton and the twins had splashed around in the river, but Dianne had been too afraid to set foot into the water.

"Don't be a goose, Dianne," Morgan had teased. *"You won't drown. We won't let you."*

Dianne had been about eight or nine. She couldn't even remember for sure where they'd been. It might have been on one of the visits to her grandparents; then again, it might have been near the house where they lived before moving to New Madrid.

"You'll splash water in my eyes," she had declared to her brothers, *"and then I won't be able to see. I'll get lost."*

"You won't get lost," Trenton had assured her. She trusted Trenton because he always took good care of her. When he'd reached for her hand that day, Dianne had hesitated only a moment.

"You won't forget me? You won't leave me by myself?"

He led her to the water, assuring her all the time that he would never let her get any farther away than he could reach. The memory warmed her. Trenton had been true to his word, just as God had been true to His.

He, too, had promised He'd never leave her.

Opening her eyes, Dianne felt the same blessed assurance she'd known as a child wash over her anew. God truly had her safely in His care. He wouldn't leave her nor forsake her. The momentary worries about tomorrow faded in light of this truth.

With her bath finished, Dianne slipped into her bedroom. The baby slept soundly and Cole relaxed in bed, reading from one of the books he'd picked up in Virginia City. The sight of such a scene filled her with great warmth and pride.

"My husband and baby—this is the finest sight I've ever known."

Cole looked up and smiled. "You're a pretty good sight yourself, Mrs. Selby." He put his book on the nightstand, then pulled down the covers from her side of the bed. "Better get in here before you get cold."

"My hair's still wet. I should dry it first."

"Nah. I don't mind. Come on."

Dianne's heart skipped a beat at the look of love on his face. He smiled lazily and winked, patting the mattress beside him. "You're just plain ornery," she said, crawling into the bed.

Cole pulled her into his arms, making Dianne feel safer than she'd felt in weeks. "I've missed you more than I can say," Cole began, kissing her damp hair. "I never want to be separated from you like that again."

"Me either." She wrapped her arms around his neck and pulled him closer. He pressed his mouth against hers. The kiss was long and lingering, blotting out any other thought of speech.

In the morning they both awoke before Lucas did. The dawn was just beginning, and the light was soft and muted. Dianne relished the moments of silence. Just being there—held by her husband before having to face the day and all its problems— somehow gave her strength.

"I love you, you know," Cole whispered against her ear.

"I should hope so. I would feel mighty uncomfortable being here if you didn't."

He chuckled. "Well, you needn't worry."

Dianne shifted in his arms to better see her husband's face. "So much has happened. I'm such a different person from the girl I used to be. There was so much fear in that girl—so many questions. Now, I know there are dangers out there. I heard you talking at dinner about the Indian Wars and the possibility of attack. But I want you to know I'm not afraid. Not anymore."

"What happened to change your mind?"

Dianne shook her head. "I don't know. I guess it's just a part of the process of becoming a woman, trusting God, learning to take one day at a time. I know, without any doubt, that troubles are still coming. I feel it strongly, but I won't live my life in fear of what might happen. For all I know, the army may well convince the Indians to go back to their reservations. The Sioux and

Cheyenne may give up willingly and return to their appointed places. But either way, this is our land—our home. This is the life we've chosen for ourselves. We must make a stand—a stand of faith."

Cole seemed to be considering her words and for a moment said nothing. Then he surprised her by slipping away from her and reaching over to the nightstand drawer. "I have a present for you. I wanted to wait until the right moment, and this seems like the best time."

He pulled out a small wooden box and handed it to her. "When we were separated these last weeks, all I could think about was how many things seemed to work against us—to keep us apart. My heart was bitter. Then God reminded me that while things had kept us apart, we had stayed together despite all the conflicts and problems that the world could throw our way."

Dianne smiled. "Yes. It's all a matter of heart—looking at the good instead of dwelling on the bad."

Cole opened the box and reached inside. "I bought this ring for you. I'd always felt bad about not having something special to give you when we married. Oh, I know I got you that little gold band, but this is something different. When you look at this, I want you to remember that we are two parts of a whole. That I'm nothing without you. That we belong together."

Dianne looked at the ring and blinked back tears. It was like nothing she'd ever known. Two perfectly matched garnets were set side by side in a circle of gold.

"They're each their own stone—but they're set together, and together they balance the whole. You balance me, Dianne. You give me hope when I'm discouraged, and you make me smile when there seems to be nothing but despair all around me. I want you to know that come what may—no matter the storm— we'll weather it together."

Dianne let him put the ring on her finger. It slipped down

to rest against her wedding band. She looked into his eyes and found all the love that she would ever need.

"Come what may," she whispered, knowing in her heart that with this man by her side, tomorrow didn't seem nearly so frightening.